Praise for FINDERS KEEPERS:

"Light romantic fun, from a writer with a lot of promise."—*Philadelphia Weekly Press*

"A Perfect 10 . . . A riveting, tightly written, edge-of-your-seat tale that pulls the reader in from page one, never letting go until the poignant finish."
—*Romance Reviews Today*

"The author's sure hand with characterization makes each twist of this emotionally laden storyline as suspenseful as any well-wrought battle scene . . . With peppy, laugh-out-loud dialogue, an outstanding cast of supporting characters and a big serving of adventure in the mix, *Finders Keepers* is guaranteed to show readers a pleasant and thoroughly entertaining time."—*SciFi.com*

"Sinclair's prose is tight and intense. You'll feel as though you are in the cockpit, the ship's controls in your hands, speeding through space with your hair on fire. I mentioned earlier that this was a keeper, but I must correct myself. It's firmly placed on the shelf marked, 'Touch this and die.'"—*Mystique Book Reviews*

"The characters are well-rounded and . . . the story is skillfully written with a number of twists and turns . . . Space opera at its best filled with suspense, double-dealing and space battles and unfolds against a background of a universe with its own political, economic and social structure . . . I thoroughly enjoyed this book."—*SFCrow's Nest*

"Would I recommend Finders Keepers to hard SF fans? Definitely! Would I also recommend it to romance fans? Absolutely! Linnea Sinclair is obviously a versatile author with a wonderful imagination, which enables her to take readers along for the ride."—*Novelspot*

"Has the 'wow!' factor in spades...Well-developed and wonderfully imaginative, *Finders Keepers* has 'exceptional merit' written all over it."—*Heartstrings*

"*Finders Keepers* is just the thing for anyone who has a soft spot for a good old-fashioned 'space opera.' The characters are well rounded and believable...It's clear that Linnea Sinclair had fun writing this story, and anyone who picks up *Finders Keepers* will have a great time reading it."—*Bookloons*

"A well written science fiction romance, with a little politics on the side...There were so many moments where I laughed out loud...This is a wonderful story that I cherish and will certainly read again."
—*BookReviewCafe.com*

"Takes the reader on a wild ride of danger and intrigue with a mismatched pair who surprise themselves by not only staying alive, but falling for each other. All this and humor, too, makes this book a real keeper."
—Jane Toombs, author of *Fire Griffin* and *Dangerous Medicine*

Praise for GABRIEL'S GHOST!

"Five stars. Captures your interest with nonstop action and suspense and keeps it as the tension

mounts... With nonstop action and a heartfelt love story, *Gabriel's Ghost* is a must buy."
—*CataRomance Reviews*

"Fine characterizations, snappy and smart dialogue, nifty world building and plenty of political and religious intrigue... Readers who enjoy romantic science fiction packed with a heady blend of adventure, action and intrigue will love *Gabriel's Ghost*."
—*BookLoons*

"The subtle weaving of events into a complex but easily followed plot makes this a book for your keeper shelf."—*PNR Reviews*

"A high-flying, sci-fi romance for a number of reasons—not the least of which is the sense of euphoria it will give readers craving credible science fiction as well as a complicated-but-fulfilling love story. There isn't a shadow of a doubt in this reviewer's mind that Bantam Spectra has a bona fide, interstellar star in this author. Prepare to be star-struck, dear reader..."
—*Heartstrings Reviews*

"Five Moons rating—outstanding, cosmic! Who said there is no good way to blend sci-fi and romance? Whoever did has obviously never read *Gabriel's Ghost*. The romantic element is wondrously, fantastically, stupendously necessary to the hard science fiction that defines a Linnea Sinclair book. What we are looking at here is the next incarnation of the genre. It's deep, visceral, and more human in that it's emotionally and— yes—sexually intense... sci-fi has never been better!"
—*MystiqueBooks.com*

"...[A] nonstop adventure ride [that] will appeal to fans of traditional science fiction, with the strongly developed technology and worlds. Yet there is a strong romantic storyline with the beautifully developed characters that is bound to charm fans of that genre as well."—*Best Reviews*

"Readers have come to expect the extraordinary from author Linnea Sinclair, but *Gabriel's Ghost* still exceeds all expectations! With the vision and texture of a poet, the heart of warrior, and the skill of a master, Sinclair creates a world of psychic gifts and shape shifters, of dangers beyond imagination and love beyond question...A tale so entrancing, so mesmerizing that readers will be absolutely blown away."
—*Midwest Book Review*

"If you're a fan of McCaffrey or Catherine Asaro, this book's for you. A nonstop thrill ride with a pace that never slows down...The sexual tension crackles and the love scenes are positively incinerating. Combine all of this with fascinating supporting characters who are never quite what they seem and a hard look at prejudice, genetic engineering and the ease with which the truth can be twisted, and you have an intellectually and emotionally satisfying book."—*Sime-Gen Reviews*

"A phenomenal book and one that deserves its place on keeper shelves all over the world...A rapid-fire, page-turning, roller coaster adventure...Sinclair has managed to mix religion, politics, adventure, science fiction and romance into one of the best reads of the year. A true winner!"—*Interludes Magazine*

ALSO BY LINNEA SINCLAIR

Finders Keepers
Gabriel's Ghost

an accidental goddess

Linnea Sinclair

Bantam Books

AN ACCIDENTAL GODDESS
A Bantam Spectra Book / January 2006

Published by
Bantam Dell
A Division of Random House, Inc.
New York, New York

ISBN-10: 0-553-58799-4
ISBN-13: 978-0-553-58799-9

Printed in the United States of America
Published simultaneously in Canada

www.bantamdell.com

OPM 10 9 8 7 6 5 4 3 2 1

WITH THANKS TO!

My Intergalactic Bar & Grille regulars, including but not limited to: Commander Carla Arpin, Lynne "Library Lady" Welch, Cy Korte, Mike Pennington, Brenda, Marty, Jennifer, Diane, Robin, Bill, Lynne, Debby, Katrina, Sumera, Ann, Liza, Cynn, Chris, Cathy, Marie, Darcy, Mischelle, Kimberly, Donna, and the rest of the wild gang. Thank you for listening to the lunatic ravings of an author when surely you could be doing better things....

Some of the best authors on the planet: Susan Grant, Stacey Klemstein, Robin Owens, Isabo "Kat" Kelly, Monette Michaels, Nancy Cohen, Ruth Kerce, and Jacqueline Lichtenberg—thank you for your friendship and guidance....

My agent, Kristin Nelson, for her spunky effervescence, and my editor, Anne Groell, for her good-natured patience....

And as always, with thanks to my husband, Robert Bernadino, who believes in me; and our resident furpersons, Daq and Miss Doozy, for their secretarial expurrrtise.

With love,
~Linnea

an accidental goddess

It wasn't the first time Gillie had hazily regained consciousness flat on her back in sick bay, feeling stiff and out of sorts. And unable to account for a missing two or three hours. Pub-crawling did have its side effects.

But it was the first time she'd been unable to account for a missing two or three *hundred years*. Not even a week of pub-crawling could explain that.

Three hundred forty-two years, sixteen hours, Simon's voice stated clearly in her mind. *If you want to be absolutely accurate.*

She didn't. Her math skills had never been her strong point. And three hundred years was a close enough estimate to cause her stomach to do flip-flops in a way a bottle of Devil's Breath never had.

The possibility that she'd died flitted across her mind—though death wouldn't have thrown her inexplicably into the future. Even so, she thought it prudent to pull her essence out of her physical self and make a cursory examination of her own body on the diag table. By all appearances, she was still short, blond, and very much alive. The readout on the medi-stat confirmed the last part of her hastily conducted diagnosis. It detailed a few bumps and bruises as well as notations on a mild concussion, no doubt the source of her blistering headache.

A headache that wasn't the least bit helped by whatever heathen concoction was being pumped into her system through the round med-broche clamped to her wrist. Med-broches! Raheiran technology rarely used such invasive things. She longed to alter its feed rate but knew her mental tinkering would likely set off some alarm. She'd almost tripped a few when she'd awakened ten minutes ago, groggy and achy, then tried to spike into this sick bay's systems.

Impatience invariably leads to sloppy work, Simon had chastised.

Sloppy work, a bitch of a headache, and a reality that suddenly did not make sense.

How in the Seven Hells had she ended up three hundred years from her last conscious moment, flat on her back in some unknown space station's sick bay? With Simon in a similar state of disarray a few decks below.

The Fav'lhir.

Ah, yes. Small matter of a large warship intent on her destruction. Obviously, the Fav hadn't succeeded. Though something *had* happened.

They're vicious and powerful, Simon, but they don't have time-travel capabilities. Neither do we. Someone or something else pulled us here. Wherever *here* was. That much she ought to find out.

She stepped away from her unconscious body on the diag table, peeked around the corner of the small room. Felt foolish and could hear Simon's wry chuckle. No one could see her.

At least, no one other than Simon, who, from his tone, was very aware she'd pulled out of her self to explore her surroundings. *Have a care, My Lady. You were injured.*

We've more serious things to consider than my few aches and pains. There were two other patients in the sick bay in much worse shape than she was. She didn't know them; there'd been no one on her ship when the Fav had attacked other than Simon and herself. The girl on the diag bed was too young to be part of the squadron she'd worked with in the Khalaran Fleet. Almost automatically, Gillie touched their essences, sending healing energy as she walked by. Then she sidestepped quickly, and unnecessarily, as a thin man in a blue lab coat hurried past and into the corridor.

She followed him and for the next fifteen minutes was thoroughly astounded, and more than a little disconcerted, by what she saw.

Wide corridors were filled with people in various modes of dress, from the utilitarian freighter-crew shipsuits to more exotic costumes with flowing skirts and elaborate fringed shawls. She noted the familiar range of skin tones—from the dusky to the pale—and hair colors—mostly browns and blacks but a few bright reds and light blonds—and heard all three Khalaran dialects. A few languages were harder to identify. Rim-world tongues, most likely, clipped and rapid in their sound.

She raised her eyebrows at the antigrav pallets

trailing behind a group of dockworkers, surprised by the pallets' advanced configuration. Raised her eyebrows further at the state-of-the-art holovid news kiosks and station diagrams near the lift banks. Those she studied carefully, listening to the chatter around her; tech talk about scanner arrays and enviro grids. That matched what she saw on the diagram suspended three-dimensionally out from the bulkhead.

The Khalaran Confederation, with her assistance, had just been developing the technology to create a deep-space station the likes of which she looked at now. At least, they had been a day ago.

Correction, three hundred and forty-two years ago.

Yet it wasn't this jump in technology that bothered her. Nor this space structure bristling with unexpected weapons and sensors and databanks. Nor her headache. Or the stiffness in her left shoulder, the result of her sudden collision with the bulkhead when the Fav'lhir ship had exploded a little too close for comfort off her starboard side.

Even the unexplained missing three hundred some-odd years failed to bother her. Or the fact that, in those three hundred some-odd years, there'd been no other Raheiran advisers in this sector. Simon had checked station security logs.

Given her people's minimal-intervention policy, that was one of the few things that made sense.

No, none of those things bothered her at all.

What really bothered her was something she heard in the corridor chatter as she continued her brief, hurried tour. Something she viewed on the news kiosks and station diagrams. And finally, something she saw as she stood before the temple's double-doored entrance, shaking her head in disbelief.

What really bothered Gillaine Davré was that during her three-hundred-some-odd-year absence, the damned Khalar had gone on a shrine-building kick and made her into a deity.

Simon? There's a huge holograph of me in this temple! But I'm not—

It appears they think you are, My Lady.

Oh, hell. Oh, damn. This wasn't a minor error in alien protocol. This was a mistake. A big one that encompassed an entire culture. Gillie shuddered at the ramifications. *We have to get away from here. Now.*

Now is not possible, I fear.

When?

Three weeks, perhaps less. There's much damage to repair.

There'll be worse damage if they find out who I am!

Calm down, Gillaine, Kiasidira. There's no reason they should. That holo's fairly old—you're in formal dress in it and your hair's quite different. And I'm finding no references to you as Captain Davré. Only as the Kiasidira. However, just to be on the safe side, I do recommend avoiding contact with any Raheiran crystal and, of course, any itinerant witches or sorcerers.

The Khalar aren't mageline.

Then we'll have no problems, will we? Just be your usual charming self for the next few weeks and no one will know a goddess walks among them.

I'm not a goddess!

Nor are you seriously injured. Therefore, if you don't return to your self rather quickly, that medical officer trying to wake you may start running tests you won't like.

Rynan Makarian frowned at the irritatingly incomplete data on his deskscreen and knew it was all his fault. It had been four months since he'd been given the command to establish a Fleet presence on Cirrus One and secure it for the Project. Station systems were still far from optimal. Cirrus One was far from optimal; the station had passed its prime well over eighty-five years ago.

"Give it to Mack. He'll fix it," someone in Fleet defense and logistics no doubt had said.

It wouldn't have been the first time it was said either. He knew his reputation for unerring efficiency preceded him. It had bestowed upon him the rank of admiral in the Khalaran's newly organized Fifth Fleet at the unlikely age of forty-three. And bestowed upon him the derelict monstrosity known as Cirrus One, to rehab into a usable headquarters for the Fifth. And, within the next four months, to have that same derelict monstrosity serve as something even more important than that: as the primary terminus for the critical Rim Gate Project.

That project, more than Cirrus One, had drawn him off the bridge of the *Vedritor* and ensconced him behind a desk—albeit a well-dented, slightly rusted one.

But it was Cirrus One that took up the majority of his time. And time was the one thing he lacked. He had little more than a month in which to get his HQ fully operational and secure. Missing supplies, incomplete data, and delayed support staff notwithstanding.

He rested his elbows on that same battered desk and leaned his forehead against his fists. Damn. There was a wisdom in imperfection. He saw that clearly now. What was that adage that Lady Kiasidira's priests used to comfort the misguided? *We are all in a continuing process of growth. There are no mistakes. Only lessons.*

Cirrus One was one hell of a lesson.

Had he allowed himself a few mistakes in his career, he might well still be on the bridge of the *Vedritor*. A mere senior captain, not an admiral with an impeccable reputation to solve the unsolvable. To rectify the—

His intercom trilled. He tapped the flashing icon, leaned back in his chair. "Makarian."

A familiar thin, dusky-toned face wavered, solidified on the screen. Doc Janek, his chief medical officer. His blue lab coat bore the *Vedritor*'s insignia. Like many things Mack had requested, Fifth Fleet uniforms were still "in transit." As supply routes went, Cirrus One wasn't in the middle of nowhere. It was just the last exit before it.

"Admiral, you asked to be notified. Our visitor from that damaged freighter's awake."

Yet one more thing to plague his schedule with delays: an unauthorized ship with an unconscious pilot. An image flashed through Mack's mind: a pale-haired young woman in nondescript spacer grays lying awkwardly on the decking, just behind the pilot's chair. Emergency lighting had tinged the small bridge with glaring shades of red, casting eerie shadows over her small, still form. Another smuggler, he'd thought at that moment, whose ambitions had far exceeded her ship's weaponry.

He had a studied dislike for smugglers, yet had felt it would be a shame if this one died. He'd caught little more than her profile as the med-techs had lifted her onto an antigrav stretcher, but it had been enough for him to mentally tag her as beautiful, before he was even aware he'd done so.

That wasn't like him. It was unprofessional, judgmental. She was nothing more than a temporary annoyance.

But she was beautiful. It made the job of questioning her a bit less unpleasant.

"On my way." He slapped off the intercom, threw one more frustrating glance at the inadequate, nonsensical data, and strode from his office.

The sights and sounds of Cirrus One assaulted him immediately. He'd thought by now he'd be used to them. Had the sights and sounds been continually repetitive, he probably would have been.

But there was always something new. Or rather, there was always *something*. His office was a few steps from the main atrium. Raucous laughter barked out from a level or two below, or possibly above, as Mack stepped into the open corridor. A man and a woman, in the blue shipsuits of a starfreighter crew, leaned against a wide metal pylon on his left. They were locked in a passionate embrace, oblivious to his presence. And oblivious to the snickers of a trio of adolescent boys in various stages of sartorial rebellion loping past, their long skirts catching between their gangly legs.

Mack shook his head and sent a mental plea to the

gods for understanding. And patience. He missed the orderly routine of the *Vedritor*.

There was a loud whoop, then a high-pitched screech. His gaze automatically jerked to the right. A flash of bright yellow and blue hurtled quickly uplevel through the atrium's center.

His hand automatically swiveled his comm set's thin mouth mike into position. "Makarian to ops."

"Ops." A familiar male voice sounded in his earpiece. "Lieutenant Tobias."

"I thought we'd solved the parrot problem."

"I thought we had too, sir."

"I just left my office." He sidestepped a merchant whose balding head barely topped the bolts of cloth stacked in his arms. Evidently someone was getting hard-goods deliveries. Where in hell were those uniforms? "Main north, Tobias. Heading uplevel. The problem's not solved."

"Logged and noted, sir."

He tapped off the mike, flicked it back down. Fleet crewmembers, whose uniforms showed mixed insignias, nodded respectfully as he passed. Stationers and freighter crew, whose clothing and demeanor showed an unholy mixture of unknown origin, simply ignored him.

Janek's sick bay was at D5-South, five levels down, on the opposite section of the ring. He headed for the stairs. Cirrus One's lifts had been known to ignore him too.

The lanky CMO turned from the med-stat panel when Mack stepped through the sliding doorway. "She's in Exam Four."

A second sliding door; this one ceased opening at

the halfway point. Mack squeezed through sideways, after Janek.

The young woman on the diag bed had her knees drawn up under the silver thermo-sheet and her arms wrapped around them. There was a flush of color on her pale cheeks, a slight curve on her lips. And an engaging, almost challenging tilt to her chin.

She was, most definitely, beautiful. But young. Couldn't be any more than twenty-five years old, though sick bay's analytics transed to him earlier had stated early thirties. Something more than her youthfulness didn't fit the smuggler's profile as he knew it. He couldn't pinpoint what it was, but then his mind seemed very reluctant to focus on business at the moment.

Janek moved to her bedside. She smiled, then her gaze found Mack.

"This is Admiral Makarian, commander of the Fifth Fleet on Cirrus," his CMO was saying, but Mack only half listened. The other half of him was unprofessionally captivated by the color of the young woman's eyes.

Green, yet lavender. Her eyes widened slightly at his introduction. He assumed the cause of her surprise was his age—he was the youngest admiral in Fleet history to date—or his uniform. His shirt, like Janek's lab coat, still had the *Vedritor*'s insignia. The bars decorating his breast pocket showed only the three for senior captain.

His admiral's bars, like the requested uniforms, had not yet materialized. Now he wished they had. For some reason, he wanted to look his best in front of her.

He shook off his uncharacteristic self-consciousness. She was just a smuggler. She was—

"Gillaine Davré." She leaned forward, extended one hand. No salute. Therefore she wasn't military, or even ex-military.

He took her hand, got a closer look at those eyes. They *were* an odd combination of green and lavender. Green with decidedly lavender flecks. His fingers tightened around hers. A man could lose his soul in eyes like those.... The direction of his thoughts jolted him. Quickly, he cleared his throat, refocused. Put a firm tone in his voice. "Miselle Davré? Or is it Captain?"

"Captain, technically. But mostly just Gillie."

He released her hand. She had a voice almost as intriguing as her eyes. Firm, yet with a sultry undercurrent. He imagined her laugh—

He had to stop imagining. He didn't imagine. He never imagined.

He stepped back, clasped his hands behind his waist. "My CMO tells me your injuries aren't serious. Your ship has suffered significant damage, however."

The exam room's utilitarian overheads were harsh, bright, but their light played through her short, pale hair in a mixture of silver and gold like moonlight and starlight. There was an almost ethereal beauty about her. Mack felt as if he knew her, but from a dream.

He halted this additional mental wandering. "Your ship also has no sanctioned Confederation ID. I need to know, Captain, just who you are. What you're doing here."

"Recuperating in your sick bay is what I'm doing here, Admiral." The edge of her mouth quirked upward slightly. "It's not as if Cirrus One was my intended destination."

Obviously, neither his rank nor his tone had managed to intimidate her. He tried to keep the frown off his face. She wasn't military. His infamous frown would be wasted on her. "Where were you headed?"

"The Ziami Quadrant."

"Ziami?" In a huntership as powerful as the *Vedritor,* that would be four months and two jumpgates. In a small freighter like hers, that could take eight months, maybe a year, if the ion storms kicked in around the Sultana Drifts again. What in hell would a young woman be doing in that godsforsaken quadrant? Cirrus was bad enough.

"My family runs a depot in Ziami. When we trade here, we run our ships under a Khalaran Kemmon flag. I was headed home, running empty. I'd already archived my Confed clearances. However, if my ship's not too damaged, I should be able to pull them up for you."

That sounded reasonable. But Mack rarely accepted reasonable, especially in explanations without documentation that might concern one of the more volatile Khalaran states, such as one of the rim Kemmons. "Which Kemmon do you trade with?"

She shrugged. "Depends on the commodity and the destination."

"No, Captain. *This* run."

"Not the Fav."

"The Fav'lhir and their Kemmons haven't plagued us for over three hundred years, thank the Lady. That wasn't my question." Yet in a way, it was. He'd watched her face when she'd answered, noted the dislike when she'd said the name of the longtime enemy of the Khalar. Not that the emotion couldn't be a sham. But she didn't strike him as a Fav'lhir agent. Plus, he'd seen her ship. That definitely wasn't up to Fav standards.

"I had a transfer for a Kemmon–Drin tri-hauler," she said after a long moment. "Then I had some personal business to take care of. I may have overstayed my clearances."

So that was it. He relaxed slightly, matching a fact to his suspicious feeling. Now he knew why she'd avoided answering his questions. Not quite a smuggler. A rim trader—and that's what he was sure she was—could have any type of interesting "personal business," from a genuine love affair to an illegal trade in drugs and weapons. Or, more likely, rune stones. Life crystals. Most of which were probably fakes but willingly snatched up in the market, as anything even remotely connected with the Tridivinian gods, or Lady Kiasidira, always was.

"When do you intend to release her, Doc?"

"I want another scan of her concussion. An hour."

"Your ship's in a repair bay on D11-South, Captain." He tried to ignore the color of her eyes, the softness of her mouth, as she leaned against the diag bed's pillows. Straightening his shoulders, he reminded himself that he wasn't in sick bay to notice such things. "You can show me those Drin clearances in one hour."

She seemed about to say something, but then only nodded and smiled.

The exam-room door opened completely this time. He took it as a signal that his departure was advisable, as well as an omen to try the lifts. Either way, he had to get out of her exam room before the decidedly unprofessional imagination he didn't have got the best of him.

Ops Command 2 was on Upper6-North. Or rather, it was being slowly integrated back into its rightful section, as Mack viewed it, of Upper6-North. Eventually, his office would be there as well. The previous administrators of Cirrus had firmly declared their priorities when they'd appropriated that square footage, as well as a large portion of ops, and transformed the space into a casino gaming parlor. One of his first projects had been the reclamation of that space back to a more functional—at least in his opinion—utilization.

For now he could deal with his temporary office. Getting a real operations and command center running was more important. The Rim Gate Project would depend on them.

He headed for the left side of ops' lowest level. A stocky red-haired woman monitoring enviro readouts glanced his way briefly and nodded. She was one of the station's civilian techies, in a wrinkled, orange-colored jumpsuit that showed no insignia. Another orange-jumpsuited man leaned over an engineering console beyond her. He was deep in argument with someone on station intercom.

Tobias was at the long communications console, his muscular frame shoved into a chair, his thick fingers moving quickly over the screen pads. Like Janek, Fitch Tobias was a former *Vedritor* officer, one of nine who'd volunteered to follow Rynan "Make It Right" Makarian to Cirrus One. Ten Fleet officers from the

Vedri plus one hundred seventy-five from other Fleet ships and postings comprised Mack's current staff, with Tobias as his second-in-command. One hundred eighty-five of his people versus five hundred fifty—give or take a couple dozen illegals—longtime residents of Cirrus. And their parrots.

That his staff was outnumbered by an eclectic, somewhat eccentric civilian population was a fact Mack rarely forgot. But that wasn't his only problem. He rested one hip against the comm console, crossed his arms over his chest.

"Still working on the avian invaders, sir," Tobias said, without raising his close-shaved head.

"I'm not here about the parrots. I've been trying to make some sense out of this past week's PSLs." Especially the ones in the Runemist sector. That's where his patrols had found the intriguing Gillaine Davré. Who occupied his thoughts at the moment only because of her ship's location in Runemist, of course.

Tobias shoved his heel down on the chair's deck-lock release. He pushed the chair to his right, slid down the track to the empty station at the secondary sensor screens. Fleet HQ on Cirrus had yet to officially open for business. Stations were understaffed. Everyone, including Mack, did double duty or more.

"This quadrant's known for unreliable perimeter sensor logs. Sir," he said when Mack caught up with him.

"Agreed, Lieutenant. But this unreliable data was a bit too regular. Plus it came out of Runemist. If someone uncreative wanted to create sham unreliable data there, that's probably what it would look like."

"Like this, sir?" Tobias's screen flickered to life.

Mack leaned his palms on the edge of the console. "Like that."

The screens in ops were better than the hastily constructed setup in his temporary office. They were on a direct link to the main databanks. His office, well... the parrots soaring up and down the atrium core were probably a more effective means of data transport than what he worked with.

He saw now what had been missing from the data on his screen. And didn't at all like what he saw.

The toe of his boot found the deck-lock tab at the base of Tobias's chair. He unlocked it. "Get me the *Vedri* on high-priority scramble."

Tobias pushed the chair to his left, sailed back to communications. "Hailing."

"I'll take it on your screen when you've reached her."

It took ten minutes—he absently timed it on ops' main clock—before Iona Cardiff's face flickered onto the screen. "*Vedritor*. Comm Officer Cardiff."

Cardiff was second shift. At least, she had been four months ago. He didn't think the *Vedri*'s new captain, his former first officer, would have changed things that quickly.

He was right.

"Transferring your call to Captain Adler's office right now, sir."

"Admiral. What can I do for you?" Steffan Adler was a short, wiry man whose light blue eyes were a contrast to his swarthy complexion. A few years older than Mack, Adler had learned—in the seven years they'd served together—that Rynan Makarian rarely made social calls. Mack could see Adler's hand poised over an open datapad, ready to take notes.

"I've got PSLs out of Runemist I don't like. We have three patrol ships posted in that sector. Need you to take a closer look."

"What do you think I might find?"

"Someone, or something, that shouldn't be there—and is doing a barely passable job of covering their tracks."

"Smugglers?" Adler's pale eyes narrowed.

"That's my best guess. Patrol may have brought in one of their friends earlier. Says her name's Davré." Mack permitted his imagination to briefly resurrect Gillaine Davré's image. But only because he was discussing her in a professional manner.

"What was she running?"

"It appears she might have been running *from* someone. Her ship had considerable damage to the starboard side. She's sitting in sick bay right now."

"Is her ship in our files?"

"I won't know until I access her clearances. Her ship was in full shutdown when we towed her in a few hours ago. We have no ID on it, or her. But she was found not far from my suspicious PSLs."

Adler glanced down at his console. "Receiving your data now, sir. We're on it. I'll report back as soon as we're in range."

The screen flickered to black, then filled with Cirrus One's logo.

There were fifteen minutes yet before Janek would release Davré from sick bay. Mack still had work to do before he met with her. He took ops' internal stairway up to Ops Main and the primary scanner console.

Stationmaster Johnna Hebbs's dark scowl greeted him as he unlocked an empty chair and slid it to an open scanner station. She leaned against the command sling, watching him with undisguised disdain. Amazing how this woman could be so beautiful yet so unattractive at the same time.

Hebbs was old guard, second in command when Stationmaster Quigley had controlled Cirrus One for the Cirrus Quadrant Port Authority. The Port Authority was a branch of the Khalaran Department of Commerce and not known for its enthusiasm for the Khalaran military. But in this instance, CQPA agreed with Fleet that Quigley—and his gambling operation—had to go. They insisted, however, that Mack retain Hebbs as stationmaster because she knew Cirrus and because she was popular with stationers. The tall brunette was popular with *male* stationers, Mack had learned. Female stationers knew better than to cross her.

Mack acknowledged the stationmaster's tight nod with one of his own, then turned his attention to the console. He brought up the logs again. Frowned. Something was definitely going on in Runemist and, with the Rim Gate Project about to launch, this was a time he could least afford interruptions. Three jumps out from the major space lanes, the Cirrus Quadrant was too remote for such unusual activity. The Runemist sector, with no habitable worlds and only a few derelict miners' rafts, even more so.

No one came through Runemist unless she had a damned good reason. She was either looking for trouble, or running from it.

The intriguing Captain Gillaine Davré had better

be prepared with some very good answers to his questions and documentation to back it all up. Or else Mack intended to make sure her troubles in Runemist would be the least of her problems.

After all, she'd just added to his.

Her ship looked terrible. But then, that had been Simon's intention. Gillie walked in silence by Admiral Makarian's side as he inspected the exterior of the starfreighter. Four loading bays—two starboard, two port—gave the stern a bulbous silhouette. Main rampway and airlock were just aft of the bridge. By all appearances, a common Rondalaise-class short-hauler, a teardrop shape of matte gray and black metal platings, one of thousands out there.

At least, that's what the passing Khalaran patrol ship's files had revealed to Simon while their ship had been cloaked and she'd been on the floor, unconscious. Thank the gods the cloaking function hadn't been damaged by the Fav'lhir fightercraft.

And thank the gods that Simon had realized long before she did, that they were not only somewhere they didn't belong, but some*when*.

It had been left to her to figure out the rest of the bad news.

"How many ships did you say fired on you?" The admiral's dark eyes narrowed as he examined the large blackened area of hull plating forward of the starboard bay door.

"Two, sir." She repeated what Simon had felt was reasonable, based on what he could draw from this station's tactical databanks. "But I never got a visual. And I don't know what my logs will show."

"Then let's find out."

Admiral Makarian was not happy. Gillie didn't need her telepathic senses to figure that out. It was in the tension in his broad shoulders, in the way the tall man moved like a jungle *pantrelon*, poised to kill.

He did remind her of a *pantrelon*, with his dark hair and eyes, his black uniform accenting his sleekly muscled body. Pure Khalar, and definitely attractive. His people had changed little in three hundred and some-odd years. Except to become a little less warlike, a little more tolerant than she remembered them. And a lot less careful.

Though Makarian might be the exception.

It's your fault.

Simon's teasing comment reached her as she palmed open the ship's main hatch. He found the temple, and her attendant goddesshood, amusing. She didn't.

It's not my fault! She could feel Makarian's breath on her hair, the heat from his body brushing hers as the hatch slid open. He didn't trust her more than five inches away from him.

The Holy Guidelines of the Goddess Kiasidira—

We're all Tridivinians. There is no Goddess Kiasidira and you damned well know it!

My Lady . . .

Stuff a sock in it, Simon. I don't have time for that right now.

The small bridge was appropriately disheveled. She sent Simon a mental nod of appreciation. She'd been out cold while he'd altered the ship into something suitable for this situation, place, and time. And done a damned good job of it.

Gillie slid into the pilot's chair, dusted some debris from the console in front of her. It was her first look at Simon's rendition, but she'd helmed a variety of starships most of her adult life. She let her fingers play over the touchpads, knowing the pads wouldn't respond right away. They weren't supposed to. Not until she and Simon could figure out who they were supposed to be and provide the wary admiral with information that would make him leave them alone. They needed privacy to effect the repairs.

She let out what she hoped was a convincing sigh of frustration. "Systems aren't responding."

Makarian leaned around her, repeated her sequence on the console. Tried two more. The screens before them flickered, then died.

"I'll need some time to work on her system synchs," she told him.

He took the copilot's seat next to her. "Don't try to play games with me, Captain. You won't succeed."

She swiveled to face him. "Sir?" Had she let something slip? Did he suspect the truth?

"This ship's on lockout. Yes, that's a safety measure to prevent hijackings. But there's not a smuggler I've boarded who didn't have his ship rigged to mimic a safety lockout, just to keep Fleet from accessing his files. And I've opened every one."

He leaned his elbows on his knees, his narrowed eyes sending a clear warning. And a clear message that he thought she was a smuggler. Not a goddess. She let out a slow sigh of relief as he continued, "You have two choices. We can do this the easy way, and you unlock those files now. Or we can do it the hard way. And you'll face not only smuggling charges, but obstruction of an investigation and any other charge I can throw at you while I'm unscrambling your codes. And unscramble them I will."

I think he likes you.

Shut up, Simon.

She put on her most conciliatory expression. "I assure you, Admiral, there's no deliberate obstruction on my part." Well, not for the reasons he thought, anyway. "My ship was damaged. Send someone belowdecks to verify that while I try to realign my databanks, if you want. Only make sure they're willing to help and not just be decorative. I've a lot of work just to get this ship operative again. The sooner I do, the sooner my existence here will cease to be a problem for both of us."

"Anxious to get home?"

Home wasn't a possibility. Home had ceased to exist, three hundred forty-two years ago. The best she could hope for was to get back to Raheiran space as quickly as possible and leave the erroneous legend of the Lady Goddess Kiasidira far behind her. However, Simon was in no condition to handle the complexities, and stresses, of transiting the Rift right now. His initial three-week estimate might have been overly optimistic. "I'm anxious to be somewhere my every move's not questioned."

One dark eyebrow lifted slightly. "Open those files."

"I can't." Simon hadn't finished constructing them. She sure as hell wasn't going to show him her real logs. The damned Khalar would probably deem them sacred texts or some such nonsense. "I need time."

He sighed. His disappointment filtered over her. She pulled her telepathic field in more tightly. It was one thing to prudently monitor the enemy. It was totally another to let his emotions become a distraction.

I told you. I think he likes you.

"The hard way, then, is it?" Makarian shoved himself to his feet.

"Admiral Makarian." She rose as well. In the small confines of the bridge, they should have been nose to nose. They weren't. They were her nose to his chest. Gillie tamped down her irritation. His size gave him the obvious advantage in an intimidation contest.

But only the obvious. To reveal the unobvious would cause more problems than she was willing to deal with.

She let her arms rise and fall to her sides in a gesture of exasperation. It wasn't totally feigned. *How much longer do you need, Simon?*

A few hours, at most. I'm still not functioning at full capacity. And this station's databanks are singularly disorganized.

He wants to see something now.

Those new trick shots of yours at billiards are quite impressive.

Simon!

"Willing to cooperate, Captain Davré?" Makarian's deep voice was a low rumble.

Simon, give me something.

I snagged a block of shipping manifests. They're not perfect. By the time you take him belowdecks, I might have them passable.

Lock him out of everything but that, then. Gillie gestured toward the bridge hatchway. "My databanks are yours, Admiral. I've nothing to hide." She prayed she had something believable to show him.

She took the ladderway stairs just aft of the bridge down the two decks to engineering. Makarian's heavy bootsteps thudded after her.

Her stomach clenched when the admiral stopped mid-corridor, dark head angled slightly to the right. His casual posture, with his hands shoved carelessly in his pants pockets, didn't deceive her. Simon's layout didn't completely match the freighter he was simulating. Makarian had just caught that.

A distinct sensation of suspicion broke through her telepathic shield. Damn it! If she locked her own senses down any further she'd be useless. It wasn't as if she were probing for his feelings; not only would that experience be chaotic and unsettling—untrained minds were loud and disorganized—but Raheirans were taught to respect others' privacy.

And as much as she understood his suspicions, she had no desire to experience them. She had to appear calm, innocent, cooperative. Not flinch every time he did.

"You've done some modifications to this ship," he said when their gazes met.

"I'm not the original owner."

He seemed to accept that. His disquiet lessened but continued to simmer as he followed her down the corridor.

She palmed open the door marked *engineering*. A small room, left and right interior bulkheads lined with long consoles, and a narrow walkway between them. It wasn't dissimilar to her ship's actual layout. Since Makarian had already caught some differences, she hoped he might see this only as further evidence of her admitted modifications.

She sat at the primary console. It showed power active. Unlike the bridge, basic screens responded here, verifying life support, fuel levels, and hull integrity. Those functions survived all but total destruction of a ship.

She brought up the ship's main databanks and stood. "Be my guest."

He gave her a glance that would have been unreadable to everyone but a telepath. He wanted to trust her, to believe her. Why, she didn't know, nor would she probe to find out. It was only a fleeting emotion she sensed. But for the moment it changed her categorizing him as the enemy. And it unsettled her.

Then it was gone, his concentration focused on the screens before him. He keyed in a string of commands, and for the next twenty minutes she watched him play games with Simon.

There was a moment of satisfaction when he found the file of manifests. She held her breath while he gave them more than a cursory glance. They looked fine to her, but she didn't know exactly what he was looking for.

They must have looked fine to him too, though, for he tagged them, refiled them, and went back to his hunt.

From that point, all she could sense from him was frustration.

Finally, he dragged one hand over his face and swiveled toward her. "You're either very, very good, Davré, or you've got a very big problem."

She felt Simon's gleeful chortle, ignored it. "I've had two system failures in the past six months. Been running on patches. This new damage compounded my already existing problems."

"You should never have left Ziami if that was the case."

"Where we stumble is never as important as how often we get up again," she quipped. Only after the words were out of her mouth did she realize her error.

An expression of mild surprise crossed Makarian's rugged features. "I've not met many Ziamians who could quote the Lady."

Damn. She'd deliberately chosen Ziami as her feigned homeport because it was loosely allied with the Khalar and didn't share the Khalarans' obsession with their Lady Goddess. That granted her a much needed anonymity, except it was difficult to be anonymous about herself. She shrugged. "I hear that stuff spouted all the time when I'm here."

"That stuff," Makarian said, rising, "forms an important basis of a lot of people's lives. My people, the Khalar, might not be here but for her sacrifice."

I was right. He does like you.

Not me, Simon. A fraud. The sincere reverence in

Admiral Makarian's voice unsettled her. "I meant no disrespect."

He locked his hands behind his waist. "I'm putting this ship under a Level Two impound. You can have access to her, but she can't leave this station. Nor can you." He strode for the doorway but stopped. When he turned back to her, his dark eyes were hard. "Be in Ops Main at 0800 tomorrow. You'll be issued a restricted ID at that time. I'll advise you then of what repairs you'll be permitted to perform. And what reports I will require you to file, daily, with me."

"But—"

"I still have a lot of unanswered questions, Captain Davré. You will provide me answers to each and every one of them. Is that clear?"

She felt as if she were back in basic training. She gritted her teeth and answered like the dutiful junior cadet she'd never been. "Yes, sir. Very."

He nodded tersely. "Cirrus has only recently come under Fleet jurisdiction. There are still some unsavory areas. Do me a favor and stay out of trouble."

She stood in the middle of engineering, jaw clenched, until she could no longer hear his heavy bootsteps thudding through the ship.

He's gone.

She knew that, but Simon's reassurance felt good. *He doesn't trust us, but for all the right reasons, I think. I'm a smuggler and I insulted his religion.*

Then we passed the test.

Had they? Gillie clearly remembered the admiral's comment about unanswered questions. She didn't know how much more scrutiny she and Simon could stand. *How are you feeling?*

Tired. Though I did enjoy the diversion. He's more knowledgeable than I expected.

She stepped over the raised hatch tread and into the corridor. She needed a stiff drink and, unless Simon had moved it, the small ready room and galley should be aft of the bridge.

He's not more knowledgeable, she told him. *You're not taking those damned three hundred years into account.*

Three hundred forty-two years, three days—

Three, already? She gave a short, dry laugh as she climbed the stairs.

Three, already. And I am considering the time factor in my appraisal of Admiral Rynan Makarian. I thought it prudent to pull his service record. You might want to look at it.

She agreed to that. Know thy enemy was almost as important as know thyself. *Is that one of your Holy Edicts, or is it found in the Lady Goddess's Guidelines for Life?*

"Those guidelines were just a game we played one night at the pub." Simon hadn't moved the ready room. Good. She tabbed in a request for Devil's Breath, neat, with a twist. Her headache had returned. It was easier to speak out loud until the pounding subsided. "None of us was sober. Someone—I don't know, maybe it was Bex or Ethan—started compiling a list of all those little quips I make." She retrieved her drink, let herself collapse in the closest chair. "Hell, Simon, most of them are yours."

I endeavor to be not only succinct but inspirational.

"And I repeat them."

And now the Khalar revere them. And you.

Gillie sipped her drink and pondered that terrifying thought while the liquor burned a trail down her throat.

She had absolutely no interest in being revered. She had absolutely no interest in being the Kiasidira either, but she hadn't had much choice in that particular matter. Though she'd avoided it for as long as she could.

Then somehow, after three hundred years, the Khalar had mixed everything up. Gotten it all wrong, right down to her name. There was no Lady *Kiasidira*. There was, or had been, she realized belatedly, Lady Gillaine Davré. Also known as Captain Gillaine Davré, Raheiran Special Forces Division 1. Also known as Gillaine, Kiasidira. Kiasidira, like Captain, was a title, not a name.

The Khalar had gotten it all wrong.

But it had been wrong for over three hundred years. Their culture, their traditions were now intertwined with this legacy of error.

A legacy she would like nothing better than to correct.

But to do so might disrupt the very people Captain Gillaine Davré had worked so hard, three hundred forty-two years before, to keep alive.

She finished her drink. Simon had another saying: you can't make decisions in a vacuum. That was why he'd spent the past few hours pilfering information from Cirrus's databanks.

It was time for her to do a little information gathering of her own. She needed to have her answers and her new persona squarely in place before she faced Makarian again. And she could think of no better places to do that than the ones he'd just about ordered her to avoid.

Mack leaned on the railing of the atrium on U6-North and listened to the parrots screech. Did the damned things never sleep? Or were there simply so many of them, they were able to set up overlapping shifts for the sole purpose of annoying him?

"Surveying your kingdom, Admiral?"

Another annoyance. He recognized Johnna Hebbs's somewhat nasal, slightly high-pitched voice behind him. Her remark could be taken as a friendly gibe. But this was Hebbs. And he was Rynan Makarian, the man who'd disrupted her kingdom. He angled around toward her.

She was almost as tall as he was. But because he leaned against the railing, his eyes were on the same level as hers. They were a muddy brown, he noted. Uninteresting and flat in a face otherwise exotically beautiful. Though it was a beauty that seemed tarnished, especially compared to Gillaine—

He halted his thoughts. Right now, Gillaine Davré probably hated him as much as Hebbs did. If he were lucky, the two would never get together and compare notes.

Hebbs stepped next to him, pressed her palms against the railing. Her long, dark braid fell over one shoulder. "Why wasn't I informed that you'd placed Davré's *Serendipity* under impound?"

"You just were." He'd come straight to ops from the repair bay on D11, although informing Hebbs had been low priority. She was CQPA, not Fleet. "The ship's in one of my repair bays. It's my problem."

"Trying to spare me extra work, Mack? Your consideration is touching." She tilted her face slightly, regarded him from under thick lashes. It was a seductive pose, a practiced pose. She'd used it a lot on him, four months ago.

Now it was a seduction underscored with a message. Johnna Hebbs had changed her game, but not her methods.

"I'm dealing with a potentially volatile issue out in Runemist. The *Serendipity* came through there."

A low trill of laughter bubbled from Hebbs's throat. "Smugglers are a way of life out here. They're not volatile if you know how to handle them. Which I do." Her lashes dipped. "I know how to handle a lot of things. Very well. Shame you chose to do things the hard way. Admiral."

He was saved from commenting by the raucous screeching of parrots as they flew past, downlevel.

Hebbs pushed herself away from the railing, cast him one last, dismissive glance, then sauntered down the corridor.

Another flash of color. Bright green and red. Up-level. Must be shift change.

All the good stuff took place in the commercial sectors downlevel—closer to the freighter docks and cheaper housing. That was true of most stations, Gillie noted as she threaded her way through the residents strolling noisily on Down10-South, and Cirrus was no exception—especially after midnight.

Midnight was arbitrary, a dirtside term, but stations had to function with inhabitants who still adhered to those planetary rhythms. Cirrus's twenty-six-hour cycle allotted the midnight to 0500 hours as off duty for most.

But off duty didn't necessarily mean sleep.

The station directory, glowing on the wall opposite her bay on Down11-North, showed the open center atrium ended at Down7—D7, as it was called. Everything in Upper—above the Main Atrium—was labeled either *officers* or *executive*. Decks just above and below the atrium, which functioned as the midpoint in Cirrus, held the pricier, more respectable restaurants and stores.

D7 was the cutoff. The end of respectability. The beginning—in the southern quadrant of the station—of the Zone. She'd picked up that unofficial designation from Simon's perusals.

The Zone was exactly where Makarian didn't want her to go. So go there she would, just as she always had.

The Khalar hadn't minded, three hundred forty-two years ago, on Traakhalus Prime. Though her tendency to go pub crawling in the districts bordering the newly constructed Port Armin spaceport had given the Khalaran chancellor a few tense moments.

She'd made sure the white-haired man understood her priorities. "How can I function as adviser to your people if I don't know them?"

After six years of hoisting beers, shooting billiards, designing ships and defense arrays, and attending to numerous births, deaths, weddings, and commencements, she'd gotten to know them very well.

She thought they knew her.

Obviously, she was wrong. They'd deified her. Naming a pub in her honor would've been far more appropriate.

There were long lines at the lifts. She heard grumbles about never-ending malfunctions as she passed by. Stairs on Cirrus seemed to be the preferred method. She took the closest set up to D9. At the top of the stairs was a cluster of kiosks almost identical to the ones at the stair landing on D11.

A voice boomed out from behind a well-laden kiosk. "Rune stones! Genuine ward stones! Get guidance from the Lady Goddess!"

The only difference was D9's kiosks' prices were a half credit higher.

"That's 'cause we got the real ones here." The merchant's small eyes glinted. He leaned conspiratorially toward her, as if letting her in on a great secret. "Thems below, they're fakes. But we got real ones. Vedris, Ladris, you name it."

She could name them in her sleep if she had to. Knowing the names and the powers of Raheiran rune stones was innate to her. Each held a separate essence, each worked a separate magic: Vedri, Ladri, Nevri, and Khal.

The merchant's flat ward stones were in a separate velvet-lined tray from the square rune stones.

"Life stones?" she asked, not seeing any of the purple-tinged crystals. Not seeing anything real at all on the trays before her, actually. For one thing, if the stones had been genuine Raheiran, she wouldn't be able to stand so close to them without their sudden glow giving away her heritage. But she hadn't sensed anything when she'd scanned the kiosk and had known even before she stepped up to the rectangular stand that she could safely do so.

Still, if the merchant kept life stones in a metal casing ... she took a step back, cautiously, as he reached under the counter.

The beady-eyed merchant smiled as he brought up a plastic tray. "You're gettin' into high prices with them, my lady."

His use of the honorific startled her for a moment. Then she realized it was part of his sales pitch.

"How much?"

"Small ones start at seven thousand."

His price startled her for much longer than a moment. "That's—!" Blasphemous, she almost said, but caught herself.

"A good deal, considering what them priests charge, eh?"

Priests charge? For a healing through life stones? Anger surged through her.

I only discovered that bit of information myself a short time ago.

Simon! That's beyond insulting. A sacrilege. It's—

Three hundred forty-two years later, My Lady. As you so aptly reminded me earlier, things have changed.

Things suck. She turned abruptly away from the merchant before she voiced her thoughts. And her ire. She needed a drink. And she needed to get to know the Khalar, all over again.

The flashing sign over the wide doorway read, FIFTH QUARTER. SHOTS. BEERS. BILLIARDS. She pushed up the sleeves of her gray shipsuit and strode inside.

The Fifth Quarter was wide, but not very deep. The bar itself looked to be constructed of sheets of leftover bulkheading, medium gray in color and dotted with bolt studs. Two billiards tables sat under low-hanging lights to her left. Real tables with bright green felt tops, not holosims. Games were in progress on both. She watched for a moment. Neither was going to end any time soon. A flicker of movement behind her signaled stools had opened at the bar.

She hoisted herself up onto one. A bar 'droid wiped a rag over the counter in front of her. "How can I serve you, miselle?"

It took her a moment to place the unit. The 'droid was humanoid in form, barrel-chested and long-armed, a modified version of a Raheiran K3T-0. She'd been working on a prototype with a Khalaran robotics firm when the Fav'lhir had made their presence known. At least some of her centuries-old legacy was correctly intact. "The house's best ale, Keto."

"My pleasure, miselle?"

What's currency here, Simon? If she hadn't been so upset over the rune-stone seller, she would've thought to ask that before she sat down.

Credits or novads, if you want to use hard coin.

Well, that hadn't changed. Though the novads she had in her pocket might well be auctioned off as antiques to a coin collector. She didn't want to open a credit file on station. It left a readable trail. Besides, she didn't intend to stay on Cirrus that long.

She fingered the small, octagonal coins in her pants pocket, glanced at a stack sitting in front of a plump woman with bright red hair. They were close enough to her to grab the image of the date stamp, duplicate it. The coins grew warm in her hand, then cooled.

Keto brought her ale.

"How much?"

"Six and a half, miselle."

Prices had gone up. A decent ale used to be no more than two novads. Ah, well. She spilled the coins on the bar.

The redhead's name was Petrina. Her companion, Tedmond, returned from the billiards tables with an unhappy expression on his well-lined face.

"From Ziami, are you?" Petrina sucked the foam off her ale. "Know Bo Grismar, of Grismar Trade?"

Hell. She'd grabbed on to Ziami in her mental forays while still in sick bay. She'd remembered it as a remote quadrant that had little to do with the Khalar, other than some minor trading. What she'd found in Cirrus's databanks led her to believe that hadn't changed, so it had seemed the perfect home for her to adopt. Now she was beginning to suspect those databanks had some serious deliberate omissions.

"Not personally. Though my cousin probably does. He's the socializer. I spend most of my time in the lanes."

"Thought everyone in Ziami knew Bo."

Gillie broke her first rule, sent a hurried apology to her goddess. The real one. *Forgive me, Ixari.* She smiled at Petrina, probed only far enough to gently pull an image from the woman's busy mind. It was like walking into a small room with three parties going on simultaneously. Gillie needed a mouthful of ale before she could answer. "I know who he is. Just don't know him personally. Big guy with a beard. Smokes those gods-awful cigars." She wrinkled her nose.

She had to break her "sanctity of privacy" rule three more times in the next hour. Good thing there was no shortage of ale on Cirrus and that Petrina was drinking a goodly share of it. For there was much Gillie didn't know about Ziami and about the rim traders who ran between there and Cirrus. No wonder Makarian had distrusted her so quickly.

"Things are going down the shitter, what with 'Make It Right' Makarian here now." Petrina was on her third ale and content to talk to Gillie, rather than ask questions. "At least, that's what my Teddy says." She glanced back at her Teddy, lining up a shot at the billiards table.

"Make It Right?" Gillie made a mental note to read the rest of that file on Makarian as soon as she returned to her ship.

"Big Fleeter with even bigger brass balls. Just made admiral, you know. 'Course then they kicked his ass out here with us lowlifes." Petrina snorted. "We're not what he's used to. Nor do we want him here. Not that Mack ain't half bad to look at. It's that attitude." She pointed one finger at Gillie's face.

Gillie knew the attitude and had to agree with

Petrina's observation, as well as the one that Makarian—Mack? She smiled to herself. She liked that—as well as the one that Mack wasn't half bad to look at. He was, in truth, extremely pleasant to look at. But there was, as Petrina said, that attitude. Not unlike the *pantrelon* she'd likened him to earlier, Mack appeared both attractive and dangerous.

"He's got my ship on impound," she admitted.

"You who they towed in earlier? Who hit you?"

"Never got a visual on them. They jammed my eyes. And my ship's not able to talk yet." Gillie knew freighter lingo, trusted it hadn't changed much over the years—that is, centuries.

"That stinks, Gillie. Mack's giving you a hard time? Figures. Traders kept Cirrus alive long before Fleet ever decided to put their credits here. Traders and, of course, those devoteds who come out here every year for the Celebration of the Sacred Sacrifice." Petrina cocked her head to one side. "That why you were headed here? Just missed it, you know. Ended three days ago."

Three days ago...Three days ago she'd been flat on her face on her ship's bridge. "No, I—"

"Maybe you can catch the next one. Pack 'em in good here. Rune-stone sellers make out with big profits. Lot of 'em are still hanging around, but most'll be gone by next week."

"I saw them."

"Buy any?"

Gillie shook her head.

"Really? Thought you would—well, it's your hair color." Petrina flicked a finger at Gillie's hair. "Lot of her followers change theirs to that blond, 'cause it matches hers, you know."

She didn't. No, she did. The infamous and unlikely Lady Goddess Kiasidira.

"But of course, they wear it real long, like she did," Petrina continued. "Yours is short."

Gillie hadn't worn her hair long in almost five years. Three hundred forty-seven years ago. The Khalar, as she and Simon had discovered in their first few hours on station, were working off some very old holos. Every one they'd seen was a version of that gods-awful staged holograph taken her first year on Traakhalus. Swaddled in a thick, purple Raheiran mage robe, her sword raised, face turned skyward, she'd felt like an idiot. A circus display. An over-dressed avenging angel.

Even she had a hard time recognizing herself.

Tedmond returned, a handful of winnings jingling, and nuzzled his face into Petrina's neck. Her answering giggle was surprisingly soft and lilting for a woman of her size.

Then the decking under the bar suddenly lurched, hard. Glasses crashed to the floor, liquid and foam flying, spilling. Bottles rattled, shattered. People tumbled from the stools, swearing as they thudded onto the floor.

Gillie grabbed the edge of the bar, hung on. Someone careened against her. Screams filled the air. The lights over the billiards tables swung precariously, sickeningly.

Then all movement stopped. The only sound that could be heard was the discordant blaring of the red-alert siren. And the low hum of the station's ion cannons powering up.

Simon?

Fav'lhir.

Shit. Images of their Raider-class fighters, studded with weaponry, filled her mind. Somehow, they'd followed her. Found her. Gillie released her hold on the bar and bolted for the corridor, her heart pounding almost as loudly as her boots.

"On my way!" Mack slapped off his bedside intercom with one hand, groped in the darkness for his uniform pants with the other. "Lights!" he ordered. Cabin illumination responded slowly as he yanked on his pants, tripped over his boots in the shadows, swore. He pulled a shirt out of his closet, barked his knuckles on the door when the floor beneath him jolted.

He swore again, but the bleating of alarm sirens swallowed his words. Snapping the tiny comm set over his right ear, he charged for the door.

The lifts were on automatic lockdown. He keyed in his override code, prayed the lifts would stay functional long enough to get him up two decks to U7. As the doors closed in front of him, he flipped up his mouth mike. "Makarian to ops. Status."

"Lieutenant Pryor. Shields at max. Cannons powering up, sir."

"ID on the bogies?"

"Not yet."

"Get Tobias on it."

"He's already checked in, sir. On his way."

Mack collided with Johnna Hebbs at the doorway to Ops Main. Her long unbraided hair hung past her waist. Her orange uniform shirt was on inside out. He grabbed her arm, steadying her. She reeked of liquor.

He should order her off duty. Even though Cirrus One was a joint venture, he had that authority in an emergency. But he didn't know what he had out there. Only that it had gotten past Cirrus's defenses, fired on the station. He needed every live body he could get, especially one who knew Cirrus as well as she did.

"You're drunk. Get some coffee." His voice was an angry growl. He released her arm. "Then get to your post."

"Go to hell," she said. She staggered away.

Voices in Ops Main were hushed, tense. Pryor was at Con-1, his white mustache seeming to bristle as he worked his screens with diligent concentration.

"What've we got?" Mack asked, reading the data over Pryor's shoulders.

Pryor's thick brows knotted. "Nothing confirmed yet, sir."

He didn't have to tell Pryor to stay on it. He knew he would.

Several stations around him were vacant. Crew slid back and forth on their unlocked chairs. A console section, unattended, lights flashing, caught his attention. Mack took the station, coordinated data with a tense-faced, overworked lieutenant. Many systems were on a temporary link, would be for another three weeks. This couldn't have come at a worse time.

He pulled his gaze from the pinched, frowning faces around him and stared at the large main screen. It showed him nothing but the black starfield. One of the secondary, smaller screens displayed a squadron of Cirrus's fighters veering away from the station in a defensive formation. Other screens showed the starfield, then the squadron from a different angle.

Sensors told him nothing.

Not one damned thing.

He waited until two more techs hurried in to assist before he thundered down the steps to Ops 2.

Tobias was at the secondary sensor console.

"What's out there?" Mack knew if anyone could answer that question, it was Tobias.

"All I can tell you right now is what isn't. The parrots." Tobias grabbed two sensor feeds, fed their data into the analytics. "But I may be able to get something on their weapons' energy signatures."

That's exactly what he would have done. When you can't find the enemy, look for what they've left behind.

He couldn't remember the name of the woman at communications. But she wore an orange jumpsuit. Not one of his people. "Can you raise the *Vedritor*?"

"Lieutenant Tobias requested that a few minutes ago, sir. Waiting on a response to our hail."

He'd buy Tobias a beer later for that one. "Contact the *Gallant* and the *Worthy*. Alert them to our situation, but don't bring them in yet." He needed those cruisers, and their patrol ships, out there. In case whoever had paid Cirrus a visit had more friends on the way.

"Alerting them now, sir," the woman replied.

He looked back toward the scanners. "Tobias?"

"Still working on it."

He took the stairs up to Ops Main two at a time.

Hebbs was at her post, her hair tied back, her shirt still inside out. A cup of coffee sat in the holder on her desk. She didn't look up as he strode past but kept her gaze locked on her deskscreen.

Sensors showed nothing. Two squadrons circled the station now. Saw nothing. The *Vedri,* on her way in, saw nothing. The *Gallant* and the *Worthy* reported all was quiet. An hour later he downgraded to yellow alert, pulled in one squadron.

He wished like hell he had an office on ops level where he could monitor everything and yet have a place to think. Dissect the data. Unravel the reports, even if they told him nothing.

He slid a chair over to the empty station next to Tobias's on Ops 2. Ops Main buzzed above him, but the tension had dissipated. The red glow of the large clock on the wall snagged his attention. It was damned near three in the morning.

"I don't like this, sir."

Mack arched an eyebrow, peered at Tobias's screen. His back hurt, his neck hurt, and if he really wanted to be honest about it, he had a throbbing headache. Bad news at this point would fit right in. "Tell me."

"The only energy signatures I was able to capture don't match anything in our recent files."

He added a sickening chill to his growing list of ailments. Someone or something unknown? It was a damned big galaxy. Fleet's official policy was that all neighboring quadrants had been scouted and confirmed harmless, but Mack didn't discount that anything could be out there. People had believed for centuries that mogras and varls were mythical monsters, from the old tales of wizards and sorcerers. Then five years ago some scientist had discovered the petrified remains of one, not far from the spaceport on Traakhalus.

He wasn't given to imagining. But he didn't rule out the impossible.

"What does it match, Lieutenant?"

"Something from our archives."

Not an unknown, then. Perhaps someone resurrecting fifty-, seventy-year-old technology. Like Cirrus One itself.

"How far back?"

Tobias sucked in a breath. "Almost three hundred fifty years. Based on galeph–trine emission patterns."

"We didn't use galeph–trine technology three hundred years ago."

"No, sir, we didn't. But the Fav'lhir did. It matches an energy signature from our files on the Fav'lhir."

It was almost four in the morning. The lines in the conference room adjacent to Ops Main had already been drawn.

Cirrus's staff stood firmly behind Stationmaster Hebbs. "Impossible," she said, when Mack informed them of Tobias's findings. Six faces topping orange jumpsuits nodded. "You Fleeters keep trying to relive those thousand-year-old legends, when the Khalar were the personal bodyguards of the Sorcerer. Battling the Fav'lhir on horseback, with swords."

"They had some pretty good-size starfighters more recently," Mack intoned tiredly.

"That was three centuries ago. The Fav haven't bothered us since then. All we had out there tonight was a couple of rim traders settling a grudge a bit too close to station." Hebbs pointed one finger at Mack. "You just want this to be some kind of military crisis so you can justify taking this station away from CQPA. Well, we're not buying it." She shot to her feet, steadier and far more sober than she'd been an hour before. Mack wondered if it had been the coffee, or the fear, that had cleared the alcohol out of her system.

Though it was a fear she was denying. He understood that. Civilians had a difficult time believing that the Fav'lhir Empire would ever take an interest in the Khalar again. Lady Kiasidira had destroyed not only their ships but their mageline.

Mack knew better. Even before he'd made the rank of admiral, he was aware that Fav agents had visited the Confederation for years, in the same way that Fleet had their resources in the Empire. But both conducted their business quietly, never doing more than that. At least, not as far as confed agents could determine. So a peace—albeit an uneasy one—had existed based on the fact that the Fav weren't capable of any large-scale aggression.

Though the Fav had rebuilt their ships. But they'd never been able to resurrect their powerful mageline— and without that, their ships' capabilities lagged far behind those of the technically superior Khalar.

"I consider the matter settled," Hebbs said.

Six orange jumpsuited forms stood, filed out after her.

Mack looked at the five who remained with him.

Tobias, Pryor, Brogan, Rand, and Janek. If the unthinkable was about to happen, he had the best by his side.

"Keep all patrols on a Level-One yellow alert," he told Tobias. He glanced at his watch. "It's late." Or early, depending on how he looked at it. "The rest of you, get some sleep. We're not going to solve anything right now."

Janek lagged behind, his dark face creased with worry. "Really think it's possible, Mack?"

That the Fav'lhir would openly attack, after almost three hundred fifty years? The Rim Gate Project could be a powerful incentive.

Or was it simply—as Hebbs had stated—that Fleet was in need of a good fight, a cause that would, yes, make the locals more amenable to Fleet's presence on Cirrus? Such as an old rivalry resurrected.

Mack knew the rivalry, the legend, well. The Khalar and the Fav had been kinsmen thousands of years ago. The Khalar had allied behind the Sorcerer, the powerful Rothal-kiarr of Traakhal-armin. The Fav had followed the Wizard, Lucial, and his sister, Melande the Witch. And been defeated when Lady Kiasidira, herself a powerful sorceress, had sided with the Rothal-kiarr.

Then, three hundred forty years ago, they'd sought out the Khalar again, not on horseback, but in starships. And Lady Kiasidira handed them defeat. Again.

Would they try a third time? It seemed unlikely. Or maybe not. He rubbed at the ache in his temples. Those ships firing on station had been no figment of his imagination, and they'd not been rim traders with bad aim either.

"I'm going to look over Tobias's analysis again," he told Janek.

"Then you think it might be a mistake?"

"I'm not thinking anything right now, Doc." Other than he'd like to close his eyes and sink into something warm and soft. With pale hair, and the most intriguing green and lavender eyes. She probably had a marvelous laugh that—

He gave himself a harsh mental shake.

"Mack?"

He waved away Janek's concerns. "I'll have more answers in a few hours."

"Get some sleep. Doctor's orders. You've been pushing yourself much too hard. And you know it."

He did. But he had no time for sleep. He had a derelict station to renovate and secure, and a reputation to uphold. And now a nightmare from the past to deal with.

He sat in the conference room after Janek left and distractedly turned his empty coffee cup in his hands. Tobias was rarely wrong. But Mack desperately hoped the lieutenant was in error this one time. The Rim Gate Project was on the verge of becoming a reality. Plus, he had over five hundred civilians on this station. Five hundred civilians who were, in his estimation, barely civilized and more prone to weeklong parties than working for a living. Rumors of the return of the Fav'lhir could cause a panic. Chaos. A mass exodus—though as he dwelled on that particular thought he had to admit it held a kind of appeal. Especially if they took their damned parrots with them.

But the rumors could also spark riots, and that definitely wasn't appealing.

The Fav'lhir...after centuries of silence. He wondered what Fleet HQ would say if he told them Cirrus One had been attacked by the Fav. Given he'd seen nothing in recent intelligence reports to suggest they were capable of such actions.

The brass in Traakhalus would most likely see it as proof that their youngest admiral was cracking under the strain of his new command. He knew of a few who'd welcome that as an excuse to take Fifth, and the project, away from him. Diplomacy had never been his strong point. He'd left his bootprints on more than a few backs on his way to the top.

Not that Cirrus One was the top. But it would be, when the Rim Gate opened. And Fifth Fleet along with it.

And that's all he'd ever wanted. Wasn't it?

"You're sure it's not too much of a strain on you?"

I've handled more than this many times, My Lady.

Gillie sipped her coffee and glanced again at the data scrolling across one of her ship's real screens. Half the bridge still emulated the freighter *Serendipity*. The other half had reverted to the Raheiran Raptor-class starcruiser. It was an odd mixture of metals and crystals, but Gillie barely noticed its disharmony. She was more concerned with what Simon was doing with, and to, Cirrus One.

Last night proved to them both that the station didn't have the means to detect the Fav'lhir, should they return.

But with Simon's help, they might.

It was taking away from his own repair time,

however, which meant another delay in their departure. That worried her. And not only that.

You have your meeting with the admiral in half an hour.

"Yes, I know, but—"

It's not your fault. We've been over and over this, Gillaine, Kiasidira, Ciran Rothalla Davré.

Gillie winced. Simon used her title and mage name only when he was losing patience with her. He'd used it twice last night.

Shall I repeat what I told you?

No. She knew it by heart, though much of her heart had trouble accepting it. The Fav'lhir ships did not follow her three hundred forty-two years into the future. She did not draw them to Cirrus One, nor did the Fav have any means to know she was here. Her presence here was not endangering the Khalar. The Khalar didn't even know Fav'lhir ships had attacked them. The official report Simon read had labeled it *friendly fire from a private dispute.*

Go meet with the admiral. He needs something pleasant to think about.

She almost choked on her coffee. "Then I'm probably the last person he wants to see."

False modesty is not a worthy attribute of a goddess such as yourself.

"Stuff a sock in it, Simon."

Mack did look like he needed something pleasant to think about. There were shadows under his eyes and a grimness in the tight line of his mouth. Gillie accepted his offer of a shabby-looking chair across from his desk. He sat in one in not much better condition.

The office, and the desk, certainly didn't match the man. Either the office was too small, or the man was too large, or both.

The desk looked as if it'd kicked around the station for seventy years. Literally.

Then she remembered what Petrina had told her last night. Stationers didn't want him here. His current office—with its plain, bulkhead-gray walls, dark deck matting, and not even a small viewport—seemed to reflect those sentiments. Though Gillie had a feeling it was the office's lack of utility, and not beauty, that annoyed the admiral.

She'd agreed with Petrina's comment that he had a definite attitude. But pretentiousness wasn't part of it.

He apparently caught her appraisal. "Temporary quarters."

"You've got a lot of other things to keep you busy on station." Busy enough, she hoped, that he'd leave her alone to make her repairs. But first she and Simon had to satisfy his requirements of ID and clearances. That was another thing Simon's interfacing with Cirrus had delayed. Tomorrow, he'd promised her.

"Tomorrow," she told Mack, when he asked that very question. He seemed to echo her thoughts. Latent telepath? She considered a light probe, decided against it. "I didn't get much done last night."

"Nor much sleep." His mouth quirked in a self-deprecating smile.

A wave of his tiredness washed over her. The man was exhausted.

"I guess things got rather hectic in ops."

"As to be expected. Probably only a false alarm. But you may hear rumors. It would be best to ignore them."

Something that felt like a warning prickled the back of her neck. "Rumors?"

He shook his head, his eyes closing briefly. "Just ignore them."

"And my ID?"

It took him several long moments before he answered her question. Several long moments where he simply stared at her. No, studied her, as if he needed to memorize something about her. Or as if he needed... just needed. The sensation pulled at her, made her want to touch her fingertips to his face, smooth away the worry lines around his eyes.

He looked away suddenly, jabbed his fingers at his screen. "Your ID. Restricted. I mentioned that, didn't I?"

"You did."

"The security office on U3-South—that's Upper3-South—will have it waiting for you. You can pick it up on your way back to your ship."

"And my reports?"

"Reports?"

"Yesterday you said you wanted daily reports on my repairs."

Dark brows slanted slightly. "It's standard regs. Until I can verify your transit docs."

She'd figured as much. Yet it sounded almost as if he was trying to convince himself more than her. "And my repair list?"

He started to speak, then closed his mouth. Stared at her again.

"You said you'd give me a list of permissible repairs," she said softly.

Tiredness. Exasperation. Frustration. And now a twinge of embarrassment. It came at her like rapid ripples on a pond.

"I really think you ought to get some sleep, Admiral. You won't do anyone any good if you collapse from exhaustion."

"Fleet pays my CMO a good salary," he snapped, his voice harsh. "I don't need some rim trader to tell me that."

"Then I suggest you listen to your CMO." Gillie rose. "I'll pick up my ID at security on my way back down."

She took the first set of stairs she saw, went quickly down two levels before he came out of his office to catch her and apologize. Which he would no doubt have tried to do if she'd waited. She'd felt his mortification the minute he lost his temper and control. He was tired and angry, but not at her.

He was angry at himself.

She caught a glimpse of him leaning on the railing at U5, his dark hair and black uniform shirt a sharp contrast to Cirrus's gray metal backdrop. Fleet officers and orange-suited techs hurried this way and that behind him, but his gaze was focused two levels below. She ducked further back, slowed her steps. Security's office was opposite his, two levels down. With Cirrus's center-atrium layout, her entering the office would be clearly visible to someone at his location.

She didn't want him waiting for her when she came out of the security office, didn't want to face a tired and apologetic Admiral Rynan Makarian. She was much more comfortable with the confident, brash, almost arrogant man she'd met yesterday.

This one caused unsettling feelings in her. Feelings that made her want to take him in her arms, caress the aches out of his shoulders and back. Aches that as a Raheiran and a healer she clearly felt.

And that made her want to allay his fears about those rumors that so distinctly troubled him. She was the Kiasidira, adviser and benefactress to the Khalar. Whatever it was, she could help him handle it.

But she couldn't risk telling him that, couldn't risk anyone finding that out. And she had to get the hell away from Cirrus before anyone, especially Rynan Makarian, did.

The next morning Gillie dutifully sent Mack the ID and clearances Simon had manufactured and tagged both to her repair report. An answer came back almost immediately, a small transnote with the simple header of *R. K. Makarian, Admiral—Fifth Fleet: My office, fifteen minutes.*

She wasn't sure what to expect: had he unraveled her lies yet? She thought not, or it would be a contingent of security personnel or perhaps temple guards, not a simple transnote, requesting her presence.

It was 0830 hours and Mack's prickly attitude of the previous day was gone, replaced by a professional demeanor that was probably, she felt, more like his usual self. More like the aggressive but respected former senior captain she'd read about the night before in the station's personnel files.

If he had a failing, it was that he worked too hard. Though Fleet probably didn't consider that a failing.

She waited while he reviewed her clearance docs and transit logs. His previous aura of suspicion had dissipated.

"Coffee?" he asked, in the middle of questioning her about recent shipments—totally fictitious shipments—with a Kemmon–Drin export firm.

She smiled, slightly surprised by his offer. "Coffee would be great."

He keyed in a request. An ensign appeared with a tray moments later.

"Thanks, Wallace. I'll handle it from here." Mack dismissed the young woman with a nod. "I've never been one to be waited on," he added as his office door slid closed. "And I never—well, I'm usually not so short-tempered. Like yesterday."

"That's all right—"

"It wasn't. My apologies, Captain."

His sincere tone tugged at her. "Apology accepted, Admiral." She smiled, took the cup of coffee he held out to her.

The following morning, coffee was waiting when she hand-carried in her repair reports. She decided Mack was simply being efficient and thoughtful. After all, it was early and they both needed coffee. No reason not to share that ritual. She showed him her datapad bearing a schematics problem—a totally fictitious problem—that he'd offered to work on for her when she'd voiced her not totally fictitious frustration the day before.

The third morning Mack had a pot of coffee on his desk, two cups, and a plate of fresh fruit.

How romantic! Your first meal together.

Stuff a sock in it, Simon! But the gesture touched

her. This wasn't the Admiral Mack that Petrina had complained about. But this was, she had a feeling, the one the crew of the *Vedritor* knew.

Gillie sipped her coffee and watched a frown crease Mack's forehead. Her latest repair report, with its fabricated damage assessment, was closer to the truth and not overly optimistic. In spite of Simon's protestations to the contrary, her ship wasn't in very good shape. The destruction of the Fav'lhir ship in the tight, unstable confines of the Rift had done considerable damage to the starboard neural interfaces that allowed Simon to integrate with and control the ship. Being the ever-efficient Simon, he'd transferred much of his functions to his portside systems. But even a Sentient Integrated MObile Nanoessence had his less-than-perfect moments from time to time.

Mack tapped one finger on a highlighted section of her report. "I have two Dal-Four Analyzers due on station this week. If they come in I might be able to spare one for a few hours. It could help trace this power fluctuation."

That would also require Simon to maintain the false image of the *Serendipity* in unerring detail while Khalaran techs crawled over her ship. He wasn't up to the strain, in her opinion. And things had gone so well to date. She didn't want to slip up now, didn't want anyone on station to even suspect who or what she was. She tried to sound appreciative but not encouraging. "There are a few things I'd like to work on first."

"If you need help—"

"Thanks. Not yet."

Something that felt like disappointment trickled

briefly through the telepathic shield she tried to maintain around him.

"You have enough to do here," she added, feeling guilty.

His dark gaze held hers for a moment. "Sometimes too much."

"Easier to fix other people's problems?" She offered him a smile. It was almost 0900. Their initial five-minute meetings had hit the half-hour mark. And their conversations were less about repairs and more about the odd quirks of living on Cirrus. She had a feeling she provided him with a diversion from some of those things he had to do.

He nodded, a glint of humor sparking in his eyes. His desk intercom trilled. He shot the screen a dismissive, somewhat annoyed glance that vanished when he looked back at her. "Tomorrow, 0830?" he asked as she stood. "If that's convenient."

"No problem."

"Good." His intercom trilled a second time. His gaze didn't move from her face. "Tomorrow, then?"

"Tomorrow." She nodded, then stepped through the opening door as she heard him answer the call with what sounded like a short sigh of frustration.

Bet you he'd rather it was breakfast in bed.

Oh, shut up, Simon.

She took a shuddering lift down to the repair bay, worked through lunch, nibbled at dinner while running three synchronized loop tests, and wondered, briefly, as her head hit the pillow, if Mack wasn't the only one working too hard on Cirrus.

She was jolted out of a sound sleep by pain searing through her. She knew immediately what it was. The strain of repairs on top of maintaining the freighter emulation, plus his constant monitoring of Cirrus's sensors, had triggered a cascade collapse in Simon's primary systems.

"Simon! Talk to me!" She dragged on the first articles of clothing her hands could find: a pair of workout shorts and an oversize sweatshirt. She stuffed her socks in her pockets and ran for the bridge.

"Simon!"

No need to shout, Gillaine, Kiasidira. I am quite . . . awake.

"Where does it hurt?" It felt like everywhere.

"Where" is not the most functional concept at the moment.

"Gods damn it, Simon! Tell me what to do!"

Calm down.

"After that?" She brought up all screens as quickly as she could, engaged four different diagnostic programs. The bridge around her shimmered, lost its metallic components. Crystal was everywhere.

Don't let anyone come into this bay. I need . . . to phase back for a while.

Phase back. Shit. More than the bridge was reverting to crystal.

She tore through the bridge hatch, raced down the corridor to the airlock. She had to secure the bay. Simon, dear beloved Simon, was coming undone.

She was late. Mack glared at the time stamp on the edge of his screen. Ten minutes late. The aroma of hot coffee was still strong, pleasant in his office.

Twenty minutes. The coffee had cooled. He

considered calling her, dismissed it. He didn't want to hear she'd simply forgotten. Forgotten him. That would hurt, though he didn't want to think about why. The gods knew he had more crucial things to fret over, between the current state of affairs on Cirrus One and the most recent PSL reports.

That should be his concern, not Captain Gillaine Davré's whereabouts. Hebbs might discount the quasilegal traffic that flowed by, and through, Cirrus as normal, but to Mack—and Fleet Command—it was an unsecure border. One that needed to be secured before the first girders and rafts of the Rim Gate Project were towed into place.

Though how Fleet thought he was going to not only rehab this station but implement effective patrols throughout this quadrant without adequate staffing or supplies was still a mystery to him.

Other than: *Give it to Mack. He'll fix it.*

Twenty-seven minutes. The fruit, carefully arranged on the plate, had ceased to glisten. And an edgy impatience wrapped around him like a damp, clinging curtain.

He worked on other reports but kept seeing the lavender and green depths of her eyes. Kept wondering what it would be like to hear her laugh. Wondering what it would be like to feel her lips against his. Wondered if his wonderings would matter to her at all.

Yesterday he'd begun to think they might. There'd been something in her smile, a warmth in her voice that had made him want to hear that same voice in a different setting, saying words that had nothing to do with datafeeds and errant system loops. Words that might answer his question of why he felt so illogically drawn to her. And why it felt so right.

Those weren't words to be said in Admiral Makarian's office. His heretofore unimaginative mind played with images of Gillaine in his arms, soft and achingly sweet against him. He wanted to rub his face against her moonlit hair, his mouth over her—

He leaned back in his chair and squeezed his eyes shut. Counted to ten. Twenty. Worked on slowing the sudden rapid beating of his heart.

He had to get control of his inexplicably unruly imagination. He had too many problems on his desk, security patrols to coordinate, repair techs with no equipment to organize. He had no time for imaginings. No time for Gillaine Davré, especially if she didn't have time for him.

Though if she did, and if he did . . . Gods, if they . . .

Thirty. Forty. Seventy-five. He took a deep breath. Let it out slowly.

One hundred.

His intercom trilled. It jolted his newfound composure. He tapped the screen, saw Iona Cardiff's face. He assembled his own into what he hoped was typically "Make It Right" Makarian.

"Captain Adler wishes to speak with you, sir."

"Put him through." He arched the stiffness out of his shoulders while he waited. His imagination seemed to be back under his control.

"Admiral Makarian. Is this a convenient time to go over some data?"

"You sent a report?" Mack glanced at his in-box on the screen. It was empty. But then, things had been known to sit for hours in ops when Hebbs was there.

"I preferred to discuss this off the record with you first."

"Tell me."

"Those PSLs from Runemist." Adler leaned back in his office chair, folded his hands over his stomach. Mack remembered that padded chair, missed it sorely. In more ways than one. "In the past twenty-six hours, our sensors have recorded small flashes of what, for lack of a better term, I'm going to call an anomaly."

"Smugglers? Fightercraft?" Or the return of those mysterious Fav'lhir ships? He'd doubled sensor sweeps since the attack, but things had been blissfully—almost eerily—quiet.

"Neither. At least, that's the best my science officer can determine."

"Not a ship of any kind."

"No."

"Then what, Captain?"

Adler pursed his lips for a moment. "We don't know."

"That's unacceptable."

"I fully agree. I wish I had something more to offer you. You requested we watch all movement in Runemist, and we are. This is the only thing we've seen. And there's no known explanation for it. Right now."

Just like the phantom ships that had attacked his station four days ago. He'd never filed a report on Tobias's findings. It would go through too many eyes before it reached HQ. The more he thought about it, the more he realized he couldn't risk a riot.

Or someone at HQ questioning his sanity.

"What's your science team's best guess?"

Adler wasn't comfortable with the question, nor his

answer. He hesitated, frowning, before responding. "It's not a wormhole. And there's never been a jump-gate at those coordinates that might disintegrate, cause . . . this anomaly."

"We're talking energy field?"

"Possibly."

"Antimatter? Black hole? Did your science team give you anything at all to work with?"

"Only this." Adler tapped his screen, brought up an image from the *Vedritor*'s science labs. Something rectangular—or at least, it had been at one time—suspended in an antigrav containment field.

Mack leaned forward. "Magnify."

The image of the object doubled, tripled, until all Mack could see was a wide, jagged sheet of crystal. It glistened in the overhead lights, giving off a faintly purple hue. There were indistinct black markings trailing across its left quarter.

Mack forced himself to blink. "Tell me, Adler."

"It's a sheet of crystal, sir."

"I can see that. Where'd it come from?"

"From, or through, that anomaly."

"Yesterday?"

"We sent a probe in. This came out."

"Why is it under containment?"

"We did that as a precaution. After we tested it."

"Is it radioactive?"

"No, sir." Adler hesitated again. "It's Raheiran."

Mack made sure the conference room door was locked securely before he tabbed the screen back on.

Steffan Adler's face came into focus. The long object behind the *Vedritor*'s captain was slightly blurred.

Mack pointed at Fitch Tobias, seated at the conference table. There was no one else in the room.

"Tell him," he ordered Adler.

Adler did. Tobias listened quietly until Adler was finished. "May I see it on close-up?"

Adler stepped aside.

Mack paced. Tobias's parents were part of the Kiasidiran temple in one of the Kemmons on Nixara. He was an unofficial expert on the technologically advanced yet mystical Raheira. If Tobias couldn't determine what this was, Mack would have no choice but to go to temple authorities on Traakhalus Prime.

He didn't want to do that. Not until he did a little more research. And had a chance to go over Tobias's report, for the tenth time, on their phantom attackers.

The Raheira and the Fav'lhir. By the eyes of the Holy Goddess. Three-hundred-year-old history repeating itself, almost to the day. If this didn't get him a permanent suite in the Home for the Devotedly Delusional, he didn't know what would.

Tobias was nodding, manipulating the image left and right, up and down. Three times he ran the vidcam's lens over the scrawling black markings, then made notes on his datapad.

Finally, he sat back. "Admiral? Captain Adler? Thank you. I think I have what I need to work with, for now."

Adler's face flashed on screen. "Admiral?"

"We'll get back to you."

The screen blanked. Mack glanced at the door one more time. Then back at Tobias. "Tell me."

"I have no reason to question what our—their science labs determined. It's apparently a large sheet of Raheiran crystal."

"From?"

"A ship."

"A ship?" Mack felt like an idiot's echo. He lowered himself into the chair across from Tobias.

Tobias put his datapad between them, tabbed the screen up at an angle. "Those black marks are Raheiran symbols. Writing."

Mack's mouth suddenly felt dry. "Can you read them?"

"I can read the part that's there."

There were times when Tobias's literal-mindedness chipped away at what little patience Mack had. This was rapidly becoming one of them. "Fitch!"

"*L'heira Ixari.*" Fitch Tobias ran one thick finger across the top of the screen. "It's part of a blessing to the Goddess of the Heavens, for protection. Most Raheiran ships carried that on their hulls."

As far as Mack knew, the Khalar had been visited by only one Raheiran ship in recent centuries. But he let that fact pass, for the moment. "And this?" He pointed to the series of markings underneath. A large section of the middle was missing.

"The first part is the Raheiran honorific *Lady*. The broken section, of course, we have no way of knowing. Most likely, given the honorific, it held the Lady's familial name. It appears to end, however, in the letters *n* and *e*.

"And this," he said, pointing to the final series of markings, "is the other part of her name." His fingers traced the markings on the screen as if he needed to re-assure himself they were actually there. "Kiasidira."

"Kiasidira." That damned echo was back, though this time it sounded distinctly strained. "Do you have any idea of what you're saying, Lieutenant?"

"Quite, sir. You know my parents—"

"I know about your parents. Tell me exactly what's sitting in the *Vedri*'s science lab!"

"A part of Lady Kiasidira's ship. That's my best guess."

"Guess? You don't guess about something like this. What are the chances it's a fake? A prank?"

Tobias laced his fingers together and cracked his knuckles with a loud pop. "Always a possibility. With most other substances, we could run a Maxor test to determine approximate age. If this were part of the Lady's ship, it should be about three hundred forty years old."

"You're talking Raheiran crystal."

"Yes, sir. I believe what you're getting at is that Raheiran crystal defies age-testing."

"That's exactly what I'm getting at. What are our options?"

"We only have one. See if we can't find the rest of the ship. Sir."

Mack had always found peace by just sitting in the Lady's temple, yet this time that sense of respite eluded him. Maybe it was because he could only spare a few minutes; his usual, twice-weekly meditations took at least fifteen. But it was a few minutes he sorely needed to try to calm the unsettled feeling hovering around him.

He left the temple, still edgy, and headed for the officers' mess on U4. All the tables were empty. It was too late for lunch, too early for dinner. He grabbed two sandwiches, then strolled quickly toward his office. If the gods were with him, there'd be a message from Gillaine. He hoped it would be friendly; it didn't even have to be an apology. Friendly would do. He needed friendly right now if he was going to navigate successfully through the rest of his day. The morning's events—and for some reason the adjective *cataclysmic* kept coming to mind—had put him more than several hours behind schedule. As well as in a decidedly unsettled mood.

The fact—if it was indeed a fact—that a portion of the Lady Goddess Kiasidira's ship should appear in a quadrant under his command might have been considered by many to be a blessing. That had also been on his mind when he'd sought solace in her temple. But given his current situation, with the rehabilitation of the Fleet's portion of the station and the lack of cooperation from Hebbs and her people, the disappearance of just about everything he requested from Fleet Procurement, and *then* the mysterious attack on the station and Tobias's supposition about the Fav'lhir, which resulted in increased security patrols, and all of this underscored by the constant screeching presence of the parrots—he couldn't forget the parrots!—given all that, this was just another item on a long list that Mack had titled, *What Now?*

Still, it was one of the more intriguing entries on that list, the appearance of Captain Gillaine Davré notwithstanding.

Temple priests were forever looking for omens to

signal the pleasure (or displeasure) of the gods toward the Khalaran people. There had been very few, as far as Mack could remember. A holy statue of Merkara toppling for no reason. A strange discoloration appearing for a brief time on a revered piece of Raheiran crystal.

Interpretations were vast and varied.

But to the best of Mack's knowledge, nothing of this sort had ever occurred before.

There were only three genuine articles that the temple authorities put forth as confirmed Kiasidiran relics. The most well known was the Lady's sacred ceremonial sword with its short blade and jewel-crusted hilt. That, according to temple historians, had been found in her quarters in Port Armin after that fateful day over three hundred years ago. It was now heavily guarded in the main temple.

He'd viewed the sword twice: one as a child traveling with his grandfather, and once while in the academy, when he'd felt the need for the Lady's special guidance.

There was also the original datapad bearing the first six of the Lady's Holy Guidelines for Life. That, too, had been found in those same quarters and was now secure in a vault under that same temple.

The least known, and least viewed, artifact was a brief section of a holovid of the Lady herself attending a celebration. The vid's encryption was fragile with age, preventing any duplication. He'd never seen it. It was said to be viewed only by the privileged and most devout of her priests, and rarely spoken of except in hushed tones.

He wondered if Tobias's parents had ever seen it.

There was, of course, a veritable plethora of one-of-a-kind, guaranteed-to-be-genuine Kiasidiran relics. Most of those fraudulent items were hawked in mass quantities by beady-eyed merchants on every station and populated world in the Khalaran Confederation. Since Raheiran crystal reacted physically only in the presence of a true Raheiran, and since Lady Kiasidira was the only true Raheiran the Khalar had seen in several centuries, these merchants were free to profess their crystals and rune stones as the real thing, without fear of refutation.

Mack even owned a few crystals. A spacer could never have too much luck. He just wasn't sure what kind of luck this latest find would bring him.

He knew that it was imperative the find be kept secret. Until he, Tobias, and the science team on the *Vedri* were very, very sure.

Because he didn't know what would be worse: a mass exodus resulting from a rumor about the return of the Fav'lhir, or a mass influx resulting from a rumor about a section of the Lady Goddess's ship on Cirrus One. Right as the Rim Gate Project was set to begin construction. A technical and tactical nightmare, if there ever was one.

He finished his second sandwich, leaned back in his hard office chair—maybe there was a spare on the *Vedri* he could appropriate—and noticed his in-box flash on his screen. A message from Gillaine had *not* been waiting when he walked in. His finger hesitated only a moment before it tapped the icon. *Admiral Makarian. Your assistance is required in Bay 15 D11 immediately.*

There was no signature. Not even a transmitting terminal designation. But he knew Bay 15, D11.

Gillaine.

He sprang from his chair.

It wasn't quite the end of main shift. Lines at the lifts were few. He grabbed the first one, keyed in a command override to keep it from stopping at other levels.

"Down-Eleven," the autovoice declared through the overhead speaker. "Fleet and Commer—"

He lunged out of the lift before it finished announcing its terminus, strode quickly down the corridor. And almost smashed his face against the sliding doors to Bay 15 when they didn't open automatically.

The palm pad showed that the autosequence was disconnected. Something was very wrong. Had he been prone to imaginings, he might almost feel it in the air.

He tapped on his mouth mike. "Makarian to ops. Put me through to the *Serendipity*."

Silence for ten, fifteen heartbeats. "*Serendipity*'s not responding, sir."

He shoved the small scancorder from his belt against the palm pad, keyed in his override commands. He should've done that to begin with.

The doors slid open.

The ungainly Rondalaise-class freighter, still showing signs of damage, was in the middle of the bay, servostairs at its bow and stern. A toolbox was at the base of the ramp. She'd evidently been working on repairs. Everything looked normal.

He trotted quickly up the ramp stairs, noticed the

exterior hatch was closed. He was about to hit ship's comm when it slid open.

But no one stood in the airlock.

A chill ran up his spine. "Gillaine?" His voice echoed in the narrow corridor.

There was no response.

He wondered if he weren't mistaken about the message, or if it weren't a prank—another prank?

Then he heard a soft, pitiful sound. A low moan.

He bolted toward the bridge, his heart in his throat.

6

He immediately recognized the small form lying in the middle of the corridor, a few feet from the bridge hatchway. It took several moments before he was convinced the small form recognized him, even though her eyes had fluttered open as he'd dropped to his knees by her side.

"Gillaine? Lie still." He made a quick appraisal, ignoring the tight, cold feeling in his chest. No visible blood or bruises, no apparent broken bones. But lots of pale, soft skin. A skimpy pair of silver-gray shorts barely covered her thighs. The bottom of the matching sweatshirt had bunched up around her waist. He pulled it down, noticed the white socks dangling from her pockets.

No shoes either.

"Gillaine."

Her gaze focused on him when he spoke her name, but other than that, she didn't respond. Had her concussion been more serious than Doc Janek had believed?

Janek. Sick bay. He had to contact sick bay.

"No." Her breathy command stopped his hand halfway to his comm set's mouth mike. "I'll be okay." She tried to prop herself up on one arm, failed.

He caught her shoulders as she slumped against him. His arms went around her, not as tightly as he would've liked. He wasn't convinced she hadn't broken something, somewhere, in her fall. He had to call sick bay, get med-techs here. But to do that he'd have to let her go.

Holding her for just a few moments longer won out.

"I'll be okay," she repeated, softly, against his chest.

He could feel her trembling. A rush of emotions, unbidden and unlikely, washed over him. He ached with the desire to protect her and from a delayed reaction to the fear he'd felt when he'd found her, lifeless, on the floor.

"You're cold." He tugged the sweatshirt more securely around her waist. It was a practical response. He understood practical. "What happened?"

"Nothing."

"So nothing put you flat out in the middle of the corridor. Tell me what you were doing before this nothing happened."

She let out a long sigh. "Repairs."

Barefoot? In shorts? And with no equipment? There was no utility belt around her waist or nearby. The only tool kit he'd seen was at the bottom of the rampway.

She pulled back slightly. Some warmth emanated

from her and color had returned to her cheeks. "I guess I pushed myself too hard." Her voice was throaty, strained. "I *will* be okay. Honest."

Damn it! He'd been staring at her again, caught by those eyes, by the dark sweep of her lashes, by the curve of her mouth...He swallowed hard, found his voice. "You belong in sick bay."

"No, Mack. Please."

"Then let's at least get you off this cold floor."

She started to stand. He scooped her into his arms. She yelped in protest.

"Objection logged and noted, Captain Davré. Now, where's your cabin?"

"The bridge will do fine."

He glanced down the length of bare leg. "You need to put some clothes on. Something warmer."

"I—oh. Just aft of the main hatch. Second door on the right. I'm sure I can—"

"You can't." He did a careful about-face. Her arms tightened around his neck. Warmth blossomed in his chest, flowed down his arms, seared his skin where he held her against him. He spied the dark outlines of the second door, headed quickly for it before he lost all control and kissed her.

His almost overwhelming urge to do that shocked him. He cordoned off his unexpected feelings. He was just naturally concerned for her. That was all.

Her cabin was plain, utilitarian, without the personal touches he would have expected from someone like Gillaine Davré. He lowered her onto a bed covered by a gray blanket, stepped back as she sat up. "Put your socks on," he told her. She probably had sweatpants in one of the drawers or the closet. He was about to ask their location when the logo and wording on her sweatshirt jangled his attention.

Khalaran Fleet Stellar Academy. Class of 5415.

"Any particular reason you chose that year?" The sweatshirt had to be a joke. It looked new, not three hundred forty-two years old.

She glanced down quickly, then up at him, her mouth making a round *O* before she clamped it shut. "No," she said after a long moment.

He arched one eyebrow.

"It was a gift."

Then something else jangled his mind. 5415. That was the year of Lady Kiasidira's Sacred Sacrifice. Come to think of it, he'd seen some of the rune-stone merchants selling shirts similar to that last week. "You said you're not a follower of the Lady."

"Simon is." She plucked the front of the shirt.

Boyfriend? Lover? Those words started a small chill invading his earlier warmth. Mack had no objection to this Simon trying to convert her. As long as that was all he tried to do.

The jealous thrust of his thoughts startled him again. "Sweatpants?" He turned away, stared at the closet behind him before she could see the emotion in his eyes.

"Bottom drawer. But I'll—"

"I'll get them." He unlatched the drawer. The gray pants were on top.

She took the pants from his fingers. "I'm fine. Really."

But Mack wasn't. He was hot and cold and losing his mind. And losing his heart to a woman who was probably fifteen years younger than him, or at least looked like she was. And who'd be gone from Cirrus, and his life, once her ship was repaired.

Which was for the better. She couldn't have come at a worse time, he told himself. He was the Fleet's newest, and youngest, admiral. Even if he didn't have the stars-and-bars to prove it yet. But maybe it was time he started acting like he did.

"I'll wait in the corridor while you change. Then you can bring me up to date on your repairs. And provide me with an estimated date for completion." He gave her one of his infamous "Don't Mess with Makarian" frowns. "I don't think I need to remind you you're tying up a military repair bay with a civilian ship."

"I have a better idea." Her eyes narrowed slightly. "I'll have a report detailing all that transed to you in an hour. That way you don't have to waste any more military time talking to this civilian captain."

"Fine."

"Good."

"I'm leaving now."

She pulled on one sock. "Bye."

"Send that report."

"Consider it done." She fluffed out the other sock.

"You won't forget."

"Nope."

"I'm leaving."

She scrunched the sock in her hand, tilted her head slightly. "Mack."

Mack. Not Admiral Makarian. He realized she'd called him Mack earlier, when he'd held her against his chest. Mack. He liked the way his name sounded on her lips. A trickle of warmth seeped through the cold wall he'd just erected around his heart. "Yes?"

"Don't let the door hit you in the ass on the way out."

Gillie slumped back, her head thumping softly against the bulkhead. *I thought he'd never leave. Simon, you okay?*

She'd been aware of Simon's presence since she'd awakened on the decking with Mack staring at her in distraught concern. But that same concern and other emotions pouring from the dark-haired admiral had kept her from fully linking with Simon.

That was a most unladylike parting comment, My Lady.

Stuff a— She unclenched her fingers from around the sock, felt Simon's low chuckle. *You're feeling better.*

I would feel very much better had my recovery not put you on the decking. It wasn't necessary for you to drain yourself to that extent.

I was worried.

And I am far more capable than you give me credit for being.

And devious. She thought again of Mack, kneeling beside her, panic lacing through him. *I locked the bay. You let him in.*

I did not. Simon sounded affronted. *He was perfectly capable of letting himself in.*

Gillie pulled on her other sock. "He just happened to be strolling by, is that it? Decided, what the hell, let's see what ol' Gillie's up to?"

She stepped into the sweatpants, knotted them. They did feel nice and warm. She'd forgotten how chilled she'd been. And how warm Mack's body had been against hers.

I have no idea what brought him here.

"Liar."

An odd mixture of tenderness and fear washed through her from Simon. *I couldn't wake you.*

She nodded, her throat suddenly tight. "I guess we both overreacted."

All three of us. He—

"Gets angry every time he gets near me. So the sooner we finish repairs, the sooner all of us will be a lot, lot happier." Gillie shoved her feet into her boots without sealing them, clomped back down the corridor to the bridge.

She'd felt more than Mack's anger. She'd felt his compassion, his attraction to her. And the fact that it disconcerted him.

But not half as much as it disconcerted Gillie.

She couldn't remember the last time a man had reacted to her purely because she was a woman. To her people, the Raheiran, she had the cumbersome distinction of being a Kiasidira. A sorceress of the highest level, marked by the gods. Someone born with talents and the responsibility that went with those talents, far above even the average Raheiran.

To the Khalar, well, even before they'd made her into a damned deity, they still tended to trip over their tongues when she was around. No matter how often she crawled through their seedier spaceport pubs— and she'd crawled through a goodly number—no matter how often she worked side by side with their drive-techs and cargo hands—and she could wield a sonic welder with the best of them—she was still a Raheiran.

Everyone wanted her to officiate at their daughter's wedding.

No one ever asked her out on a date.

But to Rynan Makarian, she was just Gillaine Davré. Rim-trader captain. Someone to have coffee with before the start of his shift. Someone to share his complaints with, about living and working on Cirrus One.

Someone to be with. Far, far too comfortably.

It would be too easy for her to get to like that. To like hearing the sound of her name on his lips, to like the steady warmth of his arms around her. To like the way his dark gaze seemed to devour her, draw her in.

It would be very easy to *more* than like that tall, undeniably handsome man with the glossy dark hair and shyly sexy, somewhat quirky smile. This *pantrelon* of a man, graceful and powerful.

But as Simon had taught her, being Kiasidira meant what you liked was often to be found on the bottom of the priority list.

Plus, she couldn't stay here. She couldn't risk someone finding out who she was.

She sighed softly, tabbed up her screen. Mack wasn't going to like her report. She didn't like her report. She didn't like the gaping hole in her ship's side either. But she couldn't tell Mack about that, couldn't tell him Simon needed two weeks to re-form new crystal and another week or more after that to temper it. Only then could she be sure it could hold the spellforms she'd weave so the ship could eventually withstand the stresses of Riftspace. Providing, of course, all other systems worked optimally.

Two weeks. She needed his precious military repair bay for two more weeks. Minimum. Then Simon might be strong enough to move the ship somewhere else to finish his recuperation. An out-of-the-way dirt-side spaceport, perhaps. Where Simon could let the ship phase back, without fear of being seen. And she could openly use her magic, without fear of being discovered. And deified.

And then they could find out just what in hell the Fav'lhir were doing back in this quadrant. Because she was the Kiasidira. She'd helped the Khalar before, and would do so again. Goddess or not, she owed the Khalar that much before she went back to Raheiran space.

In the meantime, she needed more information on current happenings on Cirrus One. Real information, not the sanitized data Simon had been finding in the station's databanks. She knew exactly where the information lived.

She sprinted back to her cabin, stripped off her sweatpants, and slipped into a plain, khaki-colored shipsuit. Funny how that particular piece of attire had changed little over three hundred years, she mused as she pushed up the sleeves. But others had. Brightly colored fringed shawls seemed to be the latest fashion find on Cirrus. Women wore them knotted at the waist, the fringes shimmying as they walked. Other than the long fringes getting snagged by too-quickly-closing lift doors or tangling in the swiveling mechanisms of the station's deck-locked chairs, the accessory was new but not unattractive.

However, she had a hard time not staring in amusement at some of the young stationers—pubescent males—in their long, side-slit skirts. Plaid. And others, both male and female, with their hair braided tightly under the chin, hanging down like a frontal tail to mid-chest.

Must be great fun when it dragged into the soup.

But functional, practical clothing had, for the most part, stayed functional and practical.

The orange-suited techies plodding up the stairs in front of her were no exception. They took the corridor at D8, her destination as well.

They kept walking. She ducked into the Fifth Quarter.

"Gillie!" Petrina, waving from a corner table. Petrina, in an orange jumpsuit. Her Teddy, cue stick in hand, nodded, heading back to the billiards tables.

"Bit of a scare we had the other day, wasn't it?" Petrina asked as Gillie swiveled a chair around, then sat. "Couple of rim traders with too much ammunition and not enough brains, I hear."

Gillie's reply was interrupted by the appearance of a short, round-faced woman with curly brown hair and a complexion the color of rich, dark honey. The patch on her light blue shipsuit read *Ander Transport*.

"Trina!" The woman grabbed the redhead's shoulder as she slid into the seat Teddy had vacated. She glanced at Gillie, then back at Petrina again. "Goddess be praised! You won't believe what I just found out."

"The magefather's agreed to let you sing at services."

"Better than that, heartfriend."

Gillie didn't know the title *magefather,* but *heart-friend* was a Raheiran term. She listened more closely.

"The *Vedritor* found a piece of the Lady's ship, out in Runemist. They're bringing it back here!"

A piece of her—my ship? Gillie frowned slightly, made sure her link with Simon was open.

Petrina fluttered her fingers in Gillie's direction. "She's not a believer, Lissy. You might want to explain."

"But her hair's . . . oh. Well, Lady Kiasid—"

Gillie nodded. "I know the story. The, um, legend." *Ixari help her, how could she keep from insulting her own people?* "Go on."

The woman called Lissy did, but only to recap what Gillie had discovered in perusing Cirrus's databanks while she lay in sick bay a week ago.

"Evil Melandan mages controlled the Fav'lhir Empire, you know. They viewed people like us"—she motioned to herself, then to Gillie—"anyone without magic talents, as 'impure,' who must be manipulated or eliminated. That's why they began threatening us, attacking our rim worlds and mining stations. This was, oh, about three hundred fifty years ago."

Three hundred forty-two years, eight days and—

Hush, Simon.

"But the Lady Kiasidira, sent by the gods—you are Tridivinian, no?"

Like the Khalar, the Raheirans worshipped the three deities: Merkara, God of the Sea; Ixari, Goddess of the Heavens; and Tarkir, God of the Land and the Underworld. Only the Khalar had recently pushed the Kiasidira into those exalted ranks as well.

At Gillie's nod, Lissy continued. "Okay, then you

understand the Lady was sent to protect us from the Fav'lhir."

No, Captain Gillaine Davré of the Raheiran Special Forces had been sent to the Khalaran Confederation because they seemed the perfect match to her somewhat irreverent, definitely un-Kiasidira-like nature. The adventurous Khalar were in the early stages of perfecting interstellar space travel. In addition to her Special Forces training, Gillie had spent her formative years stowing away on any starship she could find. When she was supposed to be studying runes and ward stones, she'd been poring over stardrive data instead. Her herb garden withered while she racked up medals in lightsword competitions. And while other adepts were on their knees in prayerful contemplation, Gillie was in seedy spaceport pubs, cue stick in hand, bent over a billiards table.

You were one of the more difficult Kiasidiras I've had assigned to me.

Life with me is never boring, eh, Simon?

"So when the Fav'lhir attacked," Lissy was saying, "the Lady and our Fleet were ready for them. We destroyed their ships. But their commodore's mother ship, the *Hirlhog,* was under control of their mageline. You know, their sorcerers, witches. It escaped. So the Lady, using magic, opened a miraculous doorway to the Rift. You know about the Rift?"

She knew it very well. A distortion of space–time maintained, and manipulated, by the Raheirans. It was much narrower and much more powerful than jumpspace. Only a Raheiran, like Gillie, could navigate it. And only crystalships could transit it and survive.

"She made the ultimate sacrifice and forced the *Hirlhog* into the Rift with her," Lissy said.

No, she didn't force the Fav'lhir ship into the Rift. It was simply crystalship versus crystalship, the natural progression of the battle. The Khalar had always been reluctant to accept that the Fav'lhir's Melandan heritage and abilities were not dissimilar to Raheiran. Their mageline had descended from the witch Melande. Only the morality of their magics—and their classifying of any nontelepathic beings as impures—were juxtaposed.

Which was why Gillie and Simon had decided to take the battle into Riftspace. Raheiran magics were stronger there.

They just never realized the destruction of a Fav'lhir–Melandan crystalship would react with those magics. And send herself and Simon almost three hundred fifty years into the future.

"She gave her life to destroy their mageline and save us." Lissy's eyes misted slightly. "And now sends us a portion of her beloved ship as a token of her continual blessing of us."

A portion of her beloved ship. How big a portion? Gillie thought of the gaping hole in her ship's side. That big? That missing piece of hull that could take weeks to regenerate?

But only hours to reintegrate. If it were in decent condition, and she could get her hands on it somehow...

Simon?

I doubt it's for sale on the open market. And the gods have strict guidelines prohibiting theft.

Gillie chewed on her lip. *I don't suppose I can just ask for it back?*

How will the Khalar handle the reappearance of the Lady Goddess Kiasidira?

There is no Lady Goddess Kiasidira!

Do you want to be the one to inform them of that? If nothing else, it will put all those kiosk merchants in a serious financial bind.

Gillie smiled innocently at Lissy. "When's the *Vedritor* due in with this holy artifact?"

Behave yourself, Gillaine Davré!

"Rumor has it, tomorrow morning."

We'll think of something, Simon. We'll think of something.

"It's unconfirmed rumor at this point." Mack laced his fingers together on his desktop, feigned a look of unconcern. Which was a sharp contrast to Senator Carlo Halbert's red-faced fury.

"Then how in Tarkir's blazes did it get across the godsdamned Confederation so fast?" Halbert's fist was clenched. He pounded it on his desktop in Drin, a Kemmon district seat on Nixara, three quadrants away, halfway between Cirrus and the Confed capital. Or had already pounded it by the time Mack saw the image. There was a slightly longer-than-normal delay in transmission due to storm interference in a nearby—in galactic distances—nebula.

"How soon will you have confirmation if this is actually part of *her* ship?" Halbert's round face wavered as the comm link fought to keep contact. "High priests from here to Traakhalus are inundating my office with calls. You're godsdamned lucky that godsdamned storm's skewed the civilian comm link and they can't reach you."

Sympathy from the gods, that one. He was grateful for the divine intervention, or whatever was preventing most of the Confederation from confirming rumors of a piece of Lady Kiasidira's crystalship sitting under guard in a bay on Cirrus One.

He had enough to deal with, given the impending arrival of the first of the highly sensitive Rim Gate generators and the continual challenges of a station that was still in far from optimal working shape, in spite of his best efforts. And a personal life that had suddenly taken a turn for the worse, probably because of his less-than-stellar efforts. He wasn't quite sure what had happened in Gillaine's cabin, only that things had gone from delightfully warm to decidedly frosty. Professionally impersonal.

And that was what he'd wanted, wasn't it?

He wasn't so sure anymore.

Cirrus, for the moment, was easier to deal with. Plus, his deadlines for the project and an upcoming admiralty inspection loomed like storm clouds on his professional horizon. He felt that pressure daily, knew his staff did too.

"The science teams and the temple here are working diligently on the find," he told Halbert. Both teams had been ever since the *Vedri* made dock early this morning. Unfortunately, someone—and he had a feeling he knew exactly who—leaked the information before his ship—before Captain *Adler*'s ship—came in.

She was the only one who'd have unquestioned access to the comm logs between his office, his temporary office, and the *Vedritor*. For all he knew, Johnna Hebbs had been listening to every conversation he'd had in his office since day one on Cirrus.

That would explain more than a few unsavory co-incidences. He couldn't prove it, so he didn't mention it. But he didn't forget it either.

He leaned back in his chair. "I'll get you the results as soon as I know, Senator."

The image wavered again. "Damned storm!" Halbert thrust a finger at his vidcam, and therefore at Mack. "You get me those results. If the comm link's down, you get them to me anyway. Even if you've got to paste feathers to the godsdamned report and fly it here!"

At last. A practical use for those parrots.

Mack rubbed his hands over his face as the link faded to black and the Cirrus One logo reappeared. The station was in a state of unheard-of excitement. Last he'd looked, they were five deep at the rune-stone-seller kiosks.

The temple, when he'd passed by earlier, was packed. It had taken the portly magefather twenty minutes to travel seven levels up to Fleet's executive docking bays. Mack had left the man with the science team hours ago. He glanced at the time stamp on his screen.

It *had* been hours. That had been at 1020. It was now 1845.

Nothing yet from the *Vedri*'s people. Nothing yet from Tobias, also ensconced with the team. Nothing he could do anything about at all. Except for one thing.

Gillaine.

In the midst of all the turmoil and titillation, it became increasingly important to him to make right—and not just because he'd been dubbed with the ungainly moniker of "Make It Right" Makarian—something that had gone very wrong with the *Serendipity*'s captain.

He had a reputation in Fleet for perfection, for attention to detail. For perseverance in the face of a problem. But not one for being a bastard.

He never berated his staff, his crew. Worked them hard, yes. Demanded one hundred percent from them, yes. It was nothing more than he demanded of himself.

If he had a personal flaw, it was that he had little tolerance for the spuriousness of politics. And an equal lack of enthusiasm for excuses. So he'd mowed down a few brass-kissers earlier in his career.

But he'd done so openly and, he wanted to believe, honorably. That was the way he'd conducted his career. The career that had been the primary focus of his whole life.

Then he'd met Gillaine Davré.

Her eyes, her smile, the curve of her mouth intrigued him. So did this sense of irreverence he sensed in her. Not a brashness, not bravado. He'd never cared for people who were cocky, overblown.

She seemed to have the ability to hold her own in any situation. And not take that same situation, or herself, too seriously.

He admired inner strength. He'd spent too many years as a Fleet officer, and too many years as the son, grandson, and great-grandson of Fleet officers, not to recognize how rare a quality that was.

He wanted to tell her that. He'd hoped their morning coffee-filled meetings might give him the opportunity to do so. They almost had. Then for some reason they'd argued again.

At least he could be sure of one thing with her. She wasn't a follower of the Lady Goddess. She wouldn't badger him for a peek at the crystal section.

"Makarian to *Serendipity*." He took a deep breath, waited. He didn't have a vidlink with her ship, only audio.

"*Serendipity*. Davré." She sounded hurried, as if he'd interrupted something.

Maybe that Simon was here, on Cirrus?

"Gil—Captain Davré. I need to speak with you." He winced at the tone of his voice. Damn it, it sounded like an official command. "If you're not busy," he added.

"Is there a problem with my repair report?"

"Your report is the only thing on my desk that makes any sense right now. I just need to—"

Her laughter bubbled over the intercom. Gods, he was right. She had a marvelous laugh! It was sexy and innocent at the same time. Real, honest. Even if she were laughing at him—no. She was laughing at everything going on, which she had to have heard about.

Cirrus One, he'd learned, had very few secrets.

"Sounds to me like you need a drink," she said. "You know the Fifth Quarter?"

Very well. "Ten minutes?"

"Ten minutes."

He made it in five, grabbed a table in the far corner, frowned his infamous frown at anyone who tried to

come near and ask about the wonderful news. The
Lady Goddess's ship. The omen. The blessing. The—

He caught a glint of moonlight and starlight as she
snaked her way through the patrons of the bar. A nod
here, a smile there. She'd barely even been on station a
week and already knew quite a few people. He fully
understood why they liked her. There was something
genuine, something warm about her. In that same
short period of time, she'd come to occupy a very
large part of his thoughts. And in spite of his best defenses was making inroads into his heart.

He unlocked a chair, held it out for her. "What are
you drinking?" he asked as she sat.

She hesitated only a moment. "Devil's Breath, neat,
with a twist."

"Good." His approval wasn't feigned. That was his
drink. He tapped in an order for two from the menu
grid in the center of the table.

"I was going to call you and apologize," she said
before he could start the conversation.

"There's no reason—"

"I'm grateful for your concern yesterday. My comments to you weren't indicative of that." She smiled
and warmth surged through him. "I understand
you've got a job to do. But you're also doing me a
tremendous favor, and I don't want you to think I
don't appreciate it."

"We've both been working too hard." He sent another glare at a stationer bearing down on him. The
woman halted, turned, fled.

"You certainly have your reasons. The Fav'lhir.
And now this."

"The Fav'lhir?" Had Hebbs decided to leak that too?

Gillie made an aimless motion with one hand. "Rumors. You warned me about them, remember?"

He had. "It's nothing for you to worry about."

"That's good to know."

"I also shouldn't have taken out my worries on you. The Confed has always extended aid to a ship in distress. If I've appeared less than cooperative, or responsive, then I'm not doing my job."

He found he was oddly disappointed that she accepted his apology without further comment. He didn't know what else he wanted to say, but there was something. Something perhaps about how his heart had almost stopped beating when he'd seen her small form crumpled on the decking. And something about how he understood her passion to repair her ship, to get back out in the lanes. He could do with a year's trip to the Ziami Quadrant just about now, with Gillaine by his side. The thought appealed to him far more than he was comfortable admitting.

A Keto 'droid brought their drinks, accepted his credit chit.

"You picked an exciting week to visit Cirrus," he said as she took a sip. "You'll have a few good stories when you get home." Another uncomfortable thought. She'd leave when her ship was repaired. A curious emptiness settled inside him.

She gave him a wry smile. "Simon—some of my friends would say my life's just a series of unusual stories."

Simon again. He decided it was time to know—for

clarification, if nothing else. "The one who gave you the sweatshirt."

"Hmm?"

"Simon." He tried to keep the emotion he felt at saying the name from surfacing. Jealousy? Ridiculous. This was simply a pleasant conversation with a lovely young woman. His attraction to her notwithstanding, there was no basis for jealousy.

But jealous he was. Or, at least, cautious.

She turned her glass around in her hands, finally gave a low chuckle. "Dear, sweet Simon." She met his gaze. "A very old friend. Who doesn't always approve of what I do."

"Maybe he cares about you."

Her small nod was almost more to herself than to him. "As I care about him. He's basically looked after me since I was four years old."

He didn't have to do the math. Simon was older. An uncle, or a grandfather figure. Relief tumbled through him. "Twenty years ago?" he quipped.

"Closer to thirty. Though right now Simon would probably tell you it feels more like three hundred." She laughed, her eyes sparkling.

"I can sympathize."

"I thought you might. I hear you're Fleet's problem solver."

It was his turn to have a wry grin play across his lips. "Cirrus is turning out to be a bigger problem than I anticipated."

"What did you anticipate?"

He shrugged. "An outdated physical plant. The usual technological incompatibilities of integrating military hardware to commercial, civilian equipment.

Some disinterest, or even mild resistance, from stationers who don't like Fleet disrupting their lives."

"But you got more than that."

He nodded. "Parrots."

"Parrots?"

"You haven't spent much time on the atrium levels."

"Not when I've got a ship to repair."

"When you finish your drink, we'll take a walk."

For the first time in over four months, Mack liked the parrots. His avian invaders. Gillaine's eyes had sparkled at the term, and she'd leaned so far over the edge of the atrium railing that he had no choice but to put his arm around her. To make sure she didn't fall, of course.

"They're beautiful!" Blue and gold flashed uplevel in front of her. Red and green fluttered down.

Shift change.

He explained his theory on that. He'd never considered himself to be particularly witty and found that her amusement delighted him. The project, the crystal section, the phantom attack, his missing supplies all slid quietly into the background. He was too busy talking—well, he had to be honest: flirting. He was too busy flirting with Gillaine Davré.

"Gillaine—"

"Just Gillie," she corrected him.

"Had dinner yet?"

"No."

"Join me at the officers' club?"

She hesitated. His heart teetered. *Too much, too fast, Mack. You're out of practice.*

"Right now?" she asked.

His heart toppled, sank. Definitely too much, too fast. She was looking for an excuse to say no. To show him his timing was wrong in more ways than one.

He should have suggested the officers' mess, not the club. Friends had dinner with friends, with coworkers, at the mess. The officers' club, even one as homely as Cirrus's, was for more serious discussions. More serious relationships.

However, he hadn't made the rank of admiral by retreating. He'd give her a choice of locales, but not activities. Or time. "Unless you'd rather go somewhere else."

The parrots screeched again. A small green one zigzagged across the atrium. Gillie watched it, but whether it truly interested her or she was just looking to buy time to phrase her rejection, he didn't know.

The parrot disappeared from sight.

She turned back to him. "The officers' club is fine. Actually, I'm getting tired of my own cooking."

With considerable effort, he prevented an idiotically foolish grin from spreading across his face. He took it as an additional good omen that the lifts were working. And that not once during dinner did his comm set ping with this-that-or-the-other minor crisis in progress.

When he decided to push his luck a bit further, Gillie agreed that dinner, again, would be a nice idea. She needed a break from her repairs. He needed a break from . . . well, he just needed a break.

Tomorrow? No, tomorrow would be pushing it,

he decided, and amended his suggestion. Day after, perhaps.

He was grinning when he entered the lift at D11, hit the touchpad for U5. Grinned all the way down the gray-walled corridor to his quarters.

Was still grinning when he touched the flashing inbox icon on the small deskscreen in his living room. Lost his grin when Magefather Rigo's pudgy, wide-eyed face appeared on the screen.

"Contact me as soon as you get this. I have received a message from Lady Kiasidira herself. Commander Hebbs and I agree this is something the entire Confederation must know about, immediately!"

Opportunities lost may not resurface, My Lady.

Gillie leaned back in the pilot's chair and ran her fingers over the half-crystal, half-metal amalgamation of the *Serendipity*'s main console. One last progress check before she went to bed. "I did agree to have dinner with him again."

But you didn't let him kiss you good night.

"He didn't try."

You didn't signal he could.

"Simon." She glared at the screen across from her even though the data was encouraging. "Mack's a nice man. Intelligent. Capable. But he's just a friend."

And in possession of a large portion of Raheiran crystal.

"Kissing him is not how I intend to get access to it. From the damage reports I've read, I'm not sure if it's salvageable. Plus, I can't think of any ploy we could use without drawing attention to ourselves." And a lot of negative publicity to Mack in the process.

Then why did you agree to see him again?

"I just told you. Because when we finally stopped arguing he turned out to be a nice man."

And?

Gods preserve her sanity. Her link to Simon was sometimes a bit inconvenient. Especially when he sensed things she wasn't yet ready to face. Such as *why* she thought Mack was a nice man.

Her increasingly positive opinion of him had nothing to do with his control of, or access to, the large portion of her ship's starboard side—though that had been her initial reason for meeting Mack in the Fifth Quarter. Not to use him to get to the crystal—using anyone was abhorrent to her—but to find out if there was any way she could do some immediate damage control. The appearance of the crystal section had sparked a renewed fervor over Lady Kiasidira. The lines at the rune-stone kiosks made her wince.

Only Rynan Makarian appeared unfazed by it. Like herself, he seemed to be looking for ways to minimize its impact.

They were unwittingly on the same side.

Then he'd shown her his parrots, entertained her with his theories, slipped his arm about her waist as she watched the creatures soar past in bursts of vivid color, and something had soared through her as well. It felt very nice when he'd held her. So nice that she'd almost turned down his offer of dinner.

She wasn't staying on Cirrus. She wasn't even who he thought she was.

She couldn't. She shouldn't. She did. Agree to dinner. Because she needed to know more about the Khalar and Cirrus One before she left.

She wrapped that fiction tightly around her, finished the progress check, and went to bed.

Simon greeted her, as he always did, with the morning's news when she woke. *Coffee's brewing, My Lady. Systems are up to sixty-two percent efficiency and mending nicely. I finished enhancing station long-range scans to filter for Fav'lhir cloaking resonances—not Raheiran, of course. That would be inopportune should we need to depart quietly.*

She sat up, stretched. "Filters activated?"

Holding off until I run a few more tests.

"Good idea. Mack's got enough problems without station techs bitching about some strange parameter in their scanner pack." She padded to the shower.

"Anything else?" she asked when the sonidryer ceased its low hum. She fluffed her short hair.

Two fights reported at the kiosks on D3. Stationers coming to blows over possession of the rune stones of peace and harmony. I gather supplies are running low.

Gillie's wry laugh was muffled by the shirt she pulled over her head.

And, oh, yes, there is one other thing making the headlines this morning.

She sat on the edge of the bed, tugged on her sock. "Let me guess. Mack's got the parrots working shifts in ops." He'd told her last night how they were under-staffed and of the problems of trying to assemble a workable HQ just one exit short of nowhere. She thought, in spite of the obvious hindrances, that he'd done a damned good job to date.

This involves you more than Admiral Makarian.

She grabbed her other sock. "Me?"

You declared Cirrus One as your official Shrine of Communion.

"I *what*?" She dropped her sock. Neither shrines nor declarations had ever been her style.

Through your ever-present link with Magefather Rigo, of course.

"Who in Tarkir's blazes is Magefather Rigo?"

Your divine consort. That also was part of your declaration. You chose him not only for his devotion, but because he's of Raheiran heritage. Through his grandmother's third cousin, I believe his bio states.

"This isn't funny, Simon."

I told you that you should have let Mack kiss you last night. He'd make a much preferable consort to Magefather Rigo.

She shoved on her sock, boots, and jacket with a barely disguised fury.

No coffee? Simon asked as she strode down the corridor for the main hatch.

"This has got to stop. It's ludicrous. Blasphemous."

If they find out who you are, in the current state of frenzy on this station, it will get dangerous.

She stopped, her hand suspended over the palm pad.

Simon was right. Stationers were already pummeling one another over fraudulent rune stones, for gods' sake.

She leaned against the hatch door. "What do I do, Simon?"

Proceed with caution. There are a number of peo-

ple who dislike this latest development as much as you do. Work through them, My Lady.

Not "them," Gillie knew as she retraced her steps to find a pot of coffee waiting for her in her ship's lounge. Him. Rynan Makarian. Whom she'd normally be sharing coffee with right now, but he'd told her last night he had an early meeting scheduled with the captain of the *Vedritor*. He seemed so disappointed, she'd invented a thruster problem and told him she needed time to work on that.

Which was just as well. She really did need time to analyze what was going on. And determine what she could reasonably do about it without revealing who she was. Could she convince Mack to question the authenticity of this magefather's pronouncement? Was station harmony, and security, more important to him than his own beliefs? She remembered the offended tone in his voice when he thought she'd belittled Lady Kiasidira's guidelines.

Damn Lady Kiasidira! Not for the first time, Gillie felt trapped by what she was. And now the Khalar had made her even more, into something she wasn't. And that something she wasn't was establishing a shrine and making proclamations, through her consort, Magefather Rigo.

She remembered Petrina's friend in the Fifth Quarter mentioning some magefather. Repairs would have to wait, again. It was time she found out more about this Magefather Rigo.

She couldn't get near the temple, but news kiosks played the holovid of the magefather's announcement over and over again. Stationers stood, transfixed and four deep, around the first two glass-fronted cylindrical kiosks she passed. Finally on D3 she found a news kiosk near an open stairway. She leaned over the railing. Magefather Rigo's round face gazed serenely back at her.

"...blessing and joyful tidings from the Lady Kiasidira. I am her humble servant. Hear her words through me, all of Cirrus One."

Gillie felt her teeth clench. *My words? Yeah, right.*

"Hear her words through me, all her beloved people of the Khalaran Confederation. From this day forth, this island in space known as Cirrus One shall also be known as her Shrine of Communion. The only true voice of the Lady shall be heard here!"

Only if I start screaming right now.

The atrium's parrots must have heard her thoughts. They screeched in agreement as they soared past.

"The only true home for the Holy Crystal shall be here, as a reminder of her sacrifice. Her essence resides in the Holy Crystal. The Lady has promised to advise me in the proper use of its powers, for the benefit of all."

On the screen, Rigo raised his hand toward a large holo-painting behind him. The camera refocused and Gillie stared, surprised, at her own profile. Well, not totally hers. The woman draped in purple mage robes with long, blond hair trailing down her back appeared a taller, older version of the Lady Gillaine in that horrible official holo. Artistic license, she assumed. No one wanted to worship a short goddess sometimes mistaken for a teenager.

Others had found her spot on the stairs, flanked her

on the left and right. A curly-haired man in orange tech overalls next to her kept murmuring, "Praise the Lady. Praise the Lady."

Gillie sighed.

"Lady Kiasidira, in her unerring wisdom, has named me her consort and keeper of her Holy Shrine. I am humbled by this honor. I am her unworthy and devoted servant."

You are also a total liar.

"I shall relay the Lady's intentions for this station to the administrators of Cirrus One. We shall work together in peace, love, and harmony. Praise the Lady!"

The image on the holoscreen switched to a well-groomed young man seated in front of the logo of Cirrus One News, his dusky face professionally serious. "That was the statement issued by Magefather Rigo this morning. Updates and reaction from Admiral Makarian and Commander Hebbs will be available within the hour. The magefather's statement will be replayed in its entirety after a brief word from our sponsors..."

Gillie trotted up the stairs, disgusted. And more than a little concerned.

Rigo—the title of Magefather annoyed her—was a blatant liar. Or delusional. Or both. But whether he had a purpose behind his pronouncement or was just capitalizing on the unexpected appearance of the crystal section, she wouldn't be able to tell without meeting him. Without probing his thoughts. And she wouldn't even have to apologize to Ixari for doing so.

But she had to get access to him first. Judging from the lines of impatient stationers at the rune-seller kiosk near the stair landing at D2, that was going to be no easy task.

Mack had graduated in the top of his class at the academy. He was trained in warfare, to analyze tactical situations. To seek holes in the enemy's defenses, use them.

Therefore, he felt he should be able to maneuver one level down and across the atrium to where Gillie leaned against the railing without being unduly accosted by any number of stationers, techies, or—gods forbid!—newshounds before he reached her.

He hadn't expected to see her this morning, but then, warrior that he was, he wasn't going to let this opportunity pass by. He'd come to several realizations after leaving her at her ship's hatchway last night, not the least of which was that he wanted to spend more time with her.

A conversation he'd chanced to overhear this morning while rushing between meetings told him he wasn't alone in that feeling. Two CQPA male staffers were talking about "the little blonde from the Ziami Quadrant" they'd met in the Fifth Quarter. A friend of someone named Petrina.

"If she needs some help with repairs," the slickly handsome one had said suggestively, "I'll be glad to show her my . . . tool."

Mack wanted to show the man the station's airlocks from the outside.

Chin thrust forward, shoulders back, Mack strode through the stationers bustling by on Main. He responded to his title with a curt nod, a slight upraised hand. "Later, please."

She turned just as he came up behind her.

"Captain Davré. Right on time." He touched her arm as if to signal she should follow.

Her eyes widened, but only slightly. For a moment he feared she might not play along. Then an impish smile crossed her lips.

"Sorry," Mack said to a pair of merchants who clearly saw their chance to get an unofficial update from Admiral Makarian. Their shirts bore the colorful logo of Cirrus's largest clothier. "Official business."

"About the Lady?" the shorter of the two asked.

"No," Mack and Gillie replied simultaneously.

Only a few tables in the officers' mess on U4 were in use. Mack knew they'd be relatively safe there. It was late morning. Everyone was either in meetings or at their post. Or coming from a meeting and stopping for coffee on their way to the next one.

About half the buffet along the inner wall was still open. Fresh fruit from the station's hydroponics glistened. Mack could smell the spicy aroma of pepperlace omelets. After a late, almost interminable conversation with Magefather Rigo and Commander Hebbs, he'd almost overslept. His day had begun with an early conference with Adler. He hadn't had breakfast, only three and a half hours of meetings. The magefather's pronouncement was the cause of most of them.

The others were the usual meetings needed to keep repairs and alterations flowing on Cirrus as they neared Fleet's deadline. An additional one after that was with his personal staff: Tobias, Pryor, Brogan,

Rand, and Janek. Topics included security issues out in Runemist and the still-unknown attacker, still officially labeled as friendly fire.

Gillie filled two cups with coffee, went to claim a table. Mack piled his tray with two omelets, sausages, and some toast.

"I'm glad to see all the excitement hasn't dampened your appetite," she said as he sat. She'd chosen a table in the corner, alongside one of the large viewports.

"Aggravation always makes me hungry." He cut one of the sausages. "And so does nonaggravation. Sure you don't want something more than coffee?"

"After coffee, maybe."

"Thought you'd be busy this morning." He remembered her comment about a clogged thruster feed.

"Curiosity got the best of me." She grinned at him over the rim of her cup. "The newsvids have been rather relentless."

"It'll pass." He hoped. Gods, he hoped. He had at least ten projects to finish and that damned deadline to meet. Fifth Fleet had to officially be in business within a month or he'd have a lot of explaining to do.

"Maybe Magefather Rigo will be transferred to Traakhalus. He's rather famous now because of all this."

"I don't see it happening right away. The temple has its procedures, not unlike Fleet. But that would be a blessing. Both the stationmaster and I have had to reschedule personnel because of this. Extra security, crowd control." He made a sweeping motion with his fork. "I've pulled the *Vedri* in on station and I really need her out there."

"Why is Fleet involved in this at all?"

"Cirrus doesn't have the science labs we do." And they didn't have Fitch Tobias. Nor was he about to let Hebbs know of Tobias's connections to the Kiasidiran Temple. Or his ability to read Raheiran. "Plus, Fleet's always claimed jurisdiction in anything to do with Lady Kiasidira. We tend to think of her as one of ours."

"Because she helped set up your Fleet."

He nodded. "And gave us basic jumpdrive theory, designed our first defensive arrays. Essentially gave us the ability to explore the Khalaran system."

"So for this you make her a goddess?"

They'd touched on this argument last night. He took a sip of coffee to wash down his omelet and to center his thoughts. He couldn't blame her for being from Ziami. If only she could spend more time here, he knew she'd understand. "You're treading on sacred ground here, Gillie."

"How would you feel," she asked after a moment, "if they made you one? A god, that is." She raised her hand when he started to reply. "Look what you're doing here. Taking a derelict station, bringing it up to standards. Introducing new technology. In the midst of all that, you've repelled some unknown attackers. Okay, rumors, Mack. But just follow me. As Fifth Fleet grows, you'll do Ixari only knows how many more things that could be taken as miraculous."

He started to laugh. "I'm flattered, but—"

"Maybe not now. But let's say five hundred years from now. When anyone who really remembers who Rynan Makarian was is dead. Only the memory of you, your legend, lives. And grows, as legends tend to do. How would you feel if you found out they'd made you, Mack, who loves pepperlace omelets and Devil's Breath, neat—"

"Not at the same meal."

"—into a god?"

"I thought we already worshipped you," drawled a familiar, and unwanted, nasal voice behind him. He felt the pressure of a hand lightly on his shoulder. Then Johnna Hebbs slid into the seat next to his. He didn't miss her appraising, scrutinizing gaze on Gillie. Nor the slightly feral smile on her lips.

He no longer wanted the rest of his omelet. Nor did he want Hebbs at this table, especially with Gillie here. "Problem in ops?"

"Just finished a staff meeting down the corridor." She looked back at Gillie again. "I'm Johnna Hebbs, stationmaster on Cirrus."

"Gillaine Davré, of the *Serendipity.*" She held her hand across the table.

"Ah. The disabled freighter we found in Runemist." Hebbs shook Gillie's hand, then released it and sat back against her chair. "Glad we could be of assistance."

Hebbs's demeanor, Mack felt, was far too friendly to a "competing" female, which was in his experience the only way the tall brunette viewed other women.

"If you need something for repairs that Mack can't get, feel free to chase me down," Hebbs was saying. "He may be our resident miracle worker, but I've been on Cirrus most of my life. I know who's got what and where it's hidden."

Far too friendly. Hebbs had no doubt called him many names, but ever since he'd rebuffed her advances during month one on Cirrus, "resident miracle worker" surely wasn't one of them. Nor was it like Hebbs to offer out her jealousy guarded equipment and spare parts without receiving something back in trade. He'd learned that during week one on Cirrus.

"I appreciate that, Miselle Hebbs."

"Johnni," Hebbs said.

"Gillie," Gillie replied.

This was not good. "More coffee?" he asked Gillie, deliberately turning his back on Hebbs.

"First time on Cirrus, right?" Hebbs asked as Gillie glanced down at her half-empty coffee cup. "You need to meet some people. I know a couple of guys who'd just...well, unless you're involved with someone back in...?"

"My ship's out of the Ziami Quadrant. And no." Gillie chuckled softly. "There's no one. Not in a long time."

Mack was very glad to learn that. He was also very unhappy it was Johnna Hebbs who'd elicited that information. And that Hebbs proposed to introduce Gillie to some of the station's available males. His mind flitted back to the one who wanted to "help" Gillie with repairs. "Captain Davré's busy with—"

"Have to take some time off," Hebbs cut in. "You know what the Lady says. *Tired minds make mistakes*. You're berthed in, what, D11? I'll get in touch with you later. We can go for a few beers. I'll introduce you to some guys who'd love to meet you."

Not if he could help it. He'd call Gillie later, find out where she was meeting Hebbs. Probably Maguire's Pub, or the Rainbow Room. He could always just happen to stop by for a drink as well.

Hebbs rose, grinning broadly down at Mack. "I

meant to tell you. Magefather Rigo's set up a news conference and special service at the temple tonight. He's going to need you there."

"Then you'll have to have those beers another time."

"It's a Fleet-only conference." Hebbs shrugged. "CQPA's not invited. I'll talk to you later, Gillie."

Mack pulverized his remaining omelet with his fork.

"Don't like meetings?"

He put his fork down and glanced at Gillie. He felt slightly foolish for being so obvious, even if it wasn't for the reason she thought. "I don't think all this publicity is advisable, at this point."

"If it's any consolation, I agree with you."

It should have been, but it wasn't. Gillie was going pub-crawling with Johnna Hebbs tonight. And he couldn't be there to stop it. He'd never cared much about his personal life before, but now he did. It was as if the gods were taking a morbid delight in thwarting his efforts with Gillie, saddling him with an antiquated space station, an overactive magefather, and now an overly friendly Johnna Hebbs. His comm set trilled. He almost dreaded activating it. "Makarian."

"Tobias here, sir. There's something . . . well, I need to speak with you as soon as possible."

Trust the gods, there was always something.

Mack had every intention of returning to the officers' club—tomorrow night for a very special dinner with Gillie. Not now, shortly before noon, with Tobias. But he no longer trusted the security of the ops conference room. He no longer trusted the security of his office. He'd get a tech team from the *Vedri* to do a sensor sweep of both, unobtrusively, soon. But Tobias's voice on his badge sounded as if he couldn't wait for that.

Mack planted his elbows on the table, cupped his hands around the mug of coffee in front of him. "Tell me."

"I have reason to believe someone's tapped into both our long- and short-range scanner arrays," Tobias said.

"Sabotage." The word hissed out between Mack's teeth.

"In the reverse sense of the word."

"Reverse?"

"The system has been unequivocally upgraded."

Tobias definitely had been working too many double shifts. Had Mack not valued the muscular man's expertise so much, had he not seen him perform flawlessly time and again over the past four years on the *Vedri,* he would've made it clear this entire meeting was a waste of time.

So he said what he had to, as calmly as he could. "Of course it's been upgraded. That's why we're here, Lieutenant."

"Yes, sir, I know that. That's not what I meant. It's not been upgraded by anyone in Fleet, or CQPA."

"What makes you so sure?"

"Because we don't have that kind of technology. Or expertise."

Mack straightened, let his palms rest on the tabletop. "Tell me everything you know. Why you believe it's not Fleet. Or Port Authority."

"There's a theoretical data linkage called NIFTY. Neural Integrator Filament Transmission Yoke. I know you've heard of it."

Mack had. Anyone who'd gone through the academy knew about NIFTY theory. Self-repairing, self-replicating units of data filament that could, for lack of a better word, think. The Khalar had never been able to achieve that technology.

But there were rumors the Raheiran had.

Mack splayed one hand toward Tobias. "The section of the crystal ship."

"I considered that it could be affecting our arrays. Ran some preliminary tests, both on Cirrus and the

Vedritor. The *Vedritor* shows no sign of NIFTY trails. We do. And only in our scanners."

Mack knew if the crystal was the cause, the *Vedri* should show trails in her systems. "Selective. Could the crystal be selective in its adaptations?"

"I can't get any tests to show the section of the crystal ship is in any way responsible for the trails. In fact, I've found two that predate the section's arrival. Sir."

"Then what's affecting the arrays? And, yes," Mack added quickly, knowing how Tobias was likely to respond in a literal fashion to questions, "I know you said we're looking at NIFTYs. But from where?"

"I'll need more time to answer that."

He didn't have much choice. "Who else knows about this?"

"I discovered it on a Team-Two assignment. Only Pryor."

Pryor was Tobias's unofficial teammate, on unofficial teams Mack had created once he realized that CQPA might be less than cooperative regarding Fleet on Cirrus. They ran their own diagnostics, kept separate logs, worked on sections of projects—sometimes even entire projects—CQPA knew nothing about.

Given Hebbs's undisguised dislike of Fleet's presence on what she perceived to be her station, these teams had been a necessary course of action.

"It stays that way," he told Tobias. "You, me, Pryor. Until we know for sure. I can't risk Hebbs... Hell, I can't risk the magefather grabbing this."

"My feelings exactly, sir."

"I want an update in twenty-six hours, Tobias. I'm

going to pull some of the *Vedri*'s crew on station for the next week, to give our people some downtime. That's all I'm going to tell Adler. We need downtime. That way no one will comment that you and Pryor aren't at your posts in ops."

"I'll tell Pryor. And I'll have an update in your files in twenty-six."

"No. Here. Verbally. Or bring your datapad and I'll transfer what you find to mine. But not through the main computers on station."

"Things that bad, sir?"

Mack shook his head slowly. "I'm not sure. And when I'm not sure, I don't take any chances."

"Well put, sir. But I think Lady Kiasidira said it first."

It took Gillie a good fifteen minutes perusing the current fashion offerings on the station's vidlink, and another five rummaging in her closet, to find something appropriate to wear while pub-hopping with Johnna Hebbs. While meeting people the stationmaster wanted her to meet. While listening to those same people talk about Magefather Rigo and Lady Kiasidira. And hopefully making sense of it all.

Her usual, nondescript flight suit wouldn't do. She didn't want anyone questioning what transport company she worked for, or with. Or what depots and spaceports she'd been to, what other captains and crew she knew. She was running out of lies. Even though she'd reviewed much of what the station had in its files, it was impossible to remember it all and keep it straight.

Simon could help, of course. He could search for answers while she pretended to think, sip her drink. But not everything was in Cirrus's files. And not everything in Cirrus's files was accurate.

Besides, she was getting damned tired of lying. It wasn't an activity she was used to.

She pulled on narrow leggings the locals termed "slinkies" and a soft sharris-wool oversize sweater, both in similar shades of pale purple. Slipped on black boots with a midsize heel that wouldn't bring her close in height to the willowy Johnna Hebbs. But at least she wouldn't look foolish standing next to her.

Your friend's entering the bay.

Gillie heard the insincere note in Simon's voice. *Friend.* He picked up on the same thing she had in the mess earlier. Johnna Hebbs wasn't here because of friendship.

"I'll meet her at the airlock." No ship's tour for Hebbs. Simon was getting tired of lying too.

Hebbs had clearly given thought to her own choice of clothing. Tight black pants had laces that criss-crossed from ankle to hip, revealing a considerable amount of skin in between. Her black jacket was open. She wore a red bustier top underneath. Dark hair fell in glossy waves to her hips.

An amazing package, Gillie thought, until you heard her voice. It had a light but annoying, whiny tone. As if everything Hebbs said was through clenched teeth.

"What a sweet outfit." Hebbs lightly touched Gillie's sleeve.

Tell her you didn't bring your hunting attire.

Shut up, Simon. She smiled at Hebbs. "Thanks. You look terrific."

She looks like she needs a keeper. With a whip. Come to think of it, she looks like she has a closet full of whips.

"We'll start at Fargo's, two levels up, since we're close," Hebbs said as Gillie palm-locked the *Serendipity.* It was for show. Simon's security was unbreachable when he wanted it to be.

"Haven't been to Fargo's. Went to the Fifth Quarter a few times."

"Fargo's is better. We'll meet Gifford there."

She met Gifford, who told her to call him Giff as he leered down at her. She also met Blaike and Jesse and Nikolay. And figured out what Hebbs's real intentions were.

Keep Gillie away from Rynan Makarian.

It was in nothing Hebbs said directly, as ale was poured and glasses were raised and music blared discordantly from quadraphonic sound mirrors around them. In Fargo's. Then in the Underground. And finally in the aptly named Rainbow Room on the Main Atrium level.

It was in the possessive way Hebbs talked about Mack. They'd worked together *very* closely for the past four months. The admiral was *so* appreciative of her help, her experience with Cirrus. Her experience. Period.

I don't care! Gillie wanted to scream at her. But the truth was, she did. Not that Mack had given her any reason to believe there was anything but a professional relationship between himself and Johnna Hebbs. If anything, she clearly heard the disdain in his voice when he spoke of the stationmaster. Given Mack's penchant for honesty, and—according to Petrina—Hebbs's well-known penchant for trading sexual services for commodities, she fully understood why Mack might not like Hebbs. But that didn't mean he might not find Hebbs physically attractive. After all, every other male in each pub they walked into openly ogled the willowy stationmaster. Why wouldn't Mack?

Because he doesn't like whips.

You're supposed to be napping. You need your rest.

A snoring sound filtered softly through her mind.

She sipped her drink—it was only her third, or was it her fifth?—to keep from chuckling out loud.

"Dance?" Nikolay laid his hand on her arm. He had a ruggedly handsome face and thick brown hair with streaks of gold. He was also only a few inches taller than she was. And significantly shorter than Hebbs.

Gillie couldn't see Hebbs being interested in him, for that reason. Which was also why, she suspected, Hebbs was glad Nikolay was clearly interested in Gillie.

"Love to." It had been years since she'd danced. Three hundred forty some-odd if she wanted to be absolutely accurate, and she didn't.

She just wanted to dance. Even if it was with Nikolay.

It was one of those neither fast nor slow songs that kept dancers together but not intimately so. She rested her arms over Nikolay's shoulders and leaned her face toward his to catch his words. He was an antiques appraiser for an export–import company. He'd probably salivate over what she had in the storage lockers on her ship.

He was also almost salivating over her. Maybe dancing wasn't such a good idea.

Nikolay edged closer. She smiled, stepped back. He gave her shoulder a little squeeze, tried to draw her into his arms. She deliberately bumped into the couple next to her.

"Oh, sorry!" She turned, stepped back from him again. "Getting a little crowded out here."

"I'll protect you." He pulled her toward him.

Hands on her shoulders pulled her away.

She half-swiveled, glanced behind her, and felt his emotions cascade through her mind before she completely saw him. Possessiveness. A twinge of jealousy. He must have come directly from the conference. He was still in his formal dress uniform and looked unequivocally, undeniably handsome.

"Mack?"

"Sorry I'm late." But he wasn't looking at her. He was glaring at Nikolay. Glaring *down* at Nikolay.

Another twinge, this time of amusement, flowed from him. Frustration, tiredness, and a little apprehension mixed in as well.

Apprehension?

He doesn't know if you want to be with Shorty.

Does he want to be with me?

Gillaine. For a goddess you can be damnably dense at times.

"Mack." She put a smile and a definite tone of welcome relief in her voice. "I'm glad you're here."

He smiled back, a slow, lazy, very sexy smile.

Suddenly it was as if there was no one else on the dance floor, no one else in the lounge. No one else, quite possibly, on the entire station but this tall, gorgeous Khalaran admiral and herself.

She let him turn her around and draw her into his arms. The music started again, a slow, lazy, rather sexy song. She realized Nikolay mumbled something but ignored it. She also realized she'd probably had a bit more to drink than she should have but ignored that too.

Instead, she rested her hands on Mack's shoulders, her cheek on his chest, and let the warmth of his body seep into hers as they danced a slow, lazy dance across the floor.

His arms tightened around her as he leaned to whisper in her ear, "Your friend's not happy."

She caught a glimpse of a sullen Nikolay leaning on the bar. And a scowling Johnna Hebbs behind him. "He's Johnni's friend. They're all Johnni's friends."

"You were dancing with him."

She shrugged lightly as she looked up at him. "Doesn't mean anything."

His half-hooded eyes seemed to twinkle slightly. "Does dancing with me?"

"I don't know . . . yet."

Heat sparked between them, surged, sizzled. She sucked in a breath as quickly and quietly as she could but couldn't stop her heart from pounding. Mack's desire fractured her empathic barriers as easily as if they were made of the thinnest crystal.

"Gillaine." His voice was thick with emotion. "I want to talk to you about 'yet.'"

She had to lick her lips before she could answer. "I'm listening."

"Not here."

Gods, why not here? It felt so wonderful, so warm in his arms, his body moving against hers. Then she caught sight of Hebbs again. She'd seen ion storms that looked less threatening.

"Because of Johnni?" she asked.

Mack's brows slanted. Then one arched. He put his mouth against her ear, his breath warm on her skin. "You think Hebbs and I—"

"I don't know." She turned her face, almost bumped noses with him. "She said . . . well, I mean . . . She's beautiful, she—"

Mack's mouth covered hers with a definite possessiveness and demanded she kiss him back. Gillie complied willingly, enthusiastically. He pulled her against him, drawing her up on her toes. She wrapped her arms around his neck as his heat rushed down her body, as the taste of him intoxicated her, as the music pounded—but not half as hard as her heart.

Couples moved around them, brushed against them as they stood in the middle of the floor. She and Mack were the only ones not dancing, but Gillie didn't care. Kissing Mack was much more important.

She forgave him for pulling his mouth from hers only because he said her name. "Gillaine."

"Umm?"

"Come with me?"

"Okay."

He took her hand, led her out of the Rainbow Room toward the nearest bank of lifts. Folded her into his arms when the lift's only other occupants exited at U5. Held her until the autovoice announced, "Level Upper-Nine. Officers' Club. Observa—"

He guided her quickly out, his arm snug around her shoulders. The club was almost empty. 'Droid servers, standing motionless by the bar, whirred into activity when she and Mack walked toward a curved couch in front of a large viewport. The darkness of space beyond was like limitless black velvet.

"Two Devil's Breath, neat, twists," Mack said. The 'droid whirred away across the carpeting.

Gillie sat on the soft couch, only peripherally aware of the twinkling hull lights on a freighter drifting by the viewport. Mack took her hands in his, brought them to his lips.

Heat sparkled down her arms, caused a near riot considerably lower.

"I want to start all over with you. From the beginning."

She didn't think where they were right now was all that terrible. "Why?"

"Because I need to ask you something. What I wanted to ask you, when we first met, except it seemed so unbelievable..."

Gods. A chill shot through her. He knew who she was. Or he suspected. With her empathic and telepathic fields dampened and a few too many drinks muddling what was still functioning in her brain, she'd misread him. He was just being kind before he became angry. Before he accused her of deceiving him and the whole station. Hell, the whole damned Khalaran Confederation.

She drew a deep breath, steeled herself. So be it. She

was tired of lying. She'd tell him the truth. Even if it meant he'd never talk to her again. "What do you need to know?"

His hands tightened over hers. "Gillaine Davré. Will you marry me?"

You said you'd answer truthfully.

Oh, gods, shut up, Simon! The man just...he just...Oh, gods. He wants to marry me?

"I know this must seem sudden." Mack's voice was soft, almost apologetic.

Gillie closed her mouth, hoped it hadn't been hanging open for any noticeable length of time. Then she decided it must have been. Because her voice was gone too.

"We've known each other for only a week," he continued. "But I think I realized the first day I met you that you were the most incredible woman to ever come into my life. You probably don't believe me." His thumb traced the edge of her hand, and a little trill of pleasure flowed up her arm. "I don't expect you to. I don't even know if you feel what I feel. I hope, given time..."

He glanced at their intertwined fingers. "Time's

something I'm not sure we have," he said, looking back up at her. "That's why I had to tell you what I feel, what my intentions are. Because when your ship's repaired it's doubtful I'll see you again. Unless I give you a reason to stay."

"But..." She closed her mouth. She couldn't say what needed to be said: *but you don't know me. You don't know who I am. What I am. What I've done. What your damned culture thinks I've done—making them set up shrines and temples all over the place because of it.*

"I know we've had some misunderstandings," Mack said.

"That was my fault." Besides, that was the easy part. Two people, overtired and overwrought, were bound to have words.

The hard part was something Mack didn't know.

Maybe something he didn't have to know.

That thought jolted her. What if...what if she spent the rest of her life here, being just Gillie? Not the Kiasidira. Not a Raheiran sorceress. Not anyone's goddess or consort. Not even a captain in the Raheiran Special Forces. But just...Gillie. Gillie and Mack.

Could she do that? Nobody had recognized her. She looked different from her official holo, and Cirrus's databanks had no record of Lady Kiasidira ever being associated with a Captain Gillaine Davré. Other than that piece of her ship, there wasn't a single shard of real crystal on station that would reveal the truth. The Khalar weren't mageline; no one would sense her Raheiran lineage. Her own people no doubt had accepted her death over three hundred years ago.

She had no reason to go home. She had every reason to stay here. With Mack. Gods. Could she?

"The misunderstandings weren't your fault." His fingers caressed hers again. "I was so unprepared for what I felt when I met you. It scared me. At first, I thought you couldn't have come at a worse time in my life. Then I realized I was totally wrong. You came at exactly the right time. The Fifth Fleet, Cirrus One, it's all going to be something to be proud of. Very proud of, and I want to share that with you."

Her heart melted at his words. He wanted her with him. And she wanted so very much to be with him, to share with him. To be part of everything in his life.

Tears pricked the back of her eyes. Her voice caught in her throat. "Oh, Mack."

"I love you, Gillie. Just give me some time to prove it to you."

He ... he loves me?

I told you so.

Gillie ignored Simon's gloating voice in her mind. She threw her arms around Mack's neck, fully intending to kiss him fiercely. He evidently had similar thoughts and met her halfway. Somewhere in the middle of it all, the 'droid server deposited their drinks on the low table, then wisely and discreetly departed.

Gillie drank in Mack's kisses instead, explored the soft thickness of his hair with her fingers. Traced the rough edge of his jaw with her thumb, then kissed him again.

The heat of his emotions suffused her. She knew if

she were to drop her empathic barriers, the entire club would probably sizzle brighter than a power-grid backwash.

He kissed her mouth, her cheeks, her eyelids, the edge of one ear, then found the soft spot at the base of her throat as she arched against him.

Her fingers clutched the smooth fabric of his uniform jacket, and it occurred to her that clothes were damned inconvenient sometimes.

But this was the officers' club on Level Upper9 of Cirrus Station. Clothes were necessary.

Mack seemed to realize that too. He pulled back slowly from where she rested against the cushions. His face was flushed, his breathing hard and raspy. "Gillaine—"

She put one finger over his lips, silencing him. "We have time."

Beneath her fingertip, his mouth spread into a wide grin.

Mack couldn't remember ever feeling like this before. His good mood was totally unshakable. Not Hebbs's narrowed-eyed glare at 0700 in ops, not Magefather Rigo's righteous blustering in his office twenty minutes later, not three short and unproductive conversations with the senator an hour after that caused the smile on his face to waver one inch.

She hadn't said no. Well, truth be told, she hadn't said yes either. But she had kissed him. Gods, how she'd kissed him! And said they had time.

That's all he wanted right now. A chance. His proposal had surprised him almost as much as it had surprised her. He'd been troubled for days, knowing she would leave, not knowing how to make her stay. He didn't want to have to rush a relationship or cram it into two weeks. His deadline in getting Fifth Fleet operational so the Rim Gate Project could launch was tough enough. But that he knew how to do, knew what shortcuts would work, what patches would hold for now.

He didn't want things to be that way with Gillie. He didn't want this to be just another brief affair, a lover left behind in a spaceport. He'd had those and found them uniquely unsatisfying.

And he knew with Gillie a short affair would be more than just unsatisfying. It would leave him wanting her for the rest of his life.

His in-box icon flashed. He tabbed up the report from the *Vedritor* he'd been waiting for, glancing at the time stamp on his screen. Two hours to lunch. Two hours until he'd see Gillie. Officers' mess, he'd told her, in a brief conversation from his apartment this morning before he headed to ops. He still had no vidlink with her ship's comm pack, something he'd have to work on. He wanted to see her smile, see the sparkle in her eyes.

For now, that would have to wait until lunch. He turned his attention, not without a small twinge of reluctance, to Adler's report.

Temporary personnel reassignments had gone smoothly. The analysis of the crystal section was completed, and a report had been forwarded to HQ on Traakhalus. That would get the senator off his back for a while. Mack knew his science team—that is, *Adler's* science team—was very thorough.

He snagged a copy of the report, downloaded it to his personal datapad. He'd give that to Tobias when they met later this afternoon.

His office door pinged. The ID strip overhead showed his CMO waiting on the other side. He tabbed off the lock. "Still no word on those supplies," he said as Janek stepped inside. His CMO's lab coat looked somewhat threadbare. Mack could see that the medalytics scanner in Janek's coat pocket was wrapped in tape.

He motioned to a chair in front of his desk. "The only thing I can offer you right now is coffee."

Janek sat, grinning, then crossed his long legs as the door slid shut behind him. "I hear one of our most impregnable defense grids has been breached."

Mack immediately stiffened, shot a glance at his deskscreen for any red-coded advisory. Nothing flashed. No alarms wailed. He frowned. "What?"

"Not what. Who."

"Who?"

Janek's grin broadened. "It's all over station that 'Make It Right' Makarian was involved in a pretty heavy make-out session on the dance—"

"Oh, shit." Mack leaned back in his chair, wiped his hand across his face. But he was still smiling when he sat forward again. "My goal was the officers' club. We were sort of sidetracked before we got there."

"You're usually not so indiscreet."

Mack heard the undercurrents of disapproval in Janek's voice. They'd known each other for a long time. Janek had also pegged Hebbs's parasitical nature before Mack had, had warned him, week one on Cirrus. It hadn't been until week three that Mack had seen the truth in his friend's words. Cirrus One was under Johnna Hebbs's control, and the stationmaster would do anything—including seducing the newly assigned admiral of the Fifth Fleet—to make sure it stayed that way. "It's not like that."

Janek's arched eyebrow signaled his unspoken question.

"Last night wasn't indiscretion. It was…" He thought for a moment. Of course it had been an indiscretion. A Fleet officer's private life was meant to be private. And a Fleet officer's flings were encouraged to be as invisible as possible. Except this wasn't a fling. "It wasn't an indiscretion," he repeated. "It was an announcement."

"Of?"

"I asked Gillie to marry me."

Janek stared at him. His mouth hung open, then closed quickly. He uncrossed his legs, leaned forward, elbows on his knees. "You're serious. This is serious."

"Yes."

"You just met—"

"I know." He waved his hand as if to brush away Janek's objection. "And if I didn't do something, she'd be gone in two weeks when her ship's repaired."

"So you're marrying her to keep her here?"

"She didn't say yes. But I don't think she'll be leaving right away either."

"That ship of hers belongs to her cousin's transport firm. I think they'd want it back."

Mack shrugged. "I might be able to get someone to tow it. Or maybe they'll send someone to ferry it. Hell, considering the shape it's in, it might just be better to junk it and sell it as scrap."

"She's agreed to this?"

"We haven't discussed it. But I doubt it'd be a problem."

Janek shook his head slightly. "After all these years, I never thought we'd be having this conversation. You, serious over a woman." He pointed one finger at Mack. "I repeat, you've known her only a short time. Are you sure her affection toward you isn't based on her need for dock space for her ship?"

"She's not another Hebbs. Believe me, Gillie is exactly what she appears to be. A warm, intelligent, vivacious young woman. A hardworking, honest freighter captain. Nothing more. Nothing less."

"And you're in love with her."

"Doc, it's almost like she's the answer to my prayers. She couldn't be any more perfect for me than if the Lady had sent Gillie to me herself."

That was, Mack thought as he hurried down the corridor to the officers' mess, not a totally unlikely possibility. The Lady was Fleet's patroness. And he had, in every way he could, tried to live an ethical and honorable life. The only lack he'd ever felt had been a personal one. But he'd accepted that was part of a career in Fleet.

Still, there'd been moments the emptiness had gnawed at him. Though not anymore. His answer to his unspoken prayers waited for him outside the doors to the mess.

He felt that damned idiotic grin claim his face. "Hi."

"Hi, yourself."

He stared down at her, damning discretion as he fought the urge to kiss her again. Knew it was safer just to guide her to the buffet line inside. There'd be plenty of time for kisses later.

A few heads turned as they found a table by the wall. But that was one of the reasons why he'd asked her to lunch in the more populated mess. Rynan Makarian was making an announcement.

"I saw last night's news conference on the newsvids this morning," she said as she stirred her coffee. "Are you really going to give the magefather half a level for this shrine he wants?"

"If it were solely up to me, no." That had been part of the purpose behind Magefather Rigo's visit this morning. The magefather wanted Mack's support, one hundred percent. Even with the Lady's latest blessing sitting not six inches away from him, Mack didn't feel he could do that. But then, as he told Gillie, it wasn't solely up to him. "Fleet doesn't own Cirrus One. We've appropriated a portion under Section 36-A-1 of our laws as required for military use. But the majority of Cirrus One is still under the auspices of CQPA and self-governing. If stationers vote to grant property to the shrine, I can't stop them. They just can't take property away from the portion already allocated for Fleet use."

"But you don't want it here."

"I don't think a major military installation and a major religious site necessarily make good neighbors." He'd said that, repeatedly, last night. "For security reasons, if nothing else."

Gillie nodded, her expression thoughtful. "Tourists can end up in the damnedest places."

"Well put, my lady."

Her spoon slipped through her fingers, splashed

down into her coffee mug. She jerked back, as if startled.

Mack's napkin was already in his hand, but the damage was minimal.

"Sorry," she was saying as he offered the napkin to her. "Sorry."

"Did the coffee burn you?"

"No, I just—it's nothing." She smiled, flexed her fingers. "After hours of holding an optic diffuser, my hand sometimes cramps."

He knew what that was like. "There's no reason to push on repairs." Not now.

"I think Fleet might want to see some progress. I *am* in their bay."

"My bay," he corrected. "I'm Fleet here. And I very selfishly would like to keep you around for as long as I can."

Footsteps behind him came closer. Mack looked over his shoulder as Pryor sidled between two tables. The white-haired man nodded but hesitated. Mack waved him over.

"Lieutenant, this is Captain Gillaine Davré. Gillie, Lieutenant Tarrance Pryor. One of the *Vedritor*'s best, whose loyalty overrode common sense when he agreed to be part of my permanent staff here."

Gillie extended her hand. "Glad to meet you, Lieutenant."

Mack noticed Pryor wasn't immune to Gillie's smile or the genuine warmth in her voice. "Captain. A pleasure. A real pleasure. I need to borrow the admiral. I promise to return him to you later, none the worse for the wear."

Gillie's responding chuckle was infectious. Pryor laughed too.

Mack touched Gillie's arm as they rose. "I've nothing scheduled late this afternoon." *Barring the usual crisis,* he thought. "Come by my office, end of main shift? We'll go for a drink."

"Want me to call first?"

He knew he'd be on the *Vedri* just before that. She wouldn't be able to reach him. Not until she had the confirmed clearances. As his wife.

By Ixari's eyes, he liked the sound of that.

"If I'm late, it shouldn't be more than ten minutes."

"If he's later than that," Pryor intoned, "I'll come take you for a drink myself, Captain."

He shot Pryor a warning look as Gillie turned away.

"Only kidding, boss." Pryor's mustache twitched.

"Parrot duty, Lieutenant. I could put you on parrot duty."

"He'll be on time, Captain. Don't you worry about that."

You're going to be late, My Lady. Leave that for tomorrow.

"I've almost got the connection. Just a few more minutes." Gillie squinted at the jumble of optic feeds in the maintenance panel, centered the diffuser, and gently and carefully traced the hairline crack that ran along a thin feedline.

You need to shower. Change.

"I'm almost there." Her hand shook slightly. She hadn't lied to Mack about the cramps in her fingers from the repair work she'd been doing. But that hadn't been the reason she'd dropped her spoon.

My Lady. Even though he'd said, "my lady," she'd heard it with a capital *M* and capital *L,* and for a moment her heart had plummeted. She thought he knew who she was, and if he did, she knew she'd lose him.

That thought made her feel sick. Mack was incredibly special to her. More than special. When she dared to think about it, as she had after he'd kissed her good night last night, she admitted she was falling in love with him.

But she didn't want to dare to think about it. Didn't want to rush it. There were still too many things that could go wrong. And she didn't want to experience the terrible pain she knew she'd feel when she lost him.

Something whispered that was still very much in the range of possibilities.

If you show up at his office sweaty and filthy, it becomes a greater possibility.

"Stuff a sock in it, Simon. I'm going. I'm going!" She shoved the diffuser back in her utility belt and pulled herself off the corridor floor with a groan.

Twenty minutes later she was leaning on the atrium railing, watching the parrots change shifts, when she heard a noise behind her. Not footsteps; there were too many of those in the open corridor competing with the noises floating up and down the atrium. But something that sounded like a grunt and a low curse.

Not Mack. In spite of Simon's dire predictions,

she was early. Main shift had more than ten minutes yet. She turned, saw a muscular young man in an officer's uniform standing awkwardly in front of Mack's office door. He held a metal case in his arms and tried to juggle that and hit the palm pad at the same time.

She waited for a group of orange-suited techs to pass, then swiftly crossed the corridor. The door opened just as she reached him. Had Mack arrived, unseen?

She followed him into the office and only as the door closed behind her realized Mack wasn't inside.

"Oh, sorry," she said.

The man spun around, clearly startled. The case tumbled from his arms, crashed to the floor.

"Gods," he said. "Goddess!" He dropped to his knees in front of the open case, its contents strewn across the carpet.

"I didn't mean to scare you. I'm waiting for Mack—for Admiral Makarian." Gillie knelt, reached for one of the glistening objects between them. And stopped.

It glowed brightly, pulsing a delicate purple hue.

Crystal. Raheiran crystal.

She raised her gaze to the man in front of her. Two stars, lieutenant's stars, dotted the front of his black shirt. His dark hair was closely shorn, making the small silver comm set ringing his right ear more noticeable. He stared at her, his lower lip trembling almost imperceptibly.

Between them, the purple glow became stronger. She could feel it sensing her, even though she was shielded.

But not shielded enough.

"Goddess," the young man said again, and she re-alized now it wasn't a curse. His voice was filled with awe, his gaze on her, unwavering. "My Lady Kiasidira."

Shit.

11

Fear raced through Gillie. What if Mack walked in to find his officer babbling about Lady Kiasidira with shards of crystal pulsing around her? "I'm not, really, I—"

"I understand. I'm an impure. Not worthy to see you."

"That's ridiculous. You're fine." Damn! That wasn't what she meant to say, but she was so unused to being worshipped.

He was nodding slowly, and she had the feeling he was only half-hearing her words. "It's like you just stepped out of the sacred holovid. You're even wearing the same clothes."

Same clothes? She'd grabbed her favorite green scoop-necked sweater and a pair of black slinkies. And what holovid? Her mind was still locked on the newsvid of Mack and Magefather Rigo. Not that vid. One with—

Herself, in the green sweater. She'd bought it to wear at Ethan's birthday at the Legacy, just outside the spaceport. A bunch of drunk tracer pilots and Captain Gillaine, Kiasidira, Davré. In the same green sweater. With the same short haircut. And Sarge, from space-port security, drunk as the rest of them, with a holovid cam, capturing it all.

She sat back on her heels. She'd thought her official holo was the only image of her out there, felt reassured because the resemblance wasn't strong. But a holovid shot a week, ten days before she'd fought the Fav'lhir in the Rift! How many other people had seen it? How many other people would recognize her? Mack hadn't . . .

Dear gods. She had to get control of this situation. She grabbed the two shards of crystal. Their power pulsed through her. She recognized them immediately as part of her ship, though their spellforms were mangled. Purple light misted up her arms as she shoved them back into the case. She slammed the lid shut with more force than was required. Her hands shook.

"You're angry, My Lady."

"No." Just scared. She made a quick mental sweep of the corridor beyond the door, didn't sense Mack. Quickly, she sought Simon, something she should have done five minutes ago.

He's still on the Vedritor, *My Lady. I'll keep watch.*

She blessed Simon, praised Ixari, Tarkir, and Merkara, and threw in a list of minor deities just for good measure. Let out a long breath she didn't realize she'd been holding. "I'm not angry. Just a bit unsettled at the moment, Lieutenant . . . ?"

"Tobias. Fitch Tobias, your devoted servant."

"I don't need servants. But I really am in need of a friend. A heartfriend."

"My Lady, I'm not worthy—"

"Fitch." She tightened her grasp on his arm. "You're wonderful. You're worthy. You're fine. And please stop calling me 'My Lady.'"

"Goddess Kiasidira."

"Not that either!"

"Instruct me. I await—"

"Gillie. Just Gillie."

He hesitated. "Gillie?"

"Gillie," she repeated. "Gillaine Davré."

This time his hesitation was slightly longer. "That's the name of Admiral Mack's girlfriend."

Who is on his way, My Lady.

Oh, damn. Oh, hell. She sucked in a deep breath. "Mack doesn't know who I am."

Amazement flooded Tobias's features. "Then you are—"

"Gillie Davré. That's the only way Mack knows me. That's the only way anyone here knows me."

"Because you're on a secret mission. Involving the admiral. To help us again."

Sounds good to me. And your devoted friend there seems to like it.

"Yes, yes, yes." She stood, tugging Tobias to his feet, which wasn't easy. The man was like a solid brick.

"I shouldn't be standing in your presence."

"You will stand in my presence. You will call me Gillie. If you can't manage that, try Captain Davré. You will not call me Lady or Kiasidira or anything remotely resembling that. And you will tell no one—and

I mean absolutely no one—who I really am. Do I make myself clear, Lieutenant?"

That finally did it. It was the tone of command ingrained in her through her military training, the thin line of her mouth, the firm set of her shoulders as she pinned him with a hard gaze she hadn't used since she first set foot in the Khalaran Confederation six years—no, three hundred forty-some-odd years ago. And knew that if she didn't somehow get their scattered, bickering military forces and motley, patchwork technology in shape, the Khalar were going to be vandalized and absorbed by the greedy and relentless Melandan mages controlling the Fav'lhir.

Gods. No wonder she felt such a kinship with Mack. They were both doing the same job.

The lock on the door behind her cycled with a click. She spun around, kicked the metal case hard with her heel. There was an audible, sharp intake of breath behind her. It had probably smacked Tobias in the ankle, she realized with a sympathetic wince.

She hoped the lieutenant understood her real message: get rid of it. And whatever you do, don't open it while I'm around.

The door whooshed sideways. Gillie sensed two things immediately. Mack was very glad to see her. And not so glad to find her locked in his office with Fitch Tobias.

"Been waiting long?" Mack asked.

"Only a few minutes."

"No, sir."

Gillie gritted her teeth as Tobias's denial ran over her words. The two of them sounded positively guilty.

Mack's gaze went over her shoulder, then down. "That's for Magefather Rigo?"

She knew what he referred to. The case with the crystal shards. She stepped as casually as she could toward his desk, as if the case and its contents concerned her not at all. Couldn't change her life, rip her heart out. Make a liar of her.

No, worse. Make a goddess out of her.

Tobias retrieved the case, shot a quick glance at Gillie before he answered. "You requested I leave it in your office."

"Not on the floor."

"That was an accident, sir."

Mack frowned. "What kind of accident?"

Don't open it. Dear gods, don't open that case!

"Nothing, sir."

"Lieutenant—"

"It fell." Tobias glanced at the case almost as if to reassure himself it was still in his arms and in one piece.

Look, but don't open, Gillie pleaded. She edged further back against the desk.

"But it didn't fall far," Tobias added hurriedly. "Everything's fine. I checked."

She gave Mack a bright smile when he turned to her. "Everything's fine," she echoed. *Just don't open the godsdamned case!*

"Bring it here." He motioned to his desk as he headed for his chair. "You know what's in there?" he asked Gillie.

"Crystal. Like the rune sellers have." She backed away from the desk, still smiling.

His mouth thinned slightly. He nodded at Tobias.

"Had there been anyone other than Captain Davré in here when you opened this, you'd be facing a serious breach of security. I'm sure you know that."

"Yes, sir. It won't happen again, sir."

Mack's features relaxed, but he kept one hand on top of the case. "If there's nothing else, Lieutenant, you're free to go."

"Thank you, sir." He gave a tight bow. "A pleasant evening to you. And you, My La—CaptainGillie-Davré." His last words moved almost as quickly as his boots.

"I may be working him too hard." Mack drummed his fingers on top of the case.

Gillie's face ached from smiling. "Oh?"

"He's usually not that jumpy. Something…" He shook his head as if arguing with himself, then patted the case. "Not something. This. His parents are with the temple. He's almost fanatically devoted to Lady Kiasidira."

"I hadn't noticed."

A rude noise sounded through her mind. Simon's snort of disbelief.

"Good thing I showed up when I did, or he would've worked hard on converting you. Especially with the pieces from the Lady's ship in here." He fingered the lock.

Gillie wondered how she'd later explain it if she were suddenly forced to bolt for the door.

"You saw the crystal?" Mack asked.

"Yes." *Don't open it. Don't open it.*

"This isn't what you've seen out there, in those kiosks. This is"—he tapped the lock—"extraordinary." There was a noted reverence in his tone, and for a moment his gaze seemed unfocused, distant. Gillie winced internally at his devotion.

"I know true crystal gives off a purple color when touched by a Raheiran," Mack continued. "But I never really believed it until I saw Magefather Rigo handle these pieces. I know he says he's only partly Raheiran, not a true one. But I saw the crystals glow."

Impossible. The word jumped into her mind so clearly, for a moment she was afraid she'd shouted it out loud. The crystals glowed when the magefather— that fat, pompous charlatan—touched them? Impossible. She would've known. Simon would've known.

It had to be a trick. Some light source, perhaps in a ring or a bracelet or a watch. She'd seen rune sellers attempt that. But the light was always uneven or too concentrated. Easily discerned as a fake.

Mack wasn't the kind of man to be taken in by trickery. But there was no other logical explanation. Unless...

Unless Rigo had a Melandan heritage. A Fav'lhir. Crystal would respond to someone with a Melandan mageline, though very faintly. And they'd have to be touching it.

"Ready for that drink?" Mack asked, standing.

A Melandan wizard. It never occurred to her the Fav'lhir might have resurrected their mageline and already be here on Cirrus One. She'd never thought to check. Not that she was in a position to take any immediate actions if they were.

Go get that drink. I'll see what I can learn.

Be careful, Simon. Dear gods, be very, very careful.

She took Mack's offered hand. "I could use a drink right about now."

"Tough day?"

No. Tough couple of centuries.

The officers' club was considerably more crowded than it had been last night, but Mack found two chairs and a small table by one of the viewports. The 'droid server whirred over, returned a few minutes later with two glasses of Devil's Breath, neat.

"You're having second thoughts, aren't you?" Mack turned his glass around in his hands. He hadn't sipped it yet.

Gillie had already taken two mouthfuls of hers. That shouldn't have been sufficient potency to keep her from understanding his question. But she didn't understand it.

Of course, her attempts to keep a light constant contact with Simon while her mind simultaneously ran through the events of the past hour weren't helping. "Second thoughts?"

He tried to smile, failed. "You've been quiet. I came on a little too fast last night, didn't I?"

A small pain fluttered around her heart. He mistook her distraction for disinterest. "I've still got a few things to work out with Sim—with the *Serendipity*." *Gods* damn *it, Gillaine!* she berated herself mentally. *Pay attention to what comes out of your mouth!* "It's not you. It's my ship, and the auxiliary thruster, and the feed coils, and... well, you know, the usual repair stuff."

She was babbling. She heard herself babbling. She shut up.

"You don't owe me for that," he said quietly. "The

Khalar have always helped a ship in distress. I don't want you to think that last night was a request for repayment."

She took a deep breath, steadied herself. "Rynan Makarian. If I thought for one minute that's what last night was about, you would have been speaking in a considerably higher voice when you left the club."

Amazement gave way to amusement. His chuckle was warm and genuine, and not without a tinge of relief. "I want us to be honest with each other, Gillie. About everything."

Her own smile felt false again, but her words weren't. "I'm here with you because I want to be. And no other reason."

He folded her hand in his. "Let me tell you this theory I have about answered prayers."

Fitch Tobias, Gillie decided, wasn't the only one devoted to the implausibly perfect, increasingly miraculous Lady Kiasidira. She tried without success to shake off the growing sense of dread that surrounded her heart whenever Mack mentioned the Lady. But the rest of the evening's conversation in the club, and during dinner, was fortunately not so divinely inspired. Nor were there any new crises setting the comm set Mack had tucked into his jacket pocket to pinging, and no dire warnings from Simon to interrupt one of the most wonderful evenings Gillie had ever had. Especially after its almost disastrous beginning.

Rynan Makarian, she realized as they debated over the dessert selection, didn't have a pretentious bone in his gorgeous body. He was a delightfully unpracticed flirt, with a dry wit and a refreshingly honest way of viewing himself and his career.

" 'Make It Right'?" He stirred his coffee, a wry grin on his face. "Someone tagged me with that years ago, when I was in the academy. Not sure if it's a badge of honor or a curse."

"Tell me about your academy days." Gillie avoided stories about herself, avoided specifics. She knew her own history, anyway. Mack interested her more.

He was into his stories about his first year as captain on the *Vedritor* by the time they reached her ship.

She leaned against him in the *Serendipity*'s airlock doorway, her hands splayed against the front of his shirt. The warmth of his body melted against hers. His kisses sent flutters of pleasure spiraling through her.

Simon kept humming the Raheiran wedding song in her mind and wouldn't shut up.

"I've got meetings all morning tomorrow. Lunch?" Mack brushed his mouth across her forehead.

"Umm," she said into his chest.

"Is that a yes?"

Tell him a midnight snack would be preferable.

I'm not rushing this, Simon. Shut up.

She tilted her face up. "Yes. That's a yes. Your office, noon?"

"I'm running a maintenance inspection on D12 just before that. I'll come here when that's done."

"That could get dangerous. I might put you to work."

"I like dangerous work." He snugged her tighter against him, smiled a slow, lazy, sexy smile. Those flutters of pleasure flitting inside her increased in intensity. Sweet Ixari! If his touch, his smile, his kisses did this to her, what would happen when he really made love to her?

A few stars may collide, a sun may go nova, but not much more than that, I'm sure.

Gillie stood on her tiptoes, claimed another kiss.

Simon resumed humming the wedding song.

Morning found Gillie flat on her back, a crystal integrator in one hand and the fractured skewings of spell-mangled crystal above her. Simon had the ship still half-*Serendipity,* half-Raptor, but assured Gillie he had his full attention on the station's news archives as he relayed back to her anything he could find on Magefather Rigo. Though as always he kept watch on the comings and goings in and around Cirrus One.

You have a visitor, My Lady.

A visitor. Not a friend. Not your husband-to-be, or blessed betrothed, or any one of the soppy romantic titles Simon had bestowed on Mack recently.

But there was no note of alarm in his announcement either. Nor would Simon have permitted anyone to enter the bay if he felt there were a possibility of danger. Gillie sat up, narrowly missing banging her head on the edge of a console, and scanned the bay.

Fitch Tobias. Nervous, unsure, and wandering around with his shaved head tilted back as he examined the damage to the *Serendipity.* Or rather, Simon's rendition of the damage to the *Serendipity.*

"Lieutenant. Good morning." Gillie trotted down the ramp.

Tobias was halfway into a reverent kneeling position before he caught himself, straightened. He decided to salute instead. "My Lady Captain."

"Gillie."

"My Lady Captain Gillie."

She bit back a sigh. "Just visiting, or is this official business?"

"Unofficially official." He locked his hands behind his back, straightened his shoulders. "Admiral Mack didn't send me, but he did ask that I trace some enhancements I found in our long-range scanners. NIFTYs. That didn't make sense until I realized Your Worshipfulness was here. Am I correct in assuming they're your Blessed Handiwork?"

She knew what NIFTYs were, had built many herself. But not lately. "I haven't..." *Simon?*

I may have been less than discreet in my efforts to safeguard this station from the Fav'lhir.

"Certain precautions have been taken." She amended her hasty denial. "But we...I didn't think they were obvious." *Damn it all, Simon! And you call me sloppy.*

My enthusiasm and diligence do at times override my better judgment, I fear.

"Not obvious, My Lady. If this station weren't in such a state of disrepair, I'd probably not even have noticed them. It's just we're so used to things not working that when they actually do work, we feel obliged to find out why."

"We. You mean, Admiral Makarian found them?"

Tobias shook his head. "He didn't see them until after I showed him my report."

"And this report. It stated I'm responsible?"

"I had no idea who was responsible, in my first report. That's the purpose of my second report. That's why I'm here." He hesitated, his mouth pursing like a child who knew his next admission was going to earn him a scolding. "My loyalty to the Fleet requires that I report to the admiral the source of these alterations to Cirrus's systems. But my devotion to you, My Lady, tells me I must also obey your commands. You've requested my help in concealing your true identity. I am honored by your faith in me. But it has put me, for the first time in my life, in an unusual position."

"You can't drink wine with your enemies and then dine with your friends," she said softly.

"May Tarkir strike me dead should I ever consider you my enemy," Tobias replied quickly, his dark eyes wide in alarm. "But I recall that was your thirty-second Guideline for Life, and I do understand your point."

"And I understand your predicament." She patted his shoulder in what she hoped was a friendly, reassuring gesture. It was like patting a medium-size asteroid. "Would it help if I said that Admiral Makarian will be informed of the source of these enhancements to Cirrus's systems as the need arises? I only ask that you let me choose when and where."

"The Fleet's long operated on a 'need to know' basis."

"Then have faith that he'll be told when I feel he has a need to know."

It might make for interesting conversation on your twenty-fifth wedding anniversary.

"You have my faith, my allegiance, my unwavering devotion." He knelt.

Gillie grabbed his elbow as he descended, pulled. She was effective only because, halfway down, Tobias must have remembered her order not to kneel. He straightened abruptly, taking her with him.

She stumbled backward, grabbing on to him as he grabbed on to her.

He looked down at her in the shock and surprise of holding a real live goddess in his arms. "Forgive me, My Lady!"

"Fitch, it's all right."

"I offer no offense!"

"Glad to hear that, Lieutenant," Mack said from behind him. "Because all I can offer her is lunch."

12

Lunch didn't sit well in Mack's stomach the rest of main shift. It disturbed him almost as much as his own thoughts, his doubts. His . . . well, yes, when he was finally ready to be honest about it, his jealousy.

Fitch Tobias was thirty-two years old. Gillie was, by her own admission, the same age. Though every time Mack looked at her he felt she was no more than twenty-five. And therein was part of the problem.

When he looked in his own mirror, he clearly saw a man who was forty-three. Ten years older than Gillie and Tobias.

Plus, he'd heard Gillie call Tobias by his first name as he'd come up behind them in their embrace. There was no other description for it. It was an embrace, even if Gillie's explanation had been reasonable and believable: they'd both bent to retrieve a crystal splicer she'd dropped and they'd collided.

It had just looked like something else when he'd walked in.

Just like it looked like *something* when he'd found them together in his office yesterday.

He leaned back in his office chair and closed his eyes. He was wrong, of course. He had to be wrong. Tobias was his second-in-command on Cirrus. Gillie wasn't another Johnna Hebbs who used and manipulated people for her own selfish purposes. Gillie was the woman he loved, the woman he hoped to marry. Who'd been sent to him, he truly believed, by Lady Kiasidira.

And the Lady would never do him harm. Though when Magefather Rigo appeared in his office doorway, he remembered that the Lady also said that for every truth, there was invariably an exception.

His exception clasped his hands at his ample middle in a pious gesture and nodded. "Gracious blessings of the Gracious Lady upon you. I feel her presence stronger every hour that I work as her consort."

"What can I do for you?" Mack motioned toward the chair, as the magefather was already headed that way.

"I wanted to update you on my plans for the Shrine of Communion. Stationmaster Hebbs and I have some new ideas. I know you'll find them as exciting as we do."

Mack doubted that, but he listened to the man anyway for a half hour without interrupting. Looked, when asked, at the layout on the magefather's small datapad. Didn't like what he heard. Liked less what he saw.

"You must know I can't assign the temple an uncontrolled docking bay." He leaned across his desk, tried to assemble a patient expression on his face. What the man wanted would create an unbelievable breach in security, not only for Cirrus, but for the Fifth Fleet and the Rim Gate Project. "Ops has to know the identity of all craft from our outer beacons on in. This is a CQPA regulation as well as Fleet."

"I, of course, understand that. And your concerns. But this is not my lowly, impure self making this request. This is from the Lady herself." Rigo's gaze briefly shot upward, though the station, being in space, had no true up or down in relation to the mystical heavens.

"And the Lady, in her brief time in physical form among us, was a stickler for security." If there was one thing Mack could quote in chapter and verse, it was Lady Kiasidira's military strategies.

"That was a long time ago. Things have changed. We have progressed according to her Blessed Plan, and she now feels we must leave behind our childish paranoia. Be willing to embrace the universe itself!" Rigo's voice shook with this last pronouncement.

Mack sincerely hoped the man wasn't about to burst into tears of devotion. "I'm sure we can find a way to do that without violating regulations. Perhaps if you pray on it a bit longer, you'll come up with another option."

"But it is not I who speaks! This comes from Lady Kiasidira. She who sacrificed for us. She has asked we create this Shrine of Communion. She has sent us a portion of her Blessed Ship as proof of her intentions. I have verified the crystal myself; you saw that. How can you deny this minor request?"

"I'm not denying anything, Magefather. Only modifying it."

"The Shrine of Communion must be just that: communion. Flawless, uninterrupted communication with those who seek her guidance. If the troubled, the weary, the hopeless must announce and register their identities in order to do so, they will not come. We have defeated and defiled the purpose of the shrine."

"Then do what I told you before." Mack smiled. He was losing patience, but at least was still trying to appear pleasant. "Put the shrine dirtside. The Cavellian government indicated they'd be willing to house it in any of their provinces. There are seven spaceports in the Ladri Kemmons alone. Another three in Bexhalla. The volume of travelers utilizing those dirtside spaceports would guarantee anyone's anonymity."

"That's not the Lady's wish." The magefather hesitated, then plowed on. "Johnna Hebbs said CQPA will agree if you will."

Hebbs had agreed to an uncontrolled bay? Mack tried not to let his surprise show on his face. Hebbs saw Cirrus as her domain, that he knew. And she resented Fleet's presence there. Of that, he had no doubt. It put a damper on what she believed was best for Cirrus—a free-for-all trading environment and gaming palace, where the likes of Johnna Hebbs could reign, receive admiration, bestow favors, and play one rim trader against another: politically, economically, and emotionally.

In previous meetings she'd made it clear she welcomed the shrine for the trade and tourists it would bring. But an uncontrolled bay—

No. She couldn't have agreed to that. He thought

again of Rigo's words. Hebbs would agree if he did. She was passing responsibility. It would be Mack's job to keep Cirrus One safe so that Hebbs's tourists could continue to line Cirrus's coffers.

He damned her greed, and her shortsightedness.

"Admiral." Rigo was frowning, clearly not happy with Mack's silence. "Do you want to be remembered in history as the man who defied Lady Kiasidira?" As if to underscore his words, he reached into the folds of his robe and drew out of small sliver of crystal, about two fingers in width and length. A faint purple mist glistened around the shard.

A faint smile touched the magefather's lips as he shoved the crystal back into his robe pocket.

Mack sat back in his chair, counted to ten. He needed the time to think, to make sure he wasn't being skillfully maneuvered into an extremely untenable— and dangerous—position as training warred with faith.

Everything he knew, everything he was, told him that an unrestricted-access docking bay on a station that housed a Fleet HQ was a disaster waiting to happen. An uncontrolled bay on any station was wrong. Simply, unequivocally wrong.

And violated, he truly believed, everything the Lady Goddess had taught the Khalar.

But Magefather Rigo's touch made crystal glow, albeit ever so faintly. Not a pinpoint glow, like the sham rune sellers with their miniature lightpens tucked up their sleeves. But an overall misting haze, like a faint lavender fog.

There was no denying who and what Rigo was.

Therefore, Mack could not deny his request. Not

unless he wanted to be logged into the annals of history as the man who ignored a direct request from the consort of Lady Kiasidira.

That would hardly qualify me as a god, he thought wryly, remembering Gillie's comment at lunch. But more of a devil. One of the damned, like a hideous mogra, a creature spawned from the sludge of the Black Swamp.

"Let me think on it a little longer," he told Rigo. And hoped Make It Right Makarian wasn't about to make one of the biggest mistakes in his life.

"I will pray for the Lady to guide you," Rigo said as he stepped to the door. It slid sideways. "In fact, even now I can hear her sweet voice in my mind, saying—"

"Oh, shit." Gillie stood in the doorway, one hand hovering over the palm pad on the right.

Rigo looked down. Gillie looked up. Mack, standing behind his desk, couldn't see the magefather's expression, but Gillie's was one of surprise. Then her eyes narrowed and he heard her unexpected soft chuckle.

"A thousand pardons. Magefather."

"Yes. Yes, child. Blessings."

Mack waited for Gillie to step back or for Rigo to squeeze by her. But neither moved for a few seconds. Then the rotund man backed up abruptly.

"Sorry. Did I startle you?" Gillie swept one hand toward the corridor. "Please."

Rigo seemed to shake himself, then, head held high, he strode through the doorway.

Gillie folded her arms across her chest, watched him go.

"I need a drink," Mack said, trying to draw her attention back to him. Something about Magefather Rigo clearly bothered her. No, angered her. He'd seen a brief flash in her eyes when she'd faced him.

It didn't make sense. She might not follow the Lady, but she was Tridivinian. She was also, he knew, remembering their earlier conversations, no more pleased with the publicity surrounding recent events than he was.

At least Gillie's understanding of regulations and security segued perfectly with his.

"Devil's Breath, neat, with a twist." Her face relaxed into a smile. "Main shift ended forty minutes ago."

Had it? He glanced at the time stamp on his screen. Damn. And he'd told her to meet him in the atrium. She must have been waiting across from his office that whole time.

He tabbed off his deskcomp. "Magefather Rigo didn't tell me he was coming by. I'm really sorry."

"That's okay. The parrots and I had a wonderful conversation." She took his offered hand.

He asked about repairs as they headed down the corridor. He wanted to take her to Maguire's. Besides the club, it was his favorite. Comfortable, unpretentious, and a tad tacky, it boasted an unusual collection of antique buttons in various framed shadow boxes on its walls. It was one of the station's original bars and so had an enviable outer-wall location. Like the club, it had large viewports, albeit only three. Unlike the club, it had well-worn Cavellian soft-tile floors in an off-hued light brown, a tarnished ceiling with a few notable laser-pistol scorches, and not one unblemished table in its large, semicircular interior.

The bushy-haired bartender's name was Murphy. Mack caught his friendly nod as he ushered Gillie to a table. He keyed in their order on the tabletop menu and leaned back in his chair. And asked the question he still hadn't forgotten, even with the magefather's unexpected visit. "Seen any more of Tobias?"

Gillie gave him a quizzical half smile. "No. Are you going to send him to check up on me again?"

"Is that what you thought?"

"You tell me why I found him poking around in my bay. Then you come in, not a few minutes later, on his tail. I wasn't born yesterday, Mack."

"Honest, I didn't. I have no idea why he was there." He didn't, but since lunch he'd wrestled with the suspicion that she and Tobias were guilty of something. And since lunch, she'd been thinking that he had Tobias spying on her. "He's been working on some system glitches..." *Because of that mysterious Fav'lhir attack,* he almost admitted, but caught himself. "And a couple of other projects for me."

"Am I one of the projects?" She laughed. "He was very nervous yesterday when I found him in your office. What was he doing there, by the way?"

"He has access. All my top officers do, especially as we don't have ops fully integrated. If he seemed nervous, it's because of the crystal."

"That didn't seem to bother him half as much as when I introduced myself. Somewhere I seem to have gained the title of Admiral Mack's girlfriend." She was trying to sound stern, but she was grinning.

He closed his hand around her fingers. "Objections?"

"None."

Drinks arrived. He tasted his, thought of what she'd just told him. Realized he'd totally misread Tobias's reactions. Yes, the lieutenant was nervous around Gillie. But it was over Mack's relationship with Gillie. And, knowing Tobias as he did, he knew how that should be handled.

Admittedly, it'd never been an issue before. He'd never had a relationship with any of his female crew on the *Vedri*. But he knew of other officers on other ships who had. And knew that saying the wrong thing to the captain's lover could be an easy route to mess-hall duty.

Or parrot duty. Even Pryor had belatedly seen that.

Not that Mack would ever operate that way. But it was something his people might be unsure about until he made that fact, and his involvement with Gillaine Davré, clear.

He sent Tobias and Gillie a mental apology. He'd misjudged them both. He should have remembered what he'd told Doc Janek. Gillie was exactly what she seemed to be. A warm, sincere, honest, and intelligent young woman.

"So what blessings did the magefather bring you?" she asked.

He hesitated only a second before telling her, giving her his honest opinion. His fears for security if the request was granted. But more than that, his fears for his soul if it wasn't.

She threaded her fingers through his. "Listen to me, Rynan Makarian. Or better than that, listen to yourself. Go drag up all those Holy Edicts you've committed to memory and pull out every single one relating to the design and operations of the Fleet. I promise you that nowhere did the Kiasidira ever state that a Fleet facility should compromise security."

"I know, but—"

"Further, nowhere did she ever state she would speak to the Khalar, or to anyone, through any kind of consort. Go back in your historical archives and read. The Kiasidira was sent as a technical adviser because of the threat posed by the Melandan mages and the Fav'lhir. Not a spiritual adviser. And not as a candidate for goddesshood."

"The day of her Sacred Sacrifice changed her purpose."

"And what exactly was this sacrifice?"

When he started to reply she held up her other hand. "What you've labeled a sacrifice was a battle maneuver. Something you've been trained to conduct. The Fav'lhir were on the edge of defeat, made one last push with their prime ship. A move the Khalar, and the Kiasidira, should've anticipated—except it was so illogical, so improbable, they didn't.

"It's unthinkable to sacrifice a crystalship in that manner," she continued. "They had their entire mageline on board. Ten Melandan sorcerers and sorceresses. Thirty-seven wizards. Dozens of adepts. The fact that the Fav'lhir did so showed their desperation. It led to their failure, ultimate defeat, and the destruction of their Melandan lineage."

"And the destruction of Lady Kiasidira as well," he added quietly.

She shook her head. "You're not listening. It was a

stupid, foolish move. It violated every known precept in tactical warfare. With their mageline gone, it left them open to be conquered by the Khalar. Except that we—except that the Kiasidira and your council had agreed years before that was not the route the Khalar should ever take. Defend your borders, yes. Protect yourselves, yes. But never to become what the Fav'lhir were: wanton murderers.

"Protect and defend." She closed her other hand on top of his. "Thousands of years ago this was the promise from the Sorcerer, Rothal-kiarr, and the Kiasidira, Lady Khamsin, to the Khalar. Protection from foes. Instruction when necessary. Retaliation and vindication from wrongs. Don't pull away from those precepts. You, not the Kiasidira, have been entrusted to maintain them. It's in Fleet's creed, it's in the vows you took as an officer. Your sworn duty is to protect the Khalaran people. Not to build temples or shrines."

"Even if the shrine honors Lady Kiasidira?"

"When the spaceport was built outside Port Armin, someone suggested that. A shrine, or at least a monument." She hesitated, shook her head slightly. "Abject foolishness. A cold and unresponsive memorial constructed from cold and unresponsive material."

"That sounds like a great line for a speech, Gillie. But I don't think Magefather Rigo is going to agree with you."

Gillie focused on him. Mack had the oddest feeling that, for a moment, she didn't know who he was. But before he could say something, that distant expression passed from her face and she laughed softly. "Sorry. Sometimes my opinions get the best of me."

"For someone who's not a follower of the Lady,

you certainly know Khalaran history for that period."
As he said that, he realized it was true. Gillie knew far
more than he would've thought she would.

"Not a whole lot else to do on freighter runs but
read. You can only play so many games of starfield
doubles against the ship's computer, you know."

That, he also knew, was true. It was a long run
from Ziami to here. Quite possibly this same Simon
who'd given her the Khalaran Fleet sweatshirt had
also plied her with Khalaran history texts.

"Remind me never to challenge you at cards," he
quipped. If she was half as good at starfield as she was
with her history recollections, they'd be more than
evenly matched. He might even find himself facing a
rare loss.

"Billiards." She laughed. "The one thing you never,
ever want to challenge me at is billiards."

"Maguire's doesn't have any tables."

She patted his hand and a playful light danced in
her eyes. "Lucky for you."

Gillie leaned against the cool metal of her ship's interior bulkhead and drew in several long, deep—and she
hoped calming—breaths.

She didn't know where Mack learned to kiss, but
by Ixari's eyes, he was superb. Better each time. Only
Simon's relentless, off-key rendition of the wedding
song kept her focused on who and what and where
she was.

Gillaine, Kiasidira, Ciran Rothalla Davré. On
Cirrus One, some three hundred forty-two years from
her last conscious moment.

And facing a big problem.

"I met Rigo." She pushed herself away from the bulkhead, moved quickly toward the bridge. The metal walls around her phased to crystal as she walked.

Was I correct in my findings? Simon had been as thorough in his research on the magefather as Cirrus's databanks permitted. But only a face-to-face meeting would hold the final truth.

"Fav'lhir." She spat out the word, plopped down into the captain's chair. The warmth from Mack's kisses had faded and was replaced by a hard, cold fury. "Son of a motherless bitch is Fav'lhir. With a Melandan line in his essence. Weak, but it's there. You know what that means."

We erred—we didn't get them all. The Melandan mage lineage is not dead.

"Not yet." She ran her hands over her console, felt the crystal respond. Spellforms laced her skin. She spoke to each one, sent them back, reassured, pulsing with power. "But obviously, they think I am. And they're counting on that fact."

She hesitated, cocked her head to one side. "Simon. Answer me this. Are you starting to get the feeling that our current location is not total happenstance? That there may be a very real reason why Tarkir chose to send us to this very place and point in time?"

Besides the fact that his granddaughter-in-lineage was long overdue to fall in love? Yes, My Lady. I'm beginning to believe that this is where you were supposed to be all along.

"I am too. So now answer me this as well. How in Merkara's depths are you and I supposed to take on the entire godsdamned Fav'lhir fleet by ourselves?"

I'm sure you'll think of something, Gillaine.

"It's not only me. I need you, Simon. And I need a fully functioning Raptor-class starcruiser. If the Fav'lhir have managed to rebuild their mageline, I don't know if even all I have—all I am—can stop them."

Mack hated his office. It was shabby and cramped. It gave him absolutely no psychological advantage when it came to confronting Johnna Hebbs. But he'd have less of an advantage questioning her motives—and her greed and her stupidity—in the stationmaster's large office with its wide viewport and even wider desk.

So the morning after a wonderful evening in Gillaine's company, Mack folded his arms over his chest and leaned back in what had to be the most uncomfortable chair in the universe as Hebbs took a seat across from him. In his shabby, cramped office. And he tried not to let his irritation show.

At least, not his irritation about his surroundings. That he was seriously annoyed with Hebbs's alliance with Magefather Rigo was no secret.

"I have stationers with families to feed, debts to pay." Hebbs folded her arms across her chest as well. This was not going to be a pleasant meeting. "Two of my hotels are now your staff dorm facilities. We lost a restaurant so you could have an officers' club. Your mess hall used to be a damned decent pub. All run by stationers. Your Fleet put my people out of work. Rigo's shrine can give that income back to them."

"An uncontrolled docking bay is sheer suicide, Johnna."

"Yeah. Death by starvation takes a little longer."

Stationers were not starving. Mack would never have permitted that. Yes, there'd been some changes since Fleet's arrival. Unemployment was—temporarily—higher. But Fleet had promised a civilian work program for Cirrus One. It had just—like most of his requisitioned supplies—taken a bit longer to materialize than anyone liked. "Fleet will have twenty new civilian positions opening here in sixty to ninety days. You know that."

"Fleet routinely turns sixty days into six months. *You* know *that*. And your twenty low-end jobs won't do a damned thing for the dozen or so freighter crew I've got sitting without postings because their ships won't dock here now."

"Their ships won't dock here now because their documentation is forged. And Fleet won't hire civilians with criminal records."

"Rigo's willing to forgive their sins."

And give them jobs. Mack had suspected as much. Security was not one of Rigo's top priorities.

But Cirrus's denizens *were* one of Hebbs's. And, though he knew she didn't believe it, one of his. They actually had that in common, and he, begrudgingly, admired her devotion to the stationers. Even if it was partially motivated by greed. But he didn't think even if he admitted that admiration, it would shift her focus from finances to safety.

Still, he tried. She seemed momentarily surprised by his half compliment; he couldn't make it any more than that. There was still a not-so-subtle flirtation in her dealings with him. A sexual agenda. He couldn't risk encouraging that.

So she gave him no encouragement when it came to changing her mind about the docking bay.

When she left his office fifteen minutes later, he wondered if Cirrus would ever provide him anything other than continual exercises in futility.

And, not for the first time, he also wondered if someone in Fleet HQ hadn't foreseen exactly that. Maybe it wasn't *Give it to Mack, he'll fix it.* Maybe it was *Give it to Mack, he's rising too fast. We need to slow him down. Or stop him by setting him up to fail.*

It took three days before Mack trudged into Gillie's bay and admitted he'd given in to Magefather Rigo's demand for an uncontrolled docking bay for the shrine. Gillie was actually surprised he'd lasted that long. There was almost unrelenting pressure—from Prime temple priests and priestesses on Trakhaalus, from Hebbs and CQPA, from the tens of thousands of devout in the Confederation and the hundreds of their kindred on station. Not to mention from within Fleet itself. And Fleet, Gillie knew, was where Mack's heart resided.

He could say what he wanted to the others, and did. But he couldn't defy a direct order from Fleet Command.

It was mid-afternoon, middle of main shift, when he showed up in her bay. He'd done that more and more over the past few days when something troubled him. It warmed her that he trusted her, needed her. This was the biggest thing troubling him yet.

"I actually considered resigning." He sat next to her on the top step of the *Serendipity*'s ramp, elbows on his knees. His fingers were knotted together, like a prayerful fist. Or a fistful of prayers.

Either way, he was angry. And mostly with himself.

"That would've accomplished nothing," she said, referring to his offer of resignation. "They'd just throw some spineless ninny in command who'd basically hand the whole station over to Rigo. You have to stay right where you are, Mack, and watch. Watch everything. Work in as many safeguards as you can."

She'd had Simon start on those two days ago. More NIFTYs, more carefully inserted this time. Nothing to bring Lieutenant Tobias sniffing around her ship.

"I'm probably overreacting. Underestimating my resources. I heard that from HQ more than once."

"You're not. Trust me on this." Even though there'd been no reappearance of the Fav'lhir ships, Gillie was still on edge. Rigo was here and Rigo was up to something. But without revealing her presence, she couldn't find out exactly what that something was. All she could do was work with, and through, Mack.

He faced her. "They've not been back. Hebbs might have been right. Just a couple of rim traders with bad aim and bad timing."

It took Gillie a minute to follow. He referred to the mysterious Fav'lhir ships, the ones she'd just been puzzling over. Not for the first time, she wondered if he didn't carry a low level of telepathy.

However, she wasn't about to reveal what she knew. "You mean those rumors? The ones you told me to ignore?"

"Did you?"

"You don't survive in the lanes by ignoring rumors."

"Well put, my lady."

He'd taken to calling her that. She no longer jumped when she heard the honorific. "So you're saying ops confirmed it was the Fav'lhir."

"Ops is myopic. Tobias confirmed it. He's an unbelievable talent, at times. Fleet had him buried in a procurement depot. I stumbled over him about four years ago, on a routine matter. Sometimes I think he can outthink even the computers. He has a phenomenal memory for detail."

Like a certain green sweater in an old party holovid. She hadn't worn it since then. Didn't want to take the chance.

"That's another reason I don't want you trying to head back to Ziami," he continued. "I don't know what's out there. And I don't—"

"Like it when I don't know what's out there. Yes, I know." She smiled wryly.

"You've been studying the Lady's guidelines again."

Shit. Was that another one? These were just things she'd always said. It was damned difficult to be herself. "The *Serendipity*'s in no condition to go anywhere. And even if we were, I'm not about to leave you all alone with this mess."

"Is that the only reason you're staying?" He studied her through hooded eyes.

"No."

"Then tell me, Gillaine Davré. Why are you staying on this godsforsaken station? I really need to hear some good news right now." His tone was light, teasing. Or trying to be. But Gillie could hear—and feel—the sad edge of failure that permeated him.

The man needed a diversion, a brief respite from his worries. If only for a few minutes. She reached up, tugged his comm set from around his ear, and tucked it in his shirt pocket. "Because I like the way you kiss."

"Do you?"

"Umm."

He lowered his face. "I like the way you kiss too." He brushed his mouth over hers, then those fingers that had been so tensely intertwined traced the line of her jaw.

She nipped his thumb as it touched her lips, opened her mouth when his own covered hers. Let herself get lost, for a moment, in his heat, his desire. In the way everything just seemed so very right when he touched her—even if everything else around them was going wrong.

His kiss deepened, his hands threaded into her hair. And his comm set trilled.

She bit back a groan of disappointment as he pulled away, rested his forehead against hers.

"Damn it." His voice was a harsh whisper. He straightened, plucking the small device from his pocket, then set it in place on his ear. "Makarian." He listened quietly for a moment, then barked out a sharp laugh. "That supply ship's finally here? It's about time. The Lady be praised. Have Brogan and Janek meet me in my office, five minutes. Mack out."

He kissed her nose. "So much for my trying to escape my office for ten minutes. Dinner might be later than usual. Depends when that ship docks."

"I'll be here."

He held her gaze for one more long minute before shoving himself to his feet and heading for the corridor.

Gillie sat on the top step, still tasting his kiss. Still feeling his dejection over losing the battle to Rigo. At least the supply ship was good news.

It's not the first battle that counts, but the last.

Which number Sacred Guideline is that? And did I say it, or did you, Simon?

Neither of us, actually. I read it in a Khalaran military text.

I wonder if the Fav'lhir know that.

The old text? I wouldn't doubt it. They've had their spies around long before Rigo appeared. Long before you did as well.

Not the text, Simon! The last battle. I wonder if that's what the Fav'lhir are thinking. That wasn't their final attempt, three hundred forty-two years ago, out by Traakhalus Prime. This will be, at Cirrus One. As soon as Rigo's private docking bay gives them access to the station.

Hardly an auspicious prize. No offense to Admiral Mack, of course.

Gillie thought on that a moment. *Maybe it's not only the station, or even Fifth Fleet, they want. Do some more checking for me. Not archives, but upcoming* schedules. Mack mentioned something about a deadline for an admiralty inspection. He said he wanted me to be at the dedication ceremonies.

Your gold gown would be perfect for that.

Simon. Find me a guest list, both for the inspection and the dedication. It'll probably be security-tagged, so be careful when you look at it. And dig out everything on this Rim Gate Project. Is this just another jumpgate, or something more? Be very, very careful with that one.

A rude razzing noise sounded in her mind.

Simon.

I will be the epitome of meticulosity, My Lady. I will be the very definition of stealth. I will be—

"Stuff a sock in it, Simon." Gillie pushed herself to her feet and went back to her repairs. She almost hit her head on the console's edge again when her ship's comm trilled.

"Davré's *Serendipity*." She flicked off the splicer, tucked it in her utility belt.

"Lieutenant Tobias." The comm was still voice-only. Deliberately voice-only. She needed the bridge to stay in crystal state in order to effect her repairs.

"What can I do for you, Lieutenant?"

"You can...that is...My Lady Captain, requesting an audience, please."

An audience? She almost asked him if he were writing a play but didn't think the devout officer would appreciate her humor. Or lack of piety. "You'd like to speak to me privately, is that it?"

"If it's not too much trouble."

"It's not. When are you off duty?"

"Rarely. I'd like to come by now, if I may."

"I'll be on my ramp." She didn't want him on her ship. And not because, as Mack had noted, Tobias had an unerring eye for detail.

She'd felt Mack's despair when he'd encountered her accidentally clinging to Tobias that day. It had been a totally erroneous assumption on his part, but that hadn't made it hurt him any less. And she never wanted to be the source of pain for Rynan Makarian. She was, however, a source of wisdom. At least that's what Tobias said, standing in stiff military attention before her. It was his way of kneeling without kneeling, she guessed.

"So you must see my dilemma. How can I be praying to you and receiving your answers through meditations when you're not there," and he gestured upward with his chin, "but here."

"You received answers from me?" This goddess stuff unnerved her.

"I . . . I thought I had. I assume prior to your physical arrival on station I had."

Not unless Tobias was a lot older than he looked. Prior to her arrival on station, she'd been on Traakhalus Prime. Three hundred forty-some-odd years ago.

"But mostly that's the function of Magefather Rigo, during services," he continued. "He hears the prayer requests of the devout and answers as you instruct him to."

"I'd like to instruct him to stuff it where—" She caught herself, stopped. Anger and indignation had surged through her at Tobias's words. She pursed her lips, looked away for a moment. Took a deep breath.

"I've spoken to Magefather Rigo only once in my

entire life. That was a few days ago. He was coming out of the admiral's office. I was going in. We bumped into each other. I think the entire content of our conversation was along the lines of 'I'm sorry' and 'That's okay.' "

"I had begun to suspect that, My Lady." Tobias seemed relieved, though not happy.

She thought she knew why. He liked Rigo's circumventing station security as little as Mack did. Tobias was the one who'd identified the Fav'lhir ship's energy signature. He knew exactly what was at stake.

She tried to understand what the devout lieutenant must be feeling. A lifelong belief, withering. This wasn't the role she wanted to perform. It was becoming harder and harder to live among the lies. And she'd be damned—literally, she thought wryly—if she'd support them.

Especially as those lies had put a Fav'lhir in a position of power on Cirrus.

"Are you here to unmask the magefather as a fraud?" Tobias asked.

Could she? She'd been so intent on Mack's problem with the uncontrolled docking bay she hadn't considered that angle. She nodded slowly, her mind working. Could she somehow set Rigo up to appear the fool? Disgrace himself? Would that be enough to keep the Fav'lhir from trying something large-scale? She felt sure she could handle Rigo. A squadron or two of Fav warships—and the possibility of mageline officers—were another matter. "It's something I'm considering."

"Please know that you can call on me for assistance."

His faith in her touched her. But it pained also. How would Fitch Tobias view her once she was revealed as a fraud? Goddesses didn't play billiards or drink beers with starfreighter crew. Everything in Tobias's deferential tone when he spoke to her underscored that. Everything in Mack's staunch defense of Lady Kiasidira, and his devout recounting of the Lady's guidelines, told her that.

How would Mack and Tobias feel if they found out she was just Gillie?

How could she face their anger at her deception, her betrayal? How could she face losing them? Especially losing Mack. She knew how highly he valued honesty.

You're not a fraud, Simon chastised her after Tobias had left and Gillie sat in the captain's chair on the bridge, one leg draped casually over the armrest. *You are a true Raheiran, and the Kiasidira.*

"But I suck at answering prayer requests."

That only proves you're wiser than you think. If people actually received all that they foolishly asked for, the universe would be vastly more confused and unhappy than it already is.

"What do you think Rigo prays for?"

Probably to live past the completion of his mission, if he indeed has one. Melandans are not known for their loyalty to impure operatives once their role is done.

"Are we so sure he's working for the Fav'lhir? I can tell you only that he has Melandan magics in his essence. That might be the result of a parental indiscretion, not indicative of his political leanings."

Which was true. She had no proof that Rigo was up to anything more heinous than his own aggrandizement.

I think it's a possibility we must strongly consider.

"Then why did those Fav'lhir ships fire on this station?"

A moment of thoughtful silence from Simon. *A message? A warning? Or even an error?*

An error on the Fav's part would be welcome. Gillie still had no answers and only one fact: she wasn't capable of stopping the Fav'lhir alone, and she couldn't enlist the Khalarans' help without revealing who she was.

"Do you have those guest lists yet? And that data on the project?" She frowned, her mind trying to sort all these problems and theories, place them in order.

The files are security-locked and require a delicate touch. I should have something within the hour.

And she had a few hours yet before she'd see Mack. She swung her leg around, stood. "I'm going to do a little poking around. Stay out of trouble, Simon."

Gillaine. There was a clear note of warning in his voice.

She ran her hands through her short hair, straightened her flight suit. "I want to take a look at Rigo's temple."

It's not his. It's yours.

She grinned. "Yeah. And maybe it's about time I put in an appearance."

Gillaine. Simon's voice stopped her at the rampway. *You stay out of trouble.*

Two hours before end of main shift meant Cirrus's corridors were populated by civilian stationers, not

Fleet or CQPA personnel. Gillie threaded her way around clusters of plaid-skirted adolescent males ogling clusters of adolescent females, whose long braids nearly covered their faces. She wondered how the first knew who they were looking at and how the second saw where they were going.

Last she remembered, the trend with teenagers on Traakhalus involved bill-fronted caps worn sideways, as if protecting one ear. And they'd all clomped around in boots laced with strange, curling shoelaces in the most fluorescent of colors.

What had she done at their age? Stowed away on a few freighters, visited a few spaceports where the only safe drink was beer in a bottle, and only if you opened the bottle yourself.

Simon probably would've preferred if she'd indulged in funny shoelaces or braiding her hair or collecting fringed scarves to wear tied around her waist. So would the priests and priestesses at Tarkir's Temple, who were forever piling penance on her when she returned from one of her jaunts. Maybe that's why she felt a little uneasy about entering the temple now. She still remembered what it was like to sit on that cold stone floor for hours, repeating the Supplications, the Minor Incantations, the Major Blessings until her mind felt as numb as her ass.

The wide double entrance doors to the temple—her temple—were locked. She shoved her hands in her pockets, sauntered past the large window. The temple's interior was dimly lit. Rows of high-backed benches curved in a half circle. Shadows clung to the paintings on the wall. She recognized the one of herself that had been behind Rigo in the those repeated announcements. A small raised platform was at the far end abutting the bulkhead, and a large, square panel was attached to it.

The panel served as a frame for what looked like a crystal carving. A lightning-bolt symbol slashing a crescent moon. But if it were crystal, real crystal, she would have felt it, even out here in the corridor.

She kept walking, found a side corridor. There had to be other entrances, or exits, for the temple. She'd worked on enough station designs to know that.

A single door marked EMERGENCY ONLY was about three quarters of the way down the narrow corridor. She gauged it would open behind the large panel. She stopped, listened, sensed. People passed in the main corridor; parrots screeched. Through the bulkheading in front of her, all was quiet.

She lay her hands against the door, felt for the locking mechanism. Tripped it skillfully, slipped inside as the door opened.

She halted it midway, told it to close. The thin shaft of light blinked out. Muddy gray darkness enveloped her. Through the gloom she could make out the edges of the large panel rising like a wall in front of her, less than a foot from where she stood.

The cloying aroma of incense hit her immediately. She stifled a sneeze. She hated incense. It would be more appropriate if her temple held the pungent tang of beer.

She slipped around the panel, stood quietly as her eyes adjusted to the dim light. A lectern was in the middle of the raised platform, its compscreen dark. A small control panel to the right of the screen was dotted with three pinpoints of red.

Over her shoulder was the lightning-and-moon symbol. Plastiglass, not crystal. But something called to her. Something she hadn't felt before. Its song was thin, weak, but familiar.

She opened her senses, probed cautiously. Whatever it was, it wasn't here. A back room. She felt the door before she saw it.

She padded quickly past the front row of benches, touched the door. It was locked. She tripped its mechanism as she had the other.

A storeroom. She was plunged into a thicker darkness when the door shut quickly behind her. The scent of incense was stronger in here. Her eyes shifted to her Raheiran vision as the silent song grew louder. The outlines of a case appeared on the bottom shelf of a two-tiered table. It was larger than the case Tobias had dropped when she'd startled him in Mack's office.

Whatever was inside was much, much more powerful than the remnants of her ship's shattered side.

She was reaching for the case when heavy footsteps thudded in the temple behind her. She dropped to her knees, probed.

Shit. Rigo. The footsteps came closer. Her heart pounded in double time with them. There was only one door for this small storeroom, with only the table against the far wall and boxes of incense stacked all around. Nothing else. Nothing to conceal her. Nothing she could hide behind. If Rigo entered the storeroom and turned on the light, he'd see her.

Footsteps again. A loud cough. He was on the other side of the door.

She flattened herself against the wall under the palm pad. When the door opened, he'd look straight in. Not down. That might buy her a few seconds, though what she'd do with them she had no idea.

She held her breath.

The door slid sideways. An idea surfaced. Risky. Rigo was partly Melandan. He'd sense her Raheiran essence the minute she unleashed it.

Maybe it was about time.

She grabbed the temple's lightning-and-crescent-moon symbol with her mind, wrenched it from the panel. It crashed against the podium floor just as Rigo's fingers found the touchpad.

The storeroom filled with light. And all shadows, and safety, disappeared.

14

"What the fuck!" Rigo's bulky form spun around.

Gillie tensed in her crouch. The moment he moved, she had to move. Silently. Opposite whatever direction he took.

He hesitated. Echoes of the crash rattled through the temple. She felt his surprise, his consternation. And a small twinge of fear.

He'd felt her. Felt something mageline. Something Raheiran.

She shut down, shielded. Didn't breathe. Her nose itched almost unbearably from dust and the incense. A sneeze would give her away.

"Fuck." He drew in a quick breath. She felt his weak probe pass over her. He shook his head, strode quickly toward the rubble on the platform.

She dashed to her left, away from him, her soft bootsteps hidden under his heavier ones. She made it as far as the rear row of high-backed benches when the wide temple doors opened. Light shot in. She dove for the floor.

Two pairs of boots. Fleet issue, it looked like to her as she lay in the shadows under the seats. They hurried down the center aisle, past her.

"Magefather," a male voice called out. "Are you hurt?"

Shit. Mack.

"No. Blessings of the Lady." Rigo's voice shook.

"What happened?"

It took Gillie a moment to recognize the second speaker. Pryor. The one with the bushy white mustache and twinkling eyes. She watched the boots move. Mack and Pryor split up, no doubt inspecting the damage. If she stood now, ran for the doors to the corridor, one of them might turn and see her.

She pinched the bridge of her nose with her fingers. Damned incense!

"The Sacred Symbols . . . fell." Rigo sounded distinctly perturbed.

"Supports are sliced clean." That was Mack.

There was a murmur of agreement, some crunching of the plastiglass under boots, a few light thuds.

"Panel's intact," Pryor said.

"Were you trying to move the panel?" Mack asked.

"I was nowhere near it. Thank the Lady. I was in the sacristy, getting supplies for this evening's service."

"Nothing unusual preceded this?"

Rigo hesitated. "I felt . . . no. Nothing. I just opened the sacristy door, tapped on the light."

"Could the door or light system trigger the symbols to fall?" Pryor stepped toward the storeroom.

"Where are your main controls for the temple?" Mack asked.

"By the entrance. There."

Gillie couldn't see where Rigo indicated. But Mack's boots headed straight for her. Her breath froze in her throat as he passed her by. She turned her face, watched as he stood by the wall. Fiddled with something, she guessed from the soft clicking and beeping sounds.

"Emergency overrides?" His voice carried clearly across the long room.

"Behind the panel," Rigo answered.

"Pryor. Go with the magefather and run a systems check. I don't want to initiate it from here in case there's a short."

"But the Sacred Symbols aren't connected to the controls," Rigo protested.

"Those symbols were sheared cleanly from their supports. The only thing I think that might do that would be a sudden energy discharge."

Or one pissed-off Raheiran, Gillie thought wryly.

"Show Pryor that emergency panel, please."

She swiveled her head again. Rigo's boots swished under his long overgown as he followed Pryor.

She hoped when they found nothing there they'd call Mack, just to verify. With the three of them behind the large panel, she could bolt out the main doors.

She let out a soft sigh. And sneezed.

Mack's boots moved quickly toward her row. She tried to curl herself into a ball, bumped her rear on the underside of the bench. His boots stopped. And she knew she'd found that trouble Simon had told her to avoid.

Again.

She peered out from under the bench and stared directly into the small point of an unholstered, and primed, laser pistol. And the most incredible look of surprise she'd ever seen on a man's face.

"Gillie?"

Thank the gods he'd said her name softly. She could hear the low rumble of Pryor's and Rigo's voices. "I can explain. Really," she whispered.

"You." Mack shook his head, then his eyes narrowed. "Damn it, Gillaine!" His whisper was harsh. He whipped a look toward the platform, then back down at her. "Stay there."

He shoved himself from between the benches and pounded down the aisle toward the panel.

Gillie's heart pounded as well. She had no idea what she was going to tell him. *The truth,* a small voice whispered inside her. She pushed it away. The truth scared her more than his anger did. Let him think she was involved in some lunatic scheme. She could deal with that.

What she couldn't deal with would be the look in his eyes when he realized who she was. She wanted to be in his arms. Not on a pedestal somewhere, worshipped.

"I don't want anyone in here until I bring in a safety-inspection team." Mack's voice rang out authoritatively across the room. "I'm sorry, Magefather, but you'll have to cancel tonight's service. Or hold it somewhere else."

Mack was angry. He was really, really angry. Gillie

listened to the expected protestations from Rigo as Pryor herded him out the door.

Then all was quiet. The bench above her squeaked. She saw the back of Mack's boots, crawled out.

An ion storm hovered in the depths of his dark eyes.

She pulled herself off the floor and sat beside him. "Hi."

"Don't tell me you had anything to do with what happened here."

"Okay."

He laced his fingers together, stared at the empty panel for a long moment, then back at her. "My office. Now."

She followed him out of the temple and down the corridor in silence. Even the parrots had nothing to say.

He perched on the edge of his desk, arms folded across his chest. "Sit."

She did.

"Tell me."

Her mind had churned the entire way over here, decided it was tired of lies but still afraid of the truth. Decided it would try for something in between.

"I don't trust Rigo," she said. "But I don't have proof yet as to why. I thought I might find answers in the temple."

"This is because of the shrine's docking bay."

"To a great extent, yes."

He let out a long sigh. "I've probably told you more than I should have about this matter. This is Fleet and Confederation politics. Normal politics. I've dealt with it my whole life. I appreciate your trying to help, but you don't know what you're meddling with."

No, she thought. *You don't. And that's why I have to.* "I think more than just the Confederation is involved here."

"There's no substantive proof the attack was the Fav'lhir."

"There's Tobias's proof."

"That wasn't enough for HQ."

"It's enough for me."

He held her gaze for a long moment. "All right." He splayed his hands against the edge of the desk. "Let's say, for argument's sake, an unfriendly faction may be involved. Let's say, and I assume this is what you're thinking, that Magefather Rigo is part of it. Those possibilities alone should tell you to stay out of this. Leave it to me, to Fleet, to handle."

"I understand."

"But you don't agree."

"Mack—"

"Damn it, Gillaine! If Rigo's involved with the Fav'lhir, you could get killed."

Again? She suppressed a derisive laugh. But his words, and his fear, told her Mack had the same suspicions she did. The same suspicions Tobias did. Rigo's motives were more than personal aggrandizement. "Someone has to stop him," she said.

"Not you," he replied sharply, then the hard lines on his face softened. He reached forward, brushed one hand through her hair. Dust shimmered in front of her eyes. "Not you."

He touched her nose with the tip of his finger. "No one's cleaned under those benches in a while."

"Incense. Damned stuff's lethal."

His gaze traveled to the utility belt at her waist. She anticipated his next question. "How'd you cut down the Sacred Symbols?"

"You know what it's like in the lanes. Sometimes the tools you need are a bit more than spec," she lied.

"Since I didn't hear you tell me that, I won't have to confiscate them. But answer me this. Why?"

She knew he wasn't asking about any fictitious, high-energy and highly illegal lasers. "Rigo's able to do what he wants because people think he speaks for the Kiasidira." She suddenly realized how she could use her desperate attempt at diversion and turn it into a method of discrediting the magefather. "I hoped people might interpret something like that as a sign of her displeasure. Especially if your safety team finds no physical explanation for it."

"The supports were obviously sheared by an intense energy source."

"Which they won't be able to produce. Or identify. You and Pryor can confirm there was no one else in the temple." She shrugged. "That's all you have to announce. Leave the rest up to gossip."

His gaze shifted away from her as he wrestled with her suggestion. But only for a moment. Then he seemed to remember who, and what, he was.

"I can't, Gillaine. You're asking me to participate in the fabrication of a rumor that could potentially destroy a man's career."

"I'm asking you simply to report what your team finds. An unknown energy source sheared the Sacred Symbols while only Rigo was in the temple. That's all."

"But I know you did it."

She stood, unbuckled her utility belt, handed it to him. "Prove it."

He took the belt but didn't look at it. "You ditched the laser somewhere between the temple and my office, didn't you?"

She smiled. It was a nonanswer. It didn't feel quite as bad as a lie.

He shook his head. "I don't trust Rigo. You know that. But I have to work things my way. My methods. Fleet's methods. I'm not going to start any rumors."

He was an honorable man. She'd known that from the first time she'd met him. She never really expected he'd go along with a plan like hers.

But that was all right. She knew who would. Tobias.

Still, Mack was a damned good kisser, even when he was angry with her. He snugged the belt around her waist, threaded the buckle. Then, with his fingers curled around her belt, he leaned back against the edge of the desk and pulled her against him.

She wrapped her arms around his neck. Easier to do when he wasn't towering over her.

His kiss was long and deep. She luxuriated in the feel of his short, thick hair against her palms, of the solid warmth of his chest against hers. His breath shuddered slightly in her mouth, sent a thousand fluttermoths soaring through her senses. Then his hands, which had been sensually massaging their way up from her waist, stilled.

He pulled back reluctantly. "I have to be in a meeting in five minutes." He stroked her cheek. "Promise me. No more adventures. Without telling me first."

"Promise."

"Dinner will be late. We can have it at my place?"

She thought of what Simon would say. "Only if I'm allowed to be dessert."

Desire flashed like a surge of heat in his eyes. Then he closed them, as if he knew she'd seen. Knew he was at the limits of his control.

Gillie knew. She teetered on the edge of her own every time he touched her.

"I'll call you. When the supply ship's cleared." He pushed her back gently, stood. "No more adventures. That's a promise, now."

"No more adventures. At least," she added huskily, "not without you."

"Damn it," he said, but it wasn't a curse. He crushed her against him, kissed her hard. She felt his body throb against hers, felt his heart pounding in time to her own.

He dragged his mouth away, rested his face against her hair. His breathing slowed. "You're very distracting, Captain Davré."

"Thank you, Admiral Makarian."

He released her. "Dinner later. And . . . dessert."

She smiled. And tried not to laugh when he almost bumped into the edge of the door on his way out of his office.

Simon was tsk-tsking her when she walked into the bay. *Not one of your more flawless performances, to be sure.*

I thought I handled Mack's questions—and his kisses—pretty well.

That, yes. I'm also aware that was no performance. But I'm speaking of your assault on your own temple.

She climbed the rampway stairs. The airlock slid open as she reached the top step. *Rigo's got something in that storeroom. That sacristy, as he calls it. I need to find out what it is.*

It contains a significant measure of Raheiran crystal.

No kidding. I was there, remember? The unknown case in the sacristy was more of a curiosity than a threat, however. She leaned against the back of the captain's chair, surveyed the readouts on the bridge. Simon was doing better, much better. But he was still far from being in fighting shape.

Interesting symbols. The crescent moon. Basic female symbolism. But the lightning bolt. That's traditionally male.

"The Sorcerer and the Kiasidira," she said out loud. "Ancient history, Simon. You taught me that."

Glad to know you were listening. I've had my doubts over the years. Do you also remember their names?

"Lady Khamsin was the first Kiasidira."

And the Sorcerer?

"Rothal-kiarr, of course. He was her magesoul. Her lover. Her husband." She also carried part of his name in her own: Gillaine Ciran Rothalla Davré.

That's his magename. What did she call him?

"She?"

Lady Khamsin.

"She called him . . ." Her mind ran over the legend, remembered the Sorcerer had often used a more common name for himself. When she found the answer, she stumbled over the name. "Rylan." She'd almost said Rynan.

Interesting, don't you think?

"It's similar. Not the same." She turned from the console, leaned over her navigation array. Refused to let her mind play with the coincidence. It frightened her, and intrigued her at the same time.

Speaking of names, I have a few more. The ones you asked me to find.

She straightened, glad the conversation was back to business. "The guest list. Who's invited to our humble abode?"

Some people who could well push us into the high-rent district. The admirals of the First, Third, and Fourth Fleets will be here for the official inspection. As will three of the Rim Gate Project's top scientists. All will stay, of course, for the dedication the following day. That's when "they" arrive.

"They?"

Prime Hostess Honora Syrella Trelmont and her daughter, Roannan Charity. The wife and daughter of the Chancellor of the Confederation.

Gods. In a less than three weeks, Cirrus would contain three of the highest-ranking officers in the Khalaran Fleet—four, counting Mack—along with key personnel from the project. And the prime hostess, the wife of the political head of the Confederation.

And a huge gap in station security that the Fav'lhir could fly a crystalship right into. To kill, if that was their intention.

Or to take hostages. And gain control of the Khalar in this, the final battle. And there was no way Gillie could stop them.

✦✦✦ 15

Mack was extremely pleased to see the supply ship arrive. He was extremely pleased that all his requisitioned items were neatly listed on the manifest. And he was also extremely pleased that clearance of the vessel took under two hours.

A record, especially for Cirrus.

And a break, for him. Dinner with Gillie would be late, but not abysmally so. There might even be time for dessert.

He stepped into the lift, sucked in a sharp breath. Held his stomach in as well. He'd been too busy the past few months to spend much time in the gym. Would she notice? He'd always considered himself in decent, if not better than decent, shape.

Unless, of course, he compared himself to Fitch Tobias.

But Gillie was having dinner with him, not Tobias. That is, providing she was still speaking to him after his reaction to her little stunt in the temple. His heart stuttered when he pictured her dust-streaked face peering up at him from under the bench.

She'd taken considerable risks because of what she believed in. And because she believed in him.

The woman was...incredible. There was no other word for it. He hoped he was worthy of incredible tonight.

Incredible waited for him at the bottom of her ramp, in a short tan-colored skirt that looked like butter on silk. On top of that, incredible wore a clingy, long-sleeved top that whispered across her when she moved.

"Hi," he said, when he found his voice. He knew he stared at her. He didn't care.

"Hi, yourself."

"My place?"

"Unless you want to have dinner on my stairs."

He folded her hand in his, couldn't stop smiling. But at least he didn't bump into the door frame on the way out again.

His small apartment on Upper5 held the wonderful aroma of a sweetly spicy stew he'd ordered from Maguire's earlier. He retrieved the bottle of wine from the refrigerator and watched Gillie turn in a slow circle in the middle of his living room.

"It looks like you." She accepted the glass of golden wine with a smile.

"Really?" He knew she meant his apartment, but beyond that didn't know quite what she meant. He didn't think she referred to the layout. His home since coming to Cirrus One was identical to many other residential apartments on the station's upper levels, with a long living-room–dining-room combination flanked on one side by an open galley—kitchen, he corrected himself. And on the other, a door that led to a decent-size bedroom. It was larger than his quarters on the *Vedri*, but smaller, he knew, than executive apartments on newer stations.

The carpet in his living-room area and bedroom was a medium gray flecked with blue, a sturdy, industrial grade. The dining room, kitchen, and two small sanifacs had white soft-tile on the floor.

His walls were a paler gray than Cirrus's corridor bulkheading. On them he'd hung his holos from the academy and all his postings, including the *Vedri*, in no special order. The four-tiered built-in bookshelf to the left of the kitchen held a few real bound books; those were special. So were the few other items secured to the metal shelves, including a plastiglass globe of Traakhalus Prime his grandfather had given him when he'd graduated from the academy. And one beer can, never opened, on a velvet cushion.

She touched it, questioningly.

"Long story." He took a sip of his wine first. "Ever hear of Captain Ward Dylannin?" When she shook her head, he shrugged. "No reason you should have. That was six, seven years ago." He knew exactly how long it was, but didn't like to remember that either. "Ward and I went through the academy together. Took our first postings on the same ship, the *Richenza*. From there, went to the *Loyal*. I guess you could say he was my best friend."

He saw by the softening in her eyes she'd caught his use of the past tense and knew where this story was going. He continued anyway. "We both made captain within four months of each other. I got the *Vedritor*. Ward got the *Nevritan*. Sister ships. Both Tarkiran-class hunterships. Right off the designer's deskscreens. And with some unexpected flaws in the power grids.

"The *Nevri* was engaged in a war-games maneuver when her power grid collapsed. Ward was trapped in engineering with his chief and two junior crew. He got the juniors out and the situation went critical. Someone had to stay in engineering or the jumpdrives would blow. And take the ship, and her two hundred nineteen officers and crew, with them. Ward was the one who stayed, and because he did, they were able to contain the explosion to just the drive room. And therefore lost only one life."

"Your friend," she said softly.

"He wouldn't have had it any other way."

"And the beer?"

"He bought it when we both made captain. First one to make admiral, he said, gets to open it." He shook his head. "Maybe when all this gets straightened out, I'll do that. For him. Though I really didn't win it fairly. If he'd lived, they might've offered Fifth to him instead of me."

She was looking at him intently, the lavender in her eyes much more noticeable for some reason tonight. "The admiralty was your destiny, Rynan, not his. Your path here is not at all by chance."

Something stirred inside him, in a very deep place he'd all but forgotten about. It was almost like a memory. One that held no pain. Only peace.

He touched her face, chided himself at the wild, romantic imaginings in his mind. "So all this—the parrots, Hebbs, Magefather Rigo, no supplies, kids in long plaid skirts—this is all my destiny?"

She was smiling. "Yes."

"And you too?"

"And me."

"How lucky can one guy get?" He tweaked her nose gently. "Dinner?"

She said yes to that too. And to more wine. And, after dinner, to coffee laced with chocolate. They sat on his low-backed dark blue couch and sipped their coffee while music spilled from his small soundmirror in the corner. He tabbed down the lights, removed the coffee cups, pulled her against him. "Come here, destiny-mine."

She laughed softly. "Just Gillie."

"Gillaine. It sounds more elegant. You have a middle name?"

"A few," she said after a moment.

This surprised him. He didn't remember one listed in her ID file. Not for the first time, he realized how little he knew of her. Whenever they were together, they talked about the station, or about himself. She must think him terribly self-centered. "Tell me yours and I'll tell you mine."

"Why? Is yours embarrassing?" She leaned her head back against his chest and looked up at him. Looked hopeful. Looking, he felt, for something to tease him about.

"Sorry, not at all. I just rarely use it. Is yours?" He could tease her just as well.

"No. Just long. And I rarely use it."

"I'm listening."

"Listening? That's a funny middle name."

"Gillaine!" He tightened his arms around her, tickled her lightly.

"Okay! Okay!" Her giggles subsided. Her gaze became serious. "Gillaine." She stopped, seemed to consider something for a moment. Took a deep breath, continued: "Ciran Rothalla Davré."

He played it over in his mind. "That's beautiful." He meant it.

"You wouldn't think so if the only time you ever heard it was when you'd been caught doing something you weren't supposed to."

"Wish I'd known that. Could've used it earlier."

She smacked his arm playfully. "Fair's fair. Tell me."

"Rynan Khamron Makarian."

She went very still in his arms. "Spell it."

"K-H-A—"

"—M-R-O-N?"

"Yes, why?" It wasn't a common name, but he felt as if it meant something to her.

"Nothing. It just figures, that's all."

"Figures?"

She turned in his embrace, slid her arms around his neck. "Destiny."

The conversation might have interested him more had her soft body not been pressing against his, her mouth only inches from his own. Her fingers traveled slowly through his hair.

He pulled her into his lap. His hand caressed her hip, then glided over the smooth, bare expanse of her thigh. His other cupped the back of her head, brought her mouth to his. She tasted like coffee and chocolate. Felt like fire in his veins.

He teased her mouth with his tongue, wanting desperately to claim her, fiercely. But wanting, knowing he would take this slow. They had time. All night. He wanted to make love to her all night, on a station one exit from nowhere, where night went on and on forever.

Her hands kneaded his shoulders, her tongue mirrored his teasings. She pulled back from his kiss, caught his lower lip between her teeth, sucked lightly. Sparks arced through him like a barrage of laser fire: hot and intense. Then she was kissing him again, and he forgot about teasing and he forgot about slow. She was warm and soft where he was hot and hard, and he could think of no better combination.

The thin fabric of her shirt seemed to melt under his hand. He cupped her breast, found the bud of one nipple blossom under his touch. Her sharp intake of breath sent heat rushing through his body. Made his mouth claim hers because he needed to taste her now, taste the passion that made her gasp. That made his own breathing ragged.

Her hips moved in a soft, sweet rhythm in his lap, stroking him. He arched against her, rasped her name. "Gillaine. Let me love you."

"Forever." Her voice was a whisper. She took his hand.

He led her into his bedroom, lifted her onto the middle of his bed. Her eyes were more lavender than he'd ever seen them; a flush of pink colored her cheeks. Her slightly parted lips drew his own like a guidance beacon, unerringly. He forced himself to keep his kisses soft, for now, though the effort almost left him shaking.

He kneeled over her to unbutton her shirt while she

unfastened his. Slipped her skirt off, then his hands stroked her warm, velvet skin, the round fullness of her breasts, the slender curve of her hips. The heat between her thighs.

The heat in his own body raged, demanded possession of her. But not yet. Not yet. There was still so much to explore, still so much pleasure he wanted to give her.

His mouth followed the trail his hands had left, and he tasted all of her. He circled her nipples with the tip of his tongue but had to stop, catch his breath. Her hands were doing some exploring of their own. Flames rose, crested inside him. Threatened to explode. His skin was sweat-slicked, heated. He groaned, fought for control.

"Love me, Rynan. Now."

He lost it. He plunged inside her. She arched her hips, her fingers raked his back. He took her mouth, branded her with kisses as the universe tilted and went into free fall.

Passions exploded. Her breath fluttered, whimpered into his mouth. A rush of ecstasy cascaded through him in a sensation he'd never experienced before. He filled her, throbbing, shuddering his release, still clinging to this ecstasy, to this spiraling sweetness. Not knowing what it was. Only that he could never get enough of it.

He could never get enough of her. Gillaine. His Gillaine.

He covered her small body with his, trailed kisses across her face, down her neck. She was still trembling.

He grabbed a handful of covers, pulled them haphazardly over them both. Rolled onto his side, drew her into his arms. There were a thousand things he wanted to tell her, to promise her, to offer her. He found he could say only her name. "Gillaine..."

"Hi."

He smiled. "Hi, yourself."

She snuggled against him.

He put his fingers under her chin, tilted her face up. The time-controlled lights in his bedroom had dimmed. He couldn't see the color of her eyes. "I meant what I said last week. I want to marry you."

She sighed. He hoped it was a happy sound. "We have time."

"How much time?"

"If you asked me that a month ago, I could have told you. I understood time then. I don't think I do anymore."

"Why?" He was usually good at riddles, but this one perplexed him.

"Because time changed. For me." She leaned her face against his chest. "I'm not trying to be evasive. A lot of things have happened in my life in the past few weeks. I don't understand them all just yet."

"I don't think I'm all that difficult to understand. Feed me. Love me. Not necessarily in that order."

She laughed softly, brought her face back up. "I can do that."

"That's all I'm asking."

"Be careful what you ask for, Rynan Khamron Makarian. You might get it."

They dozed, woke up an hour later, tangled in the covers. Made love again, talked less, kissed more. Mack spooned her against him as he lay on his side. She fit perfectly, as if their bodies had long ago been made only for each other.

When he woke the next time it was forty minutes before he was to be on duty. But her soft bottom pressing against him told him he just might be late.

He wasn't, but only because they skipped breakfast.

He grabbed a mug of coffee from the officers' mess, sipped it while he stood on the upper level of ops because it concealed the broad grin that was totally incompatible with his current surroundings. But not with the landscape of his heart. Because that was where Gillaine lived now, inside a heart that had at one time been concerned only with practicality, with his postings, his career. Devotion was a word he'd aligned with duty. Then Gillaine had changed his entire vocabulary.

He'd never been so happy in his entire life. Not even when he'd made the rank of captain. Not even when he'd made admiral.

He scanned ops again, watched his people move through their paces. Hebbs acknowledged him with a slight nod, went back to her conversation with an orange-suited worker. The willowy stationmaster had lost her aggressiveness toward him ever since he'd called her into his office. That was a good thing. He'd tired of parrying with her, of dodging her innuendos and advances.

She'd also become less vocal in her support of Rigo's shrine. Even before their talk in his office, he knew he'd lost that battle—if not to her, then to the denizens of the station who wanted the shrine, and the commerce the shrine would bring, even more than Hebbs did. He fully expected she'd gloat, throw some comments his way every chance she had.

She hadn't. He didn't know why—or what had changed her—but that, too, was a good thing.

Maybe they could finally all concentrate on the job at hand. Which was to get Cirrus fully functioning, or as close to fully functioning as they could, for the inspection and project launch in less than three weeks.

And maybe even a wedding, after that?

He brought his attention back to ops. Alter shift had already begun installing the systems' components that arrived with the supply ship. CQPA techs were elbow to elbow with black-uniformed Fleet engineers below.

They were getting somewhere now.

The time stamp on the main screen told him he had ten minutes before his meeting with Adler. He found an open console, slipped on a headset for privacy, called the *Serendipity*. The vidscreen was blank.

"Davré's *Serendipity*." Her voice sent trickles of warmth through his veins again.

"Hi."

"Hi, yourself."

He could almost hear her shy smile. "We have to get you vidlinked one of these days."

"Every time I hook it up, something else in my comm pack skews."

"We've got equipment now. I can look at it later tonight, if you want."

"Actually, I was actually thinking of a much better way to spend our time."

By Ixari's sweet eyes, so was he. He hadn't stopped

thinking about it. "Were you? Perhaps we should discuss that."

"In depth."

"In detail," he added quickly.

She laughed. "Lunch?"

"Regrettably, no. Probably not for the next few days. The toys have arrived," he said, meaning his requisitioned systems and supplies. And some prelimary equipment for the project, though those were things he wasn't at liberty to discuss publicly. "I have to make sure everyone's playing the same game."

"Late dinner again?"

"Shouldn't be. I'll talk to you later, let you know how things are unfolding." He'd talk to her, a lot. It was the only way he was going to be able to make it through the day without seeing her. He needed to hear her voice.

"I might have lunch with Petrina. She left a message."

He couldn't quite place the name. "Not a friend of our esteemed stationmaster, I hope?"

"No. A nice, happily married tech I met in the Fifth Quarter. Her husband, Teddy, thinks he can play billiards. I may have to prove him wrong one of these days."

"Be gentle, my lady."

"Won't leave any visible scars, promise."

He laughed out loud, which drew the attention of two of his crew at a console a few feet away. He turned his back on them, cupped his hand over the headset's mike. "I'll talk to you later. Gillie . . . ?"

"Umm?"

"I love you. Stay out of trouble."

"Promise."

He pulled off the headset, his whole existence warmed by her voice. He knew she cared, even if she hadn't told him she loved him yet.

But that also worried him. Because he knew Gillie. And the way she cared could damned well lead her into trouble. He didn't believe for one minute she wasn't going to fuel rumors about the shattering of the Sacred Symbols.

And he didn't believe for one minute that Magefather Rigo wouldn't do all in his power to stop her. Which, Mack realized as he strode into the corridor, was something he'd best start considering as well.

Magefather Rigo's power.

He'd just stepped into his office when his comm set and his desk intercom trilled ominously at the same time.

"Makarian."

"Hebbs here. Need you in ops. We're got a security-systems failure coming down!"

✦✦✦16

Gillie tabbed off ship's comm and closed her eyes. She let the warmth in Mack's voice wash over her and indulged herself in the remembered sensations of his kisses, the gentle yet insistent touch of his hands. Her body heated at the memory, tingled.

It'd been a long time since a man she cared about had made love to her. It felt almost as long as those three hundred forty-two years she'd traversed yet really not lived. There'd been Thaniel, an older, more serious student when she was at the university. And Kiril; charming, sexy Kiril. They'd hated basic training. Loved each other. For a little while.

Both those relationships had ended before she'd been assigned to the Khalaran Confederation.

Then in Port Armin, there'd been Ethan. Captain Ethan Tarrant, Khalaran tracer pilot. They'd been friends, close friends. She'd always felt they might have been more than friends if she hadn't been the Kiasidira.

But neither Than nor Kir nor even Ethan could make her heart race the way Mack did. None occupied her thoughts the way Mack did. And none, she knew and had always known, had really loved *her*, just Gillie. She was a Kiasidira; even to her own people, mageline all, she was an exotic enticement.

It was one of the reasons she'd never regretted leaving Raheiran space and why she'd been committed to staying with the Khalar. It was the only chance she'd ever have to be just Gillie. She'd come very close to accomplishing that with her friendship with Ethan.

It feels like you've decided to stay on Cirrus.

Her euphoric expression faded into a frown. "There are still so many unanswered questions. Issues. And not just Rigo and the Fav'lhir."

Your legendary ancestor, Rylan, once told Lady Khamsin, "Trust your heart. It's wiser than you think."

"Maybe hers wasn't in danger of being broken."

You think Mack would do that to you?

"I think he might to the Kiasidira." It had taken her six years, but she'd almost managed to be just Gillie to the Khalar. Then a Fav'lhir crystalship had exploded and everything she'd worked so hard for had unraveled. The Kiasidira hadn't been just Gillie for three hundred forty years. She was someone else, someone Tobias prayed to, someone Mack worshipped. Someone whose guidelines he'd memorized, quoted.

She didn't know what frightened her more if Mack were to ever find out who she was: that he'd hate her for lying to him, or that he'd revere her, worship her, and never touch her again.

Her chair squeaked softly as she swiveled away

from the comm console and went back to the emotionally safer topic of her research.

Magefather Rigo had opened the Kiasidiran temple in the rooms previously occupied by an Ixarian temple that had existed—unstaffed and, for the most part, unattended—for almost two years. The inhabitants of Cirrus had long been a mixture of outcasts, rarely agreeing on a preferred beer, let alone spiritual philosophy. But the worship of Lady Kiasidira, long the property of Khalaran spacers, had fit right in. So had the amiable Rigo. He showed up about six months before Mack and his people arrived. But Fleet's intention to utilize part of the station as Fifth's HQ had been announced a few months before that. It could be coincidence. Or it could be a piece of very nice planning on Rigo's, and possibly the Fav'lhir's, part.

Gillie could find no substantive proof that Rigo was involved with the Fav—not that she expected to. It wasn't the sort of thing someone would include on their resumé.

But she could see why Rigo, and Cirrus Station, would be important to the Fav'lhir.

The Cirrus Quadrant was the last to be developed. Long ignored by the Confederation, its strongest attribute now was that it wasn't overly populated. It was the perfect and logical site for the next step the Confederation was planning in its continual efforts to improve its territory: the construction of a major jumpgate directly to Traakhalus Prime, and all the worlds, colonies, stations, and industrial rafts in that sector.

Fifth Fleet was to be the guardian of that gate linking the center of Khalaran space with the rim sectors.

Rim sectors that held tremendous potential for trade, mining, and manufacturing.

That was why Mack had been so insistent in the design and setup of ops. The gate would be controlled through Fleet's facility on Cirrus. What had arrived on that supply ship, Gillie learned from studying the manifests, were components and a technology the Fav would probably love to have and control.

Technology and components they could have, through surreptitious access to Cirrus via the Shrine of Communion's docking bays. Those bays would offer access just at the time ops should be fully functioning, all those sensitive systems coming online.

And a handful of high-placed people who would make excellent hostages would be on station.

Or maybe not hostages. Victims. If the Fav were successful here—and that was a fairly big *if*—they could not only wipe out some of the Confed's key political figures but gain control of Cirrus and the Rim Gate, essentially throwing the Confederation into a serious upheaval. Even war. And with control of the gate, the Fav would suddenly have many more options on their side.

Gillie absently drummed her fingers against her mouth. The only thing in her favor was time. Nearly three weeks yet. She remembered Simon's wise warning when she'd first realized she'd been dragged three hundred forty years into the future: *Impatience invariably leads to sloppy work.*

She'd almost made a few serious mistakes. She couldn't afford mistakes now, if she was facing the Fav'lhir. Again.

Plus, she knew this was still conjecture. Rigo's push

for the shrine, his puffed-up pronouncements about being the Lady's consort, could be nothing more than an annoying ego out of control.

Yet it was all too coincidental. She hated coincidence. If that wasn't already one of her Holy Guidelines, she'd have to remember to make it one.

She shoved herself out of her chair. It was time to work on her Holy Rumors.

The Fifth Quarter was a busy place for lunch. She and Petrina were lucky to find two stools at the bar. Soup smelled wonderful as it went by on a 'droid server's tray. Gillie ordered a bowl, half-listened to Petrina's chatter about work. One of the station's larger grids had collapsed, causing a lot of shouting and scurrying around the station. But it hadn't been an environmental grid, which was Petrina's assignment, so she shrugged off Gillie's concerned questions.

"You still breathing? So am I. That's all we need to know."

Gillie turned her attention to the chatter around her. She wasn't going to have to start those rumors after all. They were already up and running on rather substantial legs.

"Lissy's upset, doesn't believe it, but I'm not sure," Petrina said when the conversation turned to the rumor. "The magefather says it's another positive sign from the Lady."

"Seems to me a positive sign would be her enhancing the Sacred Symbols, not destroying them." Gillie tried to add a note of bored disinterest to her voice.

"That's what other people are saying. Nothing like this has happened before. We'll see what goes on at the healing service this afternoon."

"Healing service?" Gillie knew she should probably pay more attention to the newsvids.

"To prove he's still the Lady's consort. A free service. Only fifteen minutes, of course, but free. Should be quite a crowd, even at that time of the day."

Gillie climbed the stairs up to the first atrium level after her lunch with Petrina. She leaned on the railing, looked up. Fourteen levels between here and the top, though not the top of the station. Just the top of the atrium. The location of the officers' club, where Mack had told her he loved her.

And the location of the observation area, where Rigo was to hold his short, free-of-charge healing service in two hours.

She understood his thinking completely. It would be mid-shift; most people would be at work. Therefore any healing he did—if he could actually do any—wouldn't be strained by a crowd of hundreds who might not let him leave when the allotted fifteen minutes expired.

Because the service was, after all, free. And as Gillie had learned, here on Cirrus, mages charged for healing.

Sheer unadulterated blasphemy. A Raheiran never charged.

So now Rigo was trying to act more Raheiran. More generous. At a time when the least amount of people could show up. In a location as far away from the bulk of Cirrus's population as he could get. Just so he could prove he still held Lady Kiasidira's favor.

Unfortunately for him, the Kiasidira had other plans.

About thirty-five people were already in line when

Gillie exited the lifts on Upper9. A few, from their dress, were merchants or administrators. But the rest clearly belonged downlevel, in the Zone.

Most were people she hadn't seen before. She wished she had.

Two were in antigrav chairs, their bodies frail, their limbs twisted. Another, an elderly woman with short-cropped white hair, knelt on the floor, her hands trembling noticeably as she prayed. Her jacket was threadbare; the orange jumpsuit underneath stained and faded. Gillie doubted she worked for CQPA. The jumpsuit was probably some tech's castoff.

They were the people who were beyond hope of even the Khalaran medical system. Or, more likely, beyond being able to pay for what that system could provide.

A small, thin young boy leaned against his father's leg. His eyes were shadowed, sunken. She could feel pain lacing through him, but he never grimaced, never whimpered.

Her heart ached. She squatted down beside him. "Hey, *chavo.*" She used the Raheiran slang term for beloved boy.

"Blessing, miselle." His voice was weak.

She glanced up at his father. He had on the plain gray jumpsuit of a freighter maintenance tech, but no ship's patch on the sleeve or pocket. He was probably out of work and, judging from the tiredness apparent in his gaze and his stance, he had been for some time. He had the same deep russet-colored hair as the boy, but his was thick and curly. The child's was sparse.

He stroked his son's head. "This gives us hope. We couldn't afford a life blessing before."

Couldn't afford a life blessing for a child in intense pain? Anger churned inside Gillie. For once she hoped Rigo did have some power. Even a Melandan could heal.

But the child needed more than a life blessing. She studied his essence, saw the rapid disintegration. Yet other signs told her it wasn't his time to pass on.

You wanted to prove the magefather a sham, Simon reminded her.

Sometimes what I want has to be put aside for what needs to be done.

She straightened, briefly touched the child's cheek. "He'll be better soon. Have faith."

She went to the back of the line.

Others came. She gave up her space, let them step in front of her. "Waiting for a friend," she explained. "Your need is greater."

It was. The small area cordoned off by station sec had swelled to capacity by the time Rigo and his attendants arrived, followed by a young man and a young woman, both in brown robes. Rigo wore the deep gold symbolizing a Raheiran mage of the Primary Order. A Ki'sidron. Or a Kiasidira.

Blasphemy, that!

Rigo nodded to his assistants. The young woman, her long hair in deep honey-colored braids, held open the small box. Rigo took out the ward stones. Vedri. Ladri. Nevri. Placed them at three points. The Khal. The stone of the powerful god Tarkir. Placed that at the high point. He stepped into the diamond-shaped area.

Gillie touched the ward stones lightly with her mind. Very low-grade crystal, their energy a thin trill.

There were some spellforms on them, enough so that the supplicant kneeling before Rigo would feel a slight relief. But that would fade.

And he or she would seek out Rigo again. Pay a fee this time.

The two assistants raised their voices in soft prayer. Gillie didn't bother listening. The words were meaningless, unimportant. She focused on the people coming, one after another, into the diamond shape made by the stones.

Some had no real need to be there. She lay a light blessing on them, sought the next. The more needy.

One woman in an AG chair was weeks from her passing. As Kiasidira, it was rarely her duty to interfere with that. *We are all here for a time, for a purpose, and then we move on.* Every Tridivinian knew that, believed that. Gillie lived that. But the Kiasidira could make the passing a joyful one. To make the transit as pain-free as possible, if there was to be pain. To gentle the essence, guide it to its next level.

That she could do. And that she did.

Rigo, she sensed immediately, couldn't. But he would, if she wasn't careful, sense her. A few times he almost did. She had to pull back, release her fingers from around the small rune stones she always carried somewhere on her. Today, they were in her left pocket. She touched the Vedri, the Nevri as needed. Drew protection from the small chip of the Khal.

She worked quietly, cautiously, and slipped out of the observation area when there were still a few supplicants left. She didn't want to chance Rigo remembering their encounter in Mack's office.

The lifts had malfunctioned again. People trudged

down the stairs, grumbling. The russet-haired man had his son in his arms, waiting for the crowd to thin.

"He's feeling better, but I don't want to strain him." The man smiled when he saw her. "Praise the Lady!"

She closed her fingers around the boy's brittle wrist. Touched his essence. She needed time with this one. But couldn't do a healing here without drawing attention to herself. And questions.

"You in school, *chavo*?"

"Sometimes," the boy said.

"What's your favorite subject?"

A small light sparked in his eyes. "Music!"

"He loves the flute," his father said. "On his better days, he can use the one in class."

She knew that. *Simon, I'm going to need a flute.*

I'll have one finished when you return.

She smiled at the boy. "You know, I have this flute someone gave me years ago. I just can't seem to learn how to play it. If I can remember where I put it on my ship, would you like it?"

"Miselle." The father was suddenly embarrassed. "There's no need for you to do this."

She raised her gaze to his. "Of course there is. A perfectly good flute should never go to waste. I'm abysmal with it."

The father swallowed hard.

"I'll bring it by later," she said, before he could object further. "Where do you live, *chavo*?"

"D-Down10." The boy stuttered out his level, then, after a nod from his father, his apartment number in his uncontained excitement.

"An hour or so?"

The father's smile was tremulous. "That would be wonderful, miselle. Thank you."

She patted the boy's hand, had taken a few steps away when the boy's high-pitched voice called out after her. "Miselle, may I ask your name?"

"Gillie," she said with a wink. "Just Gillie."

"Many thanks and blessings, just Gillie!"

She chuckled, turned again, bumped into Fitch Tobias.

"Sorry, My Lady! Captain Gillie Davré," he added quickly, his hands on her shoulders to steady her.

"If you came for the healing service, it's ended."

"I was concerned for Izaak." He pointed behind her.

Gillie glanced back. The young boy waved shyly at her from over his father's shoulders as they made their way slowly down the stairs. "Blessing to you too, Mister Toby!"

Mister Toby? Fitch must know the child Izaak. Or Izaak's parents.

"Will he be all right?" Tobias asked when she turned back to him.

She nodded. "He and I are going to have a little talk about music later. He plays the flute. I have one, and a few life stones, to share with him. He'll be fine."

"My Lady, your blessings know no bounds." Tobias suddenly grabbed her hand, kissed her fingers.

She backed away. "Don't, please!" Her voice was soft but firm.

Footsteps stopped behind her. She saw Tobias's eyes widen in alarm and knew immediately who was there.

"You seem to have an interesting effect on my officers, Gillaine."

She spun around. "Mack—"

"Admiral, sir! I was just on my way up to maintenance."

"Then carry on, Lieutenant."

Tobias looked stricken. He managed a tense nod before stiffly hurrying away.

"Mack," Gillie said again, but something in his eyes stopped her words. Something in the way he stood, hands shoved into his pockets, shoulders on a downward slant.

"We've had some datagrid problems. I've been running all over the station the past few hours. Things just calmed down."

Petrina's word echoed in her mind. And Tobias had said he was on his way to maintenance. "Tough day?"

"I thought you might be here. I hoped you were keeping your promise to me to stay out of trouble." A note of dismay was apparent even under the calm, controlled tone of his voice. Too controlled. Gillie's chest tightened. "This just wasn't the kind of trouble I was expecting to find."

17

"A flute." Gillie tugged Mack's hands out of his pockets. She knew what he thought he'd seen when he came up the stairs, found Tobias kissing her hand. A chance meeting of lovers, like one he'd thought he'd stumbled on in his office. And again in her repair bay.

Most men might have simply walked away, or said something cutting, something hurtful, then walked away.

But Mack, Gillie was beginning to understand, wasn't like most men she'd met. His sense of honor ran deep, was strong. It encompassed her, even when he thought she'd hurt him.

He frowned but didn't pull away when she twined her fingers through his. "Flute?"

"You probably passed a man carrying his son as you came up. They were at the healing service. The boy, Izaak, has been ill. But he'll get better," she added, remembering that the child *would* recover. If she made his illness sound dire, there might be questions later. "He's been too sick to attend music classes. I told him I'd bring him a flute. Tobias seemed to find my offer an extraordinary gesture."

"You play the flute?"

She grinned. "Badly. All the more reason to give the flute to the boy. He called Tobias 'Mister Toby,' by the way. I guess they know each other."

Mack curled his fingers around hers. She could feel the tension ebb out of him. "One of Fitch's weight-lifting buddies works in a downlevel secondhand store. Fitch helps out but doesn't use his rank when he's there, because some spacers—especially those who feel Fleet's presence is taking up commercial-freighter space—aren't too fond of us."

"Izaak's father had a shipsuit, but no patches."

"They're probably one of the families he's been gathering odds and ends, supply overruns for." Mack arched one eyebrow. "He thinks I don't know."

"Lucky for you, or he'd be kissing your hand too."

Mack's face finally creased into a wry smile. He glanced in the direction Tobias had gone. Clearly, he was beginning to feel his initial judgment was in error. "Sometimes Fitch can be a little too intense."

"I think he's trying very hard to be nice to me, because of you," Gillie offered. That was partly true. Tobias had the highest regard for Mack. His regard for the Kiasidira was just a little higher. "Unless, of course, you really did send him here to spy on me, and you're just trying to cover that up." She arched an eyebrow.

Mack opened his mouth to respond, closed it again. A wry smile played across his mouth. "You have a definite skill at turning tables. Ever consider a career as a negotiator? Or a lawyer?"

"Me?" Her shock was only partly feigned. She had been trying to throw Mack's suspicions back at him. It had worked last time.

"Gillie, Gillie." He squeezed her hands, released them. "Pay no attention to me. I know you're not the type to play games."

No, she wasn't. And that's why all this was starting to feel like a weight around her neck.

"I'd better go catch up with Tobias before he thinks he has parrot duty. Dinner?"

"Your office, shift's end?" The more she kept others away from Simon, the more repairs he could effect.

"Barring any more crises." He brushed her forehead with a light kiss. "Door will be unlocked. Stay out of trouble."

She tried to. She really did. Or, rather, as Simon pointed out to her about four days after the healing service, it wasn't so much that she was staying out of trouble as she was making sure the trouble she caused was in no way traceable to her.

Like the inexplicable malfunctions of the newsvid holocams during the magefather's two subsequent attempts to inform the people of Cirrus of his latest intimate chat with Lady Kiasidira. She'd been with Mack, both times, when that happened. He'd slanted her a questioning glance, but only briefly. Suspicion warred with logic, and logic won. She couldn't be in two places at once.

Nor had she been anywhere near the bank of lifts in which the portly magefather was trapped for over two hours, drawing much attention and a few quiet comments that perhaps the Lady was making her opinions known through other channels. Gillie had gone downlevel to check on Izaak, brought back a short holovid of the child playing a tune he'd written for the parrots. She was clearly visible sitting cross-legged on the floor next to Izaak. He looked, Mack commented, considerably better. And the child did have a definite talent with the flute.

And Gillie obviously had been nowhere near the lifts.

She almost gave herself away with the incident with the incense, however. When Mack didn't mention it all through dinner, she thought he hadn't heard. Or perhaps didn't see the connection.

But he had some suspicions. Empathically she picked up on them every time he touched her, brushed against her. They were small, but they were there.

He waited until she was snuggled against him on his couch before broaching the subject. "I heard another unusual thing happened to the magefather during last night's service."

"Petrina mentioned something. I didn't pay much attention."

"Oh?"

She was getting used to Mack's "ohs." It was amazing how one word could carry such a deep tone of innocence, and an even deeper tone of disbelief. She wondered if he used it on his staff, or his crew when he was captain. No doubt they lived in fear of it.

"If I told you I thought it was fitting, you'd think I had something to do with it."

"Did you?" he asked.

"Think it was fitting?" She was deliberately toying with him, and they both knew it.

His eyes narrowed slightly, but a grin played over his mouth. "No. Did you have something to do with what happened at the temple?"

"Me? Saturate ten cases of incense so none would light?" She looked up at him, her eyes wide. "How would I ever do that?"

"How'd you know there were ten cases?"

Shit. She had to remember that specificity was often the death of obfuscation. Maybe add that to her guidelines while she was at it. "Petrina." She hesitated. "Or was it Lissy?"

Mack let out a rumbling sigh.

She chuckled. "I'm flattered. You must think I have magic powers."

"I know you have. Every time I'm with you, all my troubles, all my worries disappear." He cupped her face, kissed her. "That's magic."

No, he was magic. At least, his kisses were. Warmth started at the base of her throat as his lips brushed across hers, flared between her breasts as his tongue toyed with her own. She wrapped her arms around his neck, delighted in the solid feel of him against her.

For the rest of the night, all her worries disappeared.

A few resurfaced on schedule in the morning.

There were now many more people who questioned the magefather's self-proclaimed designation as consort for the Lady. But not enough that Fleet or CQPA overturned their decision to grant him the space for the shrine. Or the uncontrolled docking bay adjacent to it.

You may have to consider an alternate plan, Simon suggested as Gillie sipped coffee on her bridge. Mack had an early meeting scheduled via vidlink with Captain Adler and several important people at Fleet HQ. She'd risen when he had, even though he told her to stay, get another few hours of sleep. But she liked watching him dress in his formal uniform, his proper admiral's Fifth Fleet uniform now. Looked forward, she told him, to taking it off later.

That had almost made him late for his meeting. It did leave them no time for coffee. Simon had coffee, and advice, waiting when she'd returned to the *Serendipity.*

We've discussed several times that our current location is not happenstance, Simon continued. *Perhaps an admission of your identity won't be as traumatic to the Khalar as you believe.*

She'd considered that. But every time she did, a small voice inside her added: *but what about Mack?*

It would be a lot less traumatic than the loss of Cirrus One to the Fav'lhir.

"I know, but..." She didn't finish her sentence. That little voice kept finishing it for her. Though she agreed with Simon's point: an attack by the Fav'lhir, even if she were somehow able to lessen its impact, would shock and disrupt the Confederation.

Almost as much as the sight of Mack kneeling in the temple late yesterday had shocked her.

"I prefer to do my reverences privately," he'd explained when he'd found her waiting outside the temple doors. "Not during open services. On the *Vedri* I had a meditation corner in my quarters."

Simon evidently plucked the image from her mind,

sensed her disquiet. *He's Tridivinian. And Fleet. Did you think he'd do otherwise?*

She took another sip of coffee before answering. It was cold. "He wasn't lighting candles to Tarkir or Ixari. He was praying to someone who doesn't exist."

Would that someone who doesn't exist like another cup of hot coffee?

"Please."

Tobias was waiting outside her repair bay when, several hours later, she returned from lunch with Mack. "A moment of your time, My Lady Captain Gillie."

She waved him inside, but not before first checking to make sure the *Serendipity* still appeared to be nothing more than a damaged and disreputable starfreighter. She suspected that if Tobias found out what her ship was, he'd steal the crystal section and try to return it to her.

She motioned to a set of servostairs near the doorway. "Sit."

"I'd feel more comfortable standing, My Lady."

So she sat. "Izaak's okay?"

"Wonderful, but I wouldn't expect otherwise."

"Then . . . ?" she prompted.

"I'm very concerned over the magefather's shrine. Renovations are almost completed, as you know. But there's one thing you may not know, and I don't mean to impugn your abilities in any way. But the shrine, and its docking bay, will open a few days before our official inspection. And the subsequent dedication ceremonies. For security reasons, identities of attendees—"

"Including Prime Hostess Honora Syrella and her daughter, Roannan Charity," she said quietly.

"You know. Of course you would. My apologies."

"I take it you have reasons to believe they might be in jeopardy?"

"Aside from the fact that we're on the rim of civilized space, have already suffered one attack by a ship believed to be Fav'lhir, and had an inexplicable security-grid failure?" Tobias rocked back slightly on his heels, continued his recitation. "And our magefather is a blatant liar, station security will be flawed by the existence of an unsecured, unmonitored docking bay, and the Fav would have much to gain if they could take control of the Rim Gate—you know about that project as well, I assume?"

"I do. And that the head of that project, Doctor Mikail Pennarton, is also on your guest list."

"He is. And, no, aside from those things, I have no reasons."

"I'll do everything in my power to keep your people safe," she told him softly. "I always have."

"I have no doubt of that, My Lady. I'm just wondering what else Admiral Mack and I can do to help you."

"Mack?" She straightened. "You've talked to him about me?"

"Only obliquely. I did mention that just because the magefather was a fraud didn't mean all our meditations were equally invalid."

Now she understood what Mack had been doing in the temple.

"He still has no knowledge of who you are, I take it?"

"No."

Tobias nodded. "By Your Will, of course."

No. Not by her will, she realized, listening to Tobias's sincere concern. By her selfishness. Her relationship with Mack was more important to her than her relationship, and the safety, of the Khalar. Again, she had to face the fact that neither she nor Simon could stop an incoming fleet.

"Your vigilance is the greatest help right now," she told him. "If and when I have need of something more concrete, I'll advise you."

"I await your command." He bowed slightly, managed to depart without grabbing her, stumbling into her, or kissing her hand. And without Mack catching him at it.

She hoped it was a good sign. She needed a sign right now, some definite guidance. The Shrine of Communion was only days from completion. The docking bay already existed. Rendering it "unsecure" or "uncontrolled" was simply a matter of assigning an open passage code to all vessels requesting one at Cirrus's outer beacon. And gaining nothing, not even ID, in return.

She toyed with the small rune stones in her pocket, careful not to drop her mental shields. Rigo would be aware of her then. Come looking for her.

She didn't want him to do that yet. But she knew now it was something that would have to happen.

Time. She'd told Mack they had time when he'd

been afraid she'd leave Cirrus after two weeks. So she'd stayed. But time was running out, anyway.

Mack seemed to sense that something troubled her. He was his usual self when she showed up at his office shortly before shift's end. The conference with HQ had gone well. They were finally taking some of his concerns seriously. An additional supply ship would dock tomorrow. And no, thank Ixari, he didn't have to be there to supervise that one. This was CQPA. Hebbs would handle it.

Then he stopped in his informal report, studied her as she perched on the edge of his desk. "You're tired. And here I am rambling on."

She let out a long sigh. "I'm fine."

He drew her into his arms. "You're working too hard."

She absorbed his warmth, let it melt into her. Gods, how she would miss this. Miss him, if he ever found out who she was. It would leave a gaping hole in her life, in her heart, larger than the one the Fav'lhir had left in her ship's side. "I'm glad Fleet's finally paying you some mind." She was. Every little bit helped.

"I'm going to pay you some mind now. Where do you want to eat tonight?"

"How about the club?" It was quiet. Because it was where he'd asked her to marry him, it was her favorite. Always would be.

"Good. I'm in the mood for a steak. Then I've got some things to show you when we get back to my place." He locked up his deskcomp, ushered her out the door.

"What things?" she asked as the lift chugged up-level.

"Some boxes I had in storage. They came in on the supply ship the other day, but this is the first chance I've had to get around to them. I'll only show them to you if you promise not to laugh."

"Holovids from your academy days?"

"Even before that."

Sweet heavens. Childhood holos of Mack, perhaps. She glanced up at him, tried to picture him as an angelic child. Failed. Started to chuckle.

"Get it out of your system now," he warned, taking her hand as the lift came to a stop. "No laughing once I show them to you."

He would tell her nothing more all through dinner, tortured her by making her wait, insisting they have coffee at the club. When they returned to his apartment, he pretended he'd forgotten where the boxes were.

"I'll find them tomorrow," he said.

She grabbed a handful of his uniform jacket. "Tonight, Admiral. Now."

He pulled them out of a storage cabinet in his small kitchen, unstrapped them. Put them on the low table in front of the sofa.

"That's Trevan, Alec, and me." He handed her a holo of three boys, ranging in age from ten to fifteen. Mack and his brothers. Tallest and eldest, he was in the middle. Gangly, young Mack glared at the camera, sporting a noticeable black eye.

"What happened?"

"Brotherly love. Trevan's a year younger than me. He's better at squareball. I was a better skater, better at ice shot. We were playing squareball that day. On opposite teams."

She smiled broadly. "And this?" Three younger boys, amid lots of foliage. Mack still the most serious of the group.

"Years before that. We had a tree fort. My first command."

There were more than just old holos. Some team medals, a piece of fossilized rock, a small jar of coins. Old music vids.

"Can you believe I used to listen to that stuff?" He handed the thin slats to her. Gillie looked at the unfamiliar names and song titles and shook her head.

"Me either." He took them back, tossed them into the box.

"Where did you suddenly find all this?" It seemed like something he might have kept on board the *Vedritor.* Yet he'd said it had come in on the supply ship.

"Alec had it. I told you he's an archaeologist with the Novidian Museum, didn't I?"

He had. And that Trevan was with Fleet medical, on a station near the Ladrin colonies. "No offense, but this stuff's hardly museum quality."

Mack smiled. "These are things my parents had. After the shuttle accident, Alec ended up with them because, well, he's usually dirtside. Easier for the lawyers to track down."

His parents' death five years before had brought the three brothers closer together. Mack had told her how he looked forward to her meeting Trev, and Alec and his wife.

"What else do you have in there you don't want me to see?"

He rummaged, came up with a narrow metal case,

the kind that usually contained a set of lightpens. An expression of delight crossed his face. "Praise the Lady, I knew I hadn't lost this. My grandfather gave it to me. Trev always said it wasn't real. That's probably because I got it, and he didn't."

"Brotherly love?"

Mack jiggled the lid carefully. "Brotherly jealousy." He flipped the lid back, turned the case toward her. "What do you think?"

She didn't have to think. The crystal's presence sang through her the moment the lid cracked open. She sucked in a short breath and slid abruptly backward on the couch. The purple glow spread from the slender piece of true crystal like wine spilling from a goblet. It flared outward, found her, enveloped her in a light cloak of lavender. Then settled, its spell-form merging with her essence, and faded to a muted glow.

Mack stared at her, his knuckles whitening as his fingers tightened around the case. She could feel confusion, apprehension, and fear churn through him.

Her own mind reeled. Her heart felt as if it had stopped beating and would never start again.

"Gillaine?" His voice rasped.

She closed her eyes briefly as if by doing so she could erase the lavender mist between them. Sought for a way to explain it all to him, to make it right. Something Mack would know how to do. Her own skills in that regard had suddenly dissipated.

But she knew she had to start. And decided to start with the least amount of information. Never volunteer more than is absolutely necessary. Lady Kiasidira's Guideline Number Twenty-two.

Her whole life hinged not only on her next words but his response to them. She took a deep breath, hoped she had the right words. Hoped her voice would carry over the pounding of her heart.

"I'm Raheiran."

18

"Raheiran." Mack echoed the word, his face devoid of emotion.

"Yes."

"True Raheiran."

She glanced down at her hands knotted in her lap, at the mist lightly swirling over her skin. He could see that as well as she could. It wasn't doubt that made Mack question, but shock. She knew that. "Yes."

He started to speak, stopped, his dark gaze unreadable. His flat demeanor made her insides feel tight. She told herself he was a professional, schooled to minimize his reactions. Tried to reassure herself that at least he hadn't dropped to his knees in abject reverence, as Tobias had. Mack would be lost to her then. His Lady Goddess was someone distant, unapproachable, who belonged in a shrine. A coldness washed over her as if she were already on a pedestal somewhere, the air around her dark and chilled. She prayed he'd believe that she was only a rim-trader captain, albeit a Raheiran one.

She let out a short, tense breath. "I wanted to tell you. But with everything going on, I was afraid to."

His gaze flicked to the slender crystal. A bright lavender energy pulsed softly through it. Gillie knew Mack had seen the crystal glow when Rigo touched it, knew its brightness and color had been nothing like what he saw now.

"There hasn't..." He stopped, swallowed hard. "There hasn't been a true Raheiran here in over three hundred years."

Three hundred forty-two and—

Shut up, Simon. Not now! It felt as if Mack had taken a few steps back from her, though neither of them had moved. There had to be a way to close that distance. She damned herself for not having answers concocted before this. She should have known her lies would undo her eventually. She should have known Mack would react this way.

She waved one hand lightly, surprised to see it wasn't shaking from the hard pounding of her heart. "Actually, we come through off and on." That, too, was a lie, but she had to prevent him from labeling her appearance as something unique. "We try to be discreet about it when we do. We're not all goddesses. Sorceresses," she corrected quickly.

"You're saying your people have been here all along?"

"We've maintained trade relationships with a lot of systems for years. Centuries." That was true, but in a more limited sense than she needed Mack to believe.

"Yet, you didn't want the Confederation to know

you were here." Mack spoke slowly. She could almost see his trained, logical mind trying to pull her information together. But whether it was to understand her or to catch her in her lies, she didn't know.

"Our technology is far advanced from yours. We've had experiences with other alliances that wanted to exploit that, artificially accelerate their growth. That's not our purpose." That was why Kiasidiras and Ki'sidrons were carefully, and only under the strictest conditions, placed as advisers.

"It's not just your technology that's advanced."

"Granted, we have some natural abilities the Khalar don't." She spread her hands in a helpless gesture. "But then, Izaak can play the flute. I can't. That doesn't make him better, or worse, than me. Or more powerful. He just has a different talent."

"Raheiran talents are *very* different."

"To you. I grew up with them." With empathic resonances and the ability to diagnose and heal by touch. And telepathy, telekinesis, matter manipulation. The last three were less common, their occurrence signaling a stronger mage essence, naming one a sorcerer. Or, in Gillie's case, burdening her with the title and responsibilities of a Kiasidira.

He glanced down at the case, at the purple glow hovering between them. Suddenly, she thought she knew part of the problem. She could almost hear him labeling himself as Tobias had: an impure. The hurt was plain in his eyes when he looked back up. "I understand that your people need to keep a low profile here. But not why you couldn't tell me, personally. Did you think I couldn't be trusted, that I'd exploit you?"

Her heart clenched at his words, almost as tightly

as his fingers clasped the case. Yet he didn't resist when she took it from him. She closed the lid, slid the case onto the tabletop. The lavender mist wavered, faded. "I didn't tell you because I didn't want you looking at me the way you are now."

He straightened slowly, as if the import behind her words forced him back. "How—?"

"A curiosity. An oddity to be examined, or worse, to be put on a pedestal. On display." She crossed her arms around her waist, hugged them to herself. Her heart pounded. All the warmth she'd sensed from him over the past two weeks was gone.

She'd lost him. Not because he disliked her, hated her for lying, or even feared her. But because she was the stuff his people's religion was made of. That damned her and glorified her at the same time.

"When Tobias dropped the crystal in your office that day," she continued softly, "he ended up on his knees in front of me. Bowing and babbling prayers and stuff. It was scary."

His dark eyes widened briefly. "Is *that* what that's been all about?"

"I think he wants me sitting in a shrine somewhere."

"You think that's what I want?"

"I don't know." Her voice wavered. She honestly didn't know what he wanted now, with this tense coldness between them. She kept seeing the image of Rynan Makarian, kneeling in reverence before her holo in the temple.

"I thought Raheirans could tell what other people are feeling or thinking."

"I can tell you're upset. But I don't go—I can't go,"

she corrected herself quickly, remembering she was supposed to be an ordinary Raheiran, "probing into people's minds. I'm not mageline," she lied. "Empathic readings aren't the same as telepathy."

"You sense emotions, but not actual thoughts."

She nodded, agreeing to the lie.

"But if you can sense emotions," he continued, "you know I care about you."

Care. Not love. Oh, gods. She didn't know if she'd lost ground or was gaining it. Some of the warmth had seeped back into him, but he was still far from the man she knew, and loved, as Mack. This was Admiral Rynan Makarian, on yellow alert, shields up, full sensor probes gathering data. And waiting.

She forced a tremulous smile. "Even though I'm Raheiran?"

"Does it matter to you that I'm not? That I'm," he hesitated, "an impure?"

She hated that word. "That's an absurdity! There are no pures or impures. We don't think that way."

His fingers splayed as if he considered reaching toward her. He closed them into a fist. She could feel his confusion warring against desire. That she was Raheiran bothered him deeply. But she wasn't sure now if it was because of what she was or because she'd lied.

"I didn't tell you, or Doc Janek, when I first got here because I didn't intend to stay. Especially after I saw the temple, all the rune-stone sellers—"

"You arrived just after the celebration of the Day of Sacred Sacrifice."

No. She arrived exactly the day she'd left, three hundred forty some-odd years notwithstanding. The day she and the Fav'lhir had clashed in the Rift. A day that had created, for the Khalar, her "Sacred Sacrifice," honoring a death that had never occurred. Eliciting a mourning for someone still alive. She wouldn't blame the Khalar if they became righteously pissed if the truth were to come out.

She couldn't blame Mack for his hesitancy, his distrust. He'd been raised on legends of the perfect, the revered Raheira. It must be sobering to meet one who could so easily manipulate and bend the truth.

But then, no one had ever made him into a deity.

"All I know is it seemed as if anything remotely Raheiran had been turned into a religion. It—" Angered her. Infuriated her. It wasn't Mack's fault, but it was his deeply held belief. She had to tread carefully. "It disconcerted me. I didn't want to add to all the excitement."

Mack nodded slowly. Emotions shifted around in him, settled. The settling encouraged her. He was sorting, analyzing. He was Mack. "The news media might have tried to make something of it, yes."

"Then I met you." She chanced a second tremulous smile. "I needed to be sure you were interested in Gillie. And not because crystal glows when I'm near it."

He shook his head. "I would never—I don't use people for who they are, what they are. I thought you knew that about me. That's why I've had such a problem with Hebbs. I told you about that."

He had, a few nights before, dispelling what little jealousy she'd had over the sultry stationmaster whose interest in Mack had been based solely on his rank and position. "I didn't think you'd use me," she responded softly. "But I wanted you to know just Gillie first."

"You should have told me before now." It was a request. His voice was equally as soft, and held no tone of accusation.

"I'm sorry, Mack. I really am. If you're angry, I accept that."

"You know I'm not."

She did. Surprisingly, no anger emanated from him. An unsettledness, yes. But even that was dissipated by a growing warmth. "You are disappointed, though."

He sighed. "I was trained to know that when captured by the enemy, you tell as little as possible. I guess I never thought of myself as the enemy."

His analogy pained her, literally, her empathic senses broadcasting back to her his expectation of rejection. "I don't—you're not! But I was afraid I'd lose you. I thought—" Her control shattered. Her voice broke. "Damn it!" she rasped, wiping the heel of her hand across her damp eyes.

"Gillaine. Don't cry." His voice was as raspy as her own.

"I'm not. I'm fine. I—" The rest of her words were lost in the fabric of his shirt as he crushed her against his chest. Strong hands stroked her back. She clung to him, took long, deep breaths. Felt only love, only warmth. Only desire.

"I'm sorry," she whispered against his neck.

"Hush. It's all right." He nuzzled her face with soft kisses. The pain in her heart abated with each touch of his lips.

She kissed him back, gently, softly, tried to put into

her touch all the tenderness she felt. All she wanted to give. Not confusion. Not lies.

He framed her face with his hands. She wondered if he saw "just Gillie," or someone else. She still sensed something uncertain in him. "Sure you're not angry?"

"Surprised, really. But at least, finally, certain things make sense."

She closed her eyes, rested her cheek on his shoulder. "As in incense?" She couldn't help herself. Gods, she was getting like Simon.

A low groan rumbled in his chest. "I don't suppose you want to explain that comment?"

"Nope."

He tucked his fingers under her chin, raised her face. And it was Mack she saw looking at her again. The Mack she knew. His dark gaze was full of promises, of understanding. Then he frowned slightly. "You've been against Magefather Rigo from the start. But he's—"

"He's not." This much she could tell him now. If she could convince Mack of the threat Rigo represented, maybe the Khalar could take steps to stop him. "He's not Raheiran, Mack. He's Fav'lhir. Possibly Melandan."

She felt the information jolt him.

"That's what brought you to Cirrus?"

"I'm here by accident." Or Tarkir's design. Which often looked like accidents to the naïve.

"But about Rigo, you're sure?"

"I wasn't until I bumped into him in your office."

He leaned back against the couch. Wiped one hand down his face. "Gillie, this is serious."

"I'm keeping an eye on what he's doing. As best I can."

"That's why you were in the temple. At the healing service."

"That's also why we have to stop that docking bay from going uncontrolled. I can't prove anything right now other than he has Melandan in his essence. It doesn't automatically mean he's allied with the Fav, but it does mean I don't trust him until he can prove to me he isn't." The words tumbled out of her. She was surprised how good it felt to tell him this, to share some of the responsibility with Mack.

And she hadn't lost him. By Ixari's eyes, he knew she was Raheiran but he was, for the most part, just being Mack. Although more Admiral Makarian right now. But that was okay. The information he had before him demanded that.

"It's not your job to monitor Rigo."

That definitely was Admiral Makarian speaking, in a voice that held all the authority of command. It was a side of him she hadn't seen very often in their private time. Aggressive, definitive, and—she felt too—a bit overprotective. Very much the *pantrelon* she'd likened him to when they'd first met. She squeezed his arm. "Who better than me? Who has more right than me?"

He stared at her. Not, as she felt before, as an oddity. But because what she said sank in.

He pulled her back into his arms, held her tightly for a moment. "What you know about Rigo is too important. I have to—"

"Confront him? With what proof? Me?" She shook her head. "I'm your best secret weapon right now."

His hands massaged circles against her back—but if he was reassuring her of his feelings, or reassuring himself she really existed, she didn't know. Nor would she probe to find out. She hadn't lied to him totally about that. Except in the most dire of circumstances, an unauthorized intrusion into another's private thoughts was—

Unthinkable, Simon put in with his usual timing.

She raised a mental eyebrow at his word choice.

Couldn't resist, he told her. Then: *so your worst fear has come to pass and the universe has not dissolved to dust around you.*

Not my worst. Second to the worst, perhaps. Mack still didn't know she was the Kiasidira. Gods, she hoped he liked older women. About three hundred forty-two years older.

You intend to tell him?

Not unless I absolutely have to. Simon, I like being just me. Gillie. Now that Mack knows I'm Raheiran, we can do more about Rigo. I might not have to tell Mack who I am.

How are you going to explain me if you don't?

Well, yes. There was that part of it. Simon. A basic starfield-variety Raheiran wouldn't be linked to a sentient nanoessence energy field.

Why should I have to explain anything? Mack would never ask me to sell my ship. As long as the Serendipity's here, you're safe.

Does that mean I'm still invited to the wedding?

Simon . . .

Yes, My Lady. A sock. I'm searching for a sock right now.

Mack woke, as he always did, ten minutes before his cabin lights started the morning sequence. Gillie was curled against him, her breath soft on his shoulder.

Her hair, pale as moonlight, was ruffled. He thought about smoothing it, just because he loved to touch her. But he didn't want to wake her. Not yet. Not until he had his fill of gazing at her, seeing her now not only as a woman, not only as his lover, but as a Raheiran. A people empowered by the gods. He'd been taught that since he was a child.

He remembered what she'd said, remembered her eyes glistening with tears, and felt slightly guilty. She wanted to be, as he often heard her call herself, just Gillie. She was, to him. She truly was. Everything about her, from the way she wrinkled her nose, to her intriguing laugh, to the unending compassion he sensed in her, was just Gillie. Very Gillie.

Yet when the crystal's purple glow had embraced her, he'd known that just Gillie had taken on another quality. One that had, he admitted reluctantly, scared him. Awed him more than he was comfortable with, even if she wasn't mageline. Why now, after more than three hundred years? Had she brought a message? She'd denied she was here because of Rigo. Could there be something important about to happen?

Except it hadn't been three hundred years. *We come through off and on,* she'd said. But discreetly. Not openly. Because others had tried to exploit the Raheira. And because of the rune-stone sellers, the shrines. He'd clearly heard the disgust in her voice.

But wasn't that Lady Kiasidira's wish? Generations of magefathers and magemothers had deemed it so. He had questions, lots of questions. The heat of her body next to his convinced him his questions could wait. He traced the line of her shoulder.

Her eyes fluttered open. "Hi."

"Hi, yourself." He brushed his mouth across hers. She wrapped her arms around his neck, and when the lights slowly came on a few minutes later he barely noticed. Didn't notice much of anything save for Gillie for another twenty minutes after that.

"You want to shower first?" He ran his hand down her arm, over the curve of her hip. Her skin, like his, was damp with the heat of their lovemaking.

She smiled. "If you had a bigger shower, you could join me."

Regrettably true. A larger apartment—and shower—might be on the agenda soon. "I'll make coffee instead."

When he carried her cup in she was wrapped in his robe, toweling her hair. She'd brought a few items of her own clothing to his place last week, but not a robe. He told her to use his. He liked the way it kept her scent, keeping her with him even when she wasn't there.

He followed her movements, seeing Gillie and yet seeing someone else for the first time. No, the second. He'd seen Gillie—*Gillaine*, he corrected himself, as her formal name sounded more Raheiran. He'd seen the real Gillaine last night, sitting on his couch, an intense but ethereal purple mist wrapping around her.

Raheiran. Kinspeople of the gods. That phrase lingered in his mind, no matter how hard he tried to ignore it.

He thought of those questions he wanted to ask. Some he'd broached last night, but they'd talked far more of Magefather Rigo and what could be done. That was the crucial issue right now. Their discussion had kept them awake until well after midnight. Made him realize that as much as he didn't want Gillie involved, she had to be. She was, as she'd said, his best secret weapon.

She tapped his arm with her hairbrush. "Are my ears on upside down?"

"Hmm?"

"You're staring."

He grinned self-consciously. "Are all Raheirans blond?"

She wrinkled her nose in response. "Don't be daft. Are all Khalarans dark-haired?"

"Lots."

"Not all."

"Lady Kiasidira was. Blond," he added. He caught the slight but immediate tension around her eyes. The same thing had happened last night. When the topic was Gillie's life, or when he mentioned Lady Kiasidira, there was a tension. Was there something else she didn't want him to know?

Maybe not something, but someone? He thought of Simon. An older man, like an uncle, from all she'd told him. There could be another man, a lover. Ex-husband. He didn't want to dwell on that.

Her reaction to Lady Kiasidira was more understandable. She'd briefly mentioned last night that the Lady wasn't part of the Tridivinian belief. The Raheirans didn't view her as the Khalar did.

She handed him a fresh towel. "You're going to be late, and no, we're not all blondes. And," she added as he stripped out of his underwear, "Kiasidira is a title, not a name." She smacked his bare behind playfully. "Not that it's going to change anything after three hundred forty-two years."

"What do you mean, a title?" He tabbed on the sonic shower, not the water spray, and leaned out of the bathroom to catch her answer.

"It'd be like calling you Admiral Admiral."

He ducked back in, thought about what she'd said as he quickly showered. Realized that while he always said, "Lady Kiasidira," Gillie said, "*the* Kiasidira." Like *the* captain. Or *the* admiral.

She was already dressed when he came out. She handed him a hot cup of coffee. He pulled on his pants, took a big mouthful of coffee, grabbed a black shirt. "So what was her name?"

"Who?"

"Lady—the Kiasidira."

A slight shrug accompanied her answer. "Damned if I know."

That surprised him. Lady Kiasidira—old habits die hard, he realized with a grimace—had been sent by the Raheirans. Granted, that was almost three hundred fifty years ago. But that wasn't all that much time. "Wouldn't your people have records?"

"Of course. But it's not the kind of data I've needed as a freighter operator."

True. Something about her demeanor, about the way she handled herself, made him forget she was a freighter captain, not military, where data accumulation surpassed being an art and evolved into an obsession. "Could you find out?"

Another shrug. "Probably. But, Mack, look at what you're asking. You really want me to challenge your people's belief system after all these years? I'm telling you because . . . well, because I'm telling you. This isn't for public consumption."

"Part of her name was on the section of the ship." He remembered Tobias trying to spell it out. He wondered if his second in command knew the distinction between name and title. After all, he'd been raised in a household closely tied with a Kiasidiran temple. Tobias had once told him he'd even viewed the Sacred Holovid of the Lady, taken only a few days before the Sacred Sacrifice.

He was also the only other person who knew Gillaine was Raheiran. "Did you tell him?"

"Tell who what? Mack, when you don't get enough coffee you can be totally incoherent. Drink up, please."

He sipped, then spoke. "Did you tell Tobias that Kiasidira's a title?"

Gillie closed her eyes for a moment. "I might have, in passing. Why?"

"Because he knows you're Raheiran." As he spoke he realized he was slightly jealous of his brawny second in command, who'd known first.

Gillie padded over—she'd not put on her boots yet—and kissed him lightly. Jealousy. Had she'd sensed his jealousy, responded?

"He found out accidentally," she said, pinning him with a stern look.

She definitely sensed his jealousy.

"So did I."

"I would've eventually told you. Not him, if I'd had a choice."

He smiled down at her. "When?"

"Twenty-fifth wedding anniversary?"

He laughed. The fact that she intended to share not

the information but that anniversary with him dispersed what little jealousy was left.

Gillie's hand hovered over the comm link in Mack's quarters moments after the door closed behind him, then stopped. She had to talk to Fitch Tobias, update him, but not this way, not here. Not where it might leave a record of the call, or worse, a copy of the conversation for Mack to listen to.

She'd worked so very hard to gain Mack's acceptance of her Raheiran heritage last night. When it had finally come, her relief, her joy, had been almost inexpressible. Simon had been right: one of her worst fears had been faced and the universe had not evicted her. More importantly, neither had Mack. He knew she was Raheiran. He loved her. Life was damned near perfect. Except for one thing.

She palm-locked his door on the way out. *Simon, where's Tobias?*

There was a moment of silence while Simon searched. *In operations, lower level.*

Alone? Could she reach him there on a public link? She still didn't like the idea. Mack had intimated station security was not uncompromisable, partly due to technical lapses and partly due to his unconfirmed belief about Hebbs's snooping.

I take it you don't mean is ops fully staffed. No, he's working with Pryor.

He needs to know that Mack knows I'm Raheiran. He needs to know Mack doesn't know I'm the Kiasidira. She tapped her foot impatiently as she waited for an available lift. *Suggestions?*

The admiral is headed for ops. I suggest we discount an in-person chat there.

Not in ops, that was for sure. The lift arrived. Gillie hesitated, waved in a group of Fleet personnel ahead of her. A flash of blue and green hurtled up the atrium. Over the din of voices she heard the jaunty notes of a flute. Izaak had taken to serenading the parrots. *Can you ruffle a few feathers, Simon?*

My Lady?

The parrots. Can you do something to excite them, agitate them? Gently, of course. They seem to be Izaak's and Tobias's pet project.

Excellent unintentional pun. And idea. Give me a few moments. I'll see what I can do.

Gillie headed for the stairs and one level up to Ops Lower. Mack had at least a five-minute lead. He should be through ops and on his way to his office by the time she got there.

Then she could grab Tobias in the corridor. She only needed a minute or two to put a few words of wisdom, and warning, in his ear. To prevent what might be a potential disaster from coming out of his mouth.

As usual, the lifts were crowded when Mack arrived. It was ten minutes to main shift. Upper5 housed several Fleet offices and a large section of Fleet officers' residences. Mack's quarters on U5 were only one level down from ops. He strode past the lines of black-uniformed personnel, nodded at those awake enough to recognize him, and headed for the stairs.

Others, both in Fleet black and CQPA orange, had the same idea.

He exited at Upper6 and was greeted by the screeching of parrots. Ops Lower was a jumble of movement. The aroma of fresh coffee mixed with the stale odor of coffee gone cold. Mack threaded his way toward Pryor, who was bent over a station, and tapped him lightly on the shoulder. "Where's Tobias?"

"You just missed him, sir. Something's got the parrots going again."

Mack shook his head. "This is more important. Executive conference, half hour, officers' club." He wished the *Vedri* was still on station, but he needed her out on patrol. Perimeter Sensor Logs had picked up some odd activities again. He'd fill Adler in later, on a private link. "I'll grab Tobias, you comm the rest of our team. We have to talk about this docking bay. The Shrine of Communion opens for business tomorrow."

He trotted back to the corridor, spotted Tobias's brawny form walking doggedly ahead of him, head angled toward the open atrium. Mack could see the glint of a bioscanner in Tobias's right hand, also angled toward the open atrium.

And a pylon, dead ahead, maybe a foot in front of the single-minded lieutenant.

"Tobias!" He raised his voice to carry over the din, then, feeling like an idiot, flicked up his mouth mike. "Makarian to Tobias, priority. Turn around. Now."

The younger officer jerked to a stop. He turned quickly. "Admiral?"

Mack was three steps behind him. He grabbed Tobias by one shoulder, guided him around. "You should watch where you're going."

Tobias lay his left hand against the curved metal pylon. "Thank you, sir. That would have been embarrassing."

"Not painful?" Mack grinned. Of course, given Tobias's physique, it might have been more painful for the pylon.

"Only momentarily. The parrots—"

"Forget about them for now. I've got Pryor calling

a team meeting. We have new information to consider about the shrine. But I need to speak to you, alone, first."

"About the shrine?"

"That, and about a young woman named Gillaine Davré."

Gillie leaned her back against the pylon and didn't dare breathe. Her heart stuttered in her chest. She'd missed Tobias by seconds. Inches. If Mack hadn't called out she would've already been stepping around the wide metal support beam, reaching for the lieutenant. Mack's voice, and Simon's warning, had sounded in her ears and mind at the same time.

She almost did step out when she heard her name mentioned. But something—fear? insecurity?—held her back, made her legs and her mind freeze. She had no rational explanation for being just outside ops. She had to trust that Tobias would remember and adhere to her admonition to him: *tell no one I'm the Kiasidira until I directly give you permission to do so.*

That included his CO, Mack. She prayed—no, beseeched—Ixari, Tarkir, and Merkara to bestow on Fitch Tobias the wisdom to keep his damned devout mouth shut.

Mind link. She could try for a full telepathic link with Tobias, but that not only violated every principle she'd ever been taught but was emotionally frightening for the unexpected recipient. A full link was more than just peeking in to glean information, as she had with Petrina. There was no way she could predict what would happen if she tried for full contact with an untrained, unprepared mind. She was trying to prevent damage, not cause it.

Mack's and Tobias's voices faded away. She closed her eyes briefly, then shoved herself away from the pylon before someone questioned her odd position.

Sorry, My Lady.

Maybe it'll be all right. This was the price, she knew, for weaving lies. Probably excellent subject matter for a few meditations. Even a guideline or two. But right now, she had other things to think about.

Like the hidden, locked box in Rigo's sacristy. The one with the soft, plaintive song. She had to take another look around that temple, especially now that she had Mack's implicit approval to continue her work. That approval meant more to her than she'd thought it would.

Where's Rigo this morning? she asked as she waited in line for a lift. Her breathing had slowed to normal. Better to think about the annoying magefather than what Tobias might be telling Mack right now, undoing everything she'd tried so hard to keep together last night.

Station systems show he's not left his quarters since 2315 last night. Shall I peek?

Please. Simon's link with Cirrus's computers provided him with information not only from ops, but from security. And security always monitored all public areas and offices, in case of an emergency. But they weren't foolproof.

Simon's link with Cirrus's computers also provided him with the ability to eavesdrop if a computer monitor was activated in a certain location and was not privacy-locked. She hoped Rigo was up cooking breakfast with the news on, or reading his mail.

He was. *At least a half dozen doughnuts and coffee*, Simon informed her. *But then, his training's in theology, not nutrition.*

Shame that Mack wasn't talking with Tobias in his office. Simon might have been able to listen in there as well. Then at least she'd be prepared with answers. Or excuses and apologies.

She pushed that problem out of her mind, concentrated on tripping the lock on the temple's back door.

The crystallike moon symbol had been repaired, she noticed as she crouched in the semidarkness. The light that filtered in through the corridor window only added to the irregularity of the shadows she needed for cover. She heard nothing other than her own breath.

A sneeze threatened as she laid her hand against the sacristy's lock. Damned incense. It must have dried out after the dousing she'd given it.

The door opened. She slipped inside, crouched down again until the door closed. The hidden crystal's voice was thin but unrelenting. Quickly, and as quietly as possible, she moved the boxes of supplies aside.

She pulled the case from the lower shelf onto a space she'd cleared on the floor. Ran her hands over it, felt the crystal inside strongly now. Unlike the cases Tobias and Mack had had, this one was plexicast, not metal. It couldn't damper its contents the way the others had. She found that odd; Raheiran crystal was almost always stored in metal to prevent its being a disruptive force.

Of course, since there hadn't been any true

Raheirans around in over three hundred years, perhaps that precaution had ceased to be necessary.

She found the lock, felt for its patterns. Stopped cold as something answered from within.

But not out of fear. Out of recognition.

My Lady? Simon's concern came through clearly. *Visitor?*

All is still clear. But something's disturbed you.

This is...was mine. She touched the lock more confidently now, her mind racing with questions.

Simon tried valiantly to keep pace. *I have no idea. What? What? Of course, I'm listening! But you're rambling, Gillaine Kiasidira. What sword? There are hundreds of ceremonial—*

Gillie lifted the sword from its silk-lined case, hefted it in her hand.

Oh. Simon understood. *That sword.*

The small room pulsed with a deep purple mist that swirled, not only from the crystalline blade but from the jewels and rune stones covering the hilt. Then the spellforms, recognizing her essence, muted, returned to the sword.

It wasn't really, Gillie knew, a sword. It was too short. But it was too long to be called a dagger.

It was also hers; had been hers since she was small.

I left it in my quarters at the port, a couple weeks— a few hundred years ago, she corrected. *But what in hell Rigo's doing with it...* She didn't finish the thought. Couldn't. She had no idea what Rigo was doing with it. Or if he even knew what he had.

I think we have to assume he does, My Lady. Therefore, stealing it is not advisable.

I'm not stealing it. She secured it under her jacket.

You can't steal your own things. But I can't leave it here. It's a desecration.

He may notice it's missing. Perhaps he uses it in a special service?

Then we'll just have to get him another one. You have its pattern on file. Duplicate it for me—not out of true crystal, of course.

That will take me at least two hours.

She knew that. *There aren't any services scheduled today. I checked.* She'd learned her lesson from last time.

You'll have to break in to the temple again to replace the false one. I'm not fond of that idea.

Last time, I promise.

She repacked the box, stacked the incense, almost missed Simon's soft grumbling. *I've heard that one before.*

You'll hear it again. She slipped out of the small room, locked it behind her. Then slipped as quietly, and easily, out of the back door of the temple.

She was almost to Down11 when she heard the shouting. Then a woman's mournful wail. She took the stairs two at a time, following the noise.

Simon! Can you find out?

Lift malfunction of some kind, he replied after a long moment. More people were running with her. The shouting grew louder.

Her heart plummeted when she saw the open lift doors. And a familiar flute on the decking nearby.

Izaak.

Simon, the child!

Two large men were restraining a thin dark-haired

woman who stood at the edge of the open lift shaft. "Izaak! Jared!"

"Mama!" came a thin reply.

Gillie grabbed the arm of a woman in a blue freighter uniform. "What happened?"

"Door opened. Lift wasn't there. Kid bolted forward, not looking. The man grabbed for him, fell." The woman's voice was strained. "It's not the first time. Damn it! How many have to die?"

"Did anyone call security? Medics?"

"Sure." The woman's mouth thinned to a tight line. "Don't see them rushing here, do you? And them's the only ones who got the access codes to get in the shaft from below."

Gillie used Simon's link to grab a datapath to sick bay. Doc Janek wasn't on duty. The CQPA doctor there was in surgery with a critical case. The only med-techs she could spare were still trying to log out their gear.

Security was on the way, but without medical, they'd be little help.

Simon? How deep is the shaft?

Five more levels, though civilian access halts one down, at D12. Station schematics show only maintenance tunnels after that. But there's a lift stopped at M5, one below D12. Two levels down. That may be where they are.

Gillie bolted for the stairs. *Guide me there.*

Save for a matched pair of 'droid maintenance workers dismantling a sound mirror at the far end of the bar, the officers' club was blessedly empty for most of

Mack's meeting. The few who wandered in for coffee weren't there long enough to hear the hushed exclamations of surprise and disbelief when Mack quietly reported that a true Raheiran was on station. And had brought news that Magefather Rigo might not be all he purported to be.

"You're sure this Raheiran's true, not just someone with a grandmother who claimed Raheiran lineage a generation ago?" Doc Janek had his elbow on the table, his narrow chin against his fist. Everyone leaned forward. These weren't words that should go further than the table.

"Could be a she," Josza Brogan posited. She was a willowy young woman with short curly dark hair. Her degrees in linguistics and psychology made her a valued part of the *Vedri*'s tactical team, in spite of her youth. "The admiral didn't say."

"The admiral's not going to say," Mack said. "Which doesn't mean I don't trust all of you. I do. But this is my friend's request. And yes, Doc. I'm sure." He nodded at Janek. "Crystal doesn't lie."

"When the magefather touched the crystal, it glowed," Pryor pointed out.

"Dimly. And he had to touch it. That's not how crystal reacts to a true Raheiran." Mack waited for the next question. He'd handpicked his team because he knew they would question. Five people who agreed with everything he said would be useless.

Donata Rand splayed her hand toward him. "Why does our Raheiran friend think the magefather's a fraud?" Rand had been with Fleet security for over ten years. Her sturdy frame had been in the middle of more than a few bar fights.

"Our friend," Mack said, deciding he'd use that term to keep from inadvertently saying Gillie's name, "has been suspicious of the magefather for a few weeks. These suspicions were confirmed when our friend bumped into Rigo outside my office the other day. Raheirans are empaths—"

"—and telepaths," Tobias said.

"—and can read a person's emotions. And something they call an essence. Rigo's essence is Melandan. Fav'lhir."

Pryor and Brogan jerked upright. Rand closed her eyes, shook her head. Janek clenched his hands together. Tobias was nodding.

More questions were fired. Mack answered. Then plans surfaced. Ideas gelled. They'd worked this way for almost five years. It was a comfortable and profitable combination.

"I need an illegal tracer on all ships logging in for the shrine once it opens. Tobias? This has to be completely outside of CQPA's systems. I need it terminaled somewhere other than Fleet property."

"Maguire's, sir. Murphy won't ask and he's one hundred percent trustworthy."

Mack liked that idea. He could sit there with Gillie and no one would be the wiser.

"You're going to want backup security for the inspection and dedication," Rand said. "I'll handle that."

"Coordinate it with Pryor." Mack gestured to the white-haired man. "No one works alone. Watch who's around you. Watch who's watching you."

Rand nodded. "Which brings me back to our Raheiran friend. Who's watching this friend?"

"I am." Mack met her gaze evenly.

"That's not prudent, sir. With all due respect, this is my area. You're going to be involved, even distracted, by the inspection and the arrival of our guests. You'll be part of certain ceremonies. There's no way you alone can guarantee the safety of this person."

Trust Donni Rand to find the one hole in his plans. He wondered if he'd avoided thinking about Gillie's safety because he knew she'd scoff at the idea.

"We are your team," Rand continued. "I appreciate your concerns over this friend's identity, but it's my opinion you're jeopardizing safety for privacy."

"Tobias knows who our friend is."

Rand shot an appraising look at Tobias. "And he doesn't have enough to keep him busy? He's going to be running that tracer in addition to everything else he's doing now."

"She's right, Mack," Janek said.

"It's not totally up to me." Mack opened his hands in obvious frustration. He'd promised Gillie he wouldn't tell anyone, other than Tobias, of course.

A strange, and short, conversation that had been, when he told Tobias he'd found out Gillie was Raheiran. His second in command had seemed elated, then, suddenly, had become very quiet. But Fitch Tobias often had strange moments. Mack brushed the memory aside, turned to Rand. "Our friend set this condition of anonymity."

"Then he, or she, is a fool. Begging the admiral's pardon," Rand said, but she was smiling.

"I'll take your wise words under advisement." He placed his palms on the tabletop. "Anything else?"

A series of negative nods followed. "Good. You all know your projects for the next twenty-six hours. Keep in touch with me, with Tobias." He shoved himself to his feet. "May the Lady guide you and protect you."

Datapads snapped shut, chairs swiveled, boots thudded softly away on thick carpeting. All except Doc Janek, who leaned back in his chair and regarded Mack in much the same way he had in Mack's office weeks ago, when he'd teased about the breach in defenses.

"Problem, Doc?"

Janek shook his head. "It's Gillaine Davré, isn't it? Our, or should I say *your*, friend."

Mack forced his expression to remain neutral. "I can't answer that."

"You just did. You didn't say no."

"Doc—"

"I was going to tell you something, but you've been busy." He motioned to the chair Mack had just vacated, indicated he should sit. "Something odd happened when she was in sick bay. I didn't pay much attention to it at the time. But when I was going over the logs for the week, it stood out. Puzzled me. When you said we had a Raheiran on station, it all fell into place."

Mack leaned his elbows on the chair's armrest. "Tell me."

"We had two critical cases come in just before Captain Davré arrived. That worker who fell down the lift shaft when the doors opened unexpectedly. Again. And a girl, no more than fifteen, with a serious congenital heart problem. They were in sick bay with Davré."

He shrugged, followed the movements of the 'droids working on the sound mirror for a moment. "In a top-notch sick bay, both were solvable. But you know I've bitched about the state of my equipment for months. It should have taken that worker over a week to recover. The girl, I thought all I could do was make her comfortable. Hope to transfer her to a better facility in-system."

"What does Gillie have to do with this?"

"The worker recovered two days later. The girl's scans show no defects at all."

"Mistakes. You said your equipment's faulty."

"Not that faulty. And not good enough to fix those things."

"Neither can Gillie," Mack said quietly. "She doesn't have any mage powers."

Janek arched one eyebrow. "Should I thank Rigo for the healings?"

Mack remembered how he'd found her at Rigo's healing service, worried over the little boy with the flute. Izaak. The child just had a bad case of bronchitis, she'd told him. She'd given him some herbal teas, a ward stone for strength. She wasn't, she'd insisted, a mage. And definitely wasn't a sorceress.

He didn't want to believe Gillie would lie to him. She—

—wouldn't lie, but she would omit. Had omitted being Raheiran until he'd opened the case with his grandfather's crystal. Had omitted what she'd known about Rigo, working instead on her own. He closed his eyes for a moment, shook his head.

Gillie, Gillie. You have no reason to lie to me.

He opened his eyes. He didn't want to ask the question, but knew he had to. And damned that part of himself that gave him no choice. "Tell me everything you know about a little boy named Izaak Neal."

20

Gillie splayed her hand against the access panel and deactivated its lock. Her heart pounded, but that was more from her mad run down the stairs than from fear. She knew what she had to do. She knew she could do it. All she needed was time.

Izaak was on top of the stalled lift, bruised but alive. His father, Jared, was a more serious matter. Somehow he'd tumbled from the flat roof of the lift and wedged against the shaft wall. Gillie eased onto the narrow walkway on the other side of the panel, crouched down in the darkness. Light from the open door above filtered down weakly. She could see Izaak's outline. But only with her Raheiran senses could she find Jared, his father. The lift blocked not only the light but, fortunately, anyone's view from above.

"Izaak? It's Gillie. Mister Toby's friend who gave you the flute." She dropped part of her mental shields, took another scan of the child, as she was closer now. He was terrified, but nothing his mother's arms couldn't fix.

"G-G-Gillie? I lost my flute."

"It's up there in the corridor. We won't worry about that now. I'm going to try to help your father, okay?"

"Okay."

"You stay there. Don't try to come down here. Understand?"

"Understand."

She pulled her belt from around her waist, held it in both hands. Softly recited ancient words, drawing spellforms into being. The belt lengthened, took on metallic form. She hooked one end on the metal railing edging the walkway, lowered herself down.

"Jared?" With one hand she moved her fingers over him until she found his shoulder, then his neck. His life essence was weak.

She opened her senses further. Massive internal bleeding, broken arm. Pain. Intense pain. She adjusted her grip on her cable, inched down further.

The life stones in her pocket called to her, but he was almost beyond their help.

"G-Gillie? Is my father okay?" Izaak's voice caught in a sob.

His mother's screams, and the angry shouts of stationers, echoed down the shaft.

Simon. This is not an easy decision. Saving Jared meant she might risk being seen, identified.

You saved Izaak because it was not his time.

Nor was it his father's. She knew that. She knew it as well as she knew her own name. Gillaine, Kiasidira, Ciran Rothalla Davré.

She whispered the words only a true Raheiran had the right to say: *"T'cai l'heira, Ixari. T'cai l'heira, Merkara."* She drew her sword and touched the flat of its blade against Jared's crumpled form. *"T'cai l'heira Raheira, Tarkir."*

The short sword flashed a bright purple light that enveloped her and Jared like water filling an empty vessel. She pulled it into herself, sent it through Jared's essence, cleansing, strengthening, healing. His eyes flickered open briefly, but that wasn't what worried her.

It was a young boy's hushed voice a few feet above her. The golden hue of a Raheiran Kiasidira now surrounded her, merging with the ethereal purple glow of the crystals, and she knew he could see it. "Goddess! Goddess!" But for the high pitch, he sounded too much like Tobias.

She touched Jared's forehead, cheek, and chin with her index finger, whispered blessings, sealing her spell-forms. Holding Jared together until the med-techs could arrive.

Security is at the stairs, Lady Gillaine.

She shoved the sword under her jacket, glanced up at Izaak, silhouetted by the dim light above. In spite of her instructions, he was hanging over the edge of the lift's roof.

"Izaak."

"You're not just Gillie, are you?"

"Sometimes I am. But I need your promise not to tell anyone what you saw me do. Will you keep that secret for me?"

"Promise. And my father?"

"Will be fine. The doctors are almost here. I have to

go." She hauled herself up the cable, reformed it back into her belt. "You're a very brave boy."

"Sometimes I am."

She smiled, shoved herself through the accessway, and remembered to skew its lock permanently open just as bootsteps sounded in the corridor.

Gillie desperately needed a hot shower and a drink. But she waited a half hour for Simon to intercept reports on Izaak's father from sick bay. And another twenty minutes after that to see what the news media made of the incident. Much publicity was given to the fact this was the third lift accident in as many months. But in spite of Izaak's shy admission that he'd prayed to the Lady Goddess Kiasidira for help, there was no follow-up. No interview with Magefather Rigo or, worse, further questioning of the child. For now, the story seemed to center more on malfunctions than miracles.

She finally permitted herself the luxury of a shower and was pulling on her soft purple sweater when her comm link trilled. "Davré's *Serendipity*."

"It's Mack." He sounded tired, annoyed.

She sucked in a quick, apprehensive breath and held on to the hope that he hadn't heard any reports of an odd purple mist or golden glowing lady in a lift shaft on Down12.

But then, Rigo's shrine opened tomorrow. Maybe that was the reason for his annoyed tone. Not the mysterious purple mist or golden glow. And not his talk with Tobias, which still weighed heavily on her mind. But she assumed if the trouble were either Tobias or

Izaak, Mack would've tracked her down long before now, not waited a half hour before she was to meet him for dinner.

"Hi, yourself." She put a lightness she didn't feel into her voice, replied with what had become their unofficial, playful greeting. Even if he hadn't opened with his unofficial part. It was one other reason she knew something was wrong. "I just have to run a brush through my hair and then—"

"I can't. Gillaine, I'm sorry. Dinner's out tonight. I've got things to cover yet with Tobias, Donata Rand."

"Want me to pick up something from Maguire's, bring it to your office?"

"Thanks, but no. I might not be here."

"You have to eat sometime. I'll wait."

"I don't know when we'll be through."

Damn. A small tendril of fear wove around her heart. "Sounds like things aren't going well," she prompted, hoping he'd at least allude to what troubled him. She knew he wouldn't mention Rigo specifically on the comm link. But she needed something more than just this strong note of frustration she heard in his voice. She needed to know it wasn't because of her.

"More like too many things. Just too many things right now."

"Can I help?"

Silence. A long silence. At least, it seemed that way to Gillie.

"That's something we may have to talk about," he said finally.

"Sure." An icy pain laced through her. "What time will you be home?"

"I'll call you."

"That's okay. I'll wait up—"

"On the *Serendipity*. I'll call you on the *Serendipity* if it's not too late."

This time the silence was hers. He was not only canceling dinner, he was canceling her spending the night with him. The pain around her heart swelled, tightened.

"I love you, Mack." Her voice had a slight tremble.

"I love you more than you can possibly understand, Gillaine." He hesitated. "I'll call you."

The comm link clicked off.

"Simon!" Gillie dropped her hairbrush, headed for the bridge. "Find Tobias. Now!"

My Lady, it may not be what you think. He did say he loved you.

"More than I could possibly understand. I don't like the sounds of that." She stepped over the hatch tread, shoved herself into her seat. "Five, eight years ago—give or take a few hundred—some guy penned love poems to Ixari, remember? 'Devotions to My Goddess' or something, he called them."

She ran her hands over the console. Crystal flared, misted, swirled. "Find Tobias yet?"

Working on that and, yes, I remember the book.

"He said the whole thing was a *higher love* that exists only on a spiritual realm. He called it the love that one cannot possibly understand, except through prayer and meditation. This was how he loved his goddess."

I'm sure Admiral Mack didn't mean it that way.

"I'm not. Where's Tobias?"

Conference Room 3 on Upper6, near Ops Lower.

"What's he working on?" She prayed he wasn't pulling up a copy of that holovid of her in the bar, the one where she wore her green sweater. As far as she'd been able to determine, the only copy existed on Traakhalus. But she knew he'd seen it; he'd recognized her from that vid. Her searches of Cirrus's databases didn't include what Tobias might have in his personal files.

He's viewing a layout of the shrine. And several docking bays. It appears there may be some last-minute changes.

She let out the breath she was holding. Last-minute changes could well be the total reason behind Mack's demeanor. They could also be good news. Anything that delayed the shrine, and Rigo, was good news.

She could fully understand why Mack wouldn't say that on the comm link.

Maybe she was wrong. Now that she thought about it, she couldn't see Tobias betraying her trust. She couldn't see anyone in security giving credence to the ramblings of a scared little boy. And Tobias and Izaak were the only ones who knew who she was.

She took her hands off the console, flexed her fingers. Mack would call her. She felt more sure of that now. He would call her, want her with him. Everything would be all right.

She repeated that three more times in her mind, tried to engrave it on her trembling heart: everything would be all right, everything would be all right, everything would be all right.

She took a deep breath, refocused. "What else are

you finding on the shrine? On the official and unofficial channels?" Mack had said perhaps she could help. It wasn't a matter of *perhaps*. She could help. She didn't see why she had to wait for him to ask. Doing something was better than sitting around, fretting.

Nothing on the shrine you don't know. But wait. Here's something. Rigo's been checking incoming ship schedules. I believe he's waiting for someone.

Good. Something to think about other than what Mack might be thinking about. "Probably just a handful of temple sweepers."

Temple sweepers usually don't travel on a Class-1 staryacht.

Gillie raised an eyebrow. No, they didn't. Could the prime hostess be arriving early? But the chancellor's wife would travel on a Fleet ship, under guard. A Class-1 staryacht was luxury. Decadent luxury. "Passenger list?"

Simon was quiet while searching. *Only one. A gentleman traveler by the name of Carrick Blass. Owner and captain of the* Windchaser.

Carrick Blass? The name meant nothing to her. But his sole status on the ship told her he either had incredible wealth or incredible connections. He also had Rigo anxiously awaiting his arrival.

She decided to find out why. If nothing else, it would keep her from wondering when Mack was going to call and what he would say when he did.

There was the typical dinner-hour crush in the corridors. Groups of Fleet personnel in black mingled with civilian families, rebellious plaid-skirted sons in tow. Young girls had finally removed the cascading braids from their faces but taken to decorating them in glittery face paint. Gillie waited in line for a lift. The executive docking bays were far uplevel, on U8. No staryacht worth its class would dock lower level.

She exited on Upper8. She wasn't far from ops, on U7 and 6. Once she checked out this Carrick Blass she could wander downlevel, perhaps catch Mack in the corridor.

She needed to see him, if only for a few moments.

There were six executive docking bays that opened into a general waiting area. Very plush, by Cirrus's standards. All the chairs were padded, none was ripped, and the stains on the carpeting were almost not noticeable.

Three men in merchanter tunics talked animatedly near Bay 5. At Bay 4, a lone woman sat near the doorway, datapad open in her lap, fingers tapping distractedly on its edge. Whoever she waited for appeared to be late.

Rigo was the only person at the doorway for Bay 2, his back to her. He shifted from foot to foot, his long clerical robes swaying slightly.

Gillie slid onto a bench behind some potted ferns in the middle of the room. Rigo had no reason to suspect anything if he saw her; she didn't even know if he'd remember her from their one brief encounter. But she also didn't want to take any chances.

She would face him sooner or later, over very serious matters. The less he noticed her before then, the better.

Her wait stretched to five minutes, almost to ten, before she heard the thump and clunk of a ship locking down to the decking grapples. She relaxed, stretched out her legs. Another ten minutes yet. She knew the routine.

It was exactly ten when the doorway swooshed open. She peered through the palm fronds. Rigo raised one arm, waved. Stupid, because he was the only one waiting at the doorway. And the man stepping through was the only one coming out.

She rose, walked briskly to her right as if heading for Bay 1. Rigo's back was to her, but as she glanced over her shoulder, she clearly saw Carrick Blass.

He was almost as tall as Mack. Perhaps the same age. At this distance, it wasn't easy to gauge that. But his light hair was thick, his form under his expensive suit, trim. He was definitely handsome, but whether that was a natural attribute or one financially enhanced, she couldn't tell. She stopped at a news kiosk, looked past it at him. Dropped her mental shields a few degrees, scanned.

Slammed her shields shut, plastered herself against the wide curve of the kiosk. Her heart pounded. A sick feeling rose in her stomach from the brief, almost vile, contact.

Melandan. Carrick Blass was Fav'lhir. Not a weak Melandan heritage, like Rigo. But true mageline. A—

Impossible, Simon's voice said in her mind.

No, not impossible. It's been over three hundred years. She swallowed her anger, her frustration. Every bit of intelligence she, and the Khalar, had gathered over three hundred years ago had convinced her that the entire Fav mageline had been on that ship. That was why she'd had to risk everything: the prize was worth any sacrifice.

But they'd been wrong. She'd been wrong. *The*

Fav'lhir are back, Simon. And they have a true mage-line sorcerer in their ranks.

Her hand shot to her hip, grasping for the sword that wasn't there. The sword Rigo had secreted. The one she'd found, which slept in her cabin.

She hadn't thought to carry it, hadn't thought she'd need it yet. When the other admirals, when the prime hostess arrived, yes. She'd be ready, on the defensive.

But now? A Melandan sorcerer within reach and she with no sword, no quick means to confront him, other than a battle of pure magics in which destruction would be rampant, innocents could get killed.

Then this was not meant to be the time, nor the place, My Lady.

She gritted her teeth, watched Rigo and Blass walk by, unchallenged.

It was late, near midnight, but Mack had to talk to Gillie now. In person. This wasn't something to do over a comm link. And it wasn't something that could wait until the morning.

He trudged up the *Serendipity*'s rampway stairs, hands shoved in his pockets. The airlock door slid open before he could take his hands out and slap at the intercom on the freighter's hull.

Gillie, still dressed for dinner, he noted with a pang of guilt. Her lavender and green eyes looked distinctly troubled.

He shrugged lightly. "Hi. Can I come in?"

"Hi, yourself. And since when do you have to ask?" She stepped back, motioned toward the corridor.

She had a pot of coffee on the table of her small ready room. He eased into a high-backed chair next to her, gratefully accepted a hot cup.

"Lots of things going on?" she asked.

"Yes." But where to start? With the most troublesome. No, the second most troublesome. He wasn't ready to face the most troublesome yet.

Coward, said a small voice in his head. He reluctantly agreed and added *selfish* to the description. He was selfish. He loved Gillie more than he'd ever thought possible. He wanted her in his life. He just wasn't sure anymore what that would entail.

He put down his coffee. "I've run into a problem."

"With the shrine, or with me?"

"A little of both."

"Tell me."

Funny. "Tell me" had always been his line. And she said it with the same authority he did. The same authority that now wasn't going to make her very happy. "I need this docking bay."

Incomprehension flickered across her face, followed by an expression of relief. "That's it? You need this bay? So I'll move—"

"I've got nowhere to put your ship. That's the problem. Gillie, I'm sorry. We've had to make some last-minute alterations because of Rigo's shrine. And because of the upcoming dedication ceremony. And other issues"—he couldn't tell her what they were—"attendant to that."

"You need me to leave."

"No. I . . ." He swept his hand out. "Your ship's beyond repair. Maybe it's time you faced that fact."

"A few more weeks—"

"I can't give you even a few more days. I need this bay, and there's nowhere I can store the *Serendipity*. She's not in good enough shape to tether to an exterior dock. I contacted some people I know in scrap and salvage. They'll buy her from you for parts. You'll get a good price for—"

"No!" Her denial held a mixture of anger and anguish. She shoved herself to her feet, almost knocking over her coffee cup. Mack caught it in time, righted it.

"You can't scrap Si—the *Serendipity*. You don't understand. He's not—" She turned abruptly, then stopped a few feet from the table, her back to him, hands clenched at her sides.

Her reaction startled him. He assumed she'd be upset, even a little angry. She'd put a lot of time in trying to repair this ship. He understood that. But she was not only angry, she was afraid. He could almost sense a wave of cold fear shooting through her at the mention of the scrap dealer.

She turned back to him. "I'm sorry." Her shoulders slumped slightly. "I know the problems caused by the shrine. And I know, I've heard rumors of who'll be on station for the dedication. I understand the position you're in. But scrapping my ship is not an option."

"If you're worried about a place to live, you can stay with me. I want you with me." He did. He wanted her with him, and that was all that mattered. A ship was just an object. Hell, she could have the whole Fifth Fleet if she wanted it.

He smiled, but she didn't smile back. He grasped at the most likely reason for her distress. "With the money you'll get, you can pay off your cousin, or whoever owns this ship, for the loss."

"I own it. The ship's mine."

"Your papers—"

"Are false. Mack, I thought you figured all that out by now."

He knew some of them were forged. He didn't think all of them were. "Because you're Raheiran."

"Yes."

He didn't see the problem. "So the ship's yours. Then the money's yours. You can use it as down payment on another Rondalaise."

"This isn't a Rondalaise." All emotion left her eyes, her face. Her voice was quiet. "It's a Raheiran ship. Your friends in the scrap business couldn't even come close to recompensing the value."

"It's a freighter."

"It is not."

Something in the formal way she phrased her denial caught his attention. It made him think about his other problem, the one he didn't want to deal with right now. Gillaine Davré's creative omissions. "Then what is she?"

"A Raheiran Raptor-class starcruiser. And *his* name is Simon."

21

Mack stared at the woman standing stiffly before him, arms folded over her chest. She trembled slightly but her face was impassive, almost distant. She was afraid, angry. Because she'd just admitted her ship was a Raheiran starcruiser named Simon.

She'd named her ship after her elderly friend? For some bizarre reason, that's the first thing that popped into his mind. Incongruously so, given the fact she'd just admitted her ship's true origins—and Raptor-class meant crystalship, didn't it? He had a lot more serious things to consider than why she'd named it after some old man.

"Gillaine—"

She held up one hand. "Yes, I know. I'm sorry. I should've told you." She raised her arms, then let them fall to her side in an exasperated motion. "Be angry at me, be righteously pissed at me if you want. But for gods' sake, listen to me, Rynan Makarian. Because something very serious is happening. And the fact that you're sitting in a Raptor is the least of your worries."

A thousand things whirled through his mind. He pushed them all aside, including the hurt that Gillie didn't trust him. Again. But he trusted her enough to listen when she asked. "Tell me."

"Rigo met a visitor tonight. The man came in on a staryacht. Name's Carrick Blass. Mean anything to you?"

It did, but he didn't know what in hell Blass was doing here. Or why Blass's appearance concerned Gillie. "Big money. I mean, big money. He's had dinner more than a few times with the chancellor. He's here?"

"He's more than here." She leaned on the back of the chair next to him. "He's Fav'lhir. True mageline. A Melandan sorcerer."

Something hot and cold jolted Mack's body at the same time. "Impossible."

She smiled thinly. "That opinion's been voiced. But I saw him. I . . . can tell. Just as I know what Rigo is. This Blass makes Rigo look like the merest novice."

"When did he arrive?"

"Few hours ago. Executive Bay Two. His ship, the *Windchaser,* is still there."

He leaned his fist against his mouth. A few hours ago. By the gods, he could've had Tobias on it already, hacking into the ship's systems. Finding answers. "I wish you'd called my office."

"This is beyond Tobias's capabilities. Blass's ship has spellforms woven all over it."

His eyes narrowed at the echo in her words. "You said you couldn't read my thoughts."

"I don't have to. I know how your people, how you, work. It's what I would've done in your place. Put Tobias on it. But putting Tobias on it would've gotten him killed. You don't fuck with a sorcerer's ship."

He suddenly realized what was different about Gillie. It wasn't that her demeanor was distant, almost cold. It was more like she'd suddenly been put in charge of saving the universe, and knew how. There was a firmness in her tone, a directness in her gaze. A no-time-for-nonsense attitude. It was everything Fleet called the *presence of command*.

He'd sensed this before from her. Actually, the very first time he'd met her, in sick bay. But he'd discounted it, because she'd said she was a freighter operator. But freighter operators didn't own a Raptor-class star-cruiser. And freighter operators wouldn't know how to move behind the scenes as she had, working information on Rigo and the shrine.

And freighter operators, even Raheiran ones, would've gone to the authorities for help when a Fav'lhir sorcerer showed up. Gillie hadn't. But she'd known the ship was locked down with spellforms.

Which told him something else. She'd tried to get in. Tried to do what he would've told Tobias to do and might well have gotten his second in command killed. Yet she'd survived.

"You're Raheiran military, aren't you." It wasn't a guess. It was the logical conclusion to the facts as he now knew them, including the inexplicable healings in Janek's sick bay. And the miraculous recovery of a little boy named Izaak. Khalaran history books were clear on what it took to be in the Raheiran Special

Forces. Healing talents—mageline talents—were one of the requirements.

She nodded.

A thousand questions whirled through his mind, and heart, at her confirmation. He chose one from his mind, shelved the ones from his heart for a later time. "Rank?"

"Captain."

"You're not just an empath."

She looked away, clearly uncomfortable. He waited, aware that he'd slowed his breathing in anticipation of her answer. Aware he already knew what her answer would be. It was part of that logical conclusion.

"No," she said softly, when she turned back. "I'm sorry. I know I have a lot of explaining to do."

He'd already received some explanations. "Doc Janek thanks you for saving Izaak's life."

Color flooded her cheeks.

"There were two others in sick bay when you were admitted. They're both fine. Better than they should be."

She crooked an eyebrow at him. "Old habits die hard."

"Including not breaking cover until you're forced to?" He couldn't yet voice what he was afraid to ask, if sleeping with him was part of her cover. He didn't know what he'd do if she said it was, only that the hurt would be more than he'd be able to bear.

Then he remembered she was very likely more than an empath.

She took the chair next to him, her hands resting on

the tabletop as if she wanted to reach for him but was unsure.

Well, he was unsure too. He sucked in his fear, took her hands. "I've got a Fav'lhir sorcerer on station, a fraudulent magefather, some very valuable people showing up shortly, and all I can think about is where you'll be sleeping tonight." He shook his head. "Damned foolish, wouldn't you say?"

"Then that makes two of us. I don't want to lose you, Mack."

"And jeopardize your mission?"

She tried to jerk her hands back, but he held on.

"Sorry." He saw the anger flash in her eyes. His comment, and its timing, wasn't the best. She knew how highly he placed honesty. She had to know what had happened bothered him deeply. He hesitated, then plowed ahead. "But I've been lied to about too many things."

"I never lied about loving you. If anything, my life would be one damned bit easier if I didn't."

"But you don't trust me." He didn't really think that was true but needed to hear her deny it.

There was a bleakness in her expression when she answered. "In order to try to stop the Fav'lhir, I may have to shatter some of your people's long-held beliefs. Quite honestly, this has been tearing me apart. Because I won't just be hurting the Khalar when I do this. I'll be hurting Rynan Makarian. That almost made me decide to do nothing at all." Her voice dropped to a harsh rasp.

"The only way you could hurt me," he said softly, "is by not being a part of my life."

"And the Khalar? You have some interesting ideas

about me, about Raheirans. Most are based on stories, old legends. But these are legends your people hold very dearly. It's not my job to destroy something that's been a part of your culture for hundreds of years."

"What is your job? Besides feeding me and loving me," he added before she could misinterpret his question, think he was angry. Surprisingly, he wasn't.

With her admission of her military status, things fell into place. Her evasiveness when they'd first met, her reluctance to admit she was Raheiran. She'd been trained as he'd been trained: when you find yourself somewhere you don't belong, keep a low profile. Volunteer as little as possible.

Yet she'd become involved with him. He hoped, he truly wanted to believe, that had nothing to do with her being Raheiran or his being a Khalaran admiral. He could no longer imagine life without her. It wouldn't be a life at all, just a shell. He tightened his fingers around hers.

She responded with a small smile. "My official title is military adviser. I'm trained to work with developing cultures, not destroy their beliefs. But then Blass showed up." Her smile faded. "I may not have a choice here."

"A Raheiran–Khalaran alliance against the Fav won't destroy anyone's beliefs." Except maybe the Fav'lhir's belief that they could take over the Confederation again. He didn't quite understand the unease he sensed in her.

"I'm not officially here. I don't have the authority to make commitments, promises."

"But you said your people come through here

frequently. Isn't there a squadron or contingent close that could assist—"

"No." She cut him off, shaking her head. "Believe me, we've . . . I've scanned."

Something didn't make sense. "Why did your CO send you in alone?"

"Do you remember that anomaly Captain Adler told you about?"

"Out in Runemist."

"I was caught in it. Dragged here by mistake. My ship was damaged."

"You came through a natural wormhole?" That's what the Rim Gate Project would simulate. If a wormhole was already here, though, Fleet had to know. It could seriously affect the operations of the artificial gate, possibly even scrap the entire project. "Our people have probed this entire area, found nothing like that."

"Because it wasn't a wormhole. It was a problem in Riftspace."

Mack knew about Riftspace. Or rather, he knew about the theory, and the legend, of Riftspace. It was a place where science and magics merged. The Khalar had no access to it. Only the Raheira did. Then he remembered Blass, a Melandan mage working with the Fav'lhir. His gut tightened. "Is that how Blass came here?"

"His ship's spellforms show no signs of Rift transit. At least, not this trip."

Blass's ship could run through Riftspace. "But you said it's a staryacht. Not a crystalship—"

"And the *Serendipity*, to you, is a Rondalaise freighter." She pinned him with a narrow-eyed look.

A crystalship masquerading as a staryacht. A crystalship owned by a Melandan mage. That was how the Fav'lhir had engineered their surprise attack almost three hundred fifty years ago, by using the knowledge of the mageline. A mageline that had been destroyed, eradicating that knowledge and those abilities to travel in the Rift undetected.

But it hadn't been destroyed. Blass was here. Mack's heart felt heavy as he reluctantly pushed aside his concerns over his relationship with Gillie and focused on a threat the Khalar had never wanted to face again. The Fav'lhir, with the power of mageline magics behind them.

Blass's crystalship...wasn't the only one. A Raheiran Raptor-class starcruiser, Gillie had stated that in describing the very ship he sat in now. A crystalship. A *Raheiran* crystalship.

"What do you need me to do?" he asked.

"Find me a place for Simon. I can't take on the Fav'lhir without him."

Mack swiveled slowly around in the captain's chair and fought the urge to pinch himself. For the moment, his worries about Blass and the Fav'lhir were relegated to the background. He'd already done all he could through a terse conversation with Tobias, who would relay his instructions to Rand. Watch Blass. Monitor all the comings and goings around the *Windchaser*. But nothing more, because he and Gillie agreed they weren't in a position to play their hand yet.

So for now he let himself be amazed by the fact that he was sitting on the bridge of a Raheiran

Raptor-class starcruiser. A crystalship. The rumble of her—*his,* he corrected—sublights was faintly audible.

This was not at all the bridge he'd seen before. This was magnificent. At least, he thought it was, though he had no idea what he was looking at. Other than the viewports and screens, all instrumentation was foreign, not only in labeling but in form. There were no touchpads, no screen points, no click tabs. Just crystal. He ran his hands over a console area that had to be the captain's. The crystal felt smooth, cool. But there were slight differences in texture. Very slight.

Gillie came up beside him, touched a square area. Light blossomed in a deep green, ran up her arm. She moved her fingers. More colors misted, flowed.

She pulled her hand away. The crystals still glowed, but no longer sent their colors toward her.

"Enviro systems check." She sat in what he assumed was the copilot's seat, looked quizzically at him.

"It's going to take me a while." Not to understand the instrumentation before him. That he doubted he ever could. But to accept what he was seeing. A crystalship. Gillie. No, Captain Gillaine Davré. He knew she had to have some serious mage talents, even though she hadn't admitted to more than being a healer. And, obliquely, a telepath.

She wanted to be with him. She loved him. That was the most amazing part of it all.

"But I'll get used to it," he added, seeing the edges of her mouth dip slightly.

A part of her smile returned. "I'll need my seat if we're to move this ship."

He vacated it, took the copilot's chair. "Ops will only see a freighter?" Cloaking and emulations functions were theory to him.

"Simon can split images. They'll see the *Serendipity*." She tapped at a crystal section on her right. It pulsed a light blue. "Davré's *Serendipity* to Cirrus Traffic Control. Ready when you are. Will activate bay door on your signal."

The signal came through. He didn't know how a Raheiran crystalship could interface with his station, but it did.

Gillie sent the corresponding command to open the bay doors.

Simon was, she'd assured him, quite capable of accepting an exterior dock. Her later damage reports to Mack had been designed to give him reason to keep her on Cirrus. She hadn't wanted someone questioning why she was here, or her relationship with him.

He had two out-docks available: one on Level D6, another on Upper7, one level down from the executive bays. Gillie had immediately opted for Upper7. Blass's *Windchaser* was on U8. She wanted to keep an eye on him.

The idea raised his protective instincts. Then reality took hold. She was mageline Raheiran. He'd agreed but made sure she knew he wasn't thrilled about it.

Docking took ten minutes. He heard the thump of the hatchway against her ship's airlock and was surprised when he left the bridge to find himself in a Rondalaise freighter corridor. He looked over his shoulder. Crystal glistened dimly. The bulkheading around him was dull gray metal.

He shook his head, keyed in the interface commands on a familiar-looking instrument pad adjacent to the airlock. Answering commands flashed from the ramp.

The airlock opened. Fitch Tobias's close-shaved head appeared. "Everything optimal, sir?"

"Optimal. Thanks."

"Blessings of the Goddess upon you, sir. Good night."

"Actually, it's more like good morning." Gillie leaned against the gray corridor wall behind him.

The airlock door hissed closed as he turned. He glanced at his watch.

"About three hours' worth." He rubbed the back of his neck and felt suddenly more tired than he had in weeks. But then, it had been a rather energetic day. Starting with Gillie's revelation of her Raheiran heritage last night. Ending with him, a little more than twenty-six hours later, standing in a crystalship belonging to an officer in the Raheiran Special Forces. And everything else that had happened in between.

"The shrine opens end of main shift, right?" she asked. "We should get some sleep."

He grinned. Her *we* was encouraging. "Mind if I stay here?" He didn't think he could make it even down two levels to his quarters. Nor did he want to.

"I'd like that."

He slipped his arm around her waist. "So would I. Just please, tell me. Is there anything else about you I should know?"

She leaned her head against his chest, sighed. "Yes, but, Mack, if we get into that now, neither of us is going to get any sleep at all tonight."

Oh, gods. There was more. More than being Raheiran mageline. More than being a Raheiran officer.

"Don't," she said softly, and he knew she sensed his disquiet.

"Just one question. Then no more, I promise."

She tensed slightly, but her face was calm when she looked up at him. "Go ahead."

"Are you...married? Or involved with another guy back—"

Laughter bubbled over his words. "There's no one else. Never really has been. Just you." She pulled his mouth down to hers, kissed him thoroughly.

Mack found out he wasn't quite as tired as he'd thought.

Gillie woke to her cabin's semidarkness and the warmth of Mack's body against hers. She should wake him, have coffee. Go find out what a Fav'lhir sorcerer was doing on Cirrus One.

You had your chance last night to tell him all.

That was this morning, Simon.

Why didn't you?

She sighed softly. *Because I'm hoping I won't have to. I think I can still accomplish what needs to be done without sullying the image of their Lady. If someone requires an explanation, I'll blame my connection with Special Forces, my mageline talents. That way the Khalar can keep their Lady, and I won't lose Mack.*

He's stayed with you this far.

I want to keep it that way. Start coffee, will you?

Gillie sat up, stretched. Mack grumbled something, rolled over.

Already started. And, My Lady...

Hmm?

Thank you for not selling me to the salvager.

Oh, Simon. Gillie grabbed her robe, pulled it on. *You're my best friend. I'd be lost without you.*

Speaking of lost, you'd best wait for the admiral. The ship's still in interior crystal phase. The galley lounge is not where he remembers it to be.

When she came out of the shower, Mack was awake and dressed. "I'm going to stop at my place, change into a fresh uniform, then I'll be in my office."

"Coffee?" She knew he felt the pressure of time. But she needed to cover a few more things before they tackled the shrine's opening and the ceremonies that preceded it. And Blass.

"I need that, thanks."

He took a wrong turn out of her cabin. She grabbed his arm, guided him down the silver crystalline corridor. "This way."

Simon had added a touch of chocolate to the coffee this morning. *Show-off,* she teased. She handed Mack a cup, then sat next to him. "I'm going to pull what I can from the *Windchaser*. Should have something for you before Rigo's opening."

Alarm flashed in his eyes. "Are you sure you can handle a spellformed ship?"

"You're sitting in one."

"Then Blass could know you're here."

"I'm not the fool he is. And his ship's not—" She hesitated. Damn, it was so hard to separate what she felt safe in telling him. So hard to know where to draw the line. But he had to know. She chanced it. "His ship's not sentient."

"Sentient." His coffee cup stopped halfway to his mouth.

"The *Windchaser* is what we call *essenmorgh*. Without soul-life. It's powered by crystal similar to Raheiran crystal. But that crystal functions strictly as an amplifier. Not a generator."

"Sentient," Mack repeated. At least he'd put his cup down. "The *Simon* is a sentient ship."

"Simon is the sentience. He's a life form that resides in the crystal of this ship."

Mack glanced up quickly, then, as if realizing the absurdity of his action, faced her. "Simon's part of this ship?"

"Say hello, Simon." Gillie winced as soon as she said the words, knowing how his wry, and sometimes literal, nature would interpret her request and turn it into an echo. *Politely!* she added.

"Good morning, Admiral Makarian. I trust the coffee is to your liking?" Simon's well-modulated voice issued from the comm panel on the wall.

Mack's head swiveled to the panel behind him. It took a few seconds before he was able to answer. "It's . . . it's fine. Thank you."

"You needn't face the comm panel, sir. I'm not actually there. Feel free to converse with me in a more comfortable position if you wish."

"Right." Mack looked back at Gillie and was unsuccessful in keeping the surprised expression from his face. "Why do I have the feeling that with you, it's always going to be something?"

"Trust me, sir," Simon said before Gillie could reply. "It's not a feeling, it's a fact."

Gillie tapped her spoon against her cup. "I'm sure Mack's more interested in the *Windchaser* than my troublesome history, Simon."

"A formidable crystalship, currently emulating a Class-One staryacht. But she is, as Captain Davré has told you, *essenmorgh*. Her spellforms require Blass's input and upkeep, where I am capable of creating and adapting my own."

Mack started to look back at the comm panel, caught himself. "So you've gotten into her systems?"

"Captain Davré and I were able to obtain some information last night, before Blass returned to his ship. The risk of detection increases when he is on board. I'll be able to do more once he leaves. We assume he's here for the opening of the shrine."

Mack nodded. "What do you have so far?"

"It took me several hours last night to break Blass's codes," Simon explained. "That's why I asked Captain Davré to have you delay your departure this morning. So I could bring both you and she up to date. It appears Blass is here not just to spend time with his friend Magefather Rigo. He's also here to spend time with the woman of his dreams. At least, that's what he's written in his letters to her."

This odd bit of news surprised Gillie. Simon had said nothing earlier. One of these days she was going to have to break him of his theatrical tendencies. "Why should we be the least bit concerned with his love life?"

"Because his lover is the chancellor's wife, Honora Syrella."

Blass was involved with the Khalaran chancellor's wife? Gillie blinked, hard, as if by doing so she could block from her mind's eye the sinister implications in that liaison.

Disbelief, then disgust, showed on Mack's face. "That's impossible."

"Sadly, evidence states otherwise. As does her impending arrival."

"Here?" Mack's hand was halfway to his comm set when it trilled. He flicked it up. "Makarian." Then he fell silent, listening, frowning. Gillie had a feeling she knew why.

"Confirmed at our outer beacon? Halbert and the prime hostess?" Mack's questions were terse. And the answers he received through his earpiece didn't make him happy. "Damn it!" Then: "Alert Rand. I'll be in ops in ten. Makarian out." He faced Gillie, his dark eyes narrowed. "This is far beyond Rigo's capabilities."

"I know," she said softly, feeling his confusion and frustration. "But not beyond Carrick Blass's. And not beyond the Fav'lhir's."

22

Gillie leaned against the airlock wall and watched Mack thunder through the gangway connecting the *Serendipity* to the station. His voice, and his anger, was directed at whoever was at the other end of his comm set. But it carried clearly in the confined space.

"We should have been notified before this, and Halbert damned well knows that!"

She didn't doubt that Senator Halbert did. She also didn't doubt that Prime Hostess Honora Syrella Trelmont wielded considerable power.

Not unlike Carrick Blass.

I need his magename, Simon. Among other things. She shoved herself away from the wall, headed for her bridge.

He's still on board the Windchaser, *My Lady.*

Doesn't fancy Cirrus's hotel accommodations, I guess. She swiveled her chair around, ran her hands over the console. Colors crested, flared. *Let's see what we can find without disturbing his beauty sleep.*

After an hour of frustration, Gillie didn't care if she disturbed Blass's beauty sleep or not.

But Simon did. *I still advise caution,* he said as she headed down the corridor in search of hot coffee. *As you and Admiral Makarian agreed last night, we gain nothing by tipping our hand too soon. If you force a confrontation, innocents might be injured. Or killed.*

Gillie perched one hip on the edge of the small conference table in her ready room, coffee mug in her hands. The pungent aroma was reassuring, comforting. So was the fact that Mack had accepted her military status with only the most minor of qualms, though she had the feeling there would have been more personal questions last night had they not also been concerned over Blass's arrival. Mack was Khalaran military; he prioritized. And priority right now was the safety of Cirrus One.

She took a short sip of the hot liquid before answering. "Blass isn't as good as he thinks he is. Okay, his spellforms are fairly complex. But we got in before—"

When he was not in residence.

"—and I think I understand him a little better now."

The Fav'lhir have obviously not forgotten how you broke through their warding shields three hundred forty-two years ago. So they have taken to layering their spells.

"We only know Blass does. I can't say for sure that's a result of their defeat."

I think we can assume that.

"Assume? Simon." She grinned wryly. "You were

the one who taught me to never assume. Because to assume makes an *ass* out of *u* and *me*. Didn't I make that one of my guidelines?"

In this case, I think history speaks for itself. Their mageline did reappear and has learned something. Therefore, let's also assume that's not the only thing they've learned. I advise caution.

"I will be the very definition of caution. The epitome of caution. The—"

Lady Gillaine.

"Umm?"

Be careful. You're starting to sound like me.

Gillie retrieved the small metal case from her cabin, placed it on the ready-room conference table. Touched a panel on the wall on her left. It misted open. She chose four warding rune stones from within, cupped her hand around each one, whispered to it before withdrawing it.

Ladri. For clarity, openness of mind.

Nevri. For wisdom.

Vedri. For strength, loyalty, honor.

Khal. For power and protection.

She placed each one on opposite sides of the case. Then touched her index finger to her forehead, spoke the ancient Raheiran words...

"*T'cai l'heira, Ixari.*"

...her thumb to her cheek...

"*T'cai l'heira, Merkara.*"

...and last, her index finger again to her mouth.

"*T'cai l'heira Raheira, Tarkir.*"

The table lowered to the floor, its surface rippling as a mage circle appeared on its top. Gillie again named the stones softly as she lay them on their corresponding symbols. "Vedri, Ladri, Nevri, Khal."

The circle shimmered, pulsed. A silvery curtain misted up from its edges, surrounded the circle and the stones. Gillie stood before it, hands raised, palms out. Energy crackled against her skin. The curtain parted, closing behind her as she stepped through.

She sat, cross-legged, in the middle, drew the case into her lap. Unlocked it with a touch. The glow of her short crystal sword flowed out like a rushing river, wrapped around her. She closed her eyes and tilted her head back, letting its warmth, its power, its song run through her. It was a familiar song, yet wildly exotic each time she encountered it.

She clasped the jeweled hilt of the sword in both hands. The crystal's power surged through her. She answered with her own. Felt Simon's shields close around her. Nodded her thanks, even though they'd done this many times before.

I'm ready, My Lady.

She stepped out of her Self and took Simon's offered hand.

Mack spied Donata Rand standing in front of Hebbs's station in ops. Neither woman looked particularly happy. Mack sympathized. He was still trying to process everything Gillie'd shown him, told him. He couldn't afford to delve into his emotions until this latest crisis was under control.

But he did know that some of his current displeasure at Halbert and the prime hostess's untimely arrival did, illogically, have Gillie's name on it. Sometime during the early-morning hours, his heart and mind had begun to swap theories. His professional understanding of her actions had taken to bickering with his personal feelings for her as he tried to meld Gillie, the woman he loved, with the Raheiran Captain Davré. And not everything melded to his satisfaction. For that reason he let Rand handle Hebbs. He knew when he wasn't at his best. And right now he wasn't.

Hebbs scrolled down the personnel roster on her screen. "Sure, I can give you live bodies, but not ones with Code-A security clearances." She glanced up at Mack. "If Fleet had been a little more aggressive in clearing my people, we wouldn't be in this situation."

He had no argument. HQ hadn't been expedient in reviewing the files he'd sent to them three months ago. "I should have pushed them more. I didn't. I know that and accept the blame."

"We had no idea, no warning, the prime hostess would travel without the usual chancellery security team," Rand put in. "She and Halbert have only the senator's three personal bodyguards."

"That doesn't mitigate the fact that HQ's had three months to clear Hebbs's people and hasn't." Mack shook his head.

"Who *can* you give us?" Rand leaned on the edge of Hebbs's console, frowned.

"No one with your clearances." She squared her shoulders, as if bracing for a fight.

Mack had no time to fight. He needed live bodies.

"I'm willing to waive that," he put in evenly. And was rewarded, finally, with a lessening of tension around Hebbs's eyes. And a knowing—perhaps for the first time sympathetic—nod. Regardless of the cause of this problem, it was in both their best interests that it was cleared up now. "Who can you give us that, in your opinion, is best suited to this situation? I trust your guidance here."

Hebbs nodded slowly. "I've got fifty-seven sec cops on station under Sergeant Bridger's command. To be honest, they're more used to breaking up drunken brawls than babysitting dignitaries. But there are eight, maybe ten, who I think handle high-profiles well. That's what you'll need."

Ten plus fifteen of Rand's people with Code-A clearances might work, at least to get them through the ceremonies in the shrine. He'd considered calling the *Vedritor* in. Now he might not have to. Especially with the prime hostess on station, he needed his best warship out there, watching. Ready.

Because Blass was on station too. He didn't know who else might be coming in behind him.

"Trans their files to my office," Rand said to Hebbs. "Have them report to me in a half hour."

"That's not enough time," Mack told Rand as they left ops. She followed him through the flow of traffic, leaned on the railing of the atrium when he did. They kept their voices low. The public corridors weren't the best place to have these kinds of discussions, but Mack no longer trusted the confines of his office. Or any office. And he no longer laid his suspicions on Hebbs. Not since Gillie had told him about Rigo and Carrick Blass.

"We don't have a choice in the matter, sir." She glanced at her watch. "You said you'd fill me in on this new problem. It shouldn't take Hebbs more than five minutes to get those files to me."

Mack nodded. Through Tobias, he'd relayed only the barest of outlines to Rand. A comm-set conversation was the least secure of all. "I'll lay it out quickly. You know Rigo's a risk, possibly Fav'lhir. Last night Carrick Blass arrived, quietly, to meet with him."

"*The* Carrick Blass?" Rand raised one eyebrow. "Left his sailing yachts and posh parties to come here?"

"We have reason to believe he's Honora Trelmont's lover." Mack waited until Rand's gape of surprise passed. Then hit her with the second fact. "He's also Fav'lhir. A Melandan mage."

"Blass?" Her voice was a harsh rasp.

"Confirmed."

"By your Raheiran friend?"

He nodded.

"And you trust this person, this information—"

"Completely."

"You've seen proof?" Rand was not one to take anything on face value. She'd been in Fleet long enough to know leveling charges against a well-placed higher-up could be a ticket to a dishonorable discharge.

"Of Blass's love affair? No. But of my friend's identity? Would a Raheiran crystalship be acceptable as proof?"

Rand's mouth opened and closed again. "Here? On Cirrus?"

"Don't go looking for it. You won't find it. It's cloaked, can change its appearance."

Rand's fingers tightened on the railing. She stared at a flock of parrots darting downlevel. "Gods. Goddess." She turned back to him. "That crystal section.

It must have come from..." She stopped and made a dismissive gesture with one hand. "Sorry. I'm not thinking straight. That section couldn't have come from your friend's ship. It's from the Lady's."

"Of course."

"I'd better go get those files. We'll handle this. Don't worry, sir." Rand pushed herself away from the railing, headed down the corridor.

Mack watched her go without actually seeing her. His mind replayed her comment and his automatic answer:

That section couldn't have come from your friend's ship. It's from the Lady's.

Of course.

Of course. Gillie's ship had taken significant damage to the starboard side. The section of the Lady's ship, according to Tobias, was from the starboard side.

But the *Serendipity* was a disguise. His mind grabbed that fact, held on to it. Therefore, logically, the damage and its location were more than likely false.

It was nothing more than coincidence. There was no way that Gillie would be in possession of the Lady—the Kiasidira's ship, he corrected himself. What would a captain in the Raheiran Special Forces want with a three-century-old relic? He doubted a ship of that age would be functional after all that time. And the *Serendipity*—Simon—appeared to be functioning satisfactorily. They'd traveled halfway around the station to the exterior dock last night with no problems.

Mack hated coincidence. But he had another crisis

blossoming on Cirrus One and had no time to puzzle over it any further.

Senator Halbert's ship was due in Executive Bay 1 in fifteen minutes.

Impressive but not impossible. Gillie studied the mesh of spellforms before her that made up Carrick Blass's primary security wall. It was strengthened at the moment by the mage's presence on his ship.

A presence she could observe undetected. She was in Simon's nonphysical plane now, moving as essence, as energy. It was not without effort and it was not a form she could maintain for long. She hoped she didn't need to.

Blass's crystalship was transparent to them as they sat, so to speak, on the outer hull of Cirrus Station. Simon touched her shoulder, pointed toward the left through the shimmering wall. *That's the third time he's checked his image in the mirror. I wonder if Honora realizes her biggest rival for Blass's affection is Blass himself?*

Gillie chuckled softly. Seeing the Melandan mage primp and preen made him seem a bit less fearful.

He's devious and crafty. Even cruel, My Lady. But he is not a Ki'sidron.

It's the cruelty that worries me. She saw it in the spellforms before her. The wardings Blass created were not merely to deter intruders. They were to kill them, and quite painfully. It was what she'd warned Mack about hours before.

Carrick Blass was a powerful, learned mage. His spellforms showed creativity, even ingenuity. She couldn't examine the wardings before her and not, in her own way, admire them. The man knew his craft and knew it well.

She just knew hers a little bit better. She hoped.

Plus, she had Simon.

Thank you.

She heard the undercurrent of amusement beneath his always gracious tone. Slanted a glance at him, caught the slight twinkle in his deep lavender eyes. *Appreciative of my recognition of your superiority?*

I am hardly superior.

To Blass, you are.

Well, yes. But he is fielgha. Simon was fond of that particular Raheiran term for indescribable filth.

He is also leaving. Come on. She stood.

Simon rose also, laid his hand on her shoulder. *Wait. Let's see what wardings he takes with him, and what he leaves behind.*

Good idea. She glanced up at Simon as he studied the spellformed wall. He was in Raheiran fatigues. His close-fitting tan shirt and pants were topped by a collarless jacket of the same soft material. A short sword, in an unadorned sheath, was strapped to his thigh.

His pale hair, pulled back and bound at the nape of his neck with a thin gold cord, reached the middle of his back. Her own hair had at one time been longer—she thought of that horrible depiction of Lady Kiasidira the Khalar worshipped—but not by much.

In height, Simon was about as tall as Mack, and not dissimilar in build, though in appearance Simon would look younger. Or perhaps ageless was a better word. And it wasn't just due to the translucent gold hue that colored his skin.

She'd asked him once for a count of his years. *Not a day over twenty-five, give or take a few hundred millennia,* he'd said. He looked more the former than the latter.

Yet in spite of his youthful appearance, no one seeing him could doubt his power, his authority.

Of course, outside of herself, very few had ever seen Simon. He'd taken semiessential form, in appearance like a translucent humanoid, only twice in the years she'd known him. He was essence; physical existence in the mundane realm drained him considerably.

I have been working on that.

Beneath her gaze, Blass made his way down his ship's corridor to his airlock. *You have no need for physical form.*

Years ago, no. Life was simpler. Kiasidiras and Ki'sidrons were simpler. A blessing here. A healing there. But if I'm not to become antiquated, I need to be able to do more.

Are you saying I need a chaperone?

I'm saying that I was of little use to you when you were injured on the floor of the bridge. And little use to you when you collapsed in the corridor. Frustration tinged his words.

You sent a message to Mack, didn't you? She'd wondered how he'd just happened to come by that day. *And you let him in.* Her ship, like Blass's, was warded and sealed.

Blass is leaving. Simon ignored her question. *Let's take a look at what he's left behind. And what he doesn't want the Khalar to know.*

Gillie held out her hands. Her skin was gold hued, like Simon's. She touched the mesh of colors. They pulsed, flared. Writhed. *Easy, my pretties.* Energy was energy, whether used by Raheiran or Melandan.

Simon's fingers drifted over a section to her right. *We were once all the same people.*

She found a loose thread, plucked it gently, listened to its song. Simon's hand covered hers for a moment, blended his energy into the mix. Then he moved his fingers higher up the thread. He grasped it firmly. *Now.*

In a swift motion, she stretched the thread of energy back as far as her arm allowed, singing to it, chanting to it, stroking its colors with her mind. It vibrated under her touch. Then dissolved.

The mesh before them unraveled into a sizable, gaping hole.

Simon ran both hands around the edge of the opening, sealing the spellpoints. They stubbed off as if cauterized, their energy no longer leaking but no longer merging. *We have at best a half hour before they'll replicate.*

He held out his hand. They stepped through into Carrick Blass's ship.

23

It felt as if she were walking on shattered glass. The Melandan spellforms crackled, shifted under her feet. But that was all they did.

They may be essenmorgh, *but they recognize a Kiasidira. They cannot attack without risking destruction themselves.* Simon hesitated in a cross corridor, ran his fingers down a bulkhead. Small flashes of light exploded at his touch. *This way.*

The complexity of the wardings suddenly increased. Gillie knew, even before she saw the intricately carved door, that they'd found Blass's quarters.

She took a moment to study the door's carvings. *What is it?*

Besides ugly? Simon gestured toward a knot of forms in the center of the door. *People feeding upon each other, possibly. Or, more likely, souls devouring souls. He might well have a closet full of whips. Perhaps we should introduce him to the feisty Miselle Hebbs.*

Even Johnni doesn't deserve this. Gillie splayed her hands toward the door and found the threads she needed. She touched them in sequence, negating them, diverting their energies. When she felt their united resonance falter, she quickly tore them apart. She sucked in a sharp breath, waiting for a second unseen level of wardings to appear.

None did. Yet she didn't believe for a moment that entry into Blass's cabin would be so easy—or at least so obviously easy. She crossed the sorcerer's threshold, her sword in her hand.

She sensed the mogra seconds before it rose from the carpeted decking, slime dripping from its scale-covered hide. Instinctively she backed up, her heart pounding. There was a second flash of light on her left. Simon, sword out, by her side.

Interesting roommate, he said. She could hear the tension in his voice. It had been a while since they'd faced one of these. That hadn't been a pleasant experience either. Especially for the mogra.

Let's hope it's the only one. Gillie grasped her sword with both hands, let the crystal's power lace through her.

As if in response, the mogra's yellow eyes pulsed with an unholy light. Clawed fingers flexed on the end of two overly long forearms. Three horns crested its slick head. But it didn't charge, didn't attack. It was reading their power, just as she and Simon analyzed the mogra's. It had to know it was weaker.

Simon whispered in Raheiran, laying a warding shield behind them. If Blass had any more pets, they'd know the moment the shields were breached.

The demon hissed out a long, foul breath as

Raheiran magics prickled against its skin. Gillie's stomach spasmed at the stench. She concentrated on the demon's spellforms. Ugly, brutal things, but nothing beyond her capabilities.

Still, one always treated a mogra with respect. And caution. *Be gone, ancient one.*

The mogra's form wavered, then solidified. Gillie knew it should have vanished at her command. Therefore, it drew its energy from something else in the cabin. She should have expected that.

Simon thrust the tip of his sword at the creature. It backed up one step, then another. But its yellow gaze was fixed on Gillie.

We could kill it, Gillie suggested, *but Blass may sense that, come back to the ship.*

You know one does not kill demons, My Lady. One only returns them to the nearest available hell.

That was my original intention. It didn't cooperate. Gillie looked past the demon, past the solid forms of a long couch, plush chairs, and elegant carved tables, which existed on a different plane of energy at the moment.

To her Raheiran sight, Blass's cabin was a cacophony of spellformed colors, most of which were putrid, clashing. She sought something very dark, very deep, something feeding power to the mogra. Her senses brushed against its ragged edges.

She jerked back, startled, more startled than by the appearance of the mogra. That had been in keeping with the little she knew of Blass. This wasn't.

A mage cabinet, ancient and powerful. Like her sword, it was constructed to contain and amplify spells. But, unlike her sword, it could also contain physical objects, imbue them temporarily with spell-forms. Many a ruler in ancient times had died from drinking from a curse-filled chalice created in such a cabinet.

Raheirans never built them, never used them. Such a close concentration of powers made the cabinets unstable, their creations malfunctioning with horrifying results. To Gillie, they'd existed only in legend. Nightmares.

Until now.

For the first time a chill ran up her spine. She entertained the disheartening thought that she might have underestimated Carrick Blass.

Simon. She directed his attention to the innocent-looking object along the wall. She felt his disbelief, then his horror and anger. *Can you keep that mogra distracted long enough for me to take a look at that?*

The question is not can I, but should I? I don't like the thought of you tampering with that. It may trigger an alarm.

We need answers, a name. It will know.

It can also drain your life essence.

She knew that. If it locked on to her, she might not be able to get out, even with Simon's help. And destroying the cabinet would render her *essenmorgh*.

She held her hands out. The cabinet's spellforms chafed against her palms. *We don't have time to waste in arguing. Keep the mogra away from here.*

Simon thrust his sword at the demon again. It backed up, hissing. He arced a second swing, more aggressively. The demon scurried to the left.

Gillie took advantage of the open space, side-stepped quickly toward the small cabinet along the inner wall. She felt the movement of Simon's sword through the energy fields behind her as she carefully touched the prickly spellforms guarding the cabinet. These were dark, convoluted.

The pattern must be thousands of years old. She now knew where those two small Fav ships that attacked Cirrus had received their cloaking magics. She sent an image to Simon.

Lady Gillaine . . . A rush of apprehension bordering on fear underscored his words.

We've come this far. She found a loose spellthread. It burned against her fingertips. She gritted her teeth, pulled on it, pain lacing up her arm. She ignored it, read its form. Found another thread. This one, too, writhed, burning.

Her heart pounded as she concentrated, plucked thread after thread. *How much time do we have?*

Eleven minutes.

Gillie sent back an affirmative mental nod. A blaze of energy rushed behind her. She heard a corresponding low whine of pain from the demon. *Careful, Simon. We don't want to alert his keeper.*

He's most interested in you suddenly.

Then I must be close. Three more threads. She chose the one on the right, pulled. There! A pulse of black and yellow as the last block of spellforms writhed, curled, retreated. *Got it!*

Gillaine, be careful.

She held her breath, feeling foolish for doing so. She was out of her physical self, had no need for breathing. But it was an automatic response, helped her focus her mind. Helped her draw the energy from the sword now grasped in both hands, send it like a wave, rolling before her.

The doors of the cabinet bowed, swelled. A liquid that looked like sickly green fire undulated over the surface.

She waited. To do more now would be dangerous.

Slowly, the doors dissolved, in the space of six, ten heartbeats. It felt like forever. Blass's ship's wardings pulsed faintly but consistently on the edges of her senses. The wardings had begun to rebuild. Time was running out.

She let out the breath she was illogically holding and forced herself to stand quietly, listening. The quick slash of Simon's sword sang through the ethers. She could hear the mogra's wheezing hiss. And distantly, beyond all that, Mack's voice.

Something tightened around her heart. How would he view what she was doing, what she was? How could she truly ever explain it?

She pushed that aside, drew her mind back to the mage's cabinet. Spellforms lay broken, withered. She touched the flat of her sword against her forehead, closed her eyes, whispered a very deep, very potent spell. The air suddenly felt cloyingly thick around her. It was only then that she felt safe enough to make her request. No. She was the Kiasidira. To make her demand.

Name thyself.

The cabinet pulsed, fought against her power. She focused her mind, laced her spell with more wardings. Her throat felt dry. It had been a long time since she'd been so challenged. The cabinet was ancient, very ancient. And very strong.

She felt it shudder, a cold wave coursing through her. She drew a short breath as its sharp edge laced her essence, held on. Suddenly, the intense cold was gone. There was only an emptiness. A small, shrill voice gasped out a name: *Carrickal Grel Te'lard Blass*.

Grel Te'lard. He was of the Grel Te'lardan mage lineage. As she was of the Ciran Rothallan. She had it. Blass's magename.

We have him, My Lady. She felt Simon's almost fierce pride at her work. *We have him*.

She glanced over her shoulder. Simon had the mo-gra pinned in the corner. The demon crouched on all fours, whimpering. *Before this is all over, we should return, destroy this cabinet*. It held too much power to be left untouched. She wondered if Blass even knew what he had. It was far stronger than anything else on his ship.

Its destruction, should she and Simon decide to chance that, would have to be done carefully. It might well be set to send an alarm to the remaining Melandan mages.

Simon sprang back, reached for her. *Now!*

Their hands clasped. The demon howled. They raced over broken-glass spellforms, through a rapidly closing warding wall, and embraced the clean energy inside Cirrus One, exhausted and slightly triumphant.

They were in the executive bay waiting area, empty now of Rigo, Blass, and Halbert's entourage. A 'droid maintenance 'bot whirred inches from their boots, seeing and sensing nothing.

A wave of light-headedness washed over Gillie. Simon's arm went immediately around her waist. *I have to get you back*.

I'm okay. We have time—

Very little. He pulled her tightly against him.

The corridor around her spun and she distantly heard the raucous calls of the parrots. Then she was back in her ready room. The image of her physical self sat in quiet meditation in the center of the mage circle.

The curtain parted as she stood before it. At the last moment, she released Simon's hand, stepped through.

"It's perfect." Prime Hostess Honora Syrella Trelmont turned in a slow circle in the middle of the yet-to-be-dedicated Kiasidiran Shrine of Communion. The lights suspended over the round center podium caught the silver threads in her diaphanous tunic and pants, glistened up and down her form. The large rectangular crystal pendant hanging from a thick silver neck chain glinted as she moved. A crescent-moon-and-lightning image was carved on its surface.

Mack thought of Gillie, turning in a similar circle the first time he'd taken her to his quarters. Honora Trelmont was nothing like Gillie.

The prime hostess was in her early forties, of medium height and with a build that could only be described as sensual. And a mass of deep-red hair, arranged in the latest haphazard style, that was anything but subdued. Flamboyant, Mack decided. He'd seen her many times on newsvids, an attractive woman on the arm of her much older husband, but this was the first time he'd met her in person.

Definitely flamboyant. With a face that could be considerably childishly sweet, if it weren't for the perpetual pout on her mouth.

A pout, Mack had the feeling, that was practiced.

She turned that pout on Carrick Blass. "Don't you think it's perfect, Rick?"

"It will be." Blass stepped away from Rigo and Halbert, took Honora by the elbow. He led her to the first row of seats encircling the podium.

She looked up at him in blatant admiration. "What does it need? I'll have Admiral Makarian handle it." Her gaze flickered to where Mack, Rand, and Tobias stood a few feet away, at the foot of an aisle.

Behind them, twenty Cirrus and Fleet security officers waited, watching, at the top of the bowl-shaped shrine. Not only for anyone attempting to enter the large room, but watching Blass, on Mack's instructions. Though the prime hostess didn't know that.

Mack hoped Blass didn't either. His experiences with mages was obviously limited. Who the Tridivinians called magefathers, Mack had begun to realize, were simply theologians. Not mages at all. Not like Blass. And not like—

He pushed her name from his mind. He didn't know if Blass was telepathic. He couldn't take that chance. He focused on the prime hostess.

Blass stood before her, arms folded across his chest. "You've forgotten what we talked about earlier. There's still one more item."

Mack tamped down his surprise. He didn't know what else was needed. The shrine's opening ceremonies were due to start in three hours. Rigo had been granted the use of an auxiliary bay adjacent to the shrine in an uncontrolled capacity, as much as it had rankled Mack to do so. All other arrangements had been handled by Rand, Hebbs, and Tobias. To Rigo's satisfaction, he'd been told.

The *Vedri,* the *Gallant,* and the *Worthy* were on silent red alert. And the three defense squadrons housed on Cirrus on standby. But only Mack's people knew that.

What now? Was this something Blass wanted to stroke his ego? Or was this a different agenda? One dictated by the Fav'lhir?

Mack wouldn't know until Blass made some kind of move. That was what he and Gillie had decided, what he and Rand were waiting for.

It was a waiting game, a dangerous one. He hated them. But the only proof they had against Carrick Blass was Gillie's word. Nothing solid he could present to HQ. And to accuse a man of Blass's stature and influence without solid proof was suicidal. As dangerous as waiting was, they had to give Blass enough room to make a move.

Mack wondered if this "one more item" to be handled was that move.

Blass flicked one finger. Rigo touched Halbert's arm, ambled toward Blass, eyebrows slightly raised in question.

The prime hostess seemed to remember what Blass wanted her to say. She raised her chin slightly, turned to Mack. "We decided that it would be a fitting gesture on Cirrus's part if the week following the opening of the shrine is declared the official Week of Communion."

Mack knew an order, even an innocuous one, when he heard it. He realized he was vaguely disappointed it was something so mundane. He expected more out of a Melandan mage. "I'm sure some kind of proclamation could be issued. Have Magefather Rigo," he said, motioning to the man stepping up beside Blass, "draw something up. I'll ask Stationmaster Hebbs to sign it as well."

"Good." She glanced up at Blass. "And as part of that, I'm sure you'll agree that the entire station should permit uncontrolled access for all bays for that entire week."

Rand, next to Mack, sucked in a short, quick breath. It was not such an innocuous request after all. If permitted, it could be fatal.

"With all due respect, Prime Hostess," Mack said quickly before Donni Rand offered something a bit more blunt, "that would create an enormous breach of security. That's simply not possible."

"Then make it possible." The prime hostess's smile was cold.

Mack returned it with a thin smile of his own to hide his mounting anger. Clearly Blass was using the prime hostess's position for his own ends. "CQPA and Fleet share authority for this station. Stationmaster Hebbs and I would need direct orders from our respective HQs to do that. I doubt they'd give an order of that kind."

"There are a number of pirate gangs out there who might take that as an invitation to loot this station." Rand's tone was polite but firm. "Your suggestion is highly inadvisable. Ma'am."

The prime hostess drew herself to her feet. "Would you find this suggestion so inadvisable, Commander, if I were to tell you it came from Lady Kiasidira herself?"

"I would find it unusual," Tobias said.

Mack slanted a quick glance at Tobias. The lieutenant's input was unexpected. But the prime hostess's inclusion of the Lady was not. He'd agreed with Gillie that Rigo and Blass were using the Khalaran's fascination with the Kiasidira as a cover for their objectives regarding Cirrus. Objectives that included uncontrolled access, now not for just one bay but the whole station.

If the Fav'lhir were planning an invasion to gain control of the Rim Gate Project, there couldn't be a simpler method. A week's worth of unrestricted access was more than just Blass arriving on Cirrus. Fav operatives could infiltrate both civilian and Fleet sections. When Mikail Pennarton's Rim Gate team arrived, they'd be entering a station populated by the enemy. And delivering technology—and personnel—directly to that enemy.

The thought chilled Mack, and angered him even more. Not his station. Not while he was still in command.

The prime hostess was equally displeased by Tobias's comment. "Are you something of an authority on the Lady, Lieutenant?" There was a note of derision in her voice.

"I'm a devoted student of hers," Tobias said.

"As is Prime Hostess Honora." Blass lay his hand on the prime hostess's arm, a knowing smile forming on his lips. Suddenly, he stiffened, frowned, his eyes narrowing.

The prime hostess caught the change in his expression. "Rick?"

Rigo also looked concerned, but said nothing.

Blass's features darkened. Something cold clutched Mack's heart. Gillie. He didn't know how he knew it, but Gillie was up to something. Or had already done something.

"Just an annoying thought." Blass shot a questioning glance at Tobias.

Telepath. That possibility existed. For the second time, Mack tried to cordon off his mind.

The prime hostess touched the crystal pendant around her neck. "The Lady has imparted to Magefather Rigo that it is her desire to welcome all people to her shrine. You cannot deny her request, Admiral."

Mack glanced at Rigo, then back at the prime hostess. "I'm sorry, but I have to."

"The decision isn't yours to make." Rigo locked his hands behind his back, rocked on his heels. His long cleric's robe pulled tightly over his paunchy form. "The prime hostess has relayed a message to the chancellor. We expect an answer, a positive answer, from him shortly."

Mack had noticed that Blass seemed distracted. The man's full attention had not been on the conversation. But the mention of the chancellor drew him back in. "Handle this," Blass said to Rigo, with an abrupt motion of his hand. "I have something else to attend to right now."

The prime hostess reached tentatively for his arm, but Blass jerked away, strode toward the wide doors for the corridor.

Gillie. Gods, Gillie. Whatever you're doing, stop it. Get out of there. He could see her small, dust-smudged face peering up at him from under the temple bench, the impish glint in her eyes.

Then that image faded and he remembered another expression on Gillie's face. One of hard determination that echoed a presence of command.

Not for the first time, he wondered which was the real Gillie Davré.

He caught the slight movement of Rand's fingers to her watchband, activating a signal. Two of her best would shadow Blass. Mack fought the urge to be part of their team. Not to follow the mage but to unmask him. Confront him. Keep Blass away from Gillie, at all costs.

But now was not the time for that. Rigo had said they were waiting for a communication from the chancellor. One that could create as dire a problem for Cirrus One from without as a Melandan mage could create from within.

Mack was sure the Lady had some succinct guideline about the lesser of two evils. He just couldn't think of it right now.

He acknowledged Rigo's statement with a slight nod. "I'm sure the chancellor isn't about to put this station, all its inhabitants, at risk."

"We've been at this crossroad before, if you remember. Over the bay that is now declared a part of this shrine. That, too, was the expressed wish of the Lady." Rigo's small eyes glinted. "And it is now a fact."

"Do not underestimate the magefather's power, or mine," the prime hostess said.

Not theirs, though the prime hostess did have considerable influence. But Blass's. A Melandan mage. An unknown entity, in Mack's experience. But not, he knew, in Gillie's.

He suddenly knew what had to be done. Gillie had to talk to his team. She'd asked for anonymity, but with this new request, the situation had escalated. He needed to know if she could find out what Blass was planning and just how far the mage could go to make those plans a reality.

"I have some things to take care of before the opening ceremonies, as I'm sure you do. Prime Hostess. Magefather." He turned to Rand. "Assign three of your best people to work with Senator Halbert's security for the prime hostess. Then meet me in the conference room in fifteen minutes."

Rigo didn't want to be so summarily dismissed. "Mark my words, Admiral," he called out as Mack stepped away. "Lady Kiasidira will have the final say in this matter."

Mack shot a glance over his shoulder, but Tobias answered first. "I have no doubt of that, Magefather. No doubt at all."

24

Mack headed for the stairs and Upper7, Tobias easily keeping up with his long stride. Parrots screeched and soared. A small group of gangly adolescent boys slumped by, almost tripping on their long, side-slit skirts. The news media, thank the Lady, was nowhere in sight. Mack was becoming immune to the parrots, the kids. But reporters were one thing he wasn't in the mood to deal with right now.

Tobias seemed to pick up on that. "This isn't turning out to be as easy as we hoped, sir."

"Rand filled you in on Blass and the PH?" He used the acronym for Honora Trelmont's title.

"Distressing, sir. Disgraceful, actually."

"I think they may deserve each other," Mack said quietly as they exited onto U7. More Fleet personnel were in the corridor. Mack passed ops, grabbed Tobias's elbow when the man started to turn. "We're not going there."

"Yes, sir. Sorry. Where are we going?"

"To convince someone that her need for anonymity is far outweighed by the need for her expertise. With Blass."

"Lady Captain Gillie may not be happy about that."

"I don't intend to give Lady Captain Gillie any choice."

"I'm not sure you have that authority, sir."

Mack shot Tobias a questioning glance. They turned down a short side corridor leading to the exterior docking bays.

"She may be Raheiran," Mack lowered his voice even though no one else was in the corridor, "but she's still in our jurisdiction."

Tobias's mouth opened, then closed. "Yes, of course," he said as they came to a stop before the airlock fronting the *Serendipity*'s exterior gangway.

Mack reached for the intercom, hesitated. He wasn't fooled by his second in command's bland expression. He knew Tobias viewed Gillie with respect, and not just because she was Raheiran, or "Admiral Mack's girlfriend." But because, like himself, Tobias had seen Gillie in action, relating to people, caring about people. Tobias was worried about what Mack was going to say, and how he was going to say it.

"I'm just going to be honest with her. There's a dangerous game being played out here with Blass. She's in a unique position to provide us with answers." He paused. "I'm not any happier than you are about getting her involved. But with the prime hostess here unexpectedly, we have no choice."

He hit the intercom panel on the bulkhead. "Gillie, it's Mack. And Tobias. We need to talk to you."

When he didn't receive an answer after a minute or so, he remembered that odd, cold feeling he'd had in the shrine. And Blass's equally odd, cold look.

Of course, she could be away from her ship for any number of legitimate reasons, which would have nothing to do with Blass. Yet that coldness that had gripped his heart had hinted otherwise.

"Sir, maybe she's—"

"Mack? Hi." Gillie's voice sounded slightly breathless. "Give me a minute."

"We'll wait." Her ship was probably in crystal form. Mack realized he had no idea how much Tobias knew about the real Gillie Davré. Well, he'd be learning a lot, quickly. He trusted Tobias. Just as he trusted his entire team. He hoped Gillie would feel the same way.

She met them in the *Serendipity*'s main corridor a minute later—and it was the *Serendipity*, gray bulkheading and all. Her hair was mussed, as if she'd just dragged a clean shirt over her head. He started to reach for her, run his fingers through the moonlight softness, but hesitated. "Can we talk in your ready room?"

She nodded. They followed. He took her hands when she sat next to him. Tobias was suddenly fascinated with the tabletop.

"Something's going on with Carrick Blass, something I know you can help us with," Mack said. "I've told Tobias and the rest of my team the basics. But we need more, Gillie."

He caught the wary look in her eyes, continued.

"Tobias knew you were Raherian before I did, but he needs to know everything you've told me since then. Then we need to talk to my team."

"I think the better course of action would be for me to tell you and Lieutenant Tobias everything *I* know. Then you work the details out with your team."

"It's better coming directly from you." He squeezed her hands.

She drew in a slow breath, flicked a glance at Tobias.

"We're meeting in ten minutes." Mack put some firmness into his tone. "I need you to tell them what Blass is capable of."

"More than I like." She pulled her hands out of his, then stood. "He's Carrickal Grel Te'lard Blass. Do you know the lineage?" She directed the last question at Tobias as she moved to the head of the table.

Tobias nodded. "I've read the name in the mage charts at my parents' temple."

"It's a very old phratry. Carries a significant amount of power behind it."

"My team should hear this, Gillie."

She leaned on the back of the chair. He watched her face for emotions, was surprised when he saw none. This was the other Gillie, the captain in the Raheiran Special Forces. He didn't know her as well. That troubled him. How could the woman he loved hold so many secrets, so many layers?

"I reserve the right," she said finally, "not to explain certain methodology."

He glanced at his watch. There was no time for negotiations. He had a feeling he might not win anyway. "Agreed."

"Anything else?"

Was she reading him telepathically? Or did she just guess from the fact that he was still seated, hands folded? His own expression no doubt gave away far more than hers. "I'd like to bring my team here. To see this ship, as it really is."

Tobias straightened, as if in surprise. Mack had only told Rand what the *Serendipity* was. But not the rest of the team. There'd been no need, until now.

And Rand knew well what she could and could not say.

A wry smile played across Gillie's lips. It was the first emotion he'd seen from her in several minutes. It warmed him. "Simon agrees with you, not surprisingly," she said, her voice as soft as her smile. "Why do I have the feeling I'm being double-teamed?"

"Simon?" Tobias asked.

There *was* much his lieutenant didn't know. For some reason, that took some of the sting out of the fact that Tobias had known Gillie was Raheiran before he did. "Rand should have everyone together by now. Go bring them here. I don't want to give out our location over the comm sets."

"Understood, sir." Tobias moved toward the door.

"When you return," Mack said as Tobias stepped over the door tread, "you'll get to meet Simon."

"I look forward to it, sir."

Gillie had her arms wrapped around her waist when he turned around. Her smile had faded. Mack wasn't telepathic, but her message was clear. Something scared her. Deeply.

He rose. She stepped into his outstretched arms, held him tightly. He stroked her ruffled moonlight hair. This was the Gillie he knew. "Thank you."

"My life is always so much more complicated than I want it to be." Her voice was wistful.

"You're a complicated woman." That was an undeniable truth.

"Actually, I'm not." She looked up at him. "Feed me. Love me. Not necessarily in that order."

Those had been his words to her, the first time they'd made love. He remembered her answer. "I can do that."

"Promise?"

"Promise."

She leaned against him, sighed. He had the feeling she needed to hear something more, but he didn't know what it was. He opted just to hold her, dusting her face with kisses, until she pulled away, reluctantly.

"Tobias is back."

"On the gangway?" Maybe she had an intruder signal he'd missed. He had been somewhat distracted the past few minutes.

She shook her head. "At the corridor airlock."

Still on station. And the airlock vidcam wasn't on in the ready room. "You can tell that?"

Her response was the slight raising of one eyebrow. Then an affirmative. "I can sense someone's arrival, when I need to."

"Can Blass?"

"Let's talk to your team, okay?" She grabbed the back of the chair at the head of the table, swiveled it toward him. "Sit, Admiral Makarian. It's showtime."

Pryor, Rand, and Brogan filed in after Tobias, nodding to Mack as he stood at the head of the table. Doc

Janek greeted Gillie warmly when he came in. "You're looking very well, Captain Davré."

She accepted his hand, and his compliment, with a broad smile.

Mack waited while Rand, Janek, and Brogan sat in the remaining three chairs. Tobias and Pryor stood behind Janek, at the other end of the table.

He glanced at Gillie, then began: "May I present my team: Commander Donata Rand. Doctor Benton Janek. Lieutenant J. G. Josza Brogan. Lieutenant Commander Fitch Tobias. Lieutenant Tarrance Pryor."

Gillie stepped forward as he extended his hand in her direction. "Ladies and gentlemen, Captain Gillaine Davré, Raheiran Special Forces."

Only Brogan looked surprised, but then, she was the youngest on his team. Tobias and Janek had known Gillie was Raheiran. Pryor and Rand had no doubt guessed Gillie was the "friend" whose identity he'd been protecting.

Gillie clasped her hands behind her back, military fashion, but it was a comfortable stance, neither overbearing nor tense. "I wish we were all gathering here under more pleasant circumstances. But recent events, and certain persons on station, have decreed it otherwise. Just as they've decreed that I can't remain anonymous, as much as I'd prefer to.

"I'm in the odd position of being an official representative of my people, yet not specifically to Cirrus One. This is why I asked Admiral Makarian not to reveal my participation. Other than the admiral—and now all of you—no one in your government knows I'm here. There could be—there undoubtedly *will* be—ramifications because of this." She nodded her head slightly.

Mack understood her concern. Her actions would reflect not only on her career but on the Raheira as well. That was one of the issues she'd been struggling with.

"But I truly believe I have no choice. Or else I wouldn't have permitted you to come on board. To learn what you're about to learn. I only ask—no, demand—this: there are some questions I cannot answer. Please respect that, and understand it has nothing to do with my faith or my trust in each of you." Gillie looked pointedly at Mack. "Or that my omissions are in any way meant to hurt you.

"Now let me tell you what I know. Then we'll deal with what has to be done."

Mack leaned back, listened as Gillie became the woman he didn't yet know that well, the captain in the Raheiran Special Forces. She succinctly and professionally recapped her information about Magefather Rigo, including that he had been the one to greet Blass's ship when it arrived. She repeated what she'd told Mack and Tobias earlier about Blass. The Grel Te'lard mage lineage was old, powerful, and true Melandan. And, as such, true Fav'lhir. After more than three hundred years, they were back, once again looking to infiltrate the Khalaran system.

"He has an ancient mage cabinet. My people won't create them, but evidently the Fav'lhir have no such scruples. This one has strong, complex, and very dark spellforms."

"You've seen it?" Tobias asked.

Mack heard the note of concern in Tobias's voice

and wished he had his second's knowledge. His information on mage cabinets was based mostly on childhood scare tales.

Gillie was nodding. "That's how I found his magename. His cabinet's an *essential*; it has a living essence, an intelligence, tied, in this case, to Melandan magics."

Mack didn't like what he heard. It was one thing to ask her to work with his team. It was another to learn what she'd been doing on her own. "You said this mage cabinet is very strong."

She hesitated. "I know a few tricks. I had to have his magename, Mack. There are ways to use his name's power against him."

Rand half-raised her hand. "Why didn't you destroy it when you saw it? If that would also destroy him—"

"It wouldn't. But he would've known I was on his ship, in his quarters. He would've undoubtedly returned. Its destruction might also be capable of sending a signal to an awaiting Fav'lhir squadron. Or fleet, possibly with other mages. We'd be dealing with a problem I don't think we're ready for yet."

"A war of deep magics," Tobias said.

Mack didn't know what disturbed him more: the potential of a battle of occult powers, which would be unpredictable, dangerously chaotic from what he knew. Or the fact that Gillie had been on Blass's ship and he hadn't been there to assist.

"You're mageline, then." Rand, as always, probing, questioning.

"Yes."

"Stronger than Blass?"

Gillie pursed her lips for a moment.

"If you can't answer that . . ." Rand offered.

"I'm trying to explain it so you'll all understand. And so that Admiral Mack doesn't stop asking me out to dinner," she added, glancing again at him.

Mack smiled at her, but his mind toyed with what she admitted. She had strong mage talents. Stronger than he knew, stronger than she thought he'd be comfortable with. He wasn't sure how he felt about that; he only knew this wasn't the time to dwell on it.

Janek's chuckle broke the slight tension in the room. Mack realized he wasn't the only one hanging on her answer.

"Drop the two of us on an uninhabited world, yes," Gillie said finally. "I can take him. But that's not what we have here. Blass will use everything here against us. Against me.

"That's why the element of surprise is so important. Once Blass learns I'm here, he'll fight dirty. He won't care how many people die around him. He doesn't have to keep everyone on this station alive. I do."

"We do," Mack corrected. Her personal sense of responsibility awed him but annoyed him at the same time. This was his station, his command.

Gillie faced him. "Understand this well, Admiral Makarian. When it comes to a Grel Te'lard sorcerer, there's very little you, or the Khalar Fleet, can do. This is my territory, just as it was—" She stopped, blinked. Shook her head. "This is my fight. I'm sorry."

"It's not yours alone," Mack persisted.

"You're absolutely right. It's not." Her wry smile,

and sudden about-face, puzzled him until she continued: "I have Simon."

The ready room shifted, bulkheads sheeted in crystal, odd-shaped power panels appearing suddenly on their surface. Rand gasped, obviously surprised even though Mack had told her the truth about Gillie's ship. Brogan's head swiveled left and right. Janek only raised an eyebrow. Tobias had a strangely rapt expression on his face, looked as if he were about to drop to his knees in adoration.

Pryor cleared his throat. "The *Serendipity*'s a crystalship."

"Raptor-class," Gillie said.

"And my name is Simon." Mack heard the familiar male voice issue from the bulkhead panels. "I've worked with Captain Davré for many years now and am quite capable of assisting her in this matter."

"Incredible," Pryor said.

"Thank you," Simon replied. "I do try."

"Simon." Tobias pronounced the name slowly. "Sentient Integrated MObile Nanoessence."

"Excellent, Lieutenant Commander Tobias." Simon sounded pleased. "Quite correct."

"And the NIFTYs—"

"Later, Lieutenant?" Mack knew of Tobias's fascination with technology. Raheiran technology could easily become an obsession.

"Of course, sir. Sorry."

"Is Blass's ship like yours?" Rand asked Gillie.

"It's a crystalship, but it doesn't have Raptor-class capabilities. And it's *essenmorgh*. It has no innate intelligence, or life essence."

Rand splayed her fingers on the table. "So his ship can't assist him like Simon can."

"Not independently."

"Why did the Fav'lhir send him so ill-prepared?" Pryor asked.

"He's not ill-prepared. He's just not expecting me to be here. A Grel Te'lard sorcerer, with whatever other Fav'lhir agents are already here, would be able to seriously compromise this station. At least, long enough for reinforcements to arrive." Gillie nodded to Mack.

If the station was unsecured, on total open access for a week, reinforcements could arrive quickly. And in large numbers. Mack now had no doubt what Blass's plans were. "We found out about an hour ago that Blass, using his influence with the prime hostess and, through her, the chancellor, is demanding a week of unmonitored access to Cirrus. In celebration of the opening of the shrine. Because Lady Kiasidira told Rigo this is what she wants," he added.

An intense fire blazed in Gillie's eyes. *"Fielgha."*

"Temper," Simon intoned.

"Well put, My Lady. Captain Gillie." Tobias smiled thinly when she glanced at him. "I speak a little Raheiran."

Gillie arched an eyebrow in answer, turned to Mack. "Blass has friends out there, somewhere. If he's asking for a week of no security scans, then we can assume at best they're three, four days out. Probably much closer than that. Simon?"

"Working on it now. But my longest range is short of that."

"How far can your sensors reach?" Mack asked.

They were facing an invasion. An imminent one. Suddenly he found his heart pounding, his adrenaline racing, and it wasn't a totally unpleasant sensation.

"I recalibrated your sensors almost three weeks ago but haven't activated all the upgrades yet. I can personally tell you you're clear to six hours past your outer beacon, Admiral. But that's only thirty-two to thirty-five hours from here. Not enough."

Rand leaned forward. "The *Vedritor* . . ."

"Doesn't have my capabilities to detect cloaked ships, and the Fav'lhir may come in cloaked. That's one of the enhancements I added to your ops, by the way. Shall I activate that now?"

Mack still had to remember not to face the comm panel when he talked to Simon. "Wait. CQPA personnel aren't going to understand. I'll send Tobias and Rand to talk to Hebbs." He looked at Gillie. "I'm sorry. It seems a few more people are going to have to know at least some minimal information. I'll do what I can to keep your name out of it."

"I understand." Her voice was soft.

Rand stood when Tobias stepped behind her. "We'll make sure the uproar's kept to a minimum, Captain."

"Talk to Simon on a closed comm link through the *Serendipity*. He'll guide you."

"Understood, Captain. And . . . thank you." Rand inclined her head respectfully, hurried out, Tobias striding in her wake.

"I can request assistance from Fourth Fleet," Mack said after the door closed, "but it will take them at least three days to move ships here. We have one bay on open access starting in two hours."

Gillie frowned, clasped her hands at her midsection. "Alert Fourth Fleet," she said after a moment. "I can stop Blass from taking control of this station. But I can't stop Fav'lhir ships from attacking it. If there's a squadron out there, and they get close enough to do that, whether their sorcerer is alive or dead will matter little to them. Or us."

25

There was a long line in U4's corridor outside the shrine. Stationers were decked out in their Reverence Day best, freighter crew in neatly pressed uniforms. A few adolescent boys and girls shifted aimlessly from foot to foot, looking glum in long pants, hair neatly swept back from faces freshly scrubbed of the glitter paint that was this week's fad.

Gillie had made some changes to her own attire, though not obviously so. Under her plain, thigh-length jacket, she'd sheathed her short crystal sword. Her pockets held additional warding stones.

She slipped through the queue, saw Donata Rand waiting for her near a door marked EMERGENCY EXIT. Gillie disliked special treatment, but she needed to be inside the shrine for the opening ceremonies. She had to observe Blass and see who else, if anyone, was doing the same thing.

After her meeting with Mack and his team, she had

a strong suspicion that Blass and Rigo weren't the only Fav'lhir agents on Cirrus. Pryor had agreed, and with Simon chiming in, that had been the topic of discussion after Rand and Tobias had headed to ops. Even with the prime hostess under Blass's influence, the Fav'lhir couldn't assume that week of unsecured access would be granted. They had to have others already in place to assist their sorcerer at the proper time.

Gillie didn't know when that proper time was. But she knew it was coming up much too fast.

She caught Rand's slight nod, answered with one of her own. Rand keyed in a code on the doorpad, then ushered Gillie through.

It took a moment for her to scan the gathering. Every seat was filled by prearranged assignment. Station dignitaries, wealthy merchants, CQPA officials, and Fleet brass occupied their respective sections. The actual seating area inside the shrine was small: sixty-five seats, Mack had told her. His hand had rested casually on her shoulder as they'd reviewed the data in the ready room. She'd felt his concern, his tension. His love. The last she still savored in her heart as her mind took in the situation before her.

The stationers gathered outside would watch the ceremonies on two vidscreens placed in the corridor for that purpose. Then, after the ceremonies had ended, they'd be permitted to file through and out again.

So much for Magefather Rigo's devotion to the common person.

Editorializing? Simon had caught her train of thought.

Sorry. She went back to her cursory examination of the shrine. From her vantage point along the upper tier, she could clearly see the center podium where Rigo sat, flanked on either side by acolytes: two male, two female. All, including Rigo, wore long hooded robes, not unlike the one Gillie had worn in that awful official portrait.

A large holographic replica of which was hanging over the center of the podium in an ornate metal frame. She wrinkled her nose in distaste. Her image would appear to turn and follow people walking around the shrine.

Beneath the suspended portrait was a plexicast case on a high, four-legged stand. It was the one she'd found in the storeroom. The one that had contained her sword but now held only Simon's perfectly crafted replica. The real one was at her hip.

If Rigo intended to use it in the ceremonies, he was in for a big surprise. It wouldn't glow; it wouldn't even flicker.

She rather hoped he'd try.

The prime hostess's location was clear from the dark-suited security guards behind and on either side of her. Gillie wondered which dignitaries had been bumped from those seats in order to accommodate Honora and Senator Halbert. And Blass. He lounged diffidently on Honora's left.

Gillie scanned the rows around Blass, looking for anything tinged with a Melandan essence. It was only a low-level scan. To drop her mental shielding this close to Blass would alert him immediately to her presence.

This wasn't the time to do that.

A familiar face across from the prime hostess caught her attention. Mack, in formal dress uniform, watching her, his dark eyes unreadable at this distance. But not his authority, his undeniable presence. She thought again of the *pantrelon,* sleek and dangerous. Her heart fluttered a little, but she tamped it down.

He shifted slightly, scanned the crowd in a casual manner. She knew him well enough to know he was anything but casual. Too much was happening, not only with Rigo and Blass but with herself. More than once she'd caught him regarding her as if he'd forced himself to take a step back.

This wasn't the time to think about that either.

She gave him a slow, affirmative nod when their gazes meshed, went back to her scrutiny.

One of the young women next to Rigo rose gracefully, pulled a set of hand bells from beneath her robe. The soft tinkling sound filled the room and quieted the low chatter of voices. The harsh lights of the vidcams flared on.

She shook the bells a second time. The overheads dimmed, leaving only the center podium in the spotlights.

Rigo stood, a small box clasped between his hands. Not the sword case; that was still on its stand. He opened it, and there was a notable intake of breath in the shrine. Gillie could see the glint of crystal in the box's shallow depths. She tightened the shields around herself and her sword, because she also knew something else: the shard in the box was a piece of her ship. She was perhaps fifty feet away from it, but she could take no chances. If it responded to her, Blass would know it.

Rigo handed the box to a robed young man, held the long shard with both hands. After a few seconds, a faint purple glow misted from the shard.

It is Raheiran crystal, after all, Simon reminded her.

A more definite collective intake of breath this time.

Suddenly, the light flared, crested, almost exploded out of Rigo's hands. Gillie jerked back, surprised. The loud clatter in the shrine told her most everyone else did as well. But Rigo appeared unperturbed, continued to hold the pulsing shard, raising it above his head.

Blass. Blass, not ten feet away from Rigo, was sending power to the crystal. But to those assembled, it looked as if Magefather Rigo was the powerful one. The chosen one.

"Lady Kiasidira," Rigo said, his voice booming out in the confines of the shrine, "has spoken. She welcomes you to her Sacred Shrine of Communion."

"Fielgha," Gillie cursed under her breath, caught Rand's slanted glance and nod of approval at her comment.

Rigo placed the crystal back in its case, then closed it inside the sword stand. Then, for the next fifteen minutes, his voice droned on and on. At least, that's the way it seemed to Gillie. Meaningless platitudes were uttered, more bells chimed. The assemblage bowed their heads in meditation while Rigo chanted.

Boring, fraudulent, and a total waste of time. Except for Blass. She focused on him, watched his movements, how he leaned now and then to share some words with the prime hostess. How he liked to use his hands when he spoke; his index finger extended in what could be construed as an elegant gesture.

Gillie touched Rand lightly on the arm. She wanted to change position, see Blass in more than just profile.

"Admiral Mack says I'm to stay with you," Rand said softly. Gillie rolled her eyes but complied.

She watched Blass's expressions, the slight narrowing of his eyes, the sly curve of a smile on his mouth. He was almost too handsome, too pretty.

That could be a spellform, Simon suggested.

Gods. She hadn't thought of that. No Raheiran would ever do that. But the Melandans were different. Their patroness, Melande, was nothing if not vain. Extraordinarily, sensually beautiful, if the ancient paintings of her were accurate. But vain.

She remembered Blass primping as she and Simon had watched surreptitiously. But was it a vanity for himself, or to keep the attentions of a powerful woman like Honora Trelmont? Were there things Honora could provide Blass, besides her connection with her husband, the chancellor? Gillie knew little of the woman's own social and political ambitions. But she knew enough about Grel Te'lards to suspect Blass would grab everything he could in his pursuit of power.

They had always been one of the more dominant Melandan phratries. It surprised her not one whit now that a Grel Te'lard would be the one to spearhead a move to take Cirrus One and the Rim Gate.

But who would share power with him afterward? What bargains had been made? Honora Trelmont's involvement raised suspicions that she didn't want to touch on but may have to.

Could the Khalar be betrayed by one of their own?

If she had time, she could take his magename into her incantations, into the protection of her mage circle, and answer a lot of these questions. If she had time.

She didn't, nor did Cirrus One. Four days. That's the scenario, the schedule she and Mack's team had developed. Whatever Blass was planning would happen within the next four days.

Rand shifted slightly next to her, touched her lightly on the wrist. "The PH," she whispered through tight lips.

Honora Trelmont had risen. Rigo extended his hand, guided her up the small steps to the podium. The vidcams trailed her with their lights.

"Dear friends and kinfolk." She opened her hands, inclined her head slightly. There was a light ripple of applause. "Thank you. It is an honor to share this day with you. It is an honor to share the blessings of the Lady."

She touched the crystal pendant around her neck. "And this is a blessing-filled day. A true shrine of communion available to all, through unhampered access in its own sacred docking bay. A haven, a respite for the troubled, the weary. And, it is my dearest hope, something even more."

She paused, as if to allow her words to sink in. As if to encourage the few whispers now floating around the room. "My dearest hope, and I know it is yours as well, is to share the wisdom and the blessings of Lady Kiasidira not just with the Cirrus Quadrant but with all of civilized space. It is for this reason I've been working with Magefather Rigo and with my husband, the chancellor, to declare Cirrus One a sanctuary. To open it to all peoples in a manner that they need never fear questions when coming here."

Stepping back, she opened her arms wide, raised her voice. "To rid ourselves, once and for all, of the needs for defenses. For instruments of destruction. For this is what the Lady taught us. To seek peace, harmony, and love!"

A slight hand movement from Rigo set the bells jingling again. The murmurs of the crowd were silenced.

I really hate being misquoted, Gillie told Simon.

It doesn't appear the audience is thrilled with her suggestion.

Gillie noted several sets of narrowed eyes on Fleet personnel. They understood, more than the merchants or the dignitaries, how tragic a defenseless station could be.

"I hope to be able to announce, by tomorrow night, that this dream has been made a reality. That thousands and thousands will come to Cirrus to embrace the Lady's teachings. That Cirrus One will be a name on everyone's lips, a required destination in everyone's life."

There was a change in the crowd. Heads nodded in agreement. Gillie recognized a few of the merchants, including a woman who ran Cirrus's largest hotel. Cirrus as a required destination would mean profits, big profits, for them. They might well be willing to take the risk.

Except they didn't know the risk. They didn't know they were dealing with the Fav'lhir.

Gillie realized she was clenching her fists, her fingernails digging into her palms. Her jaw hurt from holding it closed, from holding back words she wanted to say.

They wouldn't believe her. She knew that. In her unassuming freighter uniform, she was just another crazy spacer. Unless she dropped her mental shields and her pretenses and became who she really was, who she'd been trying so very hard not to be for the past month.

No. For her whole life. She'd fought who she was her whole life. She'd never wanted to be the Kiasidira. Until now.

Right now she wanted that more than anything else. She wanted to rip away Rigo's falsity; she wanted to expose Blass for what he was. Challenge him. Destroy him, if she had to. Before he destroyed Cirrus One and the Khalar.

The prime hostess accepted a small pad from one of the acolytes and read the opening lines of a benediction. Rigo raised his hand and the assemblage stood as if one.

She caught Mack studying her from across the room. She might well lose him. It surprised her how calmly that thought came to her. She accepted that now. If he was angry with her because she lied, so be it. Maybe in time he'd forgive her, forget his anger. They could try again. But at least he'd be alive.

For if she didn't follow what she knew she had to do, she'd lose him forever. In battle. Or through the destruction of the station, and all its inhabitants, if Blass's friends arrived.

His death would be impossible to bear. His anger, she could deal with.

Rand suddenly tensed next to her. Gillie glanced at

the security commander, then followed her gaze. A group in civilian clothing, well dressed, standing quietly in an upper row. Gillie scanned the faces, saw nothing amiss. She touched Rand's arm. "Tell me."

Rand's eyes held a brief flash of surprise. "That's Admiral Mack's line," she murmured, then indicated the back of the shrine with a taut jerk of her chin. "Woman. Blue jacket, light-green shirt. Looks familiar, but I can't place her. But it's not a good familiar."

Gillie found the woman. Mid to late forties, she judged. Brown hair cut chin length. Generous mouth, short nose, ruddy complexion. More than that, at this distance, she couldn't tell. But Rand was right. There was something uneasy, something rigid in the woman's posture.

Simon? She sent the image. *See what Fleet and CQPA databases have.*

"I want to get a closer look," Rand said. "Come with me."

They walked casually toward the next aisle break. News media and security were the only ones on the top tier. Rand's uniform and insignia meant they passed unquestioned.

The prime hostess finished her recitation. Chairs squeaked and clothing rustled as everyone took their seats.

Gillie let her gaze wander over the woman in the blue jacket again. Was she alone? A balding man sat on her left but leaned slightly away from her. The body language could be unconscious or deliberate. He ducked his head, nodded as the man next to him said something. Gillie waited, but he didn't share the conversation with the woman in the blue jacket.

On the woman's right was a girl, not much more than a teenager, in a black and yellow tunic top. Two people sat next to her and, judging from the resemblance, they were her parents. The woman in blue could be an aunt, a family friend. But in the five minutes since Rand had brought the woman to Gillie's attention, neither the teen nor the balding man had interacted with the woman.

"Any better?" Gillie asked Rand over the ringing of hand bells. Rigo was saying something she didn't bother listening to.

The commander's eyes were narrowed. "Almost. It's the face. For some reason, her hair's different. Style, or just the length, maybe."

And color.

Simon! What do you have?

A woman with prematurely white hair that's been her trademark. They call her the Snow Queen. Though she answers to Faydra Trace. Commodore Faydra Trace, Fav'lhir Attack Corps.

FAC? She's FAC? The information jarred Gillie, made no sense until she remembered her own recollection was over three hundred years old. The FAC had all new players. The names she knew—Amadeo, Harrange, Starke—were long dead. She'd taken out Starke's ship herself.

Is she mageline?

Not according to Fleet information. And, no, they don't know she's here. So that means unless she was hidden on Blass's ship, she came in through your "sacred" docking bay.

An FAC commodore. Here, on Cirrus. Without Cirrus's knowledge or permission. Blass might be able to keep his associations hidden, but Trace wouldn't. It would take only moments for Mack's team to verify her identity. This might be the break, the proof they needed to stop Blass. Or at least to let him know his plans were rapidly coming apart.

"Faydra Trace." Gillie said the name softly.

Rand started almost imperceptibly, her quick intake of breath evidence of her shock. Gillie saw her hand hover over her watch, then pull away.

"Not here," she said, almost to herself.

Gillie frowned.

Rand tilted her wrist. "I can key a red alert to my people from this. But we've got to talk to Mack—Admiral Mack first. You know who she is, then?"

Gillie nodded. "She must have come in through the shrine's open bay. Or your people would've picked her up on an ID scan."

"Damned open access."

The bells chimed twice.

"And this, heartfriends and kinfolk, concludes our first shared blessing in the Shrine of Communion." Rigo's voice boomed out. The four acolytes shook their bells vigorously. Then voices in the shrine increased, people turning to one another, commenting, saying good-bye.

"I'm putting two uniforms on her," Rand said, keeping her voice low. "Have them stay on her until a pair of my undercover operatives can take over." She stepped toward a young man in Fleet blacks to her right. He was as stocky as Rand was, with short, curly dark hair. "Leyden, we've got a Code Six." She motioned him closer, spoke hurriedly in his ear. He nodded, grabbed the elbow of a wiry female security officer next to him.

Gillie watched them slip through the crowd and head for Faydra Trace. They veered off before they got to her row, climbed a parallel aisle. No one would've thought they were watching the woman in the blue jacket. They knew what they were doing.

Can you follow her, Simon?

I can track her through any active security cam.

If Rand's people lose her, let me know.

Mack and Tobias were already moving toward the exit when Gillie spotted them. Rand saw them as well.

But so did someone else. Blass. The well-dressed man was standing in front of Honora Trelmont but not listening to her. His gaze was locked on Mack's retreating figure, his mouth a thin line.

Something cold ran through Gillie, something cold and desperate and ugly. She thought of the carved doors to Blass's cabin, the forms writhing in agony. The feeling was the same.

Blass no doubt saw Admiral Rynan Makarian as the final impediment to his plans and fully intended to make him suffer for it. Even through her shields, she could feel the venom in the sorcerer's gaze. No, more than that. Blass had placed a death mark on Mack, confident in his success to kill the admiral and claim Cirrus One for the Fav'lhir.

Gillie fully intended to make Blass fail.

Gillie and Rand intercepted Mack in the corridor not far from the shrine's exit. The rumble of voices and sound of plodding, shuffling feet echoed off the dark gray bulkheads. The line at the entrance behind them was long but finally moving, as those who hadn't been permitted inside during the ceremony were allowed in. Those departing the shrine did so quickly, as if anxious to avoid contact with Cirrus's more common elements.

Gillie stepped to Mack's side, Tobias and Pryor behind her. She wouldn't tell him here what she'd sensed from Blass. Finding Trace was first priority. And as long as Gillie stayed near Mack, she felt she could counter whatever Blass tried to do. Rand appeared on his right. "Sir. We have a Code Six in progress."

Other than a slight narrowing of his eyes, Mack showed no agitation at this news. But Gillie felt the tension ripple through him. "Understood. The club's the only secure place—"

"My ship's better," Gillie put in. Blass could never board her ship. Plus, Simon could be an active participant in the discussion.

She caught a small glint of appreciation in Mack's eyes at her offer.

"Agreed," he said. "Gentlemen?" He glanced over his shoulder at Tobias and Pryor.

"Right behind you, sir."

They wove through the crowd on the stairs. Mack caught her hand in his at one point, squeezed it, but there was little time for any personal concerns. Gillie suspected that everyone's thoughts were on the Code Six: possible hostile intruder under surveillance.

Simon opened the hatch-lock door as they arrived. The interior walls of the ship glowed dimly, brightening as Gillie headed for her small ready room. Her ship was in full interior crystal phase now. There was nothing to hide.

Gillie waved Mack into the chair at the head of the table, took the one next to him. Tobias and Pryor filled the other two seats.

Rand remained standing, one hand resting lightly on the back of her chair. "We've got an FAC officer on station. Faydra Trace."

Pryor uttered something harsh under his breath. Mack folded his hands on the tabletop, his face as impassive as if Rand had just announced the officers' mess was substituting rice for potatoes. "Tell me."

"I saw a woman in a blue jacket sitting in one of the upper rows during the shrine ceremony. There was something familiar about her but not enough for me to put a name to the face. I realized later it's because she's changed her appearance somewhat. Her hair color." Rand touched her own dark hair.

"Captain Davré and I changed position to facilitate identification," she continued. "She recognized Trace, a commodore with the FAC. I immediately saw she was correct."

"Simon identified her, based on your security files," Gillie said. "I don't know Trace."

Rand's mouth started to open, then closed. Gillie guessed at her question. "I have a telepathic link with Simon, yes, Commander."

Rand nodded, but her eyes were wide. She blinked, turned to Mack. "I've got two officers trailing her and have activated a pair of undercovers to intercept. We'll pick her up for questioning on your command, sir."

"Do we know how she arrived on station?" Mack asked Rand. "If she's here on diplomatic sanction, both your office and mine would've been notified. Correction: *should* have been notified. Before I create an intergalactic incident, are we sure she's here illegally?"

"Simon checked that," Gillie said.

"Yes, sir, I did." Simon's voice spilled from the comm panel in the room. "She didn't enter through any approved terminal on station. I checked visual and palm-scan records for the past two weeks. However, two unregistered ships discharged passengers in the shrine's bay earlier. Lieutenant Tobias's tracing program listed them as the *Grateful Wanderer* and *Richford's Azure Star*. But since security cameras were disconnected I have no records there to verify who disembarked. I did, however, find a match for her palm scan in the Garamond Hotel registry. She registered two and a half hours ago under the name of Edrea Starne."

Mack's smile was thin. "A slight variation on her ancestor, Admiral Edrom Starke. He tried to take our system over three hundred years ago. Looks like history's repeating itself."

So Trace was Starke's descendant. Gillie suddenly felt old.

Rand straightened. "Shall I have her picked up for questioning, sir?"

"Do it. I'll notify HQ on Prime, just in case someone misfiled her diplomatic clearances." The tone of Mack's voice stated he knew such clearance didn't exist. "Hold her in security and don't, whatever you do, let this leak out to Halbert or the PH. Or Blass."

Rand left, taking Tobias with her. Pryor returned to ops. Mack leaned back in his chair after the door closed behind Pryor, ran his hand over his face. Gillie sensed both the tension and the tiredness in him.

"She may not admit to working with Blass," he said.

"She won't have to." Gillie waited for Mack to read between the lines of her answer.

"Sometimes I forget you're a telepath." He shook his head slowly. His tension, his weariness, overrode any other emotions she could sense from him. "You don't look ... well ... I guess we've all always thought of Raheirans as being different from us."

"We're not. Except in a few minor things."

"Sentient crystalships and telepathic talents are hardly minor." He arched one eyebrow, but at least he was smiling. "It's a good thing you're on our side."

I have been. For over three hundred years. Gillie had never felt that more strongly than now. "I need to be in on the interview with Trace from the beginning. I want her to know up front I'm Raheiran, that she can't lie. We don't have time to waste playing games with her, or Blass."

"Agreed." Mack's face became serious. "I ran a few investigations of my own. Pulled in favors, checked with reliable sources on Blass. He's been involved with Honora Trelmont for over two years, and his connections run deep. He's also taken some interesting vacations lately, out to Tynder, and Ladrin One."

Fleet maintained bases on those stations as well, Gillie knew. "Sounds like he was shopping for a place to stage his invasion."

"Or he already has people there."

Gods, yes. Had her tactical skills really deteriorated that much in the past month? She hadn't foreseen that possibility, but she should have. She looked at Mack, nodded. "Sometimes," she said, "I forget you're the admiral. You don't look . . . well . . . gruff and pompous and authoritative like others I've known."

He smiled at her lighthearted rendition of his earlier comment, but any response was interrupted by the trill of his comm set. "Makarian." He listened closely, nodded. "On our way."

He turned back to Gillie. "Rand has our Code Six in custody."

Fleet Security on Cirrus was a maze of inner offices and gray-walled corridors. Gillie followed Mack to a room not much larger than her own ready room, and not dissimilar in layout, with a long table with four chairs. But the wall by the door had additional chairs lining it. Tobias rose from one of those when Gillie and Mack walked in.

Rand stood also, then took her seat when Mack nodded. She was at the head of the table, the woman in the blue jacket at the other end. Sonicuffs locked the woman's left wrist to the arm of her chair, but she didn't seem the least bit discomforted by it. Nor by Mack's arrival.

She was a muscular woman, her skin mottled like someone who'd been dirtside, out in the atmosphere recently, and wasn't used to it. Her eyes were a dark amber color. They narrowed slightly under Gillie's scrutiny.

Not mageline. Gillie did a brief mental scan of Faydra Trace, felt nothing other than suspicion. Apprehension. No fear. She was, after all, an FAC officer. No one ever faulted Fav'lhir military training.

"Commodore Trace." Mack locked his hands behind his back, looked down at the brown-haired woman.

"You're mistaken. My name's Starne. Your officer here has my ID."

There was a small datatab on the table in front of Rand. Mack glanced dismissively at it. "Your palm scan says otherwise."

"So she said." Trace jerked her chin in Rand's direction. "Said I'm some Fav'lhir officer. Since I can't ask the Fav'lhir to present proof your files are wrong, how can I defend myself?"

"That's what I'm here to help with, Miselle Starne." Gillie stepped away from Mack, extending her hand in a friendly greeting, trusting that if Trace wanted to stay in her assumed identity, she'd accept the offered handshake. "I'm Captain Gillaine Davré," Gillie said as Trace clasped her hand. She squeezed the woman's fingers lightly and, using the power of the rune stones, opened the first small pathway to create a mind link where she could read the woman's every thought. "Raheiran Special Forces."

Trace jerked her hand back with a violent move, then appeared to realize her mistake, tried to cover her reaction. "I . . . I thought you were with legal services. Not another grunt."

"It won't work, Trace." Mack's voice was stern. "Shall we get down to business?"

"This is crazy." Trace shifted nervously in her chair. "You accuse me, then get one of your people to pretend to be a Raheiran witch."

Gillie pulled her ward stones from her pocket, placed them in a line on the table. Their purple glow ran over her hand, up her arm. "I'm not pretending."

Trace stared at the stones. "Good trick."

Gillie smiled. The fear that was so noticeably absent before now radiated from Trace like a pulsing haze. "You can believe what you choose." Gillie picked up the Ladri stone, held it between her fingers. She sent a trail of its energy toward Trace. The woman stiffened.

Gillie grasped at Trace's mind with her own. *Either you have gone totally mad, or what you see and hear is real.*

Trace's harsh gasp gave her her answer. The woman heard her—painfully, Gillie could tell, by the narrowing of her eyes, the tightness around her mouth. Even with the stones' buffer, the experience of a telepath probing to an untrained mind was a shock. For once, Gillie didn't care.

"Tell me about Carrickal Grel Te'lard Blass," Gillie said, her voice deceptively soft.

Trace shot to her feet, her left arm straining against the cuff locked to the chair.

Mack stepped quickly in front of Gillie, like a *pantrelon* protecting its own. "Sit down, Commodore."

Trace sat, but slowly. Gillie felt the woman's emotions shift, change. Gone was the innocent-victim pretense, the helpless woman involved in a case of mistaken identity. The real Faydra Trace surfaced now. Hard. Defiant. Cold. The Snow Queen.

"You'll get nothing from me." Her words were terse, aimed at Mack.

Gillie kept a light monitor on Trace's thoughts, aware that suicide was not an unlikely option. Trace appeared to wear no jewelry, so a small pill hidden in a ring or a pendant wasn't an available means. But there were other ways, other places, other methods.

The stones on the table glowed softly. Gillie kept their power active. She touched the small Vedri stone, moved it to the right. The Khal, the largest, she pushed closer to Trace. "Have you ever seen Blass do this?" she asked conversationally.

Images flashed through her mind. Carrick Blass on a ship, not his. A Fav'lhir cruiser. She knew it as Trace knew it. Just as Trace hadn't known the identity, or purpose, of the stones Blass had used that day. Only that Blass had moved the stones without touching them. Therefore, in Trace's opinion, Gillie, who needed to handle the stones, wasn't nearly as powerful.

Gillie looked up at Mack. "Blass met with her and her team about six months ago on board a ship called the *Mezatarra*. Fav'lhir Raider-class cruiser. Captain is—"

"Damn you to hell, you filthy witch!" Trace leaned forward, her face contorted in rage. "He'll kill you. And I'll be damned glad when he does."

Mack went rigid. It was something Gillie felt more than saw. He was too much the professional to let his reactions show at this point. But he was also unable to keep those same, hidden feelings from washing over her. She had to pull herself mentally away from him. His emotions, especially his protective ones toward herself, threatened to overwhelm her. Threatened to interfere with the deep link she'd established with Trace when she'd clasped the woman's hand.

She touched the stones again, adjusting their pattern. Rand watched from the other end of the table, eyes wide. Gillie couldn't see Tobias behind her but felt his approval, his admiration. She needed that. Mack unsettled her.

"The *Mezatarra*'s captain is Almer Candler." Gillie relived Trace's memory as if it were her own. "He transferred three operatives under Commodore Trace's command to Blass's ship at that time. Blass took them to Tynder Station." Mack had been right. There were other Fav'lhir agents in Khalaran space.

"Where else?" Mack asked.

Suddenly Trace moved, her right hand swinging out to knock the ward stones from the table. Mack was quicker. He grabbed her arm, yanked her to her feet.

"Don't." His face was dark, his tone, darker. If he had bared his teeth and revealed a *pantrelon*'s fangs, Gillie wouldn't have been surprised.

Trace's mouth thinned, but she sat once again.

"Mister Tobias." Mack didn't take his gaze from Trace's face. "Lock a cuff on her other arm."

"Yes, sir."

Hatred. It burned around Faydra Trace as hotly as the mage cabinet's spellforms had burned Gillie's fingers earlier. Hatred at Tobias, who firmly held her arm down while he engaged the sonicuff. Hatred at Mack, who stood silently, authoritatively. Calmly.

Intense hatred at Gillie herself. A despised Raheiran. A witch who consorted with impures.

"Where else?" Mack repeated. "I want names, locations."

Gillie drew the answers to Mack's questions from Trace's memories, in disjointed pieces at first as the woman fought as best she could, holding unrelated, nonsensical images in her mind. Thinking of songs, mathematical equations. Those things delayed Gillie but didn't stop her.

Rand took notes on her datapad.

"Send that urgent, priority-coded, to HQ, Tynder, Primus, Ladrin. Advise ops to go to yellow-alert status." Mack turned back to Trace. "It's over, Commodore."

"You can't stop Carrick Blass." Trace's voice was raspy, strained. Her disgust at having her mind so summarily raked washed over Gillie.

"That's exactly what we're doing," Mack said.

Trace thrust her chin at Gillie. "With a telepath? A mere witch?" She smiled. "You're good, Captain. But you're not Blass. If you know anything at all about a Grel Te'lard, you know you can't stop him. We will take this station away from you."

Trace's pride was her downfall. But it also presented Gillie with the most chilling revelation, one she'd feared hearing, one she had no way of stopping alone. She straightened slowly in her chair and tried to keep the note of urgency out of her voice. She didn't want to give Trace the satisfaction of knowing the information worried her. "FAC has two starcruisers and a squadron of Rover-Twos using the mining rafts in Runemist as cover."

"Damn you!" Trace realized her mistake too late.

"He's integrated some crystal technology to the cruisers," she continued, ignoring Trace's outburst. "They're emitting freighter readings but won't pass a visual." She hesitated, sorted images from Trace again. "That's what happened a few weeks ago. Those two ships that attacked—or appeared to attack—this station. Blass and Commodore Trace were testing that technology, and testing Cirrus's sensor capabilities."

Mack glanced quickly at Tobias. "Inform the *Vedritor*. Code One, full alert."

"Use my office," Rand said as Tobias rose.

Mack turned his face toward Gillie. She shook her head. "That's all she knows. Blass called her on station because he wanted her here before her ships move in. But she doesn't know what his plans are with Rigo or Honora Trelmont."

"Your loss," Trace said bitterly.

That was true. "She was scheduled to meet with Blass and Rigo twenty minutes ago. They're probably beginning to suspect something's happened." If they'd waited to bring Trace in, they might have learned Blass's entire plan. But they also could have lost her, lost precious time as well.

Mack motioned to Trace. "Rand, get one of your people to take her back to lockup, then have your team meet me at the shrine in ten. We move on Blass. Now."

27

A dozen strategies raced through Mack's mind, followed by another dozen counterstrategies. Yet in spite of all that activity, the loudest sound was Gillie's footsteps, hurrying to catch up to him. He'd told her to stay in Rand's office. Clearly, she hadn't obeyed.

"I have to go with you, Mack."

The corridors of Cirrus One had returned to their usual early-evening crush after being eerily vacant during the opening of the shrine. People bustled about their business, totally unaware that Fav'lhir ships were within attack range. Totally unaware that a Fav'lhir agent and Grel Te'lard sorcerer were on station.

Mack wasn't quite sure what the latter portended, but he knew he was about to find out. "No, you don't," he answered without glancing at her. He didn't need to see determination written on her face. It was clear in her tone. "Rand and I will handle this. It's routine."

"Then why," she persisted, as they sidestepped a worker guiding a small antigrav cart, "are you going back to your office to get your laser pistol?"

This time he did slant her a glance. The ease with which she'd taken his destination and purpose from his mind startled him. Raheiran. Mageline. He still wasn't quite used to that. "Because."

"Same reason I have to go with you. Because."

"Gillaine." He hesitated at his office door, then palmed it open, motioning her inside. The lights, sensing a presence, flickered on.

"I don't have time to argue." He tapped in a code on his deskcomp, unlocking a lower drawer. "This is official business. You may be RSF. But you said it yourself: you're not official."

"And I was back there with Faydra Trace?"

"Trace was already in custody." And had been searched for weapons. She was harmless. "What happens in Rand's office stays there. I don't have to file an official report to explain your unofficial presence."

"I *can* take care of myself." Gillie planted her hands on her hips and glared at him. She wasn't listening to his words, he knew, but reading his emotions. And bucking against his desire to protect her.

He pulled a small laser pistol and holster from the drawer, then stripped off his jacket. He was still in his formal dress uniform, with a white shirt underneath. No time to change to something more utilitarian. No time to argue with Gillie. He checked the pistol, then shoved it back in the holster.

"You're not going to stop him with that," Gillie said as he clipped the holster to his belt.

He reached for his jacket. "Blass isn't stupid. He'll

play innocent, deny our accusations, just like Trace did. He's not going to start doing magic tricks in front of the PH."

"Magic tricks." She let out a harsh breath. "Grel Te'lard sorcerers don't do magic tricks. You threaten them and they start killing people."

"I don't intend to put him in that position until he's securely in Rand's lockup." He sealed the front of his jacket.

"It doesn't matter what you intend." Gillie didn't hide the frustration in her voice. "He'll know exactly why you're there."

Mack shoved the desk drawer closed. It clicked loudly as the lock cycled.

"He's mageline, Mack. Telepathic. And he doesn't have the same scruples a Raheiran has. Faydra Trace is missing. You walk in with Rand and Tobias, he'll be in your mind immediately. You'll feel a little dizzy at first and by the time the headache and nausea hit hard, he'll already know what you intend to do, where you've placed security. Then he'll insert commands of his own, make you do things you wouldn't intend to do. Like kill one of your own officers."

His gaze shot from the data on his deskscreen to her face. He'd been monitoring station status but her words—her admission of what a mageline sorcerer could do—wrenched his attention away. Again, he realized how little he knew about Captain Gillaine Davré. Was it only her scruples that made her different from Blass?

No. Gillie might be mageline but by her own admission she was an RSF captain, not a sorcerer. Mack felt sure a Raheiran sorceress would hold a much higher rank than military adviser.

His mageline military adviser was watching him, eyes narrowed. "You can't stop Blass," she said firmly.

"He won't have time to pull my intentions from my mind. He'll be looking at Rand's best security team all around him. Eight laser pistols on full power will tell him all he needs to know."

"You're not listening. He'll kill you."

"It's been tried before. That's part of my job description."

"And stopping a Grel Te'lard is mine."

"Gillaine." Gods, he didn't want to argue with her. He traced the line of her jaw with one finger. The stubborn line of her jaw. The lavender in her eyes darkened, the color not dissimilar to the mist that had swirled over her skin from the crystal shard. She was Raherian. Blass was a sorcerer. This was something out of his range of expertise and squarely part of hers, yet there were still the political games to consider. Blass's connections to the chancellor. Honora Trelmont's presence. If things went wrong, he'd not only have to explain an RSF captain's unofficial participation but why HQ hadn't been informed RSF was involved. He felt torn between what had to be done and the way he knew Fleet would demand things be handled.

He sighed. "Have you ever faced a Grel Te'lard before?"

A corner of her mouth quirked slightly. "Few weeks ago. I destroyed one of their ships in Riftspace. That's how I ended up here."

She'd mentioned that. He'd assumed her appearance

had been an accident. But then, he'd made a lot of assumptions about Gillaine Davré, most of them wrong. Something hovered on the edges of his mind; facts that fit, yet didn't. One of these days he'd ask her for answers, personal and political. The latter was the only thing he had time for now. "Does Blass know about this?" It could well explain the timing of the sorcerer's appearance, the Rim Gate Project notwithstanding.

"He has no idea I'm here, if that's what you're asking. Actually, the Fav don't know I made it through the Rift alive."

"You're sure?"

Something hard, cold, flickered in her eyes. "If the Fav thought I was here, they'd have sent more than just Blass."

He remembered Faydra Trace's reaction to Gillie: hatred, fear. It was clear Trace knew far more than he did about Raheiran mageline talents. But then, the FAC commodore was under the command of a sorcerer. Perhaps it was time to even out the playing field.

Reluctantly, he made a decision, shoving his heart's concerns away, trying now to think only as a military officer. One who would battle it out later with HQ, if he had to. "The shrine is a public place. While I can't officially have you accompany Rand and myself, neither can I stop you from being there."

"The shrine's still open?"

"I don't like it either." Mack knew her concern was over hostages or innocents being injured. "We're trying to keep most people away. But I can't order the shrine closed without tipping our hand."

"Who else goes in with us?"

"Five of Rand's people. They know Blass will have

no regard for innocents. He's labeled *violent-hostile*. It's part of the package." His comm set trilled and he flipped it up into position. "Makarian."

"Rand, sir. Three minutes."

"On our way."

The shrine was almost empty. But *almost* was enough to add an extra layer of concerns to the ones Mack already had. As the wide double doors slid closed behind his team, he automatically noted a family with two children sitting quietly in one of the upper rows, far to his left. An elderly man, alone, below them, three rows from the podium, his head bowed. A man in CQPA orange stood below the suspended holograph of the Lady, seeming to study it. Across the way, two women trotted up the aisle steps.

The old man stood shakily, ambled for the exit. One less to worry about. One less, plus Gillie. He hadn't seen her yet, but he knew she was in here somewhere.

Rigo's office was along the back wall, a small door marked with the lightning-and-crescent-moon symbol. The door was closed. But Rigo's office had the usual vidcams. Mack was sure the magefather was aware of their approach.

Mack loosened the seal on his jacket. Rand's and Tobias's laser pistols were in plain sight on their hips. The rest of Rand's team lingered behind, waiting for Mack's signal to approach.

Rigo's office door slid open when Mack and Rand reached the edge of the raised circular podium. The portly magefather thrust one arm into the air in greeting, then hurried toward them, meeting up with them as they stepped down the other side. "Admiral. Commander Rand. Lieutenant. How can I help you?"

"I need to speak to the prime hostess and Senator Halbert." Mack recited the agreed-upon ploy to remove the PH and the senator safely, and without incident, from the scene: a coded transmit waited for them in ops. Halbert's own security plus ones under Rand's command would escort them to a secure office instead.

"Oh?" Suspicion radiated from Rigo. "All this trouble. You could've sent a message."

"Standard security procedure," Mack answered blandly. "The prime hostess requires special handling."

Rigo blinked, seemed to accept that. "Of course." The office door slid open again. Blass emerged, headed in their direction with a confident stride.

"Problems, my friend?" Blass called out as he approached. He laid his hand on Rigo's shoulder.

"We need the prime hostess and the senator in ops," Mack said before Rigo could reply. "Codelocked incoming transmit. We have an escort waiting." He looked at Rigo. "We'll return them to you here later, Magefather, if you like."

"That would be—"

Mack saw Blass's hand tighten on Rigo's shoulder.

"I'll escort them myself," Blass said.

"I'm sorry, Mister Blass. That's not possible."

"Of course it is."

Mack met Blass's gaze, intensity for intensity. "It's not."

"I'll get the prime hostess." Rand brushed past Rigo and Blass before they could stop her.

Blass's mouth thinned but he said nothing. Mack knew he'd judged the man correctly. As he'd told Gillie, Blass would stay in his role of a magnate in the Khalaran financial world and a playmate of politicians. Revealing himself as a Grel Te'lard sorcerer would only get him killed. No, Mack knew Blass wouldn't reveal that aspect of himself until he'd taken control of Cirrus. Something Mack had no intention of letting him do.

Honora Trelmont followed Rand down the short aisle, looking slightly flustered. Halbert was a few feet behind them, his jacket over his arm. A flash of moonlight and starlight caught Mack's eye. Gillie, striding aimlessly past the first row of seats on the other side of the podium. Part of him was relieved to see her, but part of him wanted her far away from here, away from Blass.

"I don't understand." The prime hostess frowned. "But if you say I need to..."

"We have an escort waiting," Rand said.

"Or we can use my security." Halbert motioned to his bodyguards standing along the far wall.

The prime hostess ignored the senator. "Rick? You're coming with us?"

Blass shot a hard look at Mack. "My presence is requested."

"Sorry." Mack's answer was quick, final. And far from contrite.

Honora Trelmont straightened. "Admiral Makarian. If I want Carrick Blass to accompany me, he will. Your permission is not required."

"With all due respect, Prime Hostess, it is. You're in a Fleet military facility. Mister Blass is a civilian and not permitted in my ops." Not now. Not ever.

"We'll catch up with him later, Honora." Halbert touched her arm. "This might be the transmit from Derron we're waiting for."

"He needs to be there. He *must* be there."

Blass's mouth curved into a small smile.

But Halbert seemed slightly taken aback by the insistent, petulant tone. "Honora—"

"Prime Hostess! I am the prime hostess, and my orders will not be disobeyed. Not by you, Carlo, and not," she added, glaring at Mack, "by you. I can have you stripped of your rank."

"Then strip me of my rank, Prime Hostess," Mack replied calmly. "That will take weeks, months. And you'll have missed this transmit, possibly from the chancellor. Possibly granting sanctuary status to Cirrus One. That was, if I remember, your purpose in coming here?"

Honora Trelmont opened her mouth as if to speak, then stopped.

"Go listen to the message, my dear," Blass said. "I'm sure Admiral Makarian will have no objection to my meeting you in the corridor later."

"You...you will be there, Rick? When I come out?" The hard tone was gone from the prime hostess's voice.

"I'll be there."

"Prime Hostess?" Rand motioned for the exit.

Honora Trelmont stepped in front of Rand, Halbert by her side. She glanced back one more time at Blass. He nodded.

Mack listened as their footsteps faded to be replaced by louder ones. Rand's team, coming up behind him.

Blass's eyes narrowed. "If you'll excuse me, I have some business back at my ship." He moved as if to follow the prime hostess.

Mack thrust out one arm, barring his way. "Not yet."

Tobias stood in front, blocking him.

Blass glanced at Tobias, then frowned at Mack. "Really, Admiral. I actually do have to check my messages. A colleague of mine seems to have forgotten an appointment. It's not as if I'm going to launch an assault on your operations center."

Mack didn't miss Blass's choice of words. Or the fact that he'd admitted Faydra Trace's absence. "We have a message from that colleague of yours. You'll come with us, now."

"Which colleague would that be?" Blass asked slowly. Deliberately. He stared at Mack.

"We'll discuss that in Commander Rand's office." Mack glanced over his shoulder as Rand's returning bootsteps sounded on the hard floor of the podium.

Blass shot a narrow-eyed glance at Rand. "Chief of Security, isn't she? Are you thinking of charging me with some crime?"

Rigo suddenly sputtered to life. "You can't be serious, Admiral! Carrick Blass is ... well, he's known the chancellor for years. He knows senators, the minister of trade. He's very influential." He waved his hand as if to shoo Mack away. "This is nonsense."

"Then perhaps the situation regarding this colleague of his is in error," Mack said smoothly. "But until he comes with us to the security office, we won't know for sure."

Rigo switched a glance from Mack to Blass, then back to Mack again. "You're making a mistake."

Mack ignored him. "Mister Blass?"

"I've no time for your games," Blass answered. "Leave me alone, or suffer the consequences."

"Is that a threat?" Rand asked tightly.

"That's a promise. Get out."

"You must leave," Rigo echoed. "This is a holy place."

Mack gave a small nod to Rand. She spoke into her mouth mike. "Khal One. Clear the shrine."

Two Fleet security officers stepped out of the shadows, moved swiftly toward the few people scattered in the seats. Their voices echoed in the tense silence. "Security emergency. Go to the exit now."

"You've no right to do this!" Rigo's face reddened.

"What kind of security emergency?" A woman's nasal voice cut short Rigo's harangue.

Johnna Hebbs, out of uniform, strode across the podium toward them, the stocky form of Officer Leyden hurrying behind. With a sinking feeling, Mack recognized Hebbs as one of the women who'd been climbing to a higher row of seats earlier. He doubted she was here off duty. More likely, she'd included herself as part of CQPA's security arrangements. And as he couldn't tell her who—and what—Blass really was, she no doubt thought Blass was being threatened. Not the one who was the threat. "What's going on, Mack? You need more officers?" She fished in her jacket for her pocket comm.

"Everything's under control. Go with Leyden now," Mack replied firmly.

"Stationmaster Hebbs." Blass's voice was cool. "You seem upset. In fact, you don't look well at all."

Hebbs gasped for breath, her eyes wide. Her hand clasped her throat, her pocket comm slipping through her fingers. She stumbled forward, blood trailing from the side of her mouth. Leyden lunged for her just as she collapsed onto the podium floor.

Mack grabbed for Blass. The sorcerer stepped back quickly and raised his right hand in a casual gesture. His mouth twisted in a feral grin. "Seems you have a minor emergency, Admiral." Hebbs's anguished moaning punctuated Blass's words. "I'll leave you to handle it."

Mack spoke into his mike, never taking his gaze off Blass. "Makarian to sick bay. Code Red, my location."

Rigo seemed frozen on Blass's right, his broad face creased in confusion. His gaze shifted nervously toward Blass, but Blass turned away.

Mack had no intention of letting him leave. Nor had Tobias, who'd sprinted forward, laser pistol drawn. "Don't move. Sir."

Mack pulled out his own pistol. "Whatever you did to her, stop it." He glanced down at Hebbs, startled to see Gillie at the stationmaster's side. The dark-haired woman was unconscious, her limbs twitching spasmodically.

There was a hardness in Gillie's face when she looked up at him. No, past him. At Blass, who watched her from over his shoulder. *"Fielgha."* She spat out the word as she rose. "Release her."

Blass's smile faded. Mack could've sworn something crackled in the air between them. Rigo took a step backward, shaking his head.

Blass's gaze zigzagged, as if reading that same something in the air. "Raheiran." His voice was flat. Mack couldn't tell if Gillie's appearance surprised him or not.

"Release her," Gillie repeated.

Tobias clamped his hand on Blass's upper arm. "Do as she—"

Snarling, Blass spun. Tobias flailed backward as if jettisoned out of an airlock. Mack whipped his pistol up, saw Blass's eyes narrow. Then pain seized Mack's chest, the air forced from his lungs. He staggered, gasping, not understanding what was happening to him, only that Blass was the source. "Bastard!" He pressed the trigger. White laser fire streaked.

Blass swung one arm in an arc. Mack's charge sparked, illogically, impossibly dissolving like a bright cloud of dust. "Fool." Blass's voice held a deadly note. The dust cloud solidified, whirling toward Mack as if sucked backed into the pistol in his hand.

"Mack!" Rand screamed his name.

Everything went purple. Mack dropped to his knees on instinct, then realized everything hadn't turned purple. Only things close to the sword inches from his face. He squinted through the haze, saw

Blass's eyes widen. Rigo's mouth opened, but no sound came out.

"Carrickal Grel Te'lard Blass," Gillie said. The purple mist hovered around her. She pointed the sword at Blass. "You will not take this station. You will not harm my people."

Mack shoved himself to his feet, his ears ringing, his chest aching. Rand's team surged up beside him, pistols drawn. He held up his hand, halting them. He'd just learned, painfully, what a sorcerer could do with a laser-pistol discharge.

And he'd just seen an RSF captain stop a Grel Te'lard. With a sword, of all things. One that was oddly like one he'd revered, years ago, with his grandfather.

"Impossible." Rigo gasped out the word. Tobias trudged over next to Mack. Blass took one step back, eyes narrowed. He clenched his right hand.

"Don't." Gillie adjusted her grip on the sword. "Don't even try it." She splayed her left hand. A ring of lavender fire flowed from the floor around Blass and Rigo.

"Very good." Blass arched one eyebrow. "Including your emulation of Lady Kiasidira's essence and sword. But immortality isn't a Kiasidiran talent. Our ship destroyed hers over three hundred years ago."

Mack didn't understand essences, but he'd recognized the sword too. Gillie must have duplicated Lady Kiasidira's sword as a means to intimidate Blass. But the sorcerer had seen through the ploy. Mack glanced at Tobias, ready to take action if Blass challenged Gillie. To his surprise, his second in command's mouth was quirked in an odd smile.

"I will take this station," Blass continued. "One Raheiran witch cannot stop me." He opened his hand. The lavender flames flickered, died.

Mack raised his pistol as Blass barked out a harsh, satisfied laugh. The sorcerer stepped forward.

No, Mack! Don't fire! Pull your team back! Gillie's voice rang, not out loud, but in Mack's mind. That startled him, halting the signal he was going to give the security team, a signal Gillie pulled from his mind. There was a sharp ache over his eyes that disappeared as quickly as it appeared. She was monitoring his thoughts.

He didn't have time to be concerned about her unexpected intrusion. Blass raised both hands. Light flared. Mack flinched, grabbing for Gillie to push her behind him. She sidled out of his reach, swinging her sword. Purple sparks cascaded, dancing up from the flames again visible on the floor. The fire shot up into the form of a burning cylinder, surrounding Blass and Rigo. The magefather fell to his knees, his arms over his head. Blass jerked backward. His face twisted in anger as he shouted something Mack couldn't understand.

But evidently Gillie did. She swore under her breath.

Blass clasped his hands together. The fire-laced cylinder exploded.

"Get down!" Gillie lashed out with her sword.

Thousands of pinpricks danced over Mack's skin. He dropped to a crouch, sighted, fired—praying Blass was too distracted to send the pistol's energy back at them again.

The security teams' lasers whined over his shoulder.

Leyden, his body protectively over Hebbs, added his shots from Mack's left.

Someone screamed but Mack didn't turn, didn't take his gaze off Blass, who was down on one knee, both hands splayed before him. Laser fire flared impotently against what seemed to be an invisible shield, sizzled, and died.

Only Gillie stood, her sword arcing through the air, deflecting what she could see and Mack couldn't. Magic. Dark magic.

"Gillie!" Damn her, she was too close to Blass. Anger and fear surged through Mack. He rose. If she could distract Blass, maybe he could tackle him. He and Tobias could—

Pain seared his body a second time. Mack's vision hazed, his throat closed. He fell, hard, on both knees, aware that his laser pistol had dropped from his hand. Something vile writhed through him, twisting, gnawing.

He heard a keening cry. Tobias, on the floor next to him, spasming in pain.

Gillie. Where was...He forced his face around. She stood, arms raised, sword over her head, and for a moment all he could think of was the holo of the Lady in the temple. Gillie's posture, the hard determination on her face, the incandescent glow of the sword— Gillie looked like Lady Kiasidira. *No,* the *Kiasidira,* his mind corrected.

Then pain blanked his vision again. His limbs felt numb. He was dying.

Blass had been right. One Raheiran witch, even an RSF captain, was no match for a Grel Te'lard.

Mack inched his hand forward, feeling blindly for

his laser pistol. Gillie had done all she could, but she couldn't stop Blass. He had one choice. He could key the pistol to overload. Turn it into a small bomb, shove it toward Blass. It was his only chance. Their only chance.

His fingers grazed the pistol. He drew it into his palm, forced his eyes to focus, and hazarded one last look at Gillie. His Gillaine. There wouldn't be a wedding. Only a funeral.

Her sword winked out as he watched. Gods, Blass had destroyed a Raheiran sword. The sorcerer struggled to his feet, his arm stretched out toward Gillie. Beads of sweat covered his face.

Mack flipped the laser pistol over, feeling for the safety. His fingers were clumsy, useless. He groaned in frustration.

"You will not take this station," Gillie repeated, her voice shaking. "You will not harm my people." She drew in a harsh breath. *"Tal tay Raheira!"*

A blue haze sparkled through the lavender mist around her. For a moment, Mack thought he saw the shape of her sword, but it was as if it were inside her, part of her. Then her skin, her clothes, glowed with a clear, golden hue.

She chanted something. Mack didn't understand the Raheiran words, but Blass seemed to. The sorcerer seemed frozen in his stance, his face contorting. His lips moved but no sounds came out, and then his lips stopped moving altogether and Blass only stared at the woman glowing with a golden light.

Golden light. Mack's mind fought to process what he was seeing. A Raheiran glowing with a golden hue. It was something he'd only read about, but he knew what it meant. It signaled the presence of a god or a goddess, as impossible as that could be.

The prickling against Mack's skin lessened. The pain coursing through his body ebbed.

He knew what that meant too. An impossible goddess had just stopped the Grel Te'lard sorcerer.

Blass backed up, stumbling over Rigo's prostrate form. "Lady Kiasidira's dead." He spat out the words.

Gillie took a step toward him. "Guess again, Grel Te'lard."

"We killed you."

"You missed."

Someone grabbed Mack's elbow. Tobias. Mack rose shakily, pulling Tobias with him, only the solid feel of his second in command's hand on his arm verifying that what he had seen and heard was real:

Lady Kiasidira's dead.

Guess again.

Blass's gaze flickered over them, then back to Gillie, his mouth a thin line. A dark haze rushed down his arms, then curled inward at his fingertips.

Gillie shook her head.

An expression of total surprise filled Blass's face. The dark mist writhed, covering him. It clung to his skin like caustic lesions. He doubled over, gasping.

"Mage cabinets are dangerous toys," Gillie said. "Once breached, they have no loyalty. But then, loyalty has never been a Fav trait."

With a roar, Blass lunged for her, a slim blade suddenly in his hand. Mack didn't think. He moved, grabbing the sorcerer in a headlock. He shoved his knee hard against the man's side. Blass bellowed harshly, thrashing out with the blade. Tobias caught Blass's wrist, squeezed until the blade clattered against the floor. Then, with a quick twist, he snapped the sorcerer's arm in half.

Something washed over Mack, like a thick wave of ice. Dark ice, deadly and infectious. It was coming from Blass. He tried to shove the man away, but the sorcerer clung to him, his breath acrid and foul in Mack's face.

Mack! Gillie's voice, calling to him. His vision filled with purple and blue, the icy cold melting as quickly as it had appeared. Blass went limp and hit the floor with a sickening thud.

Mack almost fell over. Tobias's arm around his midsection pulled him upright at the last moment. "You all right, sir?"

He sucked in a deep, rasping breath. "I'm okay." He looked at Gillie, but whatever words he'd wanted to utter died in his throat. She shimmered in the gold light, beautiful, ethereal. Divine.

He dropped his gaze. Blass lay crumpled on the floor, his legs and arms at odd angles. Beyond him was Hebbs, Leyden bent over her protectively. Blood streamed down one side of the officer's face. Mack nudged Tobias in their direction, as part of his mind still functioned as an admiral's should. "Check on Hebbs."

When he looked back, Gillie—a golden-hued Gillie—was kneeling by the sorcerer's head. His pale eyes stared at nothing, lifeless. She passed her hand over his form, not touching him. Blue light melded to purple, flowing from her fingers. "Damn him," she said softly. "He took Trace with him."

He wasn't sure he heard her correctly. He opened

his mouth, only to realize he had no idea how to address her. She was—

"Gillie." She rose. "Just Gillie. Faydra Trace is dead. That was my error. I didn't know he'd tied her essence to the mage cabinet as well."

He knew about the mage cabinet on Blass's ship. He just had no idea what part that played in what had just happened. He wasn't even sure he knew what had just happened, other than a Grel Te'lard sorcerer was dead. And a goddess was alive, after three hundred forty-two years.

Mack took his emotions, his confusion, and shoved them aside. There were Hebbs's injuries to deal with, and two of Rand's people sitting weakly on the floor. There was a hard ache in his own chest as well. Possibly from where Blass had plowed into him. Possibly from something else, something not physical at all.

The doors to the corridor opened. Mack turned. Janek and three med-techs entered noisily, a stretcher floating behind them. "Doors were locked." Janek headed for Hebbs with one med-tech. The others stopped by the injured security officers. "What in hell happened here?" Janek asked as he squatted next to Hebbs.

Gillie, no longer golden-hued, hunkered down between Tobias and Leyden. "Blass laced a spellform over her." She fished in her pockets, came up with two small stones. The ward stones Mack had seen her place in front of Faydra Trace.

She touched Hebbs's forehead then her chest with one stone, put another at Hebbs's midsection. The stationmaster stirred slightly but was still unconscious. "It'll take a few hours. Make sure she stays warm, and don't," she added, securing the stone under Hebbs's waistband as Janek and the med-tech eased her onto the stretcher, "move this."

Janek nodded, then faced Mack. "I'll send a tech to transport Blass's body to the morgue."

"I'll dispose of it," Gillie put in before Mack could reply. She rose and stepped back to give Janek and Leyden room to turn the stretcher. Rand appeared, Rigo in tow, his hands locked in sonicuffs. The magefather trembled visibly.

"Mercy, My Lady." His voice was barely above a whisper. "I beg for mercy."

Donata Rand's mouth was grim, but her eyes were round. Mack wondered if his own face wore a similar shocked expression. "He'll be in lockup, with Trace," she said.

"Trace is dead." Mack nodded toward Gillie. No, toward Lady Kiasidira. *The* Kiasidira. His goddess. "Blass . . . somehow when Blass died, he killed her."

Rand switched her glance from Mack to Gillie but said nothing, only shoved Rigo forward.

"My Lady!" Rigo wrenched around. Tobias grabbed the magefather's arm. They fell in step behind Janek. The magefather's whimperings faded.

"Mack. I'm sorry."

Her eyes were more green now than purple. Mack didn't know why he noticed that. But it was easier to think about the color of her eyes than who, illogically and impossibly, she was. He tried to shrug casually in answer to her apology. "Trace probably wouldn't have told us much more, anyway. She—"

"Not about Faydra Trace. Though, yes, I should've guessed Blass wouldn't let her live. This mage cabinet he used, it's a vicious thing. It fed him power but it also consumed him. But that's not what I..." She hesitated. "I'm sorry I lied to you." Her words came out in a rush. "I'm sorry I couldn't tell you who I am."

He had to say it. He had to hear her confirm it. "Lady...the Kiasidira. You're the Kiasidira."

"It's a long story."

"You don't owe me any explanations, My Lady."

"Damn it, Mack, don't do that!" She closed her eyes for a moment. When she opened them, they held the thin sheen of tears.

That tugged at him hard, painfully. Almost as painfully as the fact that she was a goddess, not his Gillaine. "I'm sure you had good reasons." His grandfather had taught him that: never question the whys and wherefores of the gods.

"Yes. I hate shrines." She held his gaze for a moment, then walked back to Blass's body. Mack waited a respectful distance away, watched as she took another ward stone from her pocket. She held it between her palms, then suddenly the sword, Lady Kiasidira's sacred sword, was in her hands. She slashed down quickly. Mack sucked in a breath, startled by her movements. Equally as startled when Blass's body disintegrated at her sword's touch, leaving behind only a dark, gritty dust.

A slight movement of her hand and the dust was gone.

These were things a goddess could do.

He tried to assemble his expression into something professionally neutral when she turned back to him. It didn't matter. She wasn't looking at him. Her gaze traveled over his shoulder, and he figured he understood. He was an impure. The Lady Goddess didn't have to acknowledge him, much less speak to him.

Then he heard Simon's voice, and he realized that wasn't the reason at all.

"Lady Gillaine. We have a problem. The Fav'lhir Fleet has launched an attack against Cirrus One."

29

Mack recognized Simon's voice and didn't doubt the veracity of his information. The Fav'lhir intended to take Cirrus—just a little sooner, it appeared, than he'd expected them to make that kind of a move. He didn't know if they knew their sorcerer was dead and that was the reason. He didn't care. He needed workable specifics. "How far out are they?" He faced Gillie— Lady Gillaine—when he spoke, remembering facing the speakers in her ready room and feeling foolish. It wasn't as if Simon was actually here.

She still stared over his shoulder. "Simon?"

Something prickled the back of Mack's neck. He turned. A man stood behind him. Tall, with pale blond hair pulled tight at his neck, and a tan uniform covering a well-muscled body. An RSF uniform. Mack had seen holos in history classes.

Simon. Actually here. He'd assumed by what Gillie had said—well, he'd assumed a lot of things by what

Gillie had said and now most of them were turning out to be not quite the truth—he'd assumed Simon was incorporeal. Wasn't that what a nanoessence was? Yet...

"Two squadrons are within thirty-six hours of your outer beacons. Your own sensors aren't yet able to pick them up, Admiral. I thought it prudent to alert you."

Simon. Gods, not an old man, not an elderly caretaker. But Gillie's age. Maybe younger, and looking like a god himself. For some reason that bothered Mack almost as much as the news he brought. Fav'lhir warships, a little more than thirty-six hours out, and heading for Cirrus One.

He flipped up his mouth mike. "Makarian to Ops. Incoming at thirty-six. Red alert, Condition Two. Repeat. Red alert. Condition Two." He'd upgrade to a Condition 1 when—and if—the Fav crossed the twenty-six-hour mark.

"Acknowledged," Tobias answered. He'd evidently left Rand's offices and returned to ops. That made Mack feel only marginally better. Tobias was where he could do the most good, and Fourth Fleet, if they'd been able to deploy when they'd received his earlier message, should already be on their way.

"Full staff meeting in the conference room, ten minutes," he told Tobias.

"Ten minutes, sir."

"Makarian out." He motioned to Simon. "We'll need to know everything you can tell us."

"Lady Gillaine and I will be in the conference room in ten."

Mack nodded, tried to ignore how right Simon and

Gill—Lady Gillaine looked standing side by side, tried to ignore the realization that this godlike man had been Lady Gillaine's constant companion. Tried to ignore the fact that he had an impending attack by the Fav'lhir and all he could think about was an ache in his heart. A Divine Immortal—and there was no other explanation for her existence other than immortality—wasn't for the likes of an impure Khalaran. Admiral or not.

"Thank you. Ten minutes." Mack spun on his heels and strode for the door.

"This is an unfortunate turn of events," Simon said as the door slid closed behind Mack's retreating figure.

Unfortunate? Gillie preferred *cataclysmic*. And that description fit either the approach of the Fav'lhir warships or the loss of Mack in her life.

She'd lost him. She knew that, had known it the minute she'd been forced to take true Kiasidiran form. Blass had left her no choice. He'd integrated more of the mage cabinet's ugly magics than she'd realized, was stronger than she'd anticipated. She'd just started to deal with his spellforms on Hebbs when she'd felt his power surge and grow. He intended to kill everyone in the shrine, everyone on station if he had to.

Even the added magics of her sword had done little to quell him.

With a sigh, she ran her hand through her hair. In saving Mack's life, she'd lost his love. Oh, not his de votion. That she clearly felt. Just as she clearly felt tha pedestal building beneath her feet. Pedestals, shrines altars. That's where Mack now placed her. Not in his arms. Definitely not in his bed. She had to change that somehow. Had to get him to see her as just Gillie again.

If the Fav didn't kill them both first.

"Lady Gillaine?"

She shook off her heartache, blinked back the tears threatening to flow from her eyes. "Status, Simon. How far have you gotten in updating station defenses? Can we stop the Fav'lhir? And while we're at it, mind telling me how you've managed to take full human form?" The golden hue of his Raheiran heritage was absent.

He arched an eyebrow. "I told you I've been working on this."

"To be more useful, or to keep me out of trouble?"

"A little of both. Your other questions I can answer back at the ship."

She plucked at her plain jacket. "I'll dig out my uniform. Seeing two RSF officers on their vidscreens might just make the Fav reconsider their actions. Shame we can't also present them with a squadron of Raptors."

"Actually, Lieutenant Tobias and I have been working on that as well. We just need Izaak's help."

She shot him a questioning glance.

"Parrots," he said.

"The parrots? You're joking. They're harmless. They can't leave the confines of the station."

Simon smiled. "They won't have to."

Mack's team was already assembled in the conference room adjoining Ops Main when Gillie stepped through the opening door. She headed for Mack's side out of habit. When he rose from his seat and executed a small, respectful bow, she halted abruptly. Only the slight pressure of Simon's hand on the small of her back convinced her to move again.

She wanted to run away from the distant, reverent look in his eyes and on the faces of those around the conference-room table. Rand regarded her with a mixture of awe and hope. Pryor gave a small nod, then studied his hands, folded on the tabletop. Josza Brogan wouldn't even look at her. Doc Janek's smile was tense.

Only Tobias seemed unchanged, but then, his expression around her had always held a large measure of adoration. That might disappear, once he heard what she had to say.

She'd already dampered her empathic and telepathic senses since the incident in the shrine. She tightened her shields even more now. She needed to be in control, not pounding her head on the nearest bulkhead in frustration.

She waved Mack back into his seat. She couldn't sit. She'd only end up swiveling the chair back and forth in her current state of agitation. She needed to pace. The small conference room didn't look quite large enough to burn off all her concerns, but what the hell, she'd give it a try.

"You all know Simon—though," she added with a slight motion of her hand as she strode down the length of the table, "you haven't seen him before."

Only Tobias seemed startled by her introduction. But he knew more about the Raheira than the others and probably understood how difficult it was for a nanoessence energy field to manifest in human form.

He's about to explode with questions, Simon told her. *I imagine once we've handled the Fav'lhir, he won't give me a moment's peace.*

I've never known you to complain about a willing audience for your talents.

Did I say I was complaining?

She challenged the other part of his comment. *Are you positive we can handle the Fav'lhir?*

Simon leaned his hands on the empty chair in front of him. "What time estimate have you received from your Fourth Fleet, Admiral?"

"They deployed shortly after acknowledging my request. A little less than thirty-four hours, barring any unforeseen delays."

Gillie folded her hands behind her waist. "Any reports of additional Fav'lhir activity from other quadrants?"

Mack shook his head. "The entire Fleet's on high alert, My Lady. Security teams are following up on Commodore Trace's information of other Fav agents as well."

They'd find some, of that she had no doubt. But it would probably take longer than thirty-six hours to receive any reports of success in that area. She hoped she and Cirrus One would still be around to hear it.

That's something she had to explain to the Khalar. Something she had to make Mack understand. She was here to help them, but she wasn't a goddess. She wasn't immortal. She could fail. They could all fail.

She'd have to destroy their long-held religious belief in order to make them see that. But better to destroy their belief than their lives. She saw clearly now how her attempts over the past weeks to protect them, to preserve their cultural error, had almost resulted in getting them all killed.

She drew in breath, made sure her empathic shields were tightly in place, paced off a few tense steps, then turned. "I'm not a goddess." She looked directly at Mack. He needed to understand. He was Fleet. He was their salvation almost more than she was. "Before we go any further, you must hear this. The truth. I can't save you. I can work with you, but I can't save you. I can't say magic words and make the Fav'lhir disappear."

"Of course. Free will." Tobias was nodding. "The gods are here to guide us, but we must each learn our lessons—"

"Damn it, Fitch, you're not listening!" Gillie flung her arms wide in exasperation. "There are gods and goddesses. Tarkir, Ixari, Merkara—but I am not one of them." She stressed her words. "I'm Raheiran, yes. I bear the onus of a Kiasidira. Yes. But there were dozens before me and, no doubt, have been dozens since. Kiasidira is a title, a designation of ability, not a name. We can do a few more tricks than the average Raheiran, but we're not gods or goddesses."

Mack started to say something but stopped. He was afraid. She could feel that from him. Afraid of her. He didn't understand what she was trying to tell him. It broke her heart. "Ask," she said to him softly.

"My Lady, I—"

"Gillie. My name's Gillie. Just Gillie. Now ask whatever it was you wanted to know."

"Are you the same Lady Kiasidira who worked with us three hundred forty-two years ago?"

"Yes."

"Then you're immortal."

"No."

"But . . . ?"

Gillie turned. "Simon?"

"There was an accident in Riftspace. An explosion resulting from the destruction of the Fav'lhir ship. It caused a hole, if you will, in the normal space–time continuum. Lady Gillaine and I traveled three hundred forty-two years in thirty-four minutes."

"And I was flat on the floor unconscious for most of it," Gillie added.

A noticeable silence filled the room.

"I'm not a goddess," Gillie repeated, but more gently this time. "I'm, at best, an accident. An unwitting time traveler. When I woke in your sick bay," she nodded to Janek, "Simon told me what had happened. I had no idea what to do. Of all the things I'd been trained for, discovering myself to be a goddess wasn't one of them. I'm an adviser. A military adviser. A captain in the Raheiran Special Forces. That's all."

"And a Kiasidira," Mack said.

"That only makes me a sorceress. I'm neither immortal nor omnipotent. I can make mistakes. I've already made more than a few." She hoped her candor wasn't another one.

Brogan leaned back in her chair. She looked stricken. "I've prayed to you."

"I'm sorry. I'm sure Merkara or Ixari heard you, though."

"No, they wouldn't." Brogan seemed truly upset. "You're Fleet's patroness."

"I'm not."

"You've blessed our ships," Brogan persisted.

"I haven't."

Brogan stared at her. In spite of Gillie's shielding, some of the young woman's disbelief and disappointment filtered through.

Gillie wrapped her arms around her midsection, feeling inexplicably bereft. Destroying someone's dreams hurt her more than she'd thought it would.

It will work out, Gillaine Kiasidira.

Will it, Simon? She hung her head for a moment, let his gentle reassurance wash over her. What she really wanted was Mack's arms around her. But best forget that idea, now and forever. He didn't seem any more pleased with her confession than Brogan did.

She forced her shoulders back, ran her hand through her hair, as if by doing so she could remove what was left of the woman called Gillie. It was time for Captain Davré to make an appearance.

"Those are the facts, ladies and gentlemen. You have my sincerest apologies for being a fraud. However, Simon and I are not without resources, without talents. We faced a similar situation a few weeks ago. Well, to you it was over three hundred years ago." She shrugged. "But to us it's been only a few weeks. We remember clearly how the Fav'lhir and their mages react, how they think. Fortunately for the Khalar, the Fav'lhir don't have a similar advantage. They believe they're facing only your Fleet. They have no idea that, once again, they'll be facing me."

She didn't know if she could stop them, but they

were about to feel the full brunt of her anger. She almost pitied the poor bastards. But for them, she'd have had a nice quiet life with Mack by her side. And Brogan would've had her answered prayers and Fitch Tobias would've had his Lady to revere. The Fav were still thirty hours out from Cirrus One, had yet to fire a shot, but they'd already laid waste to the gods only knew how many hopes and dreams.

Gillaine, Kiasidira, Ciran Rothalla Davré fully intended to make them pay for that, and more.

She let Simon do most of the talking after that. He was far more fluent in certain technicalities than she was and had a good rapport with Tobias and Pryor. Though Mack, she noted, seemed wary. But that might only be because Simon had helped perpetrate the fraud that was Lady Kiasidira. Mack was no doubt upset over that. Justifiably so.

He didn't object to the plans she and Simon offered. Of course, Tobias had had a great deal of input in their design, and Fitch Tobias, Gillie suspected, had been trained by one Admiral Rynan "Make It Right" Makarian.

He hadn't been happy, however, over her decision to be on the front lines. The fact that she'd been there before didn't sway him. Nor did the fact that Tobias would accompany her on her ship. Gillie found herself alternately furious with his protective attitude and secretly flattered.

He cared, even if only in some small, very respectful way. Now if she could just get him to stop calling her Lady Gillaine or, worse, Lady Kiasidira, she'd feel she'd accomplished something.

Schematics of her Raptor-class crystalship appeared

on the room's screens. Simon explained its enhanced capabilities and what functions it could share through links he and Tobias had been building on Cirrus. "And with the *Vedritor,* Admiral. Lieutenant Tobias and I have worked on plans to integrate certain elements of crystal technology on your flagship as well."

Mack's elbows were on the arms of his chair, his fingers steepled before his face. "Tell me."

"We'd hoped to have more time to do it. I don't think any of us expected the Fav to make a move this openly, this quickly." Simon looked at Tobias, who was nodding. "So while there are still some technical details to work out, we can start with your scanners and sensor array. A filter to detect a cloaked ship. Much of what we've already done here."

"What kind of cloaking capabilities do the Fav'lhir have?"

Simon swiveled slightly to face Gillie. She uncrossed her arms and stepped away from the wall she'd been leaning against for the past twenty minutes. "Rudimentary, according to what I was able to glean from Faydra Trace. When Simon and I destroyed their ship, and their mageline, the Fav also lost much of the attendant technology. So much was keyed to the Melandan mages. Foolish on their part, because there were so few to begin with." She knew of thirty-seven—not counting wizards and adepts—who'd died with the *Hirlhog.* "That's why we, the Raheira, have always had restrictions on integrating our magics into cultures that had no natural mageline. The culture would only become dependent on us for its growth, rather than learning to develop with its own talents. I think that's been proven because the Khalar have prospered, expanded into the quadrant. It's taken the Fav'lhir three hundred years to regain their space legs. And again, they're looking to a few Melandan mages to lead the way."

"Minus one Grel Te'lard," Mack said evenly.

For the first time since she'd come into the conference room, he met her gaze without lowering his eyes. Something soared inside Gillie. It was such a small gesture, the ability to look someone in the eyes as an equal. Maybe, just maybe, they could be friends. It was more than she dared hope for.

"Minus one Grel Te'lard," she agreed. "I can only guess at the holes in Blass's training because of his reliance on the mage cabinet. If he was one of their best, and he certainly seemed to think so, then much of their magic is rough, unsophisticated. Wasteful of energy," she explained, seeing Pryor's bushy white eyebrows knit into a frown. "Think of magic like music. It takes hours of practice to play a simple melody. Even more training to perform something complex. Add a good teacher," she smiled at Simon, "with an abundance of patience, and you can do more."

"Aren't there books?" Rand asked.

Gillie shook her head. "Only in the beginning, and then very few. Tarkir learned books could be stolen, fall into the wrong hands. The knowledge and the training was then given to mentors, who were granted the ability to choose their students based on not only ability but intent. Nothing's been written down since Lady Melande almost killed Rothal-kiarr. Eons and eons ago."

"But mentors could be killed, the knowledge lost," Rand said.

"If we'd remained human, yes," Simon said after Gillie nodded to him. "But a nanoessence energy field can adapt and survive in many forms."

Tobias raised one finger in the air. "As long as we're on that subject—"

"Let's get back to the original suggestion first." Mack tapped the screen. "How long would it take to upgrade the *Vedritor*'s scanners?"

Gillie exchanged a glance with Simon. "Three, maybe five hours," she said. "Simon's already established templates here. It's really only a matter of installing them."

"Would you be willing to do that? It would require your presence on the *Vedritor*, Captain Davré."

Captain Davré. Not Lady Kiasidira. Captain Davré. That caught Gillie's attention.

"Lieutenant Tobias and I can handle the *Serendipity* quite well," Simon intoned. "And in the few hours it'll take Fourth to reach the beacons, you should be able to recalibrate the ship's sensors to link with ours."

There was no overriding reason she had to be on the *Serendipity* other than it was her ship. Hers and Simon's. Simon was perfectly capable of handling the crystalship by himself. And if she was on the *Vedritor*, they could do more.

That was a logical reason for Mack to want her presence there. Her heart, however, still held out hope for the illogical. She nodded her agreement. "Absolutely."

Whatever comment he intended was cut short by the pinging of the conference-room intercom. He tapped the screen. "Makarian."

A dusky-skinned woman with dark, braided hair

nodded. "The *Vedritor*'s just confirmed with our tugs, sir. Captain Adler says they'll be at dock in thirty minutes."

"Acknowledged." He shoved himself to his feet. "I think we all know what happens from here."

Well, Gillie knew what she had to do next. She, Simon, and Tobias had a final meeting with Izaak and his father, Jared. And the parrots. It would be Izaak's job, aided by the ward stones she'd place throughout the atrium, to direct the parrots through the music of his flute. Mack's avian invaders would finally earn their keep.

But what would happen in the hours ahead with Mack on the *Vedritor,* she had no idea. She did, however, have hopes. But no guarantee she'd live long enough to see them materialize.

30

Adler might be the captain, but Mack was clearly in command. Gillie saw that in the respect written on the faces of the *Vedritor*'s senior officers, felt the trust emanate from them as they gathered in the ship's ready room, just aft of the bridge.

Mack introduced her as Captain Davré. He continued to refer to her in that way and made no mention that she knew of that she was their Lady Kiasidira. She refused to let herself think it meant anything more than his acknowledging they were now in a military situation. And it *was* her title.

Still, when they were finally left alone—Adler and his officers returning to the bridge—Gillie felt she had to say something. She turned from the viewport that was filled with the retreating image of Cirrus One. "Thank you."

Mack looked up from the data on the screen slatted into the tabletop. "You're welcome. For what?"

"For not calling me Lady Kiasidira in front of Adler or his people."

He hesitated, pursing his lips slightly. "They don't know. Rand and I decided it was best that way. The fewer who know who you are, the better."

Then his use of her name was political, not personal. That small hope withered, though she was grateful for the anonymity, whatever his reason. She'd thought her identity had been blared throughout the station. But then, Izaak and his father, while respectful, hadn't viewed her with fear. Though Izaak had known who she was because of the incident in the lift shaft. "Who does know?"

"Only my team, those who were in the shrine when Blass attacked Hebbs. Rand's team was debriefed, sworn to secrecy. Rigo's in lockup. Janek didn't know until I told him. None of his med-techs know who you are."

"They know I'm Raheiran." She'd worn the uniform openly.

"The official position of Cirrus One is that an RSF officer and her ship are assisting. That's all Adler knows as well."

Because to reveal that Lady Kiasidira was not a goddess but a fraud might cause almost as much damage to the Khalar as the incoming invasion of Fav'lhir. In a way, Gillie almost wished she'd died in Riftspace. Then the Day of Sacred Sacrifice might be real. "Then thank you for doing the damage control. I know I've created a lot of unnecessary work, a lot of problems. Simon told me, weeks ago, to trust you, tell you who I was. He was right. I should have."

Something flickered through Mack's eyes, but she

refused to allow herself to sense his emotions. He nodded slowly. "Yes."

But would you have kissed me if I had? She wanted to ask that but knew she never could. She really didn't want to know the answer. The screen in front of Mack beeped and he swiveled back. He had far more important things to think about.

So did she. She chose a seat in the middle of the table and tabbed up a datascreen. Mack raised his face at her movements. "You'll need an access code. Here." He touched his screen.

Numbers flashed on hers. She keyed it in and, using Simon's templates, began recalibrating the ship's sensors. Adler's voice on intraship requested Mack's presence on the bridge. She glanced at the time stamp on her screen. Not quite an hour had passed since they'd left Cirrus.

Mack hesitated in the doorway. "If you need anything, comm me."

"Thanks." She went back to work. From there she took on the scanners. They were a little more difficult. She had to link with Simon twice. The *Serendipity* was positioned off the *Vedritor*'s portside, the distance greater than the depth of Cirrus One but not enough to affect a Raheiran link.

She coded in Simon's suggestion and smiled as, finally, the right patterns appeared on her screen. The ready-room door slid open. The pleasant aroma of coffee assailed her.

Mack placed a mug on her right but didn't take his seat. He wandered over to the viewport at the far end of the room and leaned against the wall. He watched her. She could feel his gaze and, when she glanced at him, saw again something flicker in his dark eyes.

She swiveled her chair a quarter turn and took a chance. "Ask."

"Do I need to, if you're reading my thoughts?"

"I'm not."

His only response was silence. To her, it implied disbelief.

"A telepathic link without permission is not only painful but it violates every Raheiran precept. I've told you this before. I don't routinely read your thoughts. I respect you, Mack. I wouldn't do that. Not to you. Not to anyone." At least, not without sufficient reason and many apologies to Ixari for the intrusion. She amended her comment. "Except for emergencies."

"Is that your explanation for reading my thoughts in the shrine?"

Gods, she'd been thinking of how she'd peeked into Petrina's mind for information on a Ziami trader. Her link with Mack in the shrine had been so automatic it was almost instinctual. As well as necessary for both their survival. "I wasn't reading them. I was shielding them. You faced a Grel Te'lard sorcerer who could've sifted through your knowledge in minutes if I hadn't. I couldn't risk him finding what you knew about me. I had to . . . monitor you. It's not quite the same as reading." Nor was it easy. Protecting Mack's mind could have drained her, had the encounter with Blass gone on much longer.

"I didn't know who you were then."

"You knew my name."

"So?"

She shook her head. She'd been so comfortable

with Mack, it was easy to forget there was much he didn't know. Too much. "My magename. I'd given you my magename. If he found that, he could've used that to kill me."

He straightened, frowning. "Magename?"

"I had his: Carrickal Grel Te'lard Blass. That's what I took from the mage cabinet on his ship. That's one of the advantages I had. I had his magename. He didn't have mine."

"You never—"

"I did." Her memories of the moment were both intensely sweet and, now, poignantly painful. She glanced at the closed door of the ready room, silently uttered a small warding spell. The same one she'd said in Mack's quarters. "Gillaine Ciran Rothalla Davré. Besides Simon, you're the only one who knows that."

"You've told lots of people you're Gillaine."

"It's the combination, not just one name. I know that concept's foreign to you. Just accept that a sorcerer's magename is inextricably tied to his essence. You have that, you have the power of life and death over him."

Mack's features went slack.

"I don't even know Simon's," she added softly.

He was silent, a frown again creasing his forehead. Then he shook his head, as if arguing with himself. "Simon could—you're saying Simon could kill you."

"It's his responsibility to do so should I violate Kiasidiran precepts."

"That's unconscionable!"

"Doesn't Fleet operate on the same principles? You give orders to your staff, your crew. You have the power to discipline them if they disobey." She watched his face for a sign he understood. "It's a safe-guard, Mack," she continued. "A necessary one. To make sure no one like Blass could ever be a Ki'sidron."

He turned abruptly away from her and splayed his hand against the viewport. The starfield shimmered around him. She could see a muscle pulse in his jaw. She'd also clearly seen the disgust on his face.

She'd lost him even more, if that were possible. Who she was, what she was, represented something too foreign for him to accept. She swiveled her chair back around, feeling drained, her entire body aching.

So much for honesty. She'd just found the answer to her earlier unasked question: if she'd told him who she was, would he still have kissed her?

No.

Intraship chimed again. "Adler to Admiral Makarian. Can you meet me in my office?"

"Makarian." His voice was rough. "Acknowl-edged. On my way."

Two hours passed. Gillie finished recalibrating the scanners and linking them with the *Serendipity* and Cirrus One. Reports from the quadrant's outer beacons flowed down the left side of her screen. The Fav'lhir ships still advanced, believing they were un-seen.

But the *Vedritor* saw them very well, though data was sparse. There was a lag time for the ship to inter-pret the data from the beacons, thirty hours away.

If they had the time they'd thought they had, believ-ing the Fav'lhir were only getting undercover opera-tives in place, believing the Fav'lhir wouldn't strike until the Rim Gate was operational, if she'd known . . . So many wrong beliefs, so many ifs. What was, was.

Deal with what is. She couldn't remember if that was one of Lady Kiasidira's guidelines or not. She didn't care.

She swiveled the chair around and headed for the bridge. Adler's chair was empty, but there was plenty of activity in the semicircular room. Two communications officers were on duty, talking to the *Gallant*, the *Worthy*, and other ships in Makarian's Fifth Fleet as well as relaying information to Fourth, still thirty hours out.

Weapons was running a series of last-minute tests. Science and navigation were gleeful over her enhancements. She leaned around a few shoulders, made suggestions, played Captain Davré with every fiber of her body, because she knew the minute she let Gillie surface, the ache would start again.

The six-hour mark heralded a shift change. It was near midnight on her body's clock. She hadn't seen Mack again during her subsequent forays to the bridge. Nor had he come back to the ready room. At least, not while she was there. She clicked off the datascreen and tabbed it back down into the table. The coffee brought to her by a well-meaning ensign an hour before was cold; her dinner, barely touched.

Captain Adler had shown her to a small cabin one deck below the bridge when she'd first come on board. She headed there, stripping off her uniform jacket as the cabin's door closed behind her. Her duffel was on the floor by the bed. She could unpack. Later. She tugged off her boots, then sprawled on the bed, her arm over her eyes.

Her chest ached. She should take off the rest of her uniform. Later.

Gillaine?

'Night, Simon.

Things will work out.

She tried to swallow the lump in her throat, but it wouldn't go away. *Thanks.*

A pinging noise woke her. She opened her eyes, the glowing red numbers by her bedside informing her she'd slept for a little over five hours. She didn't remember setting an alarm and fumbled in the darkness for the clockpad. Then realized the clock wasn't pinging.

Her cabin door was.

She jerked upright, then chastised herself. No corridor alarms wailed, no emergency lights flashed. This wasn't a red alert. This was someone, probably that pair of Adler's bridge officers, a married couple, who'd tried unsuccessfully to get her to share dinner with them last night. When she'd begged off they said something about breakfast.

Well, unless they'd brought a cargo hold full of coffee, she didn't want to see them.

She fell back on the bed, squeezed her eyes shut.

The door pinged again.

Oh, hell. Oh, damn. She shoved herself to her feet and padded to the door. Good thing she hadn't stripped out of her uniform. She slapped at the lock, then raked her hand through her hair. She knew she looked a mess. Maybe they'd take pity on her and go away.

The door slid open. She blinked. The bright light cascading in from the corridor outlined a tall, broad-shouldered form.

"Mack?" Her voice squeaked. Her heart, traitor that it was, skipped a beat.

"May I come in?" His face was shadowed, his voice equally as unreadable.

"Of course." She stepped aside, remembering when their greeting was, "Hi," and, "Hi, yourself," followed by a kiss. "Is there a problem?"

The door closed behind him. He took three steps into her cabin, then stopped, his hands shoved in his pockets. He turned and she realized he'd changed out of his dress uniform into Khalaran Fleet black fatigues, though his admiral's insignia blazed clearly on his chest. He looked impeccably neat, freshly showered.

In contrast, she knew she looked like something that had crawled out of a corner of a long-forgotten cargo hold.

Then she saw the dark shadows under his eyes. Something was wrong. She sought her link with Simon. That was strong. It was something else. "What's wrong?"

"Everything."

Everything? Her mind raced. Something had happened to the prime hostess. There was another Melandan mage on Cirrus One. No, Tynder's. No. Maybe one of the inhabited worlds, a major city. Bexhalla. Maybe—

"We need to talk. There may not be time once we make meetpoint with Fourth at the beacons."

Not Bexhalla. Not the prime hostess. She motioned to the couch along the back wall. "You want to sit?"

"I'll stand."

Oh, hell. Oh, damn. She didn't like the sound of

this at all. "I'm going to sit." She padded past him and plopped down.

He studied her for three, four heartbeats. Five. Seven. "I think you know the way I am. I don't play games."

But she had. She could still hear the derision in his voice when he'd recounted the deceptions Hebbs had tried to employ. He'd referred to the stationmaster as a master games player. She wondered if she now shared that title as well. "I didn't want to. Believe me, I—"

He held up one hand. "I was nicknamed 'Make It Right' years ago because honesty and fairness is something I value highly. If there's an error, I want to correct it." He hesitated. "I've made errors in judgment here."

"No, you haven't. It's all my fault. Everything's my fault. I should've left Cirrus the next day, as soon as my ship's sublights were online."

"Then who would've stopped Blass?"

This time Gillie stared at him for three, four heartbeats.

"His plans were already in place," Mack continued. "He would've had the prime hostess convince the chancellor to grant full, open access to the station. The Fav'lhir would probably already be in control of it."

And Mack, and all his people, would be dead. He didn't say that, but Gillie knew it was true.

"We haven't stopped them yet," she said softly, not yet ready to let go of the guilt she'd wrapped around herself.

"But we have a chance. A damned good one. Because of you."

"Your people would willingly follow you into the jaws of hell, Rynan Makarian. It's not just me."

"A compromise, then. It's us." He pushed his hands back into his pockets, rocked back on his heels. "Have you ever considered that your being on Cirrus wasn't happenstance? That there may be a very real reason why you're at this very place and point in time?"

She recognized her own words, albeit in Mack's voice. And there had been only one person around when she'd said them. "You've been talking to Simon, haven't you?" She didn't bother to hide her suspicious tone.

He shrugged. "We had a chat."

She didn't know whether to laugh or cry. Hope soared, then just as quickly crashed. Simon knew how she felt about Mack. But she didn't want Mack to be here out of duty, or guilt. Or because Simon threatened to shove him out the *Serendipity*'s exhaust vents for breaking her heart. "I take it the chat was about me."

"Considering I'm facing an invasion by Fav'lhir forces, I have the prime hostess under guard on my station, the Fourth Fleet is still hours behind us, and my own Fifth Fleet is bare bones at best . . . Considering all that, it does sound somewhat surprising that all I've been able to think about is one Captain Gillaine Davré. But, yes, that's what our chat was about."

"Simon had no right—"

"Simon didn't initiate the conversation. I did. I couldn't sleep."

"Because of me?"

He nodded. "You're a very complicated woman."

"Not really." Her voice shook as she said the words

that could save her or damn her. "Feed me, love me. Not necessarily in that order."

"I thought," he said slowly, "that Simon was already doing that job."

"Simon?" Her voice squeaked as she rose to her feet. "Simon? You thought Simon and I—"

"You have this telepathic link with him. He's Raheiran."

"Yes, but—"

"A lifelong friend, you told me. You led me to believe...well, I'd pictured an elderly man. He's not elderly."

"Two thousand or so years isn't young!"

"Then you explained about magenames. How Simon controls you."

Gillie barked out a harsh laugh. "He might dispute that."

"Everything you told me led me to conclude you'd slept with me on Simon's instructions. Because you needed access to information, to people on Cirrus One. Granted, the end result was to stop Blass. But the methodology...I thought Simon encouraged you to be my lover to gain access to security, to the workings of my team."

Anger surged through Gillie as Mack's words sunk in. Anger, white hot yet icy cold. Mack thought she'd slept with him because Simon had ordered her to. Because they'd known Blass was coming and they needed to find out what the Khalar planned to do. Belatedly, she realized he'd hinted at that before, when he'd found out she was RSF. But that had been only a hint, a mention of her not breaking cover on a mission.

This was a blatant accusation, and one that said she was no better, in his estimation, than Johnna Hebbs.

She was furious, humiliated. Her chest was painfully tight, her stomach a hard knot. It took every bit of her control not to lash out and smack him across the jaw. "Whoring is not one of a Kiasidira's duties." She shook off his attempt to grab her arm as she strode past him. She stopped at the door, slapped at the palm pad with a shaking hand, then spun to face him. "Don't let the door hit you in the ass on the way out, Makarian."

"Gillie—"

"I mean it."

"Hear me out. Please. Then I'll leave."

She folded her arms across her chest and glared at him.

"Gillie, I—"

The blare of an alarm filled her cabin, echoing in from the corridor. Mack's comm set pinged. Another pinging came from her comm set, still tucked into her utility belt.

"Damn it!" Mack tapped on his mike as she flipped her own comm set over her ear. "Status!"

"Davré here," she confirmed.

"Six Fav'lhir ships, Admiral. Captain. We don't know where they came from. But they're off our starboard side and closing."

"On my way." Mack flashed her a brief, anguished look before he bolted into the corridor.

Gillie hesitated only long enough to grab her jacket. Then she tore down the corridor after him, her heart pounding as loudly as her boots.

The Fav'lhir had found her, again.

31

The *Vedritor*'s bridge was alive with noise and motion. Adler's chair was empty, but his first officer was firmly ensconced in the adjoining one, her armpad controls angled in front of her. She pushed it aside, started to rise when Mack strode in. He waved her back down. She and Adler would work best together. Mack needed to be mobile. He'd never sat long in the command chair even when he'd been captain. And he never sat still during an attack.

The data on the six unexpected Fav'lhir ships danced on a dozen screens: five Raider-class fighters and one huntership, equal in size to the *Vedri*. They were thirty-five minutes out from the *Vedri*'s position. They must have slipped past Cirrus Quadrant's outer beacons hours earlier, assisted by their cloaking abilities. Simon had warned that the few adjustments he'd been able to make to the beacons might not be enough.

They weren't. Six new ships here on his vector. Two squadrons—the original attackers Simon had seen—still closing on the beacons. And the gods only knew how many more were out there, coming in from a different axis.

A hand clasped his shoulder. "The chair's yours if you want it," Adler said.

"You know I work best right here."

Adler hesitated only a second. "Good to have you back on board, Mack."

"Thanks. Let's get to work." He turned. Gillie stood near the front of the bridge, staring at the images of the Fav ships on the viewscreen. His heart clenched. He'd failed to make things right with her, thanks to the arrival of the Fav'lhir. And thanks to his own cowardice for not coming out right away and telling her how he felt.

He'd always suspected time was a factor in their relationship. Now he knew it worked against him.

"Admiral. Captain." Iona Cardiff swiveled in her chair at communications. "The Fav'lhir ship *Mogralla* is answering our hail."

Adler pushed himself out of the seat he'd just taken and strode forward. Mack met up with him in the middle of the bridge. "On screen," he said, and looked at Gillie. She stepped back next to Cardiff, with a slight shake of her head. And no emotion in her face, or her eyes. Captain Gillaine Davré, RSF Division 1, was on duty but not yet ready to make an official appearance.

The screen blanked, flickered, then a trim, white-haired man in a red and gold uniform appeared in the center. Fav'lhir crew dotted the stations around him much as the *Vedri*'s officers did.

Mack locked his hands behind his waist. "Admiral Rynan Makarian, Khalar Fifth Fleet." He nodded at the Fav'lhir captain. "State your business, sir."

"Not much of a fleet. Admiral." The man smirked.

Mack wanted nothing more than to wipe that smirk off the Fav's face with a full complement of ion torpedoes. But there was a protocol to follow, as foolish as it seemed. He knew damned well why the Fav were here. "You're in Khalaran space. Present your clearances or prepare to be fired upon."

Something wavered in the recesses of the Fav'lhir bridge. It looked, momentarily, like a cage with a large entity inside, then it winked out.

"They're probing our shields," an officer said evenly from the science station on his left. "Unable to identify source."

"Shields holding," said another.

"This is your final warning," Adler said. "Present—"

The *Vedritor* shimmied, a movement so slight Mack wouldn't have noticed it had he been seated. But he felt it through the soles of his boots.

At the same time, he heard Gillie utter a low, and now very familiar, curse. *"Fielgha."* She moved swiftly toward the viewscreen, her right hand outstretched, her fist clenched. A glow gelled between her fingers.

The Fav'lhir captain appeared startled. "What?"

Gillie faced him. "Captain Gillaine Davré, Raheiran Special Forces, Division One. You unholy son of a bitch!" She opened her hand.

A small pinpoint of light expanded rapidly. A cage,

rimmed in fire, hung in the air before her on the *Vedri*'s bridge. It grew to over six feet tall, shimmered, vibrated, and rocked with the impact of the mogra—by the holy eyes of the gods! A mogra!—futilely slamming itself against the bars.

There was a collective sharp intake of breaths around him. Mack's fingers closed over the laser pistol holstered to his side.

Then, just as suddenly, the cage was empty, disintegrating. The mogra appeared behind the Fav'lhir captain. The man whirled, shouting something Mack didn't understand.

Another cage surrounded the mogra. The white-haired man spun back to the screen. "Filthy Raheiran witch!"

"Yes. And there's more than one of us." Gillie sounded positively gleeful.

A squadron of Raptor-class crystalships winked out of the starfield, the *Serendipity* at the lead. They blazed across the *Mogralla*'s bow. Bright blue laser fire flared against its shields.

Then, in an incredibly graceful and not unfamiliar movement, they arced and blazed back.

The parrots. Mack had listened to Simon and Gillie explain about the parrots and amplifying essences and how they could be used to create false images. But until this very moment, he hadn't truly believed it would work.

It didn't matter what he believed. The Fav'lhir saw it as real: a real, attacking squadron of Raheiran crystalships. When in fact there was only one. Assisted by the essences of his avian invaders.

"Lock ion cannons," Mack ordered the weapons lieutenant. "Fire!"

The Fav ships' shields were peppered with incoming blasts. Chatter on the *Vedritor*'s bridge was clipped, serious, as the *Mogralla* returned fire, but the Fav ships also aimed at the imaginary Raheiran squadron, wasting weaponry and man power.

The diversion created gaps in the *Mogralla*'s defenses, and the *Vedritor* took advantage of those gaps, swiftly. Decisively.

Eventually, believing they were outnumbered by a combined Khalaran–Raheiran onslaught, the Fav'lhir cooperated by retreating rapidly. Adler sent the *Worthy* and one squadron in pursuit of the four remaining fighters. The *Mogralla* and the last fighter hung lopsided in space, all but destroyed.

"That captain was a wizard," Gillie told them when the crisis downgraded to a yellow alert. "Not a sorcerer."

Adler sat in the command chair, listening to Gillie while at the same time monitoring ship's status and damage reports. "Thank the gods he was only that," Adler said, then glanced up at Mack on his left. "I understand you and Captain Davré stopped one on station. I have no desire to run up against a sorcerer, or a sorceress, myself. They're too powerful, or, should I say, power hungry. What they can do ... well, it makes them ... unnatural."

Gillie's shoulders stiffened slightly at Adler's unintended rejection. Mack fought the urge to draw her into his arms. She'd probably give him a black eye if he tried.

"We should finish up here within three hours,"

Adler was saying. "Then we'll head for the border at maximum speed so Captain Davré can recalibrate those beacons. There are six more sets after that." He motioned to Gillie. "Lieutenant Mason is putting together a list of techs for you to train. We're going to keep you and your team very busy for a while."

Gillie nodded. "I look forward to it, Captain."

Would she permit him to be part of that team? She couldn't stop him, though he didn't think she'd be happy about it. But it would give him the time he needed to make amends, time with her to make things as right as he possibly could. He still didn't fully understand her: Raheiran, Kiasidira, RSF captain. Time traveler. Accidental goddess. All in one package she liked to call "just Gillie." A woman of incredible strengths. And, as Simon had helped him see, a woman very alone and very afraid.

"Have Lieutenant Mason send that list to me in the ready room," she told Adler.

Mack followed her into the corridor. "Gillaine."

She palmed the ready-room door open and turned. The bright overhead lights danced silver and gold through her hair. There was no corresponding sparkle in her eyes.

"We still have to talk," he said.

"I'm only going to teach your people how to calibrate your sensors for cloaking resonances. Not train them in the art of seduction, if that's your concern, Admiral."

"It's not. I never meant—" His comm set pinged. "Gods *damn* it!" He flipped up the mike with a rough, impatient gesture. "Makarian!"

"Priority trans from Traakhal One." Adler's voice

was tense. "The chancellor's ship's under attack by the Fav'lhir at our Nixaran border. Their escort's been destroyed."

Shock jolted Mack's system. What in Tarkir's hell was Traakhal One doing transiting the border between Nixara and Cirrus? Coming in on a direct vector from Traakhalus, obviously. But why? Mack could think of only one reason: the prime hostess, sitting on Cirrus One.

"The chancellor's ship's been attacked," he told Gillie, then he spun and bolted back to the bridge.

Adler stood behind Cardiff, his mouth grim. "We had no advance information on his movements."

"Neither did I," Mack said, and damned Honora Trelmont, Carlos Halbert, and Blass. Whoever was responsible for sending the chancellor to the Cirrus Quadrant unannounced.

Though obviously the Fav'lhir had known. Blass, then, before he died. Or Rigo. Mack watched the data on the communications officer's screen. Ten hours separated Cirrus One from the Nixaran border, and the *Vedri* was now ten more beyond that. Fourth Fleet was twenty hours out. Even at top speeds, they'd never reach the chancellor's convoy in time.

"Where's Admiral Lloyd?"

"Third can't get there for at least thirty-six. Their hunterships were on maneuvers out by the rim."

"Advise Traakhal One we're responding immediately, with Fourth as backup."

"I've already plotted in a course, sent an advisory. If they can hang on, we'll be there in fifteen, maybe less."

"I can . . . We can get there in an hour."

Mack hadn't seen Gillie approach. She stood on Adler's right, one hand on the back of Cardiff's chair. The communications officer angled back, giving Gillie a clearer view of the data on her screen.

"One hour," Gillie repeated. She switched a glance from Mack to Adler, then back to Mack again, her brow furrowed. "Through Riftspace."

Gillie's crystalship could travel in ways his own never could. Mack had forgotten that. He pointed to the data from Traakhal One's distress call. "The Fav have two destroyers. Can the *Serendipity* handle that kind of firepower?"

"No. But the *Serendipity* and the *Vedritor* can."

"I don't understand."

She heaved out a short sigh. "I've never done this before. Simon thinks it will work, but it will require some damage control. And your complete trust."

Mack understood her reference to damage control. Gillie was going to use her abilities as a Kiasidira again, and he had a feeling Adler's officers would be witnesses. But he didn't understand how she intended to use the *Vedri*. "Tell me. Whatever you need, I'll do." He meant it.

She closed her eyes briefly. He guessed she was talking with—quite possibly *arguing* with—Simon. Her expression was unsettled and her eyes, when she opened them, troubled. "Oh, hell, oh, damn," she said softly, then turned to Adler. "I'm a mageline sorceress."

Adler's mouth opened. Then he stammered, obviously regretting his earlier remark. "Captain, I—that is, I didn't—"

Gillie held up one hand. "It's not an issue. And the

fault is more mine. If we had time, I could explain. We don't have time. Captain Adler, I need your ship. Admiral Makarian, I need your complete and total faith in me. Lieutenant Cardiff, I need you to take your hands off the communications panel for a moment."

Mack nodded to Cardiff, whose expression was as surprised as Adler's. She dropped her hands into her lap.

Gillie pulled a small ward stone from her jacket pocket and placed it on the console. *"L'heira Ixari..."* Crystal flowed, blossomed. Cardiff gasped. Adler cleared his throat.

Mack followed Gillie around the bridge as she placed ward stones at the other stations: navigations, weapons, science, ops, tactical. Crew sat back, hands in their laps, watching. Whisperings were halted by a sharp look from Adler or himself.

Ten minutes later she stood in the middle of the bridge, eyes closed, her folded hands resting against her mouth. Mack waited by Adler's chair. He'd never seen her so focused, so determined. She looked over her shoulder at him. So afraid.

She held out her hand. "Rynan Khamron Makarian. This is your calling."

Something washed over him. Something old and powerful and deep. It held echoes of a dark lake, an impregnable castle. An undying love. He knew the castle: Traakhal-armin. He knew the lake: the Khal. The love was legendary: Rylan, the sorcerer, whose magename was Rothal-kiarr. And Khamsin, the first Lady Kiasidira.

But I'm not... he started to say, then willfully pushed aside his doubts. What he was, or wasn't, didn't matter. Gillie needed him. Gillie believed in him. That was enough.

He crossed to the center of the bridge and took her hand. She touched her forehead, lips, and chest with a ward stone, then did the same to him.

"I cannot move this ship alone," she said softly. "She's not part of me, as the *Serendipity* is. But she is part of you. You supervised her design. You know her every bulkhead."

He nodded. He did.

"She trusts you. Now you, and she, must trust me."

He tightened his fingers around hers. "With my life." Then he added what he knew he had to say now. Before he ran out of time again. "I love you, Gillie."

Her eyes misted. "I love you too, Mack," she whispered. Another ward stone appeared in her right hand. She tucked it between his palm and hers, then closed her hand on top. She whispered words he didn't understand. Purple light cascaded, swirling out from between their fingers.

His hands and arms tingled. His heart raced. A bright circle arced up around them, settling quickly into the bridge floor. It glistened with gemstones. A mage circle. He'd never seen one before, but he knew that's what it was.

This is your calling. Gillie's voice rang strongly in his mind. There was no pain this time, no discomfort. *Do you accept?*

Yes.

Rynan Khamron Rothal Makarian, hear your magename.

He heard it. He wasn't sure he believed it, nor did

he know how someone like him could have one, but he heard it.

Guard it with your life. My vow to you is to do the same. Know its power. My vow to you is to honor that power. Do you understand?

I have much to learn, My Lady, but, yes. I understand.

Gillie touched the crystal stone to her forehead, then to his. The crystal felt cool, soothing, not at all what he'd expected from its brilliant glow.

Then his world, quietly and with the merest whisper of sound, exploded.

He sucked in a quick breath. The stone was gone. Gillie clasped both his hands, steadying him. It felt as if a few thousand suns had gone nova inside his body, yet there was no pain. Only ... power. A rush of energy so strong, so sweet, so vital, and yet at the same time so incredibly gentle.

The purple glow muted around them. The mage circle winked out. He was aware of the bridge crew transfixed in their seats, but he was more aware of the slight curve of a smile on Gillie's mouth. *It does take some getting used to,* she told him wryly. *Ready?*

Ready.

Simon?

Mack heard, and felt, Simon's presence. *At your command, Lady Gillaine.*

Good. She thrust her right hand in the air. Purple light raced from crystal-enhanced console to crystal-enhanced console. The starfield shifted, sliced through by a tubular crystalline pathway. *Let's go kick some Fav'lhir ass.*

32

Damn, but she's a big ship. Gillie grabbed Riftspace with one element of herself and the *Vedritor,* through Mack, with another. Her link with Simon and the *Serendipity* was more in Simon's control. There was only so much she could do. Temporarily melding the essence of a Khalaran huntership into *essenmorgh* crystal took most of her concentration and energy.

Which was one of the reasons she needed Mack. His intimate, almost instinctual knowledge of the ship guided her in weaving her spellforms. Through Mack she linked to the *Vedritor.* Through Simon she linked to the *Serendipity.* She opened herself to Riftspace and followed the *Serendipity* in.

The convergence of energies washed over her like an icy tide, as it always did. She'd forgotten to warn Mack, though, and his sharp intake of breath caught her attention. *Give it a minute; it'll settle, once it accepts us.*

His fingers tightened around her hand. They stood almost toe-to-toe in the middle of the bridge. She cupped her other hand on top of his and didn't even need to be a Kiasidira, let alone a Raheiran, to feel his heart racing. Almost as fast as his mind. He had a thousand questions.

She had answers to some. Not all. It had been up to Simon to figure out who Mack was. What he could become.

The iciness softened into a cool breeze. Gillie drew a deep breath, felt for the *Vedritor*'s position, checked their alignment with the *Serendipity*.

Mack watched her, seeing what she saw, feeling what she felt. *We're riding in the* Serendipity's *wake. She—He's actually using Riftspace. Towing us.*

There was a distinct note of surprise in Mack's comment, but Gillie didn't know if he was surprised by the fact that he'd figured out the methodology or the methodology itself.

A little of both, he admitted.

Do you feel the balance between the ships and Riftspace? Can you see the energy threads?

Not sure . . . yes!

Good. You need to keep a constant watch on that thread that's the Vedritor *and mine with the* Serendipity. *Don't watch it, feel it.*

He drew a slow breath. *Okay.*

Gillie probed for a few more minutes, let Mack get his bearings, get used to the gently invasive feel of the link. She could hear Tobias talking to Cardiff and Adler on the comm. Given the fact that she'd just yanked an entire huntership and crew into something they'd never thought they'd see, they were all doing very well.

Extremely well, Lady Gillaine. I told you that you could do this. Simon sounded inordinately pleased.

We're not there yet, she chastised him, but yes, everything flowed. Lines and links were clean, bright.

"You *can* open your eyes," she told Mack.

He blinked, stared down at her. "This," he said slowly, as if he'd just remembered how to speak, "has been one of the most extraordinary days in my life."

"If you're counting from Blass's actions in the shrine, two days. We're into tomorrow." She pulled her hands out of his, motioned to the viewport. The small shape of the *Serendipity* blazed before them, bands of blues and purples spiraling over the hull. "You and I can see the linkages, but they," she indicated the bridge officers around them, "can't. Keep that in mind."

"What do you need me to do?"

Intuitive. Mack picked up on her unspoken, even unthought need to run a systems check. She'd sensed that in him all along, but ignored it save for occasionally wondering if he had low-level telepathy. Simon had done more. Simon had been watching and, as was typically Simon, saying little until he had time to investigate Raheiran lineages and blood bonds and was sure. "Engines and shields will be most affected by this transit. Riding in the *Serendipity*'s wake buffers this ship some, but she's so much larger." Even now, Gillie could feel the drain of her own energies as she maintained the *essenmorgh* reformation of the huntership. "If there's a problem, that's where it'll start."

He touched her cheek, hesitantly. "You okay?"

Too intuitive. But then, he was linked with her. "All things considered, yes."

"I never meant—"

She held up her hand. "I know. Simon calls me damnably dense at times." Actually, it had been a litany of his for the past hour. "Mack, we have several days' worth of questions and explanations ahead of us. But right now I need to concentrate on keeping this ship in alignment. It's the biggest thing I've ever moved. I need to focus on that."

"I'll check on the shields."

She draped her hand on his sleeve as he turned away. "They don't know who you are. What happened," she said quietly. This was her own way of doing damage control.

He smiled. "I don't know who I am or what happened. What *is* happening."

"You're making history, Rynan Makarian. If you're unlucky, someone will build a shrine in your honor in a couple hundred years."

He raised one eyebrow, then headed for Adler at navigation.

Gillie ignored the furtive, quizzical stares of the bridge crew and settled back into Riftspace again. Another forty minutes and the Fav'lhir were in for a surprise. She hoped the appearance of the *Serendipity* and the *Vedritor* would be enough. She'd throw in the parrot-fueled crystalship squadron as well. What she didn't want to have to do was openly use her Kiasidiran abilities. For her sake. For Mack's sake.

Simon had wanted her to tell Adler what she was—
more than a sorceress. She'd already heard his opinions and refused. She could do what needed to be
done without that. Without losing what little nor-
malcy was left in her life.

Engine coolant levels dropped, then steadied.
Mack?

On it.

Simon offered some suggestions, but truth was,
they were learning as they traveled. Thank Ixari, it
was a short trip through Riftspace. When she and
Simon had performed rescue operations in the past,
they—

Her knees buckled. A small alarm wailed from a
console on her left. *Oh, hell, oh, damn.* She forcibly
straightened.

Gillie?

Lady Gillaine?

*Simon, help Mack with the shields. Recalibrate.
I...I need to...need to...* She fumbled in her pocket
for her ward stones, never taking her focus from the
energy threads on the viewscreen in front of her. The
stones' coolness washed through her. She sucked in
a slow breath. *Damned big ship you got here,
Makarian.*

Gillie, why don't you sit down?

Good idea. She sank to her knees in what she
hoped wasn't an overly clumsy movement. A wave of
dizziness took up residence in her head. Then Simon's
presence was strong and her vision cleared. *I'm okay.*

No, you're not. Mack sounded angry. *We drop out
of Riftspace, now.*

We'd be five hours from the chancellor's ship—

It's better than ten.

Mack, I can do this. Simon?

Someone touched her, bringing her focus back to the bridge. Mack, his hands on her shoulders, kneeling beside her. Voices around her were hushed, tense. Thirty minutes. Well, okay, thirty-three. She had to hang on to Riftspace, the *Serendipity*, and the *Vedritor* for another thirty-three minutes. That was all.

"Simon will take us out," Mack said. "It's too much for you."

No. It was too much for just Gillie. So much for her attempt at damage control. So much for her attempt at returning to Cirrus One, her true identity known only to a select few under Mack's and Rand's commands. So much for her attempt at avoiding something she could no longer avoid. She *was* Lady Kiasidira. Maybe it was time she faced that fact, once and for all.

If she didn't, the Khalaran chancellor would die, the Fav'lhir would claim a victory, and they'd attack the Confederation again and again.

It had to stop now. She had to send a message to the Fav'lhir and their mages: Lady Kiasidira was back. And she was pissed.

She palmed the ward stone, called the crystal sword's essence into her own. It tingled, ready, its song clear, loud. She knew Mack heard it; his eyes held a startled look. She nodded and allowed him to pull her to her feet. "I'm sorry," she said softly. "It's the only way."

His love and acceptance surrounded her. "You don't have to apologize for what you are."

No, she didn't. And she never would again. She

drew in a deep breath, raised her arms. *"Tal tay Raheira!"*

The *Serendipity* flowed out of Riftspace like a comet blazing across a night sky. The *Vedritor* was seconds behind it, riding the comet's tail. Mack braced for the transition this time, the icy chill slamming through his senses as they breached the veil of energy. He held on to the energy lines with one part of his mind as Gillie had taught him and watched the data on his ship's scanners with the other.

The *Serendipity* would take on the Fav Raider-class fighters. It was his job, and Gillie's, to take on the two destroyers.

The shattered image of Traakhal One's escort ship on the forward screen angered him. It was a lifeless hull, its ident blank. Khalaran fighterships protectively flanked Traakhal One, their number also reduced. Two missing, one crippled.

"Targeting destroyer one," Adler called out.

A golden-hued Lady Gillaine stood at the apex of the bridge, her sword drawn, her image an almost exact copy of the portrait hanging in every Kiasidiran shrine in the Confederation. *Now,* she said to him.

Mack poured his essence, his knowledge of his ship's weaponry, into her. She laced over that her Raheiran magics. The *Vedri* seemed to tremble with power.

Mack gave the order at her nod. "Fire."

The starboard nacelle of the large Fav'lhir ship exploded. A squadron of Raheiran crystalships, as graceful as a flock of birds, arced past the wheeling debris.

"I think we have their attention, My Lady," he said as Cardiff's console filled with noise.

Gillie shot him an impish grin, then turned. The viewscreen flickered with an image from the Fav'lhir ship's bridge. "Three hundred forty-two years ago I promised the Fav'lhir that if they threatened the Khalar, I would destroy their mageline," she told the Fav ship's stunned captain. "I keep my promises."

Mack stepped up beside her. "Surrender, or face the power of the Khalar and the Kiasidira together." He watched disbelief turn into indecision on the captain's broad face. The man was weighing the odds, just as Mack, Adler, and Gillie had. Ship for ship, they were evenly matched. If the Fav'lhir chose to fight, the Khalar could suffer heavy losses.

The *Vedri* had only two things in her favor: the assistance of a squadron of crystalships, and the unlikely appearance of a goddess. Neither of which were quite what they seemed. But the Fav didn't know that.

Something probed him. A dark-haired woman moved up behind the captain. Witch. He read her essence just as Gillie informed him of the fact. Melandan witch. The wizard captain of the *Mogralla* hadn't seen through their ruse, but that was no guarantee this one wouldn't.

It took a moment—a long, tense moment, in Mack's estimation—before the witch nodded slowly, her face grim. "Do as he says."

"Then she really is . . . ?" The captain was still undecided.

"The one the impure call Lady Kiasidira, yes." She

stared hard at Gillie. "Someday, My Lady, someday, one of Melande's chosen will learn your magename. When that day comes, you will finally die." The witch spun on her heels and strode away.

Much happened in the four hours that followed. Yet in spite of it all, in spite of the Fav ships' surrender and the chancellor's gratitude and Captain Gillaine Davré's magnificent handling of it all, Mack couldn't forget the witch's words: *someday, one of Melande's chosen will learn your magename.* It chilled him, and not because he had a magename now. But because he realized that Gillie had extended him a trust far exceeding anything anyone had offered him before or ever would again.

In all the time he'd known her, he thought she'd told him nothing of herself. He'd been wrong. She'd told him the only thing that mattered.

Two things. She'd told him her magename, and she'd told him that she loved him.

He leaned back in the ready-room chair and watched the woman he loved clear the empty coffee cups from the table and shove them into the recyc unit set into the bulkhead. Adler's senior staff, along with the chancellor's advisers, had just left after a lengthy debriefing. They were all finally headed home.

She caught his raised eyebrow and shrugged. "Old habit. The *Serendipity*'s a small ship. And since Simon couldn't help—well, not until recently. Anyway, cleanup duty was always mine."

He held out his hand. She took it and perched on the edge of the table. "You're right. A Raheiran link doesn't mean every thought, all the time." That had been another surprise. Simon's and Gillie's presence floated in and out of his mind, but gently. And rarely stayed for long.

"What brings this up?"

"You mentioned Simon. I tried to tell you before. His relationship with you, and the entire ability of Raheiran telepathy, are two errors I made. I understand that now."

"Your ancestors would be pleased. Though you still have much to learn to understand your heritage."

"Simon's made some threats in that direction." Mack smiled. "All those years I thought my grandfather was simply being devout when he kept dragging me to visit the holy Kiasidiran relics and insisting I memorize Lady Kia—your guidelines. I had no idea he was following his great-grandfather's instructions. Or that his great-grandfather was part Raheiran."

"Captain Ethan Tarrant," Gillie said.

"My grandmother once said I look a bit like him."

Gillie tilted her head, her eyes narrowing. "Now that you mention it . . ."

Mack sat upright. "You knew him?" When Simon had told him of his Raheiran ancestry, he'd thought it had been because Simon had read something in his essence. Not because he'd known Captain Ethan. But then, that hadn't been the purpose of his chat with Simon. He'd wanted to know about Simon's relationship with Gillie, not about his own relationship to a long-dead ancestor. Raheiran or not.

He did some quick mental calculations. "Gods. Captain Ethan was around when the first spaceport was built outside Port Armin, on Traakhalus Prime. That was 5411. He was—"

"In his thirties. A bit younger than you."

"Then you *have* met him."

"He was one of the few who understood why I didn't want a shrine constructed in my honor there. 'Abject foolishness,' he called it. 'A cold and unresponsive memorial constructed from cold and unresponsive material.'"

Gillie had spoken those same words to him weeks ago, on Cirrus One. It hadn't sounded like her speech at the time. He'd just had no idea she was quoting his ancestor. Who was single, in his thirties. Part Raheiran. "Just how well *did* you know Captain Ethan?"

Gillie grinned disarmingly down at him, her eyes sparkling in shades of green and lavender. She winked. "Just who do you think taught me to play billiards?"

"Ethan."

Laughing, she pulled him to his feet. "I'm sure the *Vedritor* has a rec room or holodeck around somewhere."

He wrapped his arm around her waist. "I have a better idea."

Mack studied the woman lying under him, her pale hair soft and wispy against his pillow. The colors in her eyes shifted. Green with decidedly lavender flecks. He remembered thinking that, along with his unprofessional assessment that she was beautiful.

She was. She was also Gillaine, Kiasidira, Ciran Rothalla Davré. His Gillaine. His Gillie. His somewhat accidental goddess and his very enthusiastic lover. She twined her arms around his neck. Their skin was still damp from their lovemaking. "Hi."

"Hi, yourself," he answered with a grin.

"Amazing."

"Thank you. I do try."

She cuffed the back of his head lightly. "Be careful. You're starting to sound like Simon. I wasn't talking about the way you make love to me. That is, and always has been, more than amazing. Perfect."

He brushed a kiss across her mouth. "So who's amazing?"

"Not who. What. It's been three hours and no comm sets have pinged and no alarms have wailed."

"Ah, that. Rank does have its privileges, My Lady. I left strict orders with Adler that we not be interrupted until we're within visual range of Cirrus One. Now, if only I could find a way to shut off that damned music."

"Music?"

"Can't you hear it? It's like someone's humming the Raheiran wedding song, over and over again."

Gillie squeezed her eyes shut. *Simon!*

Yes, My Lady. A sock. I'm searching for a sock right now . . .

about the author

A former news reporter and retired private detective, Linnea Sinclair has managed to use all of her college degrees (journalism and criminology) but hasn't soothed the yearning in her soul to travel the galaxy. To that end, she's authored several science fiction and fantasy novels, including *Finders Keepers, Gabriel's Ghost,* and *An Accidental Goddess.* When not on duty with some intergalactic fleet, she can be found in Fort Lauderdale, Florida, with her husband and their two thoroughly spoiled cats. Fans can reach her through her website at *www.linneasinclair.com.*